THE DEAR G

&

FUR SADIE

THE DEAR GREEN PLACE
&
FUR SADIE

Archie Hind

Edited and Introduced by Alasdair Gray

Polygon

This paperback published in Great Britain in 2024 by Polygon, an
imprint of Birlinn Ltd. This edition first published by
Polygon, an imprint of Birlinn Ltd, in 2008.

Birlinn Ltd
West Newington House
10 Newington Road
Edinburgh EH9 1QS

9 8 7 6 5 4 3 2 1

www.polygonbooks.co.uk

First published in Great Britain
in 1966 by New Authors Ltd.

ISBN 978 1 84697 686 5
eBook ISBN 978 0 85790 150 7

British Library Cataloguing-in-Publication Data
A catalogue record for this book is available on request
from the British Library.

Typeset by Palimpsest Book Production Limited, Falkirk, Stirlingshire
Printed and bound in Great Britain by Ashford Colour Press, Gosport

To Eleanor

CONTENTS

Introduction

In 1928 Archie Hind was born in Dalmarnock, an industrial part of east Glasgow. His father, a stoker on locomotive engines, worked for fifty-one years on the railways, with an interval as a soldier in World War One. Though liked by workmates and friends he was so bad a husband that when her son Archie was seven and older brother nine their mother left home with her two-year-old daughter. Ten years later the parents were reconciled; meanwhile the boys lived with their father and his widowed mother. The home Mrs Hind had abandoned, while decent and clean, was like most tenement homes in Glasgow between the wars, a room and kitchen with communal lavatory on an outside landing. Baths had to be taken in public bathhouses and Archie sometimes used these less than he wished, to stop people seeing bruises from his father's beatings. These stopped when he and his brother grew strong enough to hit back.

The brutal part of his upbringing was not the most formative part and has no place in his novel *The Dear Green Place*, where the hero's father is based on a more representative Glasgow dad, a tolerant, intelligent Marxist uncle. The mainstream of working-class thought and culture in Glasgow was the Socialism of the Independent Labour Party, the party George Orwell most favoured, and which returned seven Scottish MPs to Westminster before World War Two. After 1946 the best of these died or joined the Parliamentary Labour Party. Like most Socialists between the two great wars Archie's people had been hopeful about the Russian Revolution and would have distrusted the U.S.S.R. more if the British government had not been so friendly to Fascist Italy, Germany and Spain.

Archie grew up with a love of literature and music – he and his brother both loved singing, and he learned piping in the Boys' Brigade. Leaving school at fourteen he entered Beardmores, the largest engineering firm in Britain. It had built cars, planes, the first British airship, and still made great steam engines for ships and railway locomotives. By the late 1960s Scottish steam-powered industries were obsolete, but Archie joined the firm when World War Two was giving it a last profitable lease of life. For two years he was a messenger, reporting to Head Office on the progress of shafts and propellers shaped in the forges, turning sheds and workshops. He should have become an apprentice when sixteen, but his father wanted the higher wage Archie earned by shifting to a warehouse supplying local grocers. In 1945 or 6 he could have gone to university, since the last act of the government that brought Britain through the war had enabled any student to attend colleges of further education who passed the entrance exam. This would have been well within Archie's power; but have meant even less money for his dad than an engineering apprenticeship. Archie only left home when eighteen and conscripted into the British Army. He served with the medical corps for two years in Singapore and Ceylon.

Which tells nothing about the birth and growth of his wide erudition and strong imagination through reading, close attention to recorded music and broadcasts, and intense discussion with those of similar interests. British professional folk often think creative imaginations unlikely outside their own social class – on first reading *Ulysses* Virginia Woolf thought James Joyce (despite his Jesuit and Dublin University education) had all the faults of a self-taught working man. Who in Glasgow could see the growth of an unusual mind in a twenty-year-old ex-Beardmores progress clerk, warehouseman and demobbed medical corps private? Jack Rillie could, the Glasgow University

English lecturer who ran an extra-mural class in literature. Archie attended it and on Jack Rillie's recommendation went to Newbattle Abbey, the Workers' Further Education College in Midlothian. The Principal was the Orkney-born poet Edwin Muir who, with his wife Willa, were the foremost translators of German language novels by Broch, Musil and Kafka. Archie became a friend of both.

By now he had decided to write a book that he knew would never sell enough to support him – a book that would leave him *a failure* in the eyes of all but those who liked unusually careful writing. Soon after Newbattle Archie married Eleanor, a girl he had met through the Tollcross Park tennis club. She accepted him and his strange ambition while foreseeing the consequences, perhaps because her Jewish mother and Irish father came from people who did not identify worldly success with great achievements. Her mother had been brought from the Crimea to Scotland by parents escaping from Czarist pogroms, and like many Jews in Glasgow she attended left-wing meetings. At one of these she had met John Slane, a coalminer who learned to make spectacles while studying at night classes. They married and he became an optician successful enough, and rich enough, to buy Eleanor a beautiful Steinway grand piano and give it house room. But he hated her marriage to a man who supported his growing family by working as a social security clerk, trolley-bus driver and labourer in the municipal slaughterhouse between writing a novel that would never earn a supportive income. Archie and Eleanor made friends with writers and artists met through a new Glasgow Arts Centre which met in premises leased by the painter J. D. Ferguson and his wife Margaret Morris, founder of the Celtic Dance Theatre.

I met them in 1958 when they had three sons (Calum, Gavin, Martin) and young daughter Nellimeg, whose mental age was arrested at less than two years by minor epilepsy. Their last child Sheila was born five years later. I had recently left Glasgow Art School and the Hinds had the only welcoming

home I knew where literature, painting and music were sub-
jects of extended, enjoyable conversations. It was a room and
kitchen flat like that where Archie had been born, but in
Greenfield Street, Govan. The room held the children's bunks
so social life was always in the warm kitchen which, despite
many evening visitors, never seemed overcrowded. These were
years when London critics thought Osborne's *Look Back in
Anger*, Amis's *Lucky Jim*, Braine's *Room at the Top*, were a new
school of literature created through the agency of the welfare
state. These three works described working-class lads acquiring
middle-class women. Archie and I thought they described
nothing profound when compared with the best writings of
Joyce and D. H. Lawrence, Hemingway and Scott Fitzgerald.
We admired *The Tin Drum*, *Catch-22*, *Slaughterhouse 5*, and
found we were both working on a novel about the only struggle
we could take seriously – the struggle to make a work of art.
This has been an important theme in poetry and fiction since
Wordsworth's *Prelude*. It inspired Archie most in the poetry
of Yeats and fiction of Thomas Mann. He liked good jazz and
American Blues, the songs of Edith Piaf and The Beatles, but
thought most highly celebrated contemporary work – Beckett's
dramas, John Cage's music, abstract expressionist painting and
Warhol's Campbell's soup icons – indicated a thinning in the
rich intellectual texture of Western culture. I was not so sure,
but agreed that as writers we should maintain that texture. Our
novels were both about low-income Glasgow artists doomed
to failure, this coincidence worried us slightly, but we had
chosen that theme long before meeting each other, and had
to put up with it.

In the middle 1960s the Hinds moved to Dalkeith where
Archie worked with Ferranti's Pegasus, an early computer
filling nearly the whole floor of a building. He left that job to
finally complete his novel, and having completed it, worked
as copy-taker in the *Scottish Daily Mail*, Edinburgh, while
awaiting publication. In Milne's Bar he sometimes conversed
amicably about sport and politics with Hugh MacDiarmid. In

1966 the novel was published in Hutchinson's New Author series. Its title, *The Dear Green Place*, was Archie's translation of *glas-chu* or *gles-con*, Gaelic words that became *Glasgow*. They had previously been translated *green hollow*, *green churchyard*, *greyhounds ferry*, *dear stream*, and (in imperial days when it was the second largest and smokiest city in Britain) the *grey forge* or *smithy*. Archie's translation is now generally accepted.

All good novels are historical – describe living people in a definite place and time. *The Dear Green Place* shows a city that had grown between 1800 and 1960, becoming for almost a century the second biggest in Britain. The earliest paragraphs give the layout – a city completely unlike London, for in Glasgow the homes of labourers, tradesmen and professional folk were intermingled with parks, shops, thriving factories with smoking chimneys and districts of old industrial wasteland. The time is about the 1950s when unemployment hardly existed and most of the labour force, though poorly housed by later standards, had the better wages and working conditions promised to the trade unions by the wartime coalition government. This Scottish region of the newly established British Welfare State gives Mat Craig the chance to occasionally dodge the commercial forces that, before 1939, would have made him an industrial serf, or political activist, or even destitute. He has enough room to exercise, however painfully, what was once a bourgeois or aristocratic privilege – the free will needed to attempt a work of art. The only other twentieth-century novel I know that places a writer's struggle in an equally well imagined city is Nabokov's novel *The Gift*.

Published in 1966, *The Dear Green Place* won four prizes: *The Guardian* Fiction of the Year, *The Yorkshire Post*'s Best First Work, the Frederick Niven and Scottish Arts Council Awards. The Hinds returned to Glasgow when, as foreseen, *The Dear Green Place* had not earned enough to support them. Archie wrote revues performed in the Close Theatre and a witty, precise political column for the *Scottish International* magazine. He worked for the Easterhouse Project, a privately funded meeting place started to reduce violent crime among the young when the Easterhouse housing scheme still had few shops, no cafés, no playing-fields or provision for games and entertainment. Soon after, he was appointed to the position of Aberdeen City's first Writer-in-Residence, later becoming copy-taker for the *Aberdeen Press and Journal.*

By this time he was working on his second novel, *Fur Sadie.* *Fur* is how many Glaswegians pronounce *for,* and the title associates it with Beethoven's piano piece, *Für Elise,* in a way that will make perfect sense when you read it. The *Scottish International* published a small part in 1973, but all that Archie wrote of it is published here for the first time, for I believe it an astonishing achievement, although unfinished.

It is sometimes said that Scottish fiction has a more masculine bias than that of other lands, and though generally untrue it is true of much writing by authors like Alexander Trocchi, William MacIlvanney, Alan Sharp, Alasdair Gray and Irvine Welsh. But *The Dear Green Place* makes it hard to include Archie Hind among these and *Fur Sadie* makes it impossible. Here he *transposes* (as musicians say) the theme of artistic struggle into the person of a small, ordinary-seeming, middle-aged yet very attractive working-class housewife and mother. In a few episodes her life between infancy and menopause is presented as richly detailed, generally admirable, stunted by too little money and leisure, yet capable of much more. Most British descriptions of working-class people suggest how horrid, or comic, or admirable that they live that way. The narrative voice of *Fur Sadie* is free of such condescension. He knows that better lives are possible, and shows Sadie working for one. Her portrait is deeply historical. Her childhood is in the pre-television age when city children still sang and played in streets where motorcars were seldom seen – even professional folk seldom owned one, while coal and milk were still brought to houses in horse-drawn carts. When a middle-aged housewife, Sadie has had an electric geyser wired above the kitchen sink and no longer needs to heat cold water in a kettle. This innovation allows her time for music. There is a television set in her front room, and she can buy a second-hand piano and pay a tuner out of her housekeeping money without the expense worrying her husband. A social revolution has happened through which we see the sexual growth of a woman and man from adolescence through early marriage to late, sad maturity. No other author I know has shown a sexual relationship over many years with such casual, unsensational delicacy and truth.

And all that is essential to the tale of how a childhood friendship, and inherent, long-buried talent, at last combine with a good music teacher to bring Beethoven (no less!) alive in the mind and fingers of an apparently ordinary woman. The curious reader will wonder why this great fragment was not completed and how it might have ended. I will give my thoughts on this matter at the end of *Fur Sadie*.

This book ends with an example of Archie's journalism from 1973. I wish this book also contained a selection from his early short stories (all lost) and some playscripts from the ten commissioned and performed between 1973 and 1990. I especially remember *The Sugarolly Story*, a satirical view of Glasgow's social history from the start of World War One to the creation of Easterhouse housing scheme. This was performed by the Easterhouse Players in the Easterhouse Social Centre after Glasgow City Council at last built one. There was also *Shoulder to Shoulder*, a dramatised documentary of John MacLean's life. *The Ragged-Trousered Philanthropist*, a Scottish dramatisation of Doonan's building-trade novel, was the biggest and most successful, being the only one acted by a large professional company (7:84) in a well known theatre (The Citizens). The scripts of these have also been lost. This book must therefore be regarded as holding The Best Available Work of Archie Hind, and will deserve the attention of future lovers of Scottish literature.

The Dear Green Place and *Fur Sadie* have survived into a century where Archie's forebodings about the thinning of the

Western cultural tradition (now called dumbing-down), have come true. Intellectuals calling themselves Postmodern now say that objective truths do not exist, but are opinions in disguise. They can now lecture in universities upon anything they like because they can hold everything equally valuable, and declare many once valued things negligible. In a recent history of twentieth-century art international critics and dealers celebrate the triumph of Installation Art and announce that oil painting since Picasso is patriarchal and obsolete. Before that century ended a head of visual arts in Glasgow School of Art said no artist now needed to learn drawing. Glasgow University has a department of Creative Writing where the kind of novel Archie wrote is labelled *literary fiction*, and labelled as a genre along with crime, horror, science fiction and love stories of the sort publishers call chick lit. But when forthcoming catastrophes have moved the survivors back to serious agreement about what is important in Scottish life and art, *The Dear Green Place* and *Fur Sadie* will have survived also.

Alasdair Gray
January 2008

THE DEAR GREEN PLACE

1

IN EVERY CITY you find these neighbourhoods. They are
defined by accident – by a railway yard, a factory, a main
road, a park. This particular district was reached from the
town by a main road. On your left as you approached it was
a public park; on your right, back from the road, was a railway
embankment. Beyond the railway embankment lay stretches of
derelict land of the kind seen on the edges of big cities. Broken
down furnaces and kilns were still crumbling around where
the claypits had once been worked. This derelict area was
divided in part by brick walls, in part by some bits of drystane
dyke, in part by some straggly hawthorn. Further on than this
slag heaps and dumps for industrial refuse – here in Glasgow
they are called coups – stretched down to the Clyde. The main
road curved round the south end of the park, then entered
abruptly into the neighbourhood. If you left the tram here
and continued along the main road you pass the brownstone
tenement, the ground floor of which contains the shops, the
surgery, the pub. On the corner opposite the pub there is
an old two-storey tenement, a newspaper shop, a telephone
booth. Turning to the left here you come into a street with
rows of council houses. Further down the road is the school.
The streets traversing this are built up with red sandstone,
three-storeyed tenements. Good houses. Beyond this street
on the other side from the town were older tenements, few
of them more than two storeys in height. Beyond these a golf
course, then fields. Past the neighbourhood where the road
led on out of the city it was bounded on one side by rows
of houses, modern bungalows with raw-looking gardens, old

square stone houses with dirty windows and untidy heaps of rhododendron encroaching on the shaggy lawns. On the other side of the road are sandpits dug down hundreds of feet into the earth.

But the street with the council houses. Stand there on a Saturday morning and you'll see women coming back from the shops with their messages, their shopping baskets heavy laden, small tidy middle-aged women who clasp their purses as if they were weapons and can still tell a joint from a joint and stewing steak from brisket and make pots of broth from flank mutton. The children playing in the street are well clothed and reasonably polite. The young girl walking up towards the tram stop carries a long canvas case with a hockey stick in it and wears a fee-paying school blazer. The young men passing are mostly apprentices, the men mostly tradesmen. At eleven o'clock the group of men standing at the corner will disappear into the pub. These are the punters, the bookie and his runners. A quiet circumspect lot. You'll see an occasional brief-case belonging to one or two young men who go to the University on a Glasgow Corporation grant. Later in the afternoon the men will appear wearing their blue scarves on their way to see the Rangers playing at home at Ibrox. If these middle-aged women have to scrape a bit at least they don't have to pinch, the men can afford a pint and there are Christmas trees in the windows during the festive season. A quiet street. As these streets go a prosperous one.

In one of these council houses late on a September night there was a light still burning. It shone faintly on the windows, a dim amber light which had taken its colour from the room and from the old parchment coloured lampshade. Within the circle of light which the lamp cast on the surface of a table a man sat in the room, trying to write.

He was a short, dark, stocky man, with coarse black hair, a shadow on his unshaven cheeks. His rolled up shirt sleeves showed muscular forearms covered in dark hair which stopped sharply at the wrists. His small hands looked pale against the darkness of his arms. He was crouched over the paper on the table holding the pen in his hand tightly; his left arm was circled around the paper giving him the cramped appearance of a dull and unwilling schoolboy at his desk. For a couple of hours – ever since the other people in the house had gone to bed – he had been sitting writing.

Mat Craig looked up from his work towards the mantelpiece. The clock showed the time as ten past one. As it was usually about quarter of an hour fast then the right time would be five to one. He yawned and bowed his head over the papers again. All over the table within the circle of light shed by the lamp there were papers spread. He was sitting at the dining-table on one of the old mahogany chairs, its back shaped like a horse-collar. On the wall the miniature grandfather clock ticked slowly. The fire had stopped flickering and was now a dull glow, but he could still make out the individual books which were stuffed in the bookcases on either side of the mantelpiece – volumes of Marx, Lenin, Jack London, Daniel De Leon, translations of Anatole France, Eugene Sue, Zola. The books belonged to Mat's father but he had read them himself with enthusiasm as a young man and in some way, although his interests had undergone a considerable shift – his own collection of books represented a different milieu – he still felt a loyalty to the ideas in these books and to the ardent idealism which had made him plough his way through their dusty leaves.

On one wall of the room was a sepia-coloured photograph of a locomotive, taken about the time of the First World War, with his paternal grandfather standing in front of it, leaning on a shunting pole, with a big black moustache like a raven's wings stuck across his face. He had been a good Labour man in his day. At the side of the mantelpiece above one of the bookcases was a framed reproduction of one of Millet's toilers.

Mat was 'burning the midnight oil'. Perhaps there was a time when this act had for him the traditional connection with ideas of self-education and improvement which accompanies working-class political aspirations. But his sitting up writing now had nothing very much to do with these former hopes. Now his interests were nearer to the kind of thing represented by those names which spring to mind when we think of modern writing. But these interests, too, were apart from his need to write.

He was sitting crouched over the table and under the circle of light because he remembered something which had happened to him as a boy. He was sitting trying to recapture an experience which had happened to him a long time ago. This event, which he often recalled and which drove him to cover sheets of paper with his small cramped handwriting, was nothing more than his having once been overcome by a mood. He had been about ten at the time. The thing had happened after he had been playing football all afternoon and he had been walking home across a patch of waste ground. The late afternoon sun had burned through the dust and smoke which hung in the upper air and slanted down its inflamed pink light on to the hard packed ground round about him. His diffuse elongated shadow went before him as he walked. For no reason at all he had felt happy. A calm unaccountable feeling of pleasure.

Now, years later, he thought that he had gone through a type of mystic experience, although his happiness had in no way been ecstatic. it had been more of a commonplace satisfactory happiness unheightened by euphoria or anything in the nature of the occult. He often thought, too, that before this time, in his very early childhood, he must have gone through days of feeling like that. But by the time he was ten years old the experience must have been unusual to have retained itself on his memory. Since then he had almost repeated the experience but these repetitions were mere glimmerings, tenuous and fleeting, mere shades ...

Now as he sat writing he was remembering how he had recently felt again one of those vague repetitions. Early in the evening he had come home from work just as dusk was falling over the city. A calm September evening with the dust and grime high in the air, the street lamps just lit, and women's voices calling their children. As he walked up the road from the tram stop he could see the sky far away to the west, bright pink and blue like the illustrations in a child's book, while towards him the light changed to a light sepia. Round the street lamps there hung a soft amber fuzz of light. Away far down the road into the grey east everything was black and smudged like a graphite drawing. There was a general hum of traffic and the sound of voices. Every now and then a window in one of the tenements would light up. Mat had felt moved and happy. He walked under some trees overhanging the pavement and a cobweb touched his face which had made him remember walking through a wood as a child. The familiar sensation of warmth and excitement came over him. The feeling he always had before he would start to write.

Although he felt tired he was quite peaceful. His fatigue helped him to write. Normally when he sat down under the lamplight he felt that his body was irksome to him, with its crude physical need for movement, its continual demands. He would want to scratch, or jump, or to fidget; his senses too would always be paying attention to other things; even his intellect, curious and avid, would be pulling him outwards, away from the paper. Not to mention worry, anxiety, duty. But now in the quietness, so that he could hear the coals crackling in the low fire, in the stillness of the room, with the enclosing lamplight shining just on the page, the things which he wrote about, and the words, took on a kind of reality.

After Mat had interrupted himself by looking towards the clock on the mantelpiece he couldn't get started again. He felt sometimes that one of the disadvantages of writing out of his mood was that though he could pay attention to detail, to the sensuous surface of the writing, choosing the words carefully and, as it were, placing them on the page; although he could dream, feeling the words and the physical presences to which they referred, seeing every event, sensing their time and their rhythm, so that each sentence, each paragraph, had almost tactile existence for him, he found structure and invention impossible. Under the fatigue his mind simply refused to work so that he found his writing becoming a mere receptacle for memory and sense impressions. He had to go back reading over his work, reading through what he had written and then, following on the impetus, write another few sentences. He had to keep on doing this because of his inability to hold any general structure in his mind. As for invention, that was always done in the clear light of dawn when the mind was at its sharpest.

This time, instead of going on writing, he became caught up with some of his sentences. He usually reconstructed his sentences by an ingenious and wholly personal system of numbers, capital letters and various types of brackets, using this system to shift whole sentences back or forward in the paragraph or to adjust the position of a clause in the sentence. This created the difficulty that no one other than himself could have made a fair copy from the page, even if they could read the small cramped and practically illegible handwriting. Sometime, he thought, I'll get some pens with different coloured inks.

He had stopped writing now and with his chin cupped in his hand he sat looking at the paper. He thought that perhaps the story he was working on was quite good, and not badly written. The trouble was that good writing was ten a penny and that the story was also a little diffuse – slight. It needed some plain numb words to make it active, to get the feeling of narrative into it. And when he thought of the slightness of the thing he felt himself give an internal blush. It was slight and had a little touch of Romantic Irony in it because he didn't want to say too much, be too serious. He became so involved with everything he wrote that he was afraid of too much emotion. Rightly. On the other hand, the writers whom he admired, any real writer, knocked and slapped their material about in quite a cavalier fashion. I could do it in the morning, he thought, if only ... Sometimes he saw himself quite clearly as an object and could feel a certain amount of pity for the poor character in a cleft stick. The writer who couldn't really write.

'Damn it.' He almost spoke out loud and as he pushed the papers away from him, finishing with them, he felt suddenly a dry and brittle mood come over him. 'When I get to bed I'll do some grand writing in my head.' He lifted his feet on to the table and started to smoke a cigarette. Immediately he felt a twinge of conscience. All the writers who ever got anything done insisted on discipline. All right – discipline, work. He put his cigarette into his left hand, swung his feet down and picked up his pen. As he started to coax himself back into the mood he was tempted by the thought that the difficulty was in his point of view, or that he needed to wait a bit until he had *grown* more. A complete change of style and attitude would make it all so much easier. It was true – but it would be better to think of that later – one couldn't think and work at the same time. And work came first.

He gathered up the papers on which he had been working and clipped them together with a paper clip. Then as he put them aside he looked round the table at the bundles of manuscript. Jotters full of notes, dossiers full of bits of dog-eared paper and typescript, single scraps of paper with notes on them which he thought too valuable to throw away. He had a habit of keeping every single thing that he had written, all in a big cardboard box, and every time he sat down to write he'd spread them around him on the table for comfort. Faced with a single scrap of paper he found himself unable to write a word, but with his 'bits and pieces' about him he was able to write away quite happily. He took a bulky folder, the biggest of all his 'bits and pieces' and laid it in front of him on the table with a sigh of satisfaction. On the front of the folder, typed on a piece of white paper and stuck on, was the motto 'Rutherglen's wee roon red lums reek briskly'. Beneath that was a reproduction of the City of Glasgow's coat-of-arms

9

with its tree, its bird, its fish and its bell. Beneath that again was typed a little piece of doggerel verse which is known to all Glasgow school children.

> This is the tree that never grew,
> This is the bird that never flew,
> This is the fish that never swam,
> This is the bell that never rang.

On the coat-of-arms there were printed the words *Let Glasgow Flourish.* Mat sat and looked at it for a while, then he printed the word *Lord* in front of it and the words *by the preaching of the Word* after it, and restored the modern truncated motto to its old length and meaning.

Lord, Let Glasgow Flourish by the Preaching of the Word.

As he made the addition he smiled wryly to himself as if at some private joke. Then he muttered to himself in supplication, with ironic fervency, 'Lord, let Glasgow flourish by the preaching of the Word,' and opened the folder, exposing the first neatly typed page.

The manuscript began with the words *'The Clyde made Glasgow and Glasgow made the Clyde'.* It had been some time since he had opened the folder, though he had thought of it often with a warm feeling. As he read what he had written he was rather surprised that he only remembered it slightly. The words came to him now as almost new and he read on, curious to know what he had written these years ago. The typescript continued: *'For many centuries there were fishermen's huts around the spot where the old Molendinar burn flowed into the Clyde, where the shallows of the Clyde occurred, where the travellers crossed who made their way from the North-west parts of Scotland down to the South. Some authorities have it that this place where St Mungo, or to give him his proper Celtic name St Kentigern, built his little church was given the Gaelic name Gles Chu, meaning "the dear green place", and that the present name of Glasgow is a corruption of those two Gaelic words. The dear green place – as it must have been. Even late into the Eighteenth Century when the modern city that is Glasgow had begun to grow it was talked about as "the most beautiful little town in all Britain". In the Sixth Century St Mungo had built a mission there, building it like any inn or hostelry at the most likely place to catch the customers, or converts, at the spot where the drovers or travellers would pause before crossing the ford. Being on the West coast of Scotland its connections were with the Celtic Christian culture in Ireland and so it became an ecclesiastical town. In the Fifteenth Century a University was built and Glasgow remained a religious centre until the European Reformation when it acquired with vengeance the Protestant ethic and its natives turned their hands with much zeal to worldly things. These same natives had always been pugnacious; the Romans in an earlier day had found them an intolerable nuisance; and in the Tenth Century they maintained their reputation for pugnacity by knocking spots off the Danes down on the Ayrshire coast. Thereafter they mixed almost solely with people of their own racial type. During The Industrial Revolution when Glasgow suffered a great influx of people it was from Ireland and the West Highlands of Scotland that the people came so that even today the characteristic Glasgow type is short, stocky and dark like his very remote Celtic-Iberian forebears.*

'When St Mungo fished in the Clyde from his leaky coracle the source of the river was a different one from that of today. The old rhyme goes,

> *"The Tweed, the Annan, and the Clyde,*
> *A' rin oot o' ae hillside,"*

and this is not now the case. It is probable that, as some people claim, a farmer led the original Clyde burn, which rose away back in the hills, along a ditch and into the Elvan and thus on South into the Solway. This to prevent the burn from flooding his fields.'

Beside this sentence Mat marked the word 'avulsion'. As

he printed the word in the margin he felt a strange kind of satisfaction. Then he went on reading his manuscript.

'*It happened that about the same time the Glasgow merchants were howking at the river bed further downstream in order to make the deep channel which allowed Glasgow to become the great sea port which nature intended it to be.*'

Again in the margin beside this sentence Mat printed another word, in alternative forms '*alluvion*' and '*alluvium*'. Then he added the sentence: '*And thus the wiseacres are confirmed in their saying that Glasgow and the Clyde were mutually responsible for one another's being.*' He found the idea that the river had been tamed, or 'domesticated', for the sake of all this husbandry, that the big river had become something of a human artifact, he found this idea exciting and satisfying. The rest of the manuscript went on to describe the river itself.

'*A parochial historian refers to the "dim prophetic instinct in the country" which anticipates the wealth which was one day to come and speaks of one of the oldest traditions connected with the river, which tells of the three hundred Strathclyde chiefs who each wore a torque of pure gold "washed from the sands of Glengonar, or found in the mud of the Elvan". They say that German and English prospectors came to look for gold in the Leadhills. Mines are mentioned in the very oldest records connected with the Clyde district. Gold, however, was never found in abundance and the country had to await the coming of the modern alchemists who could transmute the grey ores and black minerals which were found in abundance into a precious form. Certainly as we move among the soft greenery of that lovely strath, from its source past the grey mossy slopes and thymy banks, through the quiet hills, still, with no other sound but the cry of the curlew, the bleat of the lamb, the hum of the wandering bee, and the splash of water on stone, down to the broad valley of its middle waters with its rolling bare countryside, then the picturesque falls and rippling affluents, the pastoral delights and musing solitudes of its great Ducal estates with their fine old trees, broad pleached alleys, and far stretching vistas; down from the idyllic and uncertain past into the reaches of the Clyde where the air begins to darken, the horizon is smudged, and intermingled with grazing fields, trees, farms, and gardens are coal heaps, pit heads, corrugated iron sheds, foundries, machine shops, bings and mills; certainly we begin to see what the centuries had waited for with bated breath, what had been anticipated by that "dim prophetic instinct". For here are the alembics, the retorts, and crucibles, funnels and furnaces, the apparatus and paraphernalia of the modern alchemists who transmute the grey ores and base metals of the district into glittering wealth.'*

Mat smiled at this section. He remembered copying from a parochial historian the plummy bits of prose. He had enjoyed the plushy sounds of the words 'rippling affluents' and 'pleached alleys' – whatever 'pleached' meant. Looking up the dictionary which was lying on the floor beside his chair he read the words: 'to intertwine the branches of; as a hedge'. Then he read on.

'*We move further along the loops which the river now takes round the towns of Hamilton, Bothwell, Blantyre, through Carmyle and into Glasgow. The mossy slopes harden into packed banks of black hardened mud, the soft greenery is a virid colour from the stretches of soda waste, the rippling affluents gush from cast iron pipes, an oily chemical sediment; we hear now the din of machinery, the thumping of hammers and the hiss and blast of steam and gas. Then the din dies down to a rattle and we come to the idyllic spot where the gentle oxen crossed and the little Molendinar burn flowed into the broad shallows of the river; the spot which the Gaels named Gles Chu, the spot where as legend had it St Mungo recovered his lost ring from the belly of a salmon. The little valley of the Molendinar is now stopped with two centuries of refuse – soap, tallow, cotton waste, slag, soda, bits of leather, broken pottery, tar and caoutchouc – the waste products of a dozen industries and a million lives, and it is built over with slums, yards, streets, and factories. A few hundred yards downstream from the broad shallows of the river there is now a deep artificial channel which will take ships of the deepest draught, great ocean-going liners. It is now spanned by bridges of steel and grey granite. We are now in the heart of the industrial world; not just the mercantile, commercial, industrial metropolis which is Glasgow, but at the heart of Industry itself, for in this spot was cradled the great movement, the Industrial Revolution, which transformed the face of the World. Take a map and a pair of compasses and insert the point of the compasses into the spot – tenderly! Gles Chu! – now transcribe a circle and you encompass the stamping grounds of many of the great men who made the Industrial Revolution possible. Adam Smith, the economist of Laisser-faire, who held the Chair of Logic and Moral Philosophy at Glasgow University. Watt, to whom we owe the steam engine; Murdoch – gas illumination; Neilson – the blast furnace; Symington and Bell – the steam ship; Rigby – the steam hammer; MacIntosh – the use of rubber; Tennent – industrial chemistry; Napier and Elder – the marine engine and screw propulsion; Paterson – the Bank of England. Here for the first time the Monteiths wove the muslin which clothed the Asiatic in his flowing robes and turbans; here were woven the zephyrs, inkles, and muslins which were to clothe the Americas: Dave Dale, before he married his daughter to Robert Owen, was carrying out experiments in industrial welfare; from here came MacAdam of the roadway and Telford of the bridges.'*

At this point Mat must have ceased to type for the manuscript continued in his small cramped hand. Instead of going on reading he took up his pen and started to make more notes. The last passage had moved him, it had evoked the memory of so many things; for where the river had taken these last loops into Glasgow had been his own stamping ground in his first years as a child, and the banks of the river with all its old factories and mills; from away out in Carmyle right into the heart of the city, right to the spot where St. Mungo had fished, all was as familiar to him, more familiar to him than the room in which he sat. He knew every waste pipe that gushed its mucky sediment into the river, every path along its bank, every forsaken spot and lonely stretch where no one but children ever went, where between long factory walls and the river there were narrow paths that led merely from one open stretch of dumping ground to the next. Here he had played as a child in the oldest industrial landscape in the world, amongst the oldest factories in the world, and it had been through this landscape that he had walked when he had once felt so unaccountably happy.

Inside one of these loops in the river he had been born, in a tenement building surrounded by factories. Nearby, in a house overlooking the yard of an electric power station, where coal trucks were shunted into a machine and tilted over to empty the coal into the furnaces, underneath the massive chimneys, here his mother had been born. And here, in the midst of the alchemist's paraphernalia, his grandfather had worked and raised his family, weaving in a nearby factory the muslins that clothed the far away Asiatic. One of his earliest memories was of getting a licking from his father when he had come home all soaked and muddy from falling into the water. On some parts of the river where the banks were very steep the children used to climb down them, then on to one of the iron pipes which projected over the water, lie down with their legs straddling the pipe and hold their hands in the mucky torrent which gushed out of its mouth. The fascination of the game was in creating a variety of effects, as for instance if the hands were pressed round the lip of the pipe the increased pressure scooted the water far out into the river in a delightful curve; another way of holding the hands over the pipe would cause the water to spread out in a smooth fan with a ragged tassel of drips at its base where it fell into the water; and there was the additional fascination of feeling the force of the water as it gushed from the pipe.

For a long time Mat sat without writing any more. He was thinking of these days long ago which his passage about the Clyde had evoked. He was trying now to remember whether his grandfather had been standing or sitting in front of the loom on the day long ago when Mat had carried his pieces of bread and cheese and the can of hot soup down to the mill where he had worked. But all he could remember were his grandfather's deft hands and the taut lines of cotton which jerked up and down at the back of the machine, and of course his grandfather's mop of white hair on top of his magnificently shaped long head. He had a fierce curve to his nose, a pair of arrogant hooded blue eyes and was as deaf as a door-post; his temper belied his appearance as he was the mildest of men and Mat remembered especially the way he would say 'Eh!' and curve his hand over the back of his ear. All his family, his children and his grandchildren called him 'Faither' and a great many myths were current in the Devlin family about him, all indicating that he was a poor man mainly because of his wilful stubborn integrity. However, he had spawned in the tenement where he lived an extravagant family of red-haired children, all talented in a completely useless way, the same as he had been. This background which that family had created, against which Mat grew up, was one which he loved to remember and which was always mingled, somehow, with his thoughts of the mucky old river about which he so often tried to write.

Mat looked up towards the clock in the room again. Its hands pointed to two-thirty which would make the real time two-fifteen. All this time he hadn't been writing at all, just sitting dreaming. Anyway he was too tired to go on. He got up and went into the scullery to drink a glass of water, then came back into the room to smoke another cigarette. He tried to count how long he had been up without sleep. He had risen that morning at seven-thirty, which was now nineteen hours away, and he had had hardly any sleep the night before. However, the next day was Sunday. He would get a long lie, a read at the papers, then perhaps it would be back to writing again.

The last thing Mat did before going through to his bedroom was to brush up the ashes that had fallen into the hearth.

2

THE OFFICE WHERE Mat worked was outside the city. Instead of the usual thing for office workers who more often travelled into the city, Mat travelled outwards. The tram took the main road out of Glasgow in the direction of Hamilton and Mat had to get off and walk down southwards towards the banks of the river. Again he was in the midst of that strange mixed landscape which occurs on the skirts of big industrial cities. There were old farmhouses, grass fields, ploughed fields, scraggy hawthorn hedges, then open spaces full of rank grass growing over the debris from the heavy engineering industry – rusty boilers, lumps of concrete with the rusty dowelling still sticking out of them – and all over this, in the early morning sun, a natural freshness with the green grass growing hard up against the frozen slag.

The factory itself was old, just a collection of brick buildings which had gradually assumed their present functions as the various different types of plant were installed in them. It was an old family business at one time, and though the family were still connected with it in a vague way it had been a couple of generations since they had anything to do with the management. The type of work done in the factory was traditional in the district. Cotton finishing – the bleaching, shrinking, singeing, and mercerising of the cottons which had been woven in the local mills. Nowadays there was as much work came from Lancashire as did locally. The mills had gone but the business had grown, become modern and fairly prosperous.

The approach to the factory was down a long hedged lane,

past a farmhouse, and a small water reservoir. On the other side of the factory, facing the river, was a row of small cottages, built of stone and very old. The part of the factory next to the cottages had been built over and around them, so that now only the stone fronts showed. They looked like little pieces of semi-precious stone set into the rough crumbling brick of the factory. Some of the factory workers lived in these little houses along with their families.

When Mat passed the old time clock he noticed that it was still early but he went upstairs to the empty office. First thing in the morning the office had a shining pristine look. Everything was either locked away in the safe or tucked away in the files and nowhere was there a single scrap of paper in sight to indicate that work was ever done in the place. The typewriters and the big electric calculating machine lay hooded on the desks, the mahogany woodwork had an opulent shine, the metal topped desks and paper racks were free of dust, the brown linoleum was waxed so that Mat's shoes skited on its surface. It was the most perfectly run office that Mat had ever had anything to do with. It had a written constitution, a system of checks and balances, a Code Napoleon, in which every possible contingency was provided for. There was a set of wooden boards with typed instructions pasted to them laying down the exact procedure for every situation which arose in the office. If a bag of nails was purchased for the use of the factory, its purchase and reception in the factory was carefully noted down and checked, the advice note was signed and filed away for collation against the account, a record of the cost was kept so that the price of any past or future purchases could be checked against the current one, then the cost was marked against a particular operation, the amounts of the bill duly noted in the various ledgers and day books in the proper double entry manner. All these tasks, with the order in which they were to be carried out, were written down on the wooden boards so that no mistake could possibly be made. Provision was made for everything except deliberate human malice. Human error was certainly not discounted and every task which involved calculation was checked twice.

The author of this system, the secretary of the firm, was a Mr McDaid, an elderly inhibited businessman of the old type, very Scottish, a kirk elder and teetotaller. He was a complete mystery to Mat. Not that Mat didn't understand and sympathise with the man's fear of risk. It was not the neurotic ulcer-creating fear of impending doom of the modern businessman that moved Mr McDaid, but an active and intelligent estimation of the kind of events to expect and the right thing to do about them. What was a mystery to Mat was how Mr McDaid got on outside the office when he was not able to put his system of checks and balances into operation. All that Mat knew about him was that he was a nervous, almost incompetent car driver and that his wife pulled down the blinds during the day to prevent the sunshine from ruining the furniture. He was quite a kindly man in many ways but fussy and rather ruthless towards the things he didn't understand. The man's perfectionism was personally irksome to Mat and depressed him in the same way that army routine had done.

Mat went through to one of the front rooms of the office and looked out over the grey muddy river. There was a fairly heavy spate on and where the river narrowed there was a rough striata running up and down the surface of the water. On the other side of the river, about three hundred yards from the office window, there was a great square brick power station completely blocking the view. A little way down to Mat's right a weir curved into the stream and the water poured over it in a smooth liquid curve. On either side of the weir masses of foliage, small tree trunks and mud had heaped up in a squalid untidy pile.

For some reason the view fascinated Mat. It was a particular kind of landscape, a mixture of human and natural industry which intrigued him. Each aspect seemed to take on and mingle with some of the characteristics of the other. The grass and willows growing along the banks of the river were grey and sooty looking; the weeds, dockens, dandelions and dog's flourish were tattered and defiantly stunted; the mud selvedge of the river showed rainbow tints from an oily sediment. But the brick buildings were heavily marked from the weather, the power station had great damp streaks running down it, the pointing on the factory was all crumbled and the bricks eaten with damp and covered with a thin green mossy slime.

There was a vague hum of machinery coming from somewhere inside the building and the faint clank of trucks from somewhere on the other bank of the river. Above it all, the roar and splash of the water.

Something could be done with this atmosphere, just simply out of the landscape. Mat remembered a description of Rome which he had read somewhere. It had been described as a kind of half buried history where everything, the houses, streets, monuments, churches were a huge physical agglomeration of the debris of history. Yet all of Rome could not have fascinated Mat half so much as the acts of the solid Scottish burghers which were embodied in this crumbling industrial landscape. There was something of their tradition even in this modern office in the bound ledgers, the carefully kept files, the records, catalogues and inventories, the meticulousness, the physical prosperity. Away on the other side of the river, hidden from Mat beneath a haze of smoke, was the old Royal Burgh of Rutherglen. That haze, that smoke, was for him a presence which caused in him the thrill of the imaginative excitement and brought out in him the lust for creation. He thought of the peculiar boast which the people of Rutherglen had and which he had written on the cover of his magnum opus – 'Rutherglen's wee roon red lums reek briskly'. This mixture of modesty, complacency, and sheer canniness thrilled Mat. He imagined these old burghers of the eighteenth century with their great heavy walking sticks, their breeches and embroidered coats, their horn snuff boxes, their freemasonry, their mixture of canniness and daring, their overwhelmingly male pursuits; and their women forming a solid domestic background with their crimping irons, warming pans, samplers, linen, and heavy cutlery and their utterly dull and regular lives. Mat felt a tremendous nostalgia for these people and their way of life. He loved the heavy solidity of the old burghers; their substantial broad fronts spread with waistcoat and fob, their great mansions, their big leather boots, their conservative art, their good plain substantial mundane safety.

Mat's thoughts were interrupted by the sound of feet on the wooden stairs. He heard the cheerful early morning sound of voices shouting to one another. He went out to the top of the stairs and shouted down.

'Hurry up you lazy bugger.'

Bill, the head clerk, was coming up the stairs making a deliberate cheerful clatter. He interrupted Mat. 'That wife of yours fairly kicks you out of bed these mornings.'

'I'm just dying to get to work.'

'Don't worry, we'll make you work all right.' Bill was opening the door into the office which he and Mat shared. Although it was a bright warm morning he wore a coat and hat. He took them off, hung them up, fumbled for his keys, fiddled about with his pens, and put on his specs all at the same time. Next door the typists were removing their coats, changing their shoes, opening cupboards and desks, taking the covers from machines.

Mat and Bill were very fond of one another but their relationship was strange. Bill felt sorry for Mat because of his gentle ways and his apparent naïveté. Mat in some strange way sensed Bill's feeling and because of this acted out the part which Bill had given him. He found himself doing this often with people. Not deliberately or dishonestly or with any intention to deceive but because he became as they saw him. Bill's attitude towards Mat was one of affectionate, slightly condescending, teasing.

Occasionally Mat went to visit Bill at his home. Before Mat's marriage he had gone regularly on a Friday night. Bill lived in one of the houses in a row of little miners' cottages just off the main Glasgow to Edinburgh road. On these visits Bill's wife, Joan, fussed and mothered Mat and made him eat too much. During one of these visits a relation of Joan's had come as well. A beautiful blonde girl with wonderful creamy skin whose beauty had struck Mat dumb. She had flirted outrageously with him, teasing him unmercifully for his bashfulness. Margaret, the blonde girl, had sat on his knee and Joan had switched the light off. Mat, in a painful mixture of lust, delight, embarrassment and misery because he was so sure that the girl was merely teasing him, grabbed Margaret by the elbow and started to rub it. Even after Joan had switched the light on again he kept on doing this without being aware of it. Margaret shrieked with delight and shouted at Bill and Joan. 'That's what he does to the girls in the dark, rubs their elbows.' Afterwards Bill made Mat drunk, Mat not being used to liquor, and while Mat talked a lot of nonsense and was comically tipsy Margaret and Bill shrieked with laughter and Joan slapped Bill on the shoulder and frowned at him for 'making a fool of the boy'. Mat went on pretending to be drunk, but all the time he was touched by their good-natured and unmalicious laughter. He felt that they were treating him as a small boy simply because they were the kind of people who had to lavish love on their friends. And he felt that their estimation of his naïveté was a measure of their own goodness and simplicity, also that their ordinary domestic happiness and Margaret's ordinary and wholesome beauty was something which he could only admire from the outside, but which he could never have. He envied them and would have loved to enter into their kind of life. Even this small share, this single visit seemed to him to be the very peak of happiness, but he felt strongly that his relationship with them was transient and the impossibility of ever becoming one of them was complete. He couldn't understand why he felt like this but he explained it to himself as the consequence of a simple moral inferiority in himself. He accepted this as a fact. Of course from any commonsense or social point of view he was as good as the next man. But he did feel that somewhere in him there was a flaw.

After Bill had opened up the safe in the main office he came bustling into the room where Mat was standing looking out into the cobbled yard. 'Weel, weel!' he said, 'this is no earning peenies for the bairns.'

Mat grinned and stopped musing. It was time to get down to work. On Monday mornings before Mr McDaid arrived they had some definite tasks to perform. Regularly every Monday they would read from the meters the gas and water consumption and calculate the amount of coal used by the boilers. These figures were related to the yardage of cloth which had been treated during the week. There was a fixed proportion, so many yards of cloth to so many British Thermal Units, under which the figures mustn't go otherwise there would be something wrong with the fuel economy. There was no whiff of gas, churl of coal or gleam of light to be used, beyond what was required in the service of production. This task was marked down on Monday's list of duties as Item One. After this a list was made out from the weekly calendar lying on the desk of the incidental correspondence, appointments, phone calls which would be made that day. Any task which might have to be deferred was marked into the calendar in its proper date. This was Item Two. Then they checked for information about any new employees in the factory. If none, they would score Item Three off the list, otherwise they would go through the procedure for new employees. File the insurance cards, note particulars into employees book, make out income tax cards, enter names into wages book, mark in wage rate, if young female arrange for medical examination, etc., then when the procedure was complete mark off Item Three from list. It went on like this. Item Four, check up and transfer; Item Five, make out list; Item Six, post up amounts; Item Seven, file and put away; and so forth. It was hardly an exciting job and sometimes Mat would be overcome with such a wave of ennui that his very bones would itch. At other times this was not so. Mat, on the contrary, would find himself immersed in his work, sitting at the high wooden desk in the warm office checking accounts with a vague consciousness of the busy sounds around him – the clicking of typewriters, the subdued hum of machinery from the factory, the muted slapping sounds of parcelling and baling from the despatch department, and the ticking of the big old clock in the waiting room – all these sounds coming through the mahogany door. At these times Mat felt content, almost happy, as if he really had a taste for this kind of work. He would immerse himself even deeper into his task and would come out of this immersion at five o'clock feeling slightly irritable and discontented, with a feeling of being interrupted.

3

HELEN WAS THE kind of girl who if she hadn't had a mind of her own would have married into the middle class. Instead she married Mat. From the fuss created by her parents one would have imagined a colossal social gap between them. Perhaps there was, but this had no effect on their personal relations. Mat met Helen quite by accident one day when he was walking through the town watching the students who were all dressed up and collecting money for charity. Helen had come up to him shaking her collector's can. She was dressed as a sailor, which showed up her strong slim figure. What had really attracted Mat had been that her big brown eyes seemed to shine with intelligence. Mat had tried to flirt with her.

'I'll give you a penny if you give me a date.'

'All right.'

Mat had put a penny into her can.

'See you next year,' she said, and ran off. Mat laughed at her trick and shouted after her. 'Good for you.'

Later he had gone into a record shop. Every two or three weeks Mat and his brother Jake put some money together and either one or the other of them would go into town and buy a record. As usual when Mat was in the shop he was tempted to buy more than he should and he bought a record of Caruso singing 'O Paradiso' from the opera about Vasco da Gama, and one of Sidney Bechet playing 'Maple Leaf Rag' along with his New Orleans Footwarmers. He came out of the shop with his records and wandered about the town watching the students as they ran about dressed in their weird costumes. For the second time Helen came up to him shaking her can in his face. Mat smiled at her.

'It seems we're fated to meet, either that or you're following me about.'

Helen peered at him then she laughed. 'It's you again.' She took the records from under his arm in a friendly way and looked at them. 'So you're a Caruso fan?' But she grimaced slightly at the jazz record.

'Don't be so narrow-minded,' Mat said.

'Huh!'

'It's good.'

'I like the Caruso, I've got one of him singing "Minuit Chretien" but . . .'

'Wouldn't you trust the ear of a Caruso fan? I'm telling you that Bechet's the greatest thing since toast.'

Helen demurred by wrinkling her nose.

'I wish I could convince you.'

'Never mind that, how about some more money for my can?'

Mat grinned slyly and took a half-crown from his pocket, and a penny. 'One's for charity, the other's for a date.'

Helen was a wee bit embarrassed. 'You'll put the half-crown in,' she said, with a kind of challenge.

'I'll not,' Mat said with confidence. 'If you're really a conscientious collector you'll not turn down half-a-crown. And I might get a chance to convert you to Sidney Bechet. You'd make one of the nicest Bechet fans there ever was.'

Helen was hesitating and Mat could see that she was tempted.

'I've got some other records I'll bet you'd like, real tempting ones – Galli-curci, Pinza, de Luca, Chaliapin . . .'

'You haven't got all these?' Helen asked dubiously.

'I have so. And how about Elisabeth Schumann singing "Du Bist Die Ruh"? Just think of it. All that and me too.'

Helen laughed, 'It's the *records* that tempt me.'

'What's it to be. The penny or the half-crown?'

'All right,' Helen capitulated, 'make it the half-crown.'

They had made a date and Mat was so exhilarated that he waved goodbye to her and jumped on to a bus going in a completely different direction from the one in which he had wanted to go. When Helen had walked away from him after they had exchanged names and had arranged to meet, Mat had noticed how, although she was short-sighted, she carried herself erect. That she didn't peer out into the world with her head held forward as most short-sighted people did, touched Mat. Sitting on the bus, thinking of her graceful step as she had walked off, Mat felt half in love with her already.

After they had gone out with one another for a while and had fallen in love, Helen's parents began to put up objections to Mat. They began to think about getting married and her parents were indignant that she would interrupt her studies just to get married to a working-class boy. They put the usual kinds of pressure on Helen and refused even to see Mat. It wasn't at all a blithe experience for them. They naturally expected their love to be smiled on by the world and found instead that it only involved them in a shockingly ugly experience.

Mat remembered his own father's advice. 'Aye, it's all right now, lad. But wait till you've had a wheen of years of marriage behind you and you'll wonder – is it a' worth it?'

'Well, you ought to know,' Mat thought. 'Hardly anybody would be born in the world if people *knew*.' But somehow he was touched and saddened by his father's tone. He knew in fact that his father was right.

They both knew that the advice given to them was right. You can't live on love. Getting a house was next to impossible. Mat's wage at the office was all right for a single bloke but it wasn't enough to keep a family. And look what Helen was used to. Young people in love are careless. They think the world will look after them. But you can't live on love. Above all this Mat had pretensions that were liable to get them into trouble. What was worse was that Helen approved and encouraged him in these pretensions.

They knew that all this was right, or at least they knew why their parents would look at things in the way they did. Like all young people, particularly when they are in love, they thought of themselves as individuals who would be exempt from the common fate. *We* won't make their mistakes. They didn't believe they would ever experience the anxieties and miseries of ordinary domestic life. The kind of erotic dwalm in which they were living convinced them of the truth of this. And they had faith in their own capacity for ordinary loyalty and understanding towards one another which would enable them to suffer what marriage had in store for them with more grace than did their sour advisers.

Although he had committed the sin of hypergamy Mat did not have any unusual motive for doing this. He loved Helen for the same qualities as he would have loved a working-class girl – for her physical beauty, for her eyebrows, her way of speaking gently, for nought, because it came up his humph, a notion, or just because of personal compatability and affection. Their accents were not all that different, nor were their table manners, their inhibitions, prejudices, politics, interests or religion.

Nevertheless, from the beginning Mat felt a sense of strain. Helen had to cut herself off completely from her parents. The fact that her parents lived outside Glasgow made this easy. But Mat felt all the time torn between the desire to 'show them' by becoming a tremendous success at something or other, in a few months, and the desire to defy them by being indifferent and not doing anything. He had, of course, to make a virtue out of necessity and take the latter course. From Helen he felt no pressure at all – she didn't give a damn, and the change from the walnut Steinway grand to the tinkly cottage piano in Mat's home meant so little to her that she'd sometimes close the lid and say, 'I wish to hell I'd my own piano.'

This pleased Mat no end.

Mat had expectations to do with his job. The firm was doing well and was very prosperous. Mr McDaid in his kind fussy way was pleased with Mat's marriage. At first Mat couldn't understand why this should be. Mat at this time could only see marriage as an erotic arrangement and it surprised him that Mr McDaid could sympathise with this kind of affair. It was only later he realised that to Mr McDaid his marriage was essentially a social affair which would make Mat more dependable, reliable, solid, now that he had become the supporter of a wife and the possible begetter of a family. However that might be, as a married man he was 'weel got' by the firm and he got a slight increase in wages as befitted his new status. His life was laid out with certainty before him and he knew that he had only to wait a little while and he would acquire all that was coming to him – responsibility, a diploma in accountancy, a house up a tiled close in a brownstone building and a good steady wage coming in every week, in lieu of love.

The few months that stretched out over Christmas during that first year of his marriage were the longest and most irksome of Mat's life – while they lasted. Later he looked back on these months with nostalgia, so latent had they been with something which it took him years to recognise and which once he had committed himself to a certain way of life he could never attain. He didn't know about this at the time because he didn't know about the nature of his flaw.

Hogmanay fell on a Friday afternoon that year and Bill and Mat had stayed behind in the office after Mr McDaid and the girls had gone home. This was a customary thing for them to do at New Year. After everybody else had gone they drank a few 'haufs' together and brought in the works manager and some of the foremen to toast one another's good health. Mat felt very relaxed and comfortable with his wages in his pocket, including his Ne'erday bonus, and a half bottle of whisky to nibble at. Some of the whisky was inside him already, making him feel warm and just a little drunk. Outside it was cold with the trees stark and a mist rising up from the river and the fields. He wore his best suit and he had that opulent feeling of good clean linen and stout shoes and warmth in contrast to the still silent bitterness, the harsh jagged look of the countryside outside the window.

Earlier that morning Mr McDaid had given everyone in the office a present – Mat and Bill had been given several shirt lengths of really expensive sea-island cotton with a soft rich finish like silk. Mat had been touched by the kindly finicky old man's delight in giving him these. It added to the festive holiday mood. Everyone was kind and happy, shaking hands and looking forward to going home to the dinners and drinks and friends, the warm rooms, the great coal fires, the tables all laid and ready, the glasses shining on the sideboard.

When they had drunk as much as the occasion required they got ready to go, and while Bill locked the outside door of the office Mat stood in the cobbled yard and waited, his breath blowing clouds in the air. Underneath the heavy overcoat he wore a new woollen scarf, on his hands he wore a new pair of kid gloves, inside his pocket he could feel the stiffness of his leather wallet where the belt of his coat pressed into it. The scarf, the gloves and the leather wallet had all been Christmas presents.

When Bill had locked the door they walked up the long leafless lane together, their shoes crunching on the thin ice over the puddles. Bill produced a box of a hundred cigarettes from his pocket and they smoked; the smoke hung in the still air after them. They weren't exactly tipsy, but as they walked they sang and crunched their feet into the frozen ruts in the lane. There were four long days of holiday and rest before they got back to work again. They had worked hard and late that week so that the wages would be ready early. In trying to finish as much work as possible in anticipation of the holidays the week had seemed long. But now it was finished and they were going back to their warm homes with the prospect of a well-earned rest before them. When they got to the little railway station they exchanged the usual parting greetings.

'All the best when it comes.'

'Don't get too drunk.'

'Behave yourself.'

'Ha! Ha! What a chance.'

'See you next year.'

Mat stood looking over the parapet of the railway bridge, watching the train stop, discharge its few passengers, then make up steam and puff its way into the distance among the chimneys, embankments, telegraph poles, signals and mist. Bill was getting a little short-sighted and while he was saying goodbye he had looked at Mat over the top of his specs. For some reason Mat was reminded of the time he had visited Bill a couple of years before. It was for this reason that he stood and watched Bill's train as it went off into the distance. He suddenly felt that Ne'erday feeling of trepidation over the year that had gone and over the year to come. This year the Christmas tree had been full as it had very seldom been and now the day was coming when time would be so radically marked. 'See you next year,' Bill had said. Then it would be back to 'auld claes and parritch', and the prospect of long featureless months before him. Yet as he stood there thinking he couldn't decide whether he trembled at the thought of change or of no change at all.

Jake was passing the corner of the street as Mat crossed from the tram stop. Mat walked quickly after him but his brother's jaunty swagger was too fast for him so Mat whistled through his teeth.

'Limpy Dan, Limpy Dan.'

Jake turned smiling. He preferred for reasons of his own to be addressed in this derisive way. As he held up the paper bag in his hand the bottles inside chinked.

'Cairry oot.'

Mat licked his lips. 'I'm for some of that.'

Jake was older than Mat, shorter in height and much stronger in build. He was neatly and snappily dressed in an expensive tailor-made suit, well-cared-for brown shoes. He liked to put on the bantering air of the older man.

'Steady on, sonny boy. It can get a grip.'

'Ah can take it,' Mat said, and they fell into step together. Neither of them drank over much, but jokes about drinking were the thing on Hogmanay.

As they walked up the road they could see their father at the window. It was characteristic of him that he was standing erect, unlike most people who stoop forward slightly to look out of a window. He was looking quite calm and serious in spite of the fact that he had had a wee smile on his face because Mat and Jake were pretending to hide the bottles. Then he disappeared and the light went out in the room. They went into the close and up the stairs, scliffing their feet, opening their coats, full of officious cheery noise. Jake whistled and shouted, 'Op-ee-en, op-ee-en.' Their father was at the top of the stairs, leaning on the banister. His big figure, even when it was leaning, looked erect and athletic.

'Wheesht,' he said, 'you noisy devils.'

Inside the house Mat and Jake took their coats off, but they kept the jackets of their suits on because it was Hogmanay. Jake went into the living-room to put the bottles on the sideboard. Mat stood at the door of the kitchenette where Helen and his mother were bustling about. Helen wore a soft woollen dress. Underneath the sink there was a bucket full of discarded wrappings and cardboard boxes. Practically all the available space in the kitchenette was covered by plates, trays, bowls, black bun, shortbread, trifle. A vague smell of roasting pervaded the lobby. In spite of the congestion everything in the kitchenette looked neat and orderly. Ma, a small, dumpy, clear-skinned woman, was wiping her hands on her apron and looking at Mat through her spectacles with the smug, self-satisfied air a woman has when everything is under control.

'I can still see the scars of battle.' Mat started to laugh at his mother, for her spectacles were marked with flour and she couldn't see him properly. She looked blank for a minute and said, 'Oh!' She took her specs off and wiped the lenses with her apron.

Mat went into the living-room where Jake was pouring out some beer into three tall glasses. Their father was sitting on a dining chair which was placed against the wall beside the sewing machine. He was leaning forward with his elbow on his knee, his chin cupped in his hand, his legs crossed and one slipper flapping. The table had been pulled out to its full size and spread on the crisp white table cloth was the best cutlery and dinner service, with glasses and paper napkins. On the sideboard were bowls of fruit, nuts and chocolates. Later there would be roast chicken, soup, gravies, sauces, stuffing, whisky, coffee, cigars, boxes of cigarettes. Mat took the glass of beer from Jake and sat in front of the fire. The women were still working in the kitchen, Mat could see through the window across to the back court, the big solid sandstone building. The windows in the tenement were now beginning to light up, showing the warm brightly lit rooms still full of Christmas decorations.

They sat sipping their beer and waited. The dinner would be ready at six o'clock. In the meantime, they sat and basked in the warm room. Nobody had switched on the lights and as it grew darker outside the bottles, the crockery, the polished furniture, the brass knick-knacks, even the apples on the sideboard, glimmered in the firelight.

Before Mat had gone into the army the Craigs had all lived on top of one another in a tiny room and kitchen in Bridgeton. A rough smoky district where the railings had been torn away in the back yard and the outside wash-houses merely a heap of bricks, the flagstones in the closes tilted at crazy angles. The building in which they stayed was all crazy and out of plumb. You went up several flights of worn dirty steps in a spiral staircase and along a wooden-floored verandah affair to the door of the house. In front of each door was an iron grill and you could look right down through the grill and through the other grills on the landings beneath, right on to the cobbled yard. The floor of the kitchen tilted towards the window and when Mat stood washing at the sink he was often near vertigo as he imagined them all being couped out into the street. In these days life had been very different. Jake had worked in the slaughter-house nearby as a 'blood boy', Mat worked as a labourer in a warehouse that sold flour and sugar to bakers. There hadn't been a lot of money and during the years when Mat and Jake had been at school they were, like their kitchen with its sloping floor, continually propped on the edge of some disaster. Often they were exposed to humiliation and abuse. Mat could remember from a very early age the Means Test man who would question the children in the street, or the collectors to whom he'd say, 'My Mammy's no' in'. Later there were the Schoolboard Inspectors and the teachers who'd examine their semmit and drawers, then the grocers and coal men and property factors who'd want money and rent. There were the neighbours who fought and squabbled out of sheer frustration and misery. His father then had done shift work, fire-drawing in a locomotive shed. He worked the coal dust into his fingers and hands and was lucky when he got a square meal seven days in the week. There was plenty of violence – beatings from his tired and exasperated parents, and in the street he saw many a furious fist fight, real accomplished stuff, skilled punching and gouging and butting. There were the women who got knocked on the head with tomato sauce bottles by their husbands. Occasionally Mat saw the razor being used or the broken bottle. Twice he had seen men being killed.

To Mat there was a deep and intimate connection between his memory and his writing. Yet he consciously eschewed all the violence and misery which had been a part of his childhood. He could remember these things but he did not consciously weave them into the stuff of his reveries, never in the same way that he did with those memories of his childhood which characterised his way of seeing things at that time. This part of his remembrance was almost like an object which he had put behind him. Sometimes it all seemed like a very long time ago.

When he had been demobbed from the army he had come back to live in this house with a bathroom, electric light, bedrooms, a living-room. This was a typical period in the life of a working-class family when the children had grown up and there was more money coming into the house. They were additionally lucky in the fact that this period in their lives coincided with the Labour Government's first term of office, with the initiation of the Health Service and decent social security. All his life up till then Mat had thought of domestic life, family life, as a life of sordidness and squalor. Then all of a sudden it had become decent.

It was because of all this that whenever he saw a big brownstone tenement with its walls plumb and its brickwork and pointing in good condition, especially in the dusk when the windows lit up, especially now, in the festive season with Christmas trees in the windows, he felt a feeling almost of ecstasy, powerful in its capacity to move him. A feeling of the slow peacefulness of time when life was full, protected, and without anxiety. This was the fourth year in which they had celebrated Ne'erday like this.

Mat stood in the lobby with his back against the wall and a glass in each hand. He wasn't quite drunk but when he finished his drinks he would be. From the kitchenette he could hear his mother talking to Helen. He had difficulty in hearing what she was saying over the sound of a set of bagpipes being played in the living-room. They were being tuned by his Uncle Tam. A scrap of conversation came from the kitchenette which he could hear: '– if he starts that politics again I'll get Dad to throw him out.' Mat looked at the row of empty bottles ranged against the wall along the floor of the lobby. He could still hear his mother's voice, raised now with indignation, 'It's politics, politics, all the time when all we want to do is enjoy ourselves.'

Mat laughed. If he knew anything Uncle Tam would be talking politics sooner or later because Jake would egg him on. While Mat sipped his beer his father opened the living-room door and the sound of the chanter slapped its way along the walls of the lobby while the floor reverberated from the boom of the drones.

'Ah want an accompanist,' Mat's father shouted. 'Jetta — Jetta. Ah want an accompanist.'

Uncle Tam wouldn't stop playing the pipes until Mat tapped the drones with the flat of his hands and the reeds locked and stopped playing. Tam stopped and looked sadly at the drones. 'A song from the old man and a drink for the piper,' Jake was shouting and Tam took the drink quite pacific. Ma was at the piano already and was pounding out an old music hall song. Mat's father sang in a gentle husky voice that nobody could hear, so unlike his powerful speaking rumble, and Ma played the same chords all the time with her left hand, beating the keys as if they were a drum. In one corner there were some young girls who were cousins of Mat and they were sitting quietly, sipping self-consciously at their sherry. They didn't appear to notice any noise going on around them. When Ma stopped playing the piano a sudden silence occurred amidst the noise. Tam's wife's voice was isolated in the middle of the silence, laughing emptily, and everybody turned at once to look at her. Propped up against the wall with his eyes shut and a drooping smile on his lips was a neighbour; a shy inoffensive wee man, a thief and ex-convict who had somehow wandered into the house. Jake had given him too much to drink and now his face was all clammy white and his upper lip beaded with sweat. Mat just managed to rescue the bagpipes from someone who was about to sit down on them. He lifted them from the stool across which they had been laid, put the drones across his shoulder and held the chanter in his left hand; he stood there feeling a bit drunk. Jake bawled at him across the room.

'Give us "The Battle of Tel-el-Kebir".'

Mat took the mouthpiece between his teeth. There was a whiff of treacle and mouldy leather from the bag. Mat blew and the tartan cloth cover filled out and stretched as the leather bag inside became tight and plump with air. As he gave the bag a quick punch with his fist the drones rasped then plopped harmonically into the simple major chord. As he tucked the bag under his arm the chanter screamed out in the dominant note of the chord. Mat always liked to play the big difficult march tunes to impress Tam because he sometimes teased him about the ridiculous ease with which anyone could be taught to play the pipes. Even the 'big music' – the pibroch – he used to say, was technically child's play, if it was also musical nonsense. Mat played while everyone stopped to listen. It was impossible to talk above the sound of the pipes in a room. Mat began to be more and more irritable as he played. There were three fat female neighbours sitting in a corner and Mat resented seeing them drinking, especially gin, like some cockney harridans. When he played 'The Mist Covered Mountains', a slow air, the three women looked soulful and woebegone; when he played 'Highland Laddie', a quick march, they became all braced up and military as the staunch wee Scottish soldiers, the bow legged kilties, went over the top with their bayonets fixed and an open razor tucked down their top hose. Mat tried out all the stock responses. He played 'The Highland Cradle Song' and they wept for the sticky weans, whom they had dragged up in a cursory and absent-minded fashion and who later became the brawling nuisances who disappeared to Canada. Uncle Tam was listening to him as if he was an artist, a virtuoso, a piping Paderewski. Mat really got to dislike the pipe music he was playing so intensely that in the end he started to play a few bars of a rumba, then a bit of an Orange song. There was a chorus of shocked 'Shs – shs – shs's' and Mat lifted his arm from the bag and stopped playing. Tam looked at him reproachfully.

'Oh! But you're a great piper, Mat. You should have been a great piper, Mat. But these kind of tunes don't fit –'

Jake had sidled up to Tam. 'D' you not think so, Tam?'

'Na! Na!'

'The Siege o' Delhi,' Jake said, 'The Relief of Lucknow, Magersfontein, Spion Kop, where the Boers whipped us, Tam. The 79th's Farewell to Gibraltar, Blue Bonnets over the Border. The Barren Rocks o' Aden, Modder River, the gatlings jammed, Gungha Din, ammunition's gone, rally round the piper boys, unsheath your Malacca canes, over and at them, here comes the Gallowgate Hielan'men. These 'a fit, Tam?' Jake nudged Tam with his elbow.

'Pipe music,' Tam was looking hurt, 'went through a period of Capitalistic and Imperialistic influence.' He stopped for a second to watch the effect of this trump, then he growled at Jake, 'And we *beat* the Boers.'

Jake giggled behind his hand.

'Hey, but listen.' Jake was holding Tam by the arm and whispering to him confidentially. 'How about the new Historical stage in pipe music? Listen. Vladimir Ilyich's welcome to St Petersburg. A good stirring march. And a wee poky strathspey wi' a set of steps to go with it – Uncle Joe's Wee Cley Pipe. Or the Don Cossack's Reel. The Kulak's Lament. Or – listen – how's this for a terrific jig – Wullie Stakhanovitch's Laying the Bricks?'

Tam wasn't very sure but he grinned a bit. Then he got up and brushed past them and sat down on the piano stool, turning his head and looking at Jake reproachfully. Mat went through into the kitchenette. In the middle of his laughter he suddenly felt horribly sick. From the living-room came the sound of voices and Tam had started to play 'Für Elise' on the piano. He often played 'classical' music on the piano, his drunken fingers stumbling on to all the wrong notes. He did this often when he was hurt and he wanted to demonstrate his cultural superiority to the rabble. He played 'Für Elise' or 'Sobre las Olas' – it was all one to him.

Helen was in the kitchenette trying to make coffee amongst a litter of glasses, beer bottles and wrappings. On the draining board there was a long cylinder of ash where a cigarette had been left to burn.

'Here,' Helen said, 'coffee!' Mat took the cup and half sat on the edge of the draining board, rubbing his face with his hand. His face was all stiff and cold and he felt quite sick, and sober.

A little later the piano stopped and singing started. Mat and Helen had put on their coats and were going out for a breath of fresh air. As they went down the stairs they could hear the voices singing sweetly in close harmony and in unison this time. Quite clearly Mat could hear his mother's voice, his aunts' voices, Jake's voice and his cousins' voices making a definite single family sound which was pitched accurately and dominated the other voices.

> 'For the lamps were shining brightly,
> 'Twas a night that would banish all sin.
> For the bells were ringing the old year out,
> And the New Year in.'

Outside in the street they saw two men on the other side of the road. They were propping one another up and staggering back and forward on the pavement. One of them kept muttering away in a drunken persuasive tone of voice, 'Ye'r all right, Jimmy. Ye'r all right,' and he was trying all the time to get a firmer grip so that he'd send them both off balance and they would stagger and reel all over the pavement again. Yet somehow they seemed to be making progress, each fit of staggers would propel them up the street for another few yards. The man called Jimmy had a gash on his brow which went from one temple to the other and the blood had flowed in a sheet, like a little valance, down over his face and the breast of his white shirt. His face, now crusted in dark blood, had a blank mask-like appearance. Helen immediately ran across the road and stood in front of the man, putting her hand on his shoulder and peering into his face.

'Could we help you?' she asked. 'You'll be needing that cut stitched.'

The man knocked Helen's hand aside and waved his arm in a heavy gesture which knocked him off balance. 'Lemme alane,' he shouted, while his mate staggered trying to keep him up. Together they staggered past Helen while Mat came up and took her by the elbow and drew her aside. The man looked back with bitterness and hate in every gesture while his mate tried to pull him on. He was muttering away in an indignant sounding voice and through his muttering all they could hear were the words 'her' and 'she'.

'Somebody did a good job on him,' Mat said.

Helen was shocked and Mat felt immediately ashamed of his reaction. He thought how much better it was to show restraint at this time of the year. It was probably a good idea at this darkest time of the winter to have a formal and ceremonious occasion for the release of inhibitions, for the release of all the hidden gaiety which was locked in men. But in Glasgow it never worked that way. There is always a cold deliberation in the Glasgow man's drunkenness, as if the drink which makes the head spin and the stomach heave still leaves in them the sober certainty of the bitterness of life and the inexorable passage of time. So when they become gay at New Year it is always in a gauche left-handed sort of way which soon degenerates into viciousness and violence and a kind of bitter sentimentality.

Standing in the street watching the bloodstained couple stagger up the street they could still hear the voices coming from the house.

'What a miserable song,' Mat said. 'It's not sad or sweet or anything – just plain dreich.' They walked up the street towards the main road, then they turned the corner and walked out towards the countryside. Mat was muttering away to Helen and shaking his head.

'God, how I hate bloody Ne'erday.'

Next morning Mat woke early feeling strangely refreshed.

Usually in the morning he felt as if he had not had enough sleep and it would take him some time before he would come to and feel like a human being. After he had been tight he always woke feeling bright in spite of spasms of nausea and remorse of conscience.

The party last night had ended as usual. Tam had called one of the innocent young girls 'a painted Jezebel'. He always associated sexual ostentation, even the mildest kind, with 'Capitalism'. He had gone home, weaving down the street, pipes squealing and out of tune, with a crowd of complete strangers weaving in a line behind his back. Jake's comment was, 'The comrades'll be on his top if they catch him.'

Mat and Helen cleaned out some of the mess in the kitchenette and made themselves some breakfast. Then they put on their coats and scarves to go out walking for a while. It was a lovely clear frosty morning full of pale orange light and an angry red-looking disc for a sun. In the street they stood for a minute exhaling their breath in clouds. As they stood wondering in which direction to walk someone waved to them from the other side of the street. They waved back and stood waiting while he came across the street to join them. It was Andrew Fotheringham, slim, very dark, his belted coat neat and his scarf tucked in trimly round his throat. He had a long intelligent face and a habit of looking upwards towards you with his eyes. Mat liked him but he didn't see much of him even though he lived just across the road. He was an engineering student and was usually too busy studying. As they shook hands together Mat felt more at home with the season. 'How'd it go?' Andrew waved the stem of his pipe in the direction of everywhere with a sarcastic smile on his face. Mat and Helen rolled their eyes up. 'God in Heaven – and you?'

'Got by.' He laughed mischievously and shook his head. They walked down the street and round the corner towards the park. The shop at the corner was closed and this reminded Helen. 'I'd better go and try and find a shop open for some bread and milk. You two go and have a dauner.'

As she walked away waving her mittened hand she looked very soft and feminine. Mat felt a twinge of pity for her that she should have become connected with him. She had a marvellous walk. Not the staccato click-click provocative walk so beloved by models, but a smooth undulating glide which for all its sensuousness Mat found appealed to the heart and the affections as much as anything else.

Andrew laughed at Mat. 'And to think I always said you'd end up with a doll.'

'You do learn something from literature.' Mat laughed. '"What is it that a man looks for in a woman? The lineaments of gratified desire."'

Andrew laughed and they walked over the street and through the park gates and along a road that dipped down towards the misty trees.

'The rest of that goes: "what is it that a woman looks for in a man? The lineaments of gratified desire."'

'Nobody will ever see that on your ascetic looking mug,' Andrew said.

'My what looking mug?'

'Ascetic.'

Mat laughed this off. He was used to casting himself in a different role. At one time he used to boast of his capacities and successes to Andrew. That was when he had seen everything through the gay blur of hedonism, when he was self-consciously reacting against the Calvinism which all Scotsmen inherit.

'I would say that you're the one that's an ascetic.'

'Uhuh! Except that I enjoy it.' Andrew was the type of man who'd just stop smoking when he had no money and refuse to smoke other people's cigarettes. 'I mean that there are certain simple desires which given good will, intelligence, a bit of – gumption – are easy to satisfy. But you . . .'

'With my complex desires . . .'

'Yes.'

'Oh, for God's sake, Andrew! I'm just a hick. Just a plain

simple guy. Sometimes I think I'm too stupid to have anything complex about me.'

'You're a bloody weirdie.'

'I don't know why you're always saying that. Just because I'm not a bloody engineer. You're not just a bloody engineer yourself come to think of it.'

Mat picked up a long twig from the pathway and smacked at the iron railing. 'Ha!' He laughed. 'Ha! A weirdie.' He smacked at the railing again and the crumpled dry leaves scattered from the end of the twig. 'Along this way.' They walked over the miniature stone bridge which spanned a burn and then turned along a dirt path which went under some trees. At the end of the path they sat down on a cold bench.

'What I'd like to do at Ne'erday is to go to bed after a few drinks – you know. A good meal, a few drinks and then to bed. Instead of all that mess. You could get up in the morning with the whole day before you.' Mat didn't quite know what he meant, nor did Andrew enquire, but sucked away at his pipe. There was a loud crack as a twig snapped some place and round about them the dusty sparrows were fussing stupidly over something hidden in the grass or buried somewhere in the frozen dirt path. Their wings made a gritty scuffling sound on the hard earth. Mat gazed at the fissured bole of a tree and looked up, blowing smoke and condensed breath at the dry twigs which poked up into the sky.

'If the whole world were reduced to the size of a billiard ball it would be much smoother,' he said.

Andrew had probably never thought of this but his head went back and he stayed silent a minute calculating, checking that Mat's statement was approximately correct. He nodded assent.

'It disturbs me to think that the world might become too small and that our activities on it might have something unnatural and reducing about them.'

Andrew pointed to the sky with the stem of his pipe. 'There's plenty of room up there.' Mat made a disgusted grimace.

'When I went out East on a boat it was this that I loved. You'd look at a boat far, far away on the horizon. Not even a boat but a smudge of smoke away far in the distance and it looked so far that it might have been halfway round the world. What I liked was to round the curve with the boat's screws churning away for hours and you knowing that you were going, say as fast as a tram car, and in half a day you'd pass round that curve, passing the old rusty tramp. And then away in the distance is another curve, another smudge of smoke, another stretch of sea. You can go on like that for days and days. Of course it's easy to reduce all that space. All you need is a jet plane. You point its nose at the Atlantic, zip – spin round the curve for an hour and zip – you're bang on top of America. But what I liked when I was on that boat was to savour every inch, hug every yard, conserve every mile. I used to look over the side of the ship and watch the dolphins swimming on the bow-wave and I'd be glad that I wasn't going any faster than any living animals. Then I used to say to myself, "the world's big".'

'The psychologists explain this, though it usually happens with time.'

'Of course with time. Except that it's much easier to reduce. You don't need jets or combustion engines. You don't have to invent anything. You only have to get up late some morning with all your routine knocked up and when you think about it time starts to go at a horrible speed. Or you remember something, something which is perhaps important to your life that happened say two years ago. And if there has been nothing happening between then and now, an event or a series of events which relate to that importance, then the two years can become all squeezed up and become like a second.'

'It's supposed to be a sign of reduced vitality in the organism.'

Mat looked at Andrew with his dark robust looks. He had served his time as an engineer, then late in life had taken a grant to go to University and now he was contentedly sitting at night studying his vectors and calculus and nuclear theory and refusing any temptation which would lure him away from his goal whether it was the proffered cigarette, the odd night out at the pictures, a line of thought or study which threatened to become too interesting, or the wee girl in whom he had become interested.

'I never make plans,' Mat said, 'for tomorrow doesn't exist. Besides it's far too near.' This remark sounded relevant to Mat. 'Do you ever worry about time?'

'No,' Andrew said. 'Never.' Mat could almost by an act of sympathetic imagination feel like him, with his healthy human long slow days. As he sat looking at his tough face he felt that he almost envied him. 'Reduced vitality?' he asked, like a patient naming a symptom suggested to him by a doctor.

They kicked their heels in silence for a while. Mat idly wondered how he could describe the freezing park around him when everything about its clamped-up frozen appearance seemed to deny the sensuousness out of which words came. Across the path there was the bole of a tree all black and fissured and around it the ground had been tramped as hard as concrete and the grass all worn. Down at the end of the little valley in which they were sitting he could see the park railings through the trees. He couldn't think of a word, but felt such an awful absence of language that his tongue and palate felt all dry and gritty, a numbness, as if everything in the world had become stuck.

When Mat looked up Andrew was pointing up the path, and he looked round to see a jaunty figure coming along the path.

'Alec,' Andrew said.

Alec and Andrew had known one another all their lives and they were close friends. Mat had come to know both of them when he came back from the army. Alec had at one time won a grant to go to Ruskin College in Oxford and he had a certain amount of intellectual sophistication. He read the weekly reviews and tried to encourage Mat to do so. He was a self-confessed fellow traveller. He had light brown hair, a high colour, a pointed bony nose. He smiled with his mouth twisted in a highly infectious way; his laughter was infectious also and he had been known to reduce a whole company of people to near hysteria by this quality of his laughter. Mat was very pleased to see him. He felt that their company, Andrew's healthy doggedness and Alec's bubbling energetic merriment, would ward off something. He knew that they suspected him of some weakness, a lack of self-sufficiency for which his desire to write was a compensation. He made up for this in their eyes by being able to keep up with them in their long logical discussions. In actual fact, although he was quicker and more mercurial than they were in discussion they often found to their surprise that he had much more stamina than they had, though they never ceased to disbelieve this slightly. Alec waved to them, then came up and stood before them with his hands in his coat pockets and his usual grin on his face.

He started to tell them of a book he had been reading. *Oblomov* it was called, by a Russian author named Goncharoff, pretending some difficulty in pronouncing these names. Neither Mat nor Andrew had heard of the book. The description which Alec drew of the book was really comical. It was full of sordid descriptions which Alec had invented for himself. Later, when they had read the book, it didn't seem quite like Alec's description of it. It was about a man, Alec said, who lay about in bed all day, spilling tea on the blankets, burning the sheets with his cigarettes, while the dust fell in clouds round about him, the paper rotted and peeled from the walls, the spiders festooned the cornices, the candelabra, the corners with great black cobwebs, the silverfish ate the books, the rugs mildewed and Oblomov lay waiting for the flood tide, the momentous decision, the apocalyptic message, the cataclysmic revelation, which never comes. Alec began to hint at the psychological aspects of Oblomov's behaviour which he thought the author intended as a satire on the kind of beliefs held by Mat. On the value of immediate gratification for instance. Mat didn't seriously or whole-heartedly subscribe to these beliefs, but he did chance his arm with ideas which seemed to them to be pretty wild. He had once suggested to them that the end of immediate gratification would be to prevent moral corruption. His idea was really quite unlike hedonism and had rather more in common with Sartre's idea of the inauthentic existence, although it was less clear in Mat's mind. They agreed with him that the rebel was the highest human type. Democratic Socialism was the greatest social idea. Yet in this society a man is recognised for what he is by what he does. He has a label on him. Doctor, lawyer, physicist, labourer, clerk. If you are born to humility and feel rebellion there are two things you can do. One is to wait carefully, plan, study, educate yourself so that in the end you can wear your label and become one with your peers, no longer humble. Or else you rebel, you demand immediate recognition of the fact that you are a man – a person. This is a question of pride, and there is a lovely paradox here for in your pride you are forced, if you stay with the principle, to accept humbly, more to demand the immediate recognition of every other man's right. 'That's why I'm an artist,' Mat would say, 'because an artist is recognised by what he is rather than what he does.' The simplicity of these ideas were later to appal Mat. He would hesitate too on the word 'artist', as he felt he couldn't confidently claim to be an artist until he had done something, nor did he notice the contradiction except as a general feeling of unease.

'Freud says that art is a compensation for failure in life and that this act of compensation is similar to the – well, say the doctor's study. In fact you are doing the same thing in a different way.'

'No,' Mat said, 'because the artist judges the creative success of his work by itself and not by his success in the world.'

'So does the doctor, surely, his success as a doctor is counted by the number of patients he cures, the success of his work.'

'Oh, but there's a difference.' For a moment Mat's thoughts were disturbed by a sudden sense of the cold. A cold wind blew down the little glade and the bare twigs cracked. 'It's – you know, laymen, us, and the doctors, we have the same standard of judgment – the health of the patient. No cure – no success. But the artist? How many artists are there – best-sellers – the sort of people who have achieved success, their drives satisfied, recognised by the world – who are a hollow sham?'

'Let me see?' Alec said. 'There must be some.' He rubbed his chin, looked upwards reflectively. 'You mean like James Joyce, D. H. Lawrence . . .'

'Ach,' said Mat, shivering with the cold. Then he pounced on an idea, 'Look – capital is the crystallisation of man's labours. An educated man is the crystallisation of other men's labours – his teachers, lecturers and that. In other words – a piece of capital.'

'Well, a work of art is the crystallisation of a man's experience – like a piece of capital.'

Mat sawed at the air with his hand, screwing his face up. Beneath all this gauche wrestling with these hard jagged ideas he had a tenuous grasp of something much richer. There were other thoughts, difficult and more complex, but only vaguely illuminated in his mind. He would have liked to stop and think about them. 'My idea of immediate gratification is that in revolt . . .' His voice trailed off.

They were all lip-service Marxists, but they were all equal in their embarrassment at the idea of economic determination which lurked beneath Marxist thinking. This conflicted with so much else that they thought and assumed.

They rose, their limbs creaking from sitting on the cold bench. It was too tough a nut to crack sitting on a cold bench in a freezing park. Alec and Andrew went forward up the path and for a moment Mat stood and looked at the slow trickle in the burn. He made a mental note of Alec's speech when he had told them of Oblomov. 'There was this man, Oblomov – a character – who lay stinking in his kip all day . . .'

The others were walking along the path now some distance away. Mat lit a cigarette and felt his mouth dry and gritty.

When they were talking he had felt a desperate urge to come to some resolution, so that he'd say: 'That's the way it is, now we can do this.' He wanted to have some idea that would have some feeling around it. He must be like Alec's description, Mat thought. Then he realised what had long escaped him about the difference between himself and the others. It was simply that he did not evaluate himself. He knew his own weaknesses as well as the others did, but he simply accepted them, for they were his own. For a while he wondered vaguely if this was pride, laziness or complacency. Then he ran after Alec and Andrew up the path, his muscles stiff with cold. He couldn't think of any idea which would warm the park.

4

THE NE'ERDAY HOLIDAYS had passed, the four precious days frittered away with the upset routine, meals at all sorts of strange times and dutiful visits to relatives. Mat felt a vague sense of anxiety at this time, and the anxiety remained. He remembered how he and Helen had made plans about their marriage. They had imagined a house of their own, Helen cooking fantastic meals, cosy nights by the fire, long slow evenings with the clock ticking slowly and Mat sitting writing, and their friends would all come and sit and eat open sandwiches, drinking coffee and talking; and music, listening to the Vienna Philharmonic under Fürtwängler on the gramophone. Instead of the vicious knockout drinks like whisky and gin they would drink wine and there would be talk, witty, relaxed, and coruscating with ideas. Out of all this Mat was sure he could write brilliant and exhilarating books. He had the young man's sense of the particularity of his thoughts, their uniqueness, and he would think like André Chenier when knocking at his head, 'There's something there'. They would gather round them a circle of friends, young, modern, talented, and their whole lives would be lived in a glow of creativeness and love.

Any young man is a bundle of possibilities, and the world which is before him is like a city seen at night with its lights shining and its gay noise; this world is a beckoning, tempting thing. You can become anything – Mat could remember the great marathon runner whom he had seen as a child at a sports meeting, and he could remember the cheers and the glory, the great wave of sound which followed the athlete after he had plodded in agony into the running track; he could remember the tiny figure of the famous centre forward running out from beneath the stand at Ibrox Park, out into the middle of the stadium and how as he stood enrapt on tiptoe his throat choked as the voices of the fans rose into a magnificent roar.

And there had been moments like this which he had shared himself, watching the oval ball's queer stuttering movement like a bat against the sun, taking it from an awkward bounce and twisting and dodging and finally being slammed down by a fourteen-stone scrum-half, the ball in his outstretched hands just six inches beyond the line and bang between the sticks. And afterwards coughing and gasping, his mind gone and the tears streaming from his eyes as the team pummelled and thumped him with joy and the team supporters shouting and his Commanding Officer running on to the field to shake him by the hand.

He could remember the excitement of his last exams at school when he had sat reading the test papers and was aware that what he knew was more than what was really required and he had sat writing, thinking only of perfection, striving to probe, not just a passable result, but a hundred per cent mastery of his subject.

Footballer, sprinter, scientist, artist, scholar. All the possibilities of mastery and skill. All these possibilities which glitter before you like a set of lights. Not just a set of bewildering choices, but a rich flowering and opening out – girls, riches, glory, ease, skill – all the rich glowing life of adult freedom and responsibility.

Yet shades of the prison house! He had read only recently that a sprinter is past his best at the age of twenty-one, and he had thought with an irony that reflected a hidden discomfort that that was one possibility to be scored off the list. And with this formal acknowledgement which he made that it was now too late for something went another more subtle change in the consciousness itself. That dew-dropped leaf seen fresh and new with only its greenness and wet is now seen through a haze of memory and association. The physical world comes to us again and again until we become tired of it and for moments become just a little bored and satiated. The adult, of course, responds to this change by going further afield. His desires become more complex, richer; and it is here that he is often drawn up short, feels the violent tug of the curb, when all this theoretical latency becomes circumscribed by the bald, brutal facts of his own individual existence. He begins to feel a slight anxiety; he finds it irksome when the little pangs of boredom come along that he has nowhere to turn. Maturity has many reserves and Mat didn't feel irked all that badly at first. Just a vague sense of anxiety. At the beginning of the new year they started to look for a house.

And so commenced a long trail round the factors' offices, scanning advertisements in the paper, reading through the cards posted up in newspaper-shop windows among the advertisements for folding prams, electric razors, fur coats (as new), three-piece suites, wringers, babies' cots, electric gramophones (hardly used), following the trail to derelict old houses kept by shabby widows, or spinsters in dressing-gowns, with rusty baths, greasy cookers and peeling mauve wallpaper; among the derelict lodging house clientele – the bachelor salesmen who cooked for themselves, the potty old maids, the young arrogant clerks, the transient labourers – all the atmosphere of seediness or petty immorality. There were the crisp spotless bedrooms with respectable landladies, fingers hooked ready for the money, or the already crowded working-class house where they had to make room for the sake of the money. They saw young flashy property agents who could tell at a glance if they could afford to pay key-money. There were dozens of flights of stairs in city offices and dozens of shaking heads through sliding glass windows.

Mat and Helen didn't lose hope. They spent long nights walking through the streets under the lamplight, talking and dreaming, Clear nights, with the lights of distant houses twinkling in the dark and the open sky above and the vague outline of hills away to the south of the city; walking over the golf course fairway.

During this time Mat acquired an unusual obsession. When he had first left school he had worked for a while in a big department store where they had put him to work in the leather goods section. There he had sold leather bags. They had been made of pigskin of the finest quality hide and their prices were always marked in guineas. Now he had the idea of working them up into some image – the remembrance of them was connected so strongly with a certain mood – and he became interested in trying to catch the quality of this mood. The bags had been so solid with an opulent patina on them that they reminded him somehow of the sheen on a Dutch painting. At this time too he bought a copy of Vermeer's 'View of Delft' and had hung it in their bedroom. Although he couldn't catch for himself the quality of this image or its usefulness for himself, he seemed to be seeing it everywhere – in the big wooden doors in churches with their great iron hinges, studded and with massive hasps – the glint of ivory or the intricate dovetailing in the drawer of an old cabinet in an antique shop – these things seemed to him to hint in some way at the pathetic urge in man to ward off the circumstantial. In the end he managed to write a story in which something of this was expressed. He couldn't quite get into the story what he felt was significant about the human artefact, to say directly how this significance touched him. Its meaning was at once so powerful and so elusive that his equipment was simply insufficient to incorporate it into a work with all the strength of its echoes and reverberations, all its shadows and glimmerings. He wrote instead a story almost straight from memory.

When he was a boy there had been an unroofed lavatory in his school with walls made of red glazed brick which were topped with half-round glazed brick tops put there to prevent boys from walking along the top of the wall. After school hours several boys would often take the urge to climb up round the lavatory and jump from one wall to another. Mat hated when they did this because the more daring ones would shout 'Feartie', and taunt anyone unwilling to climb up on the walls along with them and share their risk. He was so terrified also of the sickeningly hard concrete floor of the lavatory, that however much they taunted him he would never attempt to climb up. In a way he wasn't even ashamed of being afraid. Trees were different, being full of branches and leaves and rough bark and knobs which you could cling to, and if you slipped all you got was your knees and elbows skinned. Across the road from the school in an empty yard there was an old brick mill with an iron fire escape that went away up higher than even the roof of the school. Mat wasn't afraid to climb that and it was much higher than the lavatory walls. Of those implacable tiled walls he was afraid. Once when he had been playing at a game which the boys called 'hudgies', that is stealing rides on the backs of motor lorries, he had fallen off a lorry that had accelerated suddenly and cracked his head on the ground. He remembered how odd he had felt and how he had wandered about for some time saying funny things and not quite knowing what he was doing. Now when he looked at those dizzy, slippery walls and that hard wet lavatory floor he would think of what it would be like to fall into that awful square chasm and he would feel as if his head had gone empty and his skull had been rung like a bell.

Once Mat had come out of school with his pal Geordie and they had stood in the playground arguing about what they would do. Some of the bigger boys had already gathered about the lavatory walls and Geordie wanted to stay and climb them. Mat tried to coax him off elsewhere.

'C'mon and watch the waterworks,' he had said.

Geordie was disgusted. 'The waterworks! You're always wanting to go and watch the waterworks. There's nothing there. Nae fun.'

They had gone across to the yard beside the factory and walked up and down, arguing and scrunching their feet in the piles of broken glass which seemed to collect there. Mat couldn't understand why Geordie liked climbing the walls. Nothing, not the attraction of the bigger boys' company, not even the fact that sooner or later someone would eventually summon up the nerve to climb over into the adjoining chocolate works and come back with some cartons of stolen chocolate, could get Mat over his aversion for these walls.

'You stay if you like,' he said. 'I'm going to the waterworks.'

'The waterworks!' Geordie was scornful and as he ran away from Mat towards the school he kept turning back and shouting, 'Feartie, feartie.' Mat stood and watched him go, but he didn't care.

Near the school there were quite a few high tenements and buildings which were either warehouses or factories and all the streets around were bustling with life; the dust never seemed to settle anywhere with the continual stir. On a piece of waste ground there was a game of football going on and Mat could hear the uncomfortable gritty sound of the ball as it bounced and scraped on the stony hard packed earth. And the ragged scraping sound which the boys made as they scuffled and dunted with one another set his teeth on edge. He moved away from all this torrid congestion, looking back from time to time until a bend in the road cut out the sight of the wall. The last Mat saw of Geordie was his tiny figure straining up, his arm outstretched as someone sitting astride the wall leaned down and tried to pull him up.

The long road which led to the waterworks was very quiet. It led straight out to the banks of the river and had been so long disused that grass had grown up round the cobbles and only a rudimentary pavement was left. After Mat had rounded that bend which had hidden Geordie from sight, the road in front stretched out long and straight and empty, pointing across the river, past a collection of low greystone buildings to the countryside beyond, where some long glass hothouses reflected the rays of the sun. At the end of this road on the right-hand side were the waterworks, shallow square pits bedded with gravel which was combed by rows of curved silvery jets of water squirting from big metal pipes. These metal pipes moved to and fro across the gravel beds. The whole of the waterworks was surrounded by a high neat green-painted iron fence. Mat just stood at the fence and listened to the hiss of the water falling into the gravel.

There was nobody about except for a man in dungarees standing still just inside the furthest part of the fence. His presence only seemed to intensify the loneliness of the place. Mat felt an emotion which had something to do with the peace and quiet of the spot. Everything about it was so neat, the green-painted iron fence with not a rail bent or missing, the big metal pipes running up and down in orderly parallels, the tidy flat surface of the gravel; even the water, usually so inchoate and turbulent, was now formed out into even rows of identically curving jets and everywhere there was a quiet implacable activity. Mat stood for a while by the fence simply enjoying being there amid the peace, then he went down towards the river and made a little nest among the long grass. He sat and whittled at a stick and listened to the hissing sound coming from the waterworks. He tried to feel something of the permanence of the place, with its own road on which the grass grew and to which nobody came.

It was later, after teatime, when he was coming home from a message which his mother had sent him, that Mat met Geordie's sister. She was quite excited by the news she had to tell him, full of importance and unaware of the seriousness of what she was saying.

'Geordie fell off the lavvy wall and landed on the back of his head and he's got a mark just here' – she pointed to the back of her skull – 'and it'll never go away. I've got to go a message. Cheerio!'

When he got back to the house his mother had asked him about Geordie's accident. Her questions showed her anxiety that Mat should not be implicated in the affair.

'Were you there?'

'Naw.'

'And did you see him climb?'

'Naw.'

'Did you fall out with him?'

'Naw. I don't even know what has happened.'

'He broke his skull,' Ma said. Mat felt his head go all empty and he could imagine the cracking of bone on the hard lavatory floor. His mother continued, 'The ambulance took him to hospital.'

After this Mat sat in a corner brooding. He had to try not to think of the sheer walls from which Geordie had fallen. Instead he tried to think of the waterworks. Just about half-an-hour before bedtime a knock came at the door and his mother went to answer it. She stayed there for a long time talking and Mat could hear the women's voices rising and falling in a regular rhythm. He could hear odd phrases. 'Terrible, uhuh!' – 'Is it no' awful?' – 'Uhuh!' – 'Uhuh!' The note of the women's voices was of that avid complacency, a mixture of smugness and fear with which people discuss other people's disasters. Although the sound of their monotonous voices humming on at the doorstep increased Mat's depression, the natural tone of pity was missing which would have prepared him for what his mother told him when she came back into the room.

'I just heard there, that wee Geordie's dead.'

Mat didn't answer his mother. He tried to think about it but he couldn't. He couldn't imagine Geordie dead. He couldn't feel anything except that he was miserable and cold. All this while his mother was clucking her tongue and commiserating with herself.

'Ma? The sound of his voice startled even himself it was so desperate and cajoling. 'Can I go round to Faither's to stay the night?' By 'Faither' he meant his grandfather Devlin.

'All right,' his mother said, 'if you like, but you'd better get away before your father comes home or he'll not let you.'

Outside it had turned chilly and the street lamps were on. Mat's shadow flitted round him silently as he passed the street lamps and he felt afraid. The street was so still and he was frightened of his own loneliness and of his shadow and of the quiet street. Suddenly, while he was thinking about Geordie, he realised. All through the summer the girls had played singing games in the street. Mat could almost hear their sharp indifferent voices as they sang.

> 'Water, water, wallflowers,
> Growing up so high.
> We are all children,
> And we must all die.'

As he remembered the girls' song the night became empty and alien. As he looked up the sky seemed nothing but a vast black windy space. He fled through the street and ran up the stairs to his grandfather's house knocking desperately at the door until it was opened; then he hurried into the warm bright room with its clutter of dishes, remnants, string, screwnails, pipes, people, knobs, newspapers and its smell of tobacco and women and people; he rushed up to the fireplace and sat down on the fender with his back to the oven door.

Mat was quite pleased when he managed to finish writing the story about this experience. It was so seldom that he ever managed to finish anything now as ideas and inspiration were coming to him either in fragments or in big bald lumpy shapes. He found himself usually writing fragments or else so many long rambling processions of ideas each of which would retain their discreteness and which he hadn't the strength or the skill to fuse together. Sometimes everything seemed to congeal into a hard intractable nothingness against which his imagination would bounce and exhaust itself. But he was fairly pleased when he managed to write the story. It seemed to have something in it of that thing which was glimmering in his mind and which was so peculiarly represented by the hide bags, the Rutherglen burghers, or a Vermeer landscape.

So January, February and March went by and Mat sat up at night resisting the encroaches of time, casting his memory back and ever backwards to his childhood, writing with a sense of personal nostalgia the long accounts of his boyhood experiences, when the smoke and grime, the violence, the dizzy vertigo of life in the room and kitchen, had all been seen with a timeless sense. And further back he'd go, indulging himself vicariously in the timeless world of the Eighteenth Century Scottish burgher, writing more into his magnum opus 'Rutherglen's wee roon red lums reek briskly' which would contain all his love – but what was the object or the nature of this love he could not say.

Occasionally Mat would take a day off work and he'd go to the library and sit and write. This always caused an awful feeling of self-division in him. Like all Scotsmen Mat had inherited the Old Testament idea – this inheritance came to him through the secular facts, that work was – though it would be impossible to formulate what these ideas were; work was, of course, a curse and a bore; also it was the most valuable thing in the world; it gave you bread and butter, it was the source of your self-respect, it was the cause of great bitterness, it was the means of sustaining a decent respectable way of life, it was maintenance, protection, aliment, your stoke and your stay. Above all it was labour, it was the means to an end and Mat never suspected that it might have a value in and for itself. So although he was quite capable of enduring long hours of writing at a stretch, of sustaining intense periods of concentration even when he was otherwise fatigued, he had no doubt at all that this activity was neither labour nor work. He moralised to himself that when he took days off his work to write he was merely being lazy, indulging in temptation. In spite of his love of literature and writing he felt underneath that there was something slightly immoral in earning money by writing when it was not really working. It didn't matter to Mat how arduous he might find the task of writing, and he probably found it more difficult than most people. The fact that it was what he wanted to do precluded it from being defined as work.

It had all started when he had been staying up writing too late one night. The next morning he had felt so tired that he had lain over long in bed and had been late for work. This had made him feel unpleasant. From the day he had left school he had never been late for work, nor had he ever taken a day off. He had got himself ready very quickly and drank a cup of tea. Then he ran out of the house slamming the front door and pelting down the stairs with a piece of toast in his hand.

Outside there was a thin March sun. The first sun of the year, though the air was still cold. Mat ran up the street towards the tram stop. He suddenly halted and started to walk quite slowly. An impulse had come over him and instead of taking a tram to work he crossed over the street and took a tram going in the opposite direction altogether.

He sat on the top deck of the tram huddled against the window, beginning to feel guilty already. It was so late that the trams were now going into town fairly empty and there were the long lines of rush hour trams coming back from the centre of the town where they had discharged their loads of busy workers. In the draught-proof car Mat felt the March sun warm through the glass, though outside as they passed the cemetery in the Gallowgate there was a shifting mist rising up from the earth. At Glasgow Cross the traffic was jammed up beneath the Tolbooth, lorries speeding back and forward from the fruit market, the carriers' quarters and the warehouses, little busy vans and business men's cars all in a tangle. From the top deck of the tram there was a vista up Argyle Street of trolleys and wires. There were girls window dressing in a draper's shop and the precise policemen at the points. All the time a diastolic spasm as the streams of traffic surged and stopped, surged and stopped.

The clock on the Tolbooth showed it to be ten o'clock. Already! Normally he would have got through a pile of work by this time, and he'd have been able to look back on a morning's achievement, two long hours of work. Normally he'd be thinking, 'It's only ten o'clock', now he was thinking, 'Ten o'clock already'. This depressed him, gave him a feeling of sackcloth and ashes inside. And all the people hurrying about – errands, occupations, duties, schedules – while his day seemed to stretch out before him in rags and tatters.

When he got off the tram car he walked down Stockwell Street towards the Clyde. The pavement was jammed with people and when he walked under the railway bridge he was forced at times to wait while the commercial lorries backed in from the street underneath the archways where the carriers' quarters were, and chandlers' stores and warehouses. There was a strong composite smell of oil and sugar, and as he walked further down the street, of fish. He turned to the left, walking through the street outside the fishmarket. At the angle between the pavement and the side of the buildings there was a minuscule of dried horse dung and fish scales. There were patches of wet on the tarmacadam of the road and scatterings of grain where an impatient horse had shaken its nose-bag, a terrific flurry and scatter of hooves as a carter backed his horse into an archway, his voice ringing out in authoritative yelps, 'Hup! Hup! Hup!' and the thudding of fish boxes as the porters lifted and dumped them, their heads covered in snoods of hessian. Mat walked on underneath the railway bridges, past the sordid street markets where all sorts of junk was sold, past the rag stores and the red brick city mortuary and the Police Courts. He turned up past the gates of the Glasgow Green to the parapet of the bridge from where he could see the old Clyde, the colour of a back court puddle, winding in through the Green towards the centre of the city. Up Crown Street was a vista of dust and ashes. Mat had walked all this time with his head down, watching the toes of his shoes as they peeped in and out, in and out, from under the hem of his coat. Now as he stood on the bridge he felt the need for some sensuous stimulation, something which would destroy his grimy grey feeling of nothingness. Above the buildings the sky was harsh from a washy diffuse sunlight.

He was standing on the bridge looking over the parapet into the dirty water, at the very spot where Boswell had stood and looked at the widest streets in the whole of Europe. Gles Chu! Glasgow! The dear green place! Now a vehicular sclerosis, a congestion of activity! He felt for a cigarette in his pocket and the match which he lit flared bitterly in the cold air. The city about him seemed so real, the buildings, the bridge, the trams, the buses, so separate and hard and discrete and other. He felt again a wave of nostalgia for another kind of existence – waxed fruit, sword sticks, snuff, tobacco, shining brass valves, steam pipes, jet ware, wag-at-the-wa's, horsehair sofas, golf cleeks, cahootchie balls – all the symbols of confidence, possibility, energy, which had lived before this knotted, tight, seized-up reality which was around him had come to be.

He looked over towards where the obelisk in the park squatted, obscene. With its memories, Omdurman, Ypres, Tel-el-Kebir, screaming pipes, whisky, sweeping moustaches, regimental dinners, photographs in barbers' shops and boys with Malacca canes. Brass button sticks and old medals in junk shops. The park looked grey like a plucked fowl with its stark leafless trees. He leaned on the smooth granite parapet of the bridge easing the weight on his legs. Glasgow! Gles Chu! The dear green place!

Just as the Clyde comes into Glasgow it takes its last big loop. On the inside of this last loop is the old common land, the Glasgow Green, with its public bleaching green, its play parks, its People's Museum. To the west of the Green is the old hub of the city where the old merchants once conducted their business and built some of their houses. From this spot, but slightly to the south of the modern commercial hub of the city, the river runs nearly straight on, under the bridges and railway viaducts to the docks and the famous Clyde shipyards at Govan. Mat turned away from the parapet and started to follow the river in this direction. He moved off the bridge to the north bank of the river and walked along past the fish market again. He went past the exodus of vehicles, past the long narrow streets with their shipping offices, sundriesmen, pubs, seamen's institutes, carriers' quarters, chandlers, whisky bonds and coopers' yards. He smelled the spice, rope, tallow, flour, butter, treacle, fish and beer. He could see the varnished tops of the ships' masts, their stays and rings and splices all whipped and white with paint. There were big red funnels and spidery derricks and cranes looming over the tops of warehouses. He was walking along an almost straight mile of river. To the north was the hub of Glasgow, a piled-up heap of buildings, offices, shops, theatres, cinemas. As he looked up the long telescopic streets the magnificent views and perspectives were all blocked by a tangle of wires and roofs and chimneys and gables. On the other side of the river he could see where Hutchesontown and Gorbals lay with their broad streets and their good sandstone houses all sordid with abuse and disrepair. Mat thought of the enthusiastic Victorian citizenry who had built all this – the city fathers, all waistcoated, befobbed and frock-coated – who had accumulated all this great heap of iron and glass and steel and stone, all these great blocks of sandstone and granite. Were they really slaking an aesthetic passion? Trying to understand them sympathetically Mat felt he could understand their counting house satisfaction in this great pile-up orgy of anal-erotic vigour.

A Calvinist, Protestant city. The influx of Roman Catholic Irish and Continental Jews had done nothing to change it, even if they had given to its slum quarters an air of spurious romance. Even they in the end became Calvinist. A city whose talents were all outward and acquisitive. Its huge mad Victorian megalomaniac art gallery full of acquired art, its literature dumb or in exile, its poetry a dull struggle in obscurity, its night life non-existent, its theatres unsupported, its Sundays sabbatarian, its secular life moderate and dull on the one hand and sordid, furtive and predatory on the other. Yet Mat had to admit that all this moved him in a way that art could only be secondary to; the foundries, steelworks, warehouses, railways, factories, ships, the great industrial and inventive exploits seemed to give it all a kind of charm, a feeling of energy and promise. He thought of its need for introspection which was traditionally satisfied by the Saturday night binge, when its hero, Homer, and apotheosis in a cloth bunnet would lull his maudlin soul to rest with the drunken hymn.

'When Ah get a couple of drinks on a Saturday,
Glasgow belongs to me.'

Belongs! Belongs! Mat could understand that, too. A dirty filthy city. But with a kind of ample vitality which has created fame for her slums and her industry and given her moral and spiritual existence a tight ingrown wealth, like a human character, limited, but with a direct brutish strength, almost warm. Glasgow! Gles Chu!

Mat walked on up a long narrow street flanked by the blank backs of warehouses. Heavy lorries were roaring and bumping up and down the street and the dust stirred by their passing set Mat's teeth on edge and made his nose dry and stinging.

Later on Mat went into a working man's tearoom full of carpenters with dusty overalls and rolled up sleeves, builders' labourers with cement stained rubber boots, and lorry drivers, tense and unrelaxed even while they were eating their soup. Mat ordered a meal of rolls and sausage and tea. Afterwards he went to the old library and sat in the reading-room among the old-aged pensioners and modellers. He read all the afternoon from a volume of Hegel's work. His head went down into the book amid the teasing abstraction of the old German. He sat there the whole time utterly absorbed and completely oblivious to the hectic toiling and hurrying and scraping and worrying that was going on in the city round about him. He was captivated by the idea that the act of being might be connected with the act of forming, that consciousness might be form; and another idea which almost bounced him out of his seat so that he rocked back and forth with excitement as he read that his discrete, individual nature might depend upon the fact of his mortality. He was still excited and preoccupied by these thoughts when he noticed the pale pink lights in the offices which he could see through the steamy windows of the library. It was time to be home.

5

ONE OF THE problems of writing was what Mat called to himself the 'relativity of desperation'. People could, or rather they must, pay token admission to the plight of the drowning man who clutches at a straw. If we don't feel the pain, the water searing at the lungs, or the choking sense of strangulation, or the fluid chaotic element without solidity or ground at which the limbs clutch and thrash, or the physical panic in which the body writhes and bends, or the wild moral fear, at least we can't justify our own safety by pretending that the drowning man's writhing is excessive, that there is no real need for it. Not even if we are Glaswegians.

But what of a lesser case? A quiet undramatic desperation? The old lady who goes into the shop on the evening before she draws her pension and buys a sixpenny packet of tea. She counts her money, her pennies, and decides that she hasn't enough to buy a packet of biscuits. That's all! Maybe she has only a few years to go, a few hundred more weeks to count and divide and scrape at her pension. As the clock ticks it's a long time to live. But if you can only afford to buy biscuits two days in the week and the rest of your time is spent in a kind of hiatus awaiting next pension day, then the weeks are all broken up and shortened, time goes in skips and jumps, so many minutes and hours of that precious time is wasted just waiting, and it isn't long until she doesn't require any biscuits. So many unlived lines in her body, so many packets of biscuits uneaten, unbought. But this isn't a case that calls for excessive action, not any more than, say, the children whom Ivan went on about so much in *The*

Grand Inquisitor. You don't stand in the shop with money jingling in your pocket, watch the old lady fumbling in her purse with arthritic fingers and decide to go yelling into the street, 'Riot, murder, fire, police, ambulance! There's an old lady who can't afford a packet of biscuits.'

Not unless you want locking up.

Yet if most men live a life of quiet desperation, is it the writer's job to make real and desperate every case? Mat decided that it was. But to make too exorbitant a claim on behalf of these quiet desperations, to bare the breast and make too loud a noise, to do these things only to meet with a phlegmatic, 'What's the fuss? It isn't all that bad.' Mat decided that perhaps the writer's task was no *cri de coeur*, neither from his own heart nor another's. There was something peculiarly elusive and shifting about thinking about writing, outside the actual act of writing itself, the words and the constructions. Even there Mat had a sense that there was something fruitless and impossible in it. He had to admit to himself that he had no love for works themselves, and he made this admission with some embarrassment. His attitude was only one of respect, that words should not be abused, nor allowed to tire and exhaust themselves in the way they so often did. His feeling for language had no connection with the exotic, nor the exuberant, nor the exciting. On second thoughts he thought that he did love words, but he was a poor lover, inactive and faithless. His own writing never had that quality put into it which he *did* admire in others, say panache, daring, excessiveness, presumption. He would be sure to say to himself eventually, 'What's the fuss?'

He supposed that this was why he was sitting here doodling and exhausted with his mind running in circles. Just sit down and write, was what they'd say. Mat just sat down, and here he was with his imagination fluttering round him like a bat loose in a room, evasive and jerky. No amount of effort, thinking, will, could enable him to pin anything properly on the page. He felt the abrupt division between the tight inflexibility of his moral concerns and the indulgent whimsy of his thoughts. For a while he was exhilarated by the tempting idea that poetry, verse with all its formality, its pattern, its discreteness –

> 'A starlit or a moonlit dome disdains
> All that man is,
> All mere complexities,
> The fury and the mire of human veins.'

– the idea that here in poetry within the very rigidity of its structure he would find a way of resolving all doubt. This thought, which came to him from time to time, seemed to loosen something in Mat, excited him with the notion that he would find liberation and freedom in the tight formality of poetry. But it was the very strength of the lust which this temptation forced into him, so that his hands would shake and his body tremble at the thought of creating verse. It was this very strength which defeated him, for immediately there would spring up the nagging conscientious objection, the obtrusive sense of a reality that would not permit poetry. 'An agony of flame that cannot singe a sleeve.' He dismissed the whole idea with a shrug, with a keelie ironic sense of his limits. 'Mat Craig – Poet.' He had a living to earn, and the thought of poetry seemed to him the wildest of irresponsibilities. He thought again, 'Mat Craig – Poet.' For a wild moment he felt the electric tingle that Yeats' poem engendered in him, then he shrugged again. 'Huh!' He was really in the doldrums.

Mat was an omnivorous reader. He read everything which came his way: novels, poetry, philosophy, criticism, psychology, politics, history, sociology, but he had not yet read one single writer whom he would want to call Master. This didn't mean that he was incapable of admiration. As if in contrast to the dullness of life at the office and at home he became really interested in exotic literature. The American novelists attracted him, Hemingway, Faulkner, Scott Fitzgerald. *Tender is the Night*, with all its cadences of promise and disappointment which he understood so well himself, moved him to tears. He admired without reserve Faulkner's tough adherence to his material, Hemingway's great craft, and Steinbeck's exuberance. But he considered also how uncomfortable he might feel in Cannery Row or amid all the blood-letting, castration, violence, ambition and pride. There were other exoticisms, too, even more attractive because they were of the spirit – the virtuosi – Pound, Joyce, Eliot, Cummings, and especially Yeats – the men who represented to him the freedom which seemed to him to be the only element in which he could be happy. Sometimes he delighted in hugging to himself his experience of reading Djuna Barnes' *Nightwood* or Durrell's *Black Book*. This especially when everything, his work and the limitations of his life, became tedious and irksome. These writers created in him the illusion of having reserves.

Yet he could accept nobody as master and paradoxically enough it was because of the immense superiority of talent which these men possessed which made him unable to imitate them. He had no gift of the gab so it was useless for him to know that Joyce could spin his way out into art. He admired their manners but could not use them and he often yearned for a writer who would painstakingly plod his way into art. He would be the man under whom Mat would serve his apprenticeship. After this Mat would dream of his canny magnum opus, read up more about the Rutherglen Burghers and their wee roon red lums and go back to soaking himself in the atmosphere of provision and accounting in the regular office in Carmyle.

The lamp was shining over the papers on the table. He looked through the screed of paper which was covered by his small handwriting and wondered how he had ever had the energy to cover all that paper. He couldn't remember ever writing any other way but slowly and painstakingly and he found it surprising that he had written such a bulk. He was busy riffling through the manuscript and enjoyed the mere material existence of all the written words on the paper when he heard Jake's alarm go off. The clock showed the time as five – which would make it four forty-five. Mat felt a strange sense of unreality when he thought that he had sat here at the table for the whole night.

Through the thin walls of the house he could hear Jake muttering to himself, then there was a loud thump. Mat got up from his chair and went through into the kitchenette to put on the kettle and make himself a pot of coffee. He could hear Jake up now and making gurgling sounds in the bathroom. When Mat had finished making the coffee he lifted the pot and came back into the living-room. The papers were spread all over the table and Mat sat and looked at them while he sipped his coffee. He prepared himself in the cold dawn for the overwhelming sense of disgust which he would feel looking at the suddenly cold pages, the children's jotters which he used to write in, the diffident tentative struggle not to say too much. He supposed that if he kept his feet on the ground, wrote good wholesome social realism, he would not feel anything like this revulsion.

Jake came in and crossed slowly over to the kitchenette. He was in his stocking-soles, yawning and scratching himself. As he passed Mat he raised his hand solemnly, muttered 'Hi, genius!' and went into the kitchenette. Then he did a double take, poking his head back round through the door.

'Struth! You still up?'

'No, it's no' me. There's coffee in the pot.'

Jake loved coffee. He also refused to drink it on principle. It was an intellectual drink for people who sat up all night writing. He also loved books but he hid his love covetously.

'Not for me, thanks,' Jake said. He opened the lid of the coffee pot and grimaced. 'How you drink that stuff. Me, I'm for the old cornflakes. Sharpens your gums.' He made a face like a man with all his teeth missing, pulling his lips over his teeth and sucking in his cheeks. While Mat laughed he was off on another tack, kneeling on the carpet and searching beneath the couch for his shoes. 'Where's the old how-de-ye-does? Have you been up all night?'

'Just been doin' a wee bit scrievin' you know.'

'Aye, a' night.'

'Well, you know what the poets say.' Mat started to sing.

'And the best of all ways,
To lengthen our days,
Is to steal a few hours from the night, my dear.'

'Aye, there's a difference between casual stealing and doin' the professional burglar. Maybe you'll lengthen your days the noo, but you'll shorten them in the end, I'm thinking.' Jake was half-serious, but Mat ham-acted with his forefinger and thumb gripping the bridge of his nose. 'The artist's fate, dear boy.'

'As you say.' Jake was unimpressed. He had found his shoe and he went to the table and looked over Mat's shoulder at the pages scattered on the table. 'What's all this guff you're writing anyway?' He sounded a bit aggressive.

Mat spoke diffidently, 'It's just a lot of notes. Ideas. Chancin' my arm.' He felt embarrassed by his need to justify all this to Jake. If he was a real writer he wouldn't need justification. But Jake had gone back to his usual bantering tone.

'Just writing doon a' the answers?'

'Some o' them . . .'

'Shining up the sentences. Struth! I wonder what folk'll say if you ever dae anything wi' a' that and they find out we've reared a poet in the house?'

'I'm not a poet.'

'No, now, laddie, don't be modest. It's not such an –

heh! – accomplishment! See I could dae it myself. Eh! Let me see.

> '"Says she to me,
> 'Is that you?'
> Says I, 'Who?'
> Says she, 'You!',
> Says I, 'Me?',
> Says she, 'Aye!',
> Says I, 'Naw!',
> Says she, 'Well it was awful like you!'"

'See! Nae bother! If I can dae it so can you.'

'Naw. I'm just an old Calvinist. It's you that's the poet in this hoose.' Mat continued Jake's bantering tone. 'You know your approach to life is – eh – predominantly aesthetic.'

'Get away. Flattery'll get ye naewhere. He! Whit would the lads in the slaughter-house say?' Jake curved his hands above his head and stood up on one toe, wavering about with one leg flailing the air. 'Aesthetic! Ha! Ha!'

'It *is* you know. It is because there is no room for the aesthetic because the good and the true are no longer equated that you indulge in self mockery. You scoff at something which is in yourself because in a capitalist society it is unmarketable – useless, and a sequitur – bad, or at least, almost so.'

Jake started to grin and Mat realised that he was too sensitive to Jake's banter. Jake had merely been teasing him into making one of his pedantic speeches so that he could pull his leg, for he was now intoning in a nasal voice. 'Who'll bid for one aesthetic sensibility – who'll bid?'

But Mat felt that he had to justify himself, to tell Jake that his loyalty to his father's books on the shelf still stood. He went on arguing the case with Jake and himself about the moral nature of art. He proposed to Jake the notion that art was the ingredient which was missing from modern political and social life. For instance, their father, who had now grown indifferent to politics. Jake acknowledged some of the Marxist criticism because he could use it as a base for his cynical humorous attacks on the working class. As Marx says, the working classes are exploited, and being exploited they are mugs. Tame mugs. Jake didn't hold to any serious side of any belief and it was this serious side that Mat was interested in showing him – the need to care. As he went on formulating his ideas to Jake he became more and more embarrassed and ended up by using Jake's own flippant style. 'Life's dead,' he was saying, 'if you'll excuse the paradox. People don't care. They've nothing to believe in and less to believe with. Well?' Jake raised his eyebrows in interrogative half hoops, but Mat ignored him and went on. 'Who has the monkey gland injections? Who's going to slip the body politic the old needle so that it'll jump up and begin to worry whether it's bored or cold or hungry or damn near annihilation? Who's going to take the plain old ethical hen and stick on a few peacock's feathers, who's goin' to brush up the auld claes, who's goin' to heat the porridge? The politicians? The scientist? The Church? Not on your life. It'll be –'

But Jake was in before him. Pulling Mat's arm up in a boxer's salute of victory he shouted. 'Our Matthew! Hurray!' Mat took one of his thickest jotters and beat time on Jake's head with each syllable. 'There's nae – use – talking – to – you – at – all.'

'Chuck it.' Jake was laughing. 'Here! I hope you haven't bitten off more than ye can chew. You ought to write a book. Ha! Ha! Get the Seventh Day Adventists to take you up.' He started to mollify Mat. 'Never mind – let me see it sometime. Maybe give me a bit of education.'

'Aye. I'll give you a look if you're nice and behave yourself.'

Jake suddenly started to put on his shoes. 'I'll have to get a gildi on though. Must catch the corporation transport or I'll disappoint that wee conductress.' Then he was away into the kitchenette pouring out the cornflakes, shouting at Mat, 'You're going to be tired the day at the old darg. You don't want to be at this game too often. Instead you should be in there keeping that wee wife of yours warm. I don't know what's wrong wi' you young fellows noo-a-days – no enthusiasm.' He came back into the living-room and started to clear a place for himself at the table by picking up the papers and throwing them gently at Mat.

'Here! That's great literature you're chucking about.' Mat started to tidy the papers up.

'Aye, but a man can't live by great literature alone.' Jake slapped his stomach. 'It's got to make room for the bread and butter. The chuck comes first.'

'You're right about that,' said Mat, 'we've got to eat. Sustain the old inner man. Keep body and soul together.'

Jake was bending down tying his shoelaces. He looked up quickly. 'Eh? Since when have you been getting worried about the corporate body?' He pointed a finger at his stomach.

'Since it started to worry me. As a matter of fact the bones are beginning to show.' Mat pulled the lining from his pocket. 'Starvation is looming round the corner.'

'Here, have a cornflake.' Jake held out the cornflake, his whole body and face in the pose of a man tight with his purse and refusing even to be asked for a loan. Mat started to laugh.

'It's a packet I need.'

'Of cornflakes?'

'No, the other thing.'

'Oh, I see. So that's the way it is. So.' He rubbed his hands gleefully together. Jake was a great one for borrowing money on a Thursday night and he was always getting teased for it. Now the boot was on the other foot. He made Mat go through their usual pantomime of grovelling for the money, kissing his shoes, begging. 'More alms for the love of Allah.' Then he was at the table again eating his cornflakes speedily.

'How much?'

'A couple of fivers.' Mat was sitting on the floor propping himself up on his arms.

'A couple of fivers? Ten quid? What have you been doin'?

Been on the cuddies? You always were an awful man for the long shots.'

'That's for mugs like you.'

Never before in his life had Mat borrowed money. At least not real borrowing, like ten pounds. Jake and he passed half-crowns and ten-bob notes back and forward without taking much account of them. Jake's favourite approach when borrowing money from Mat was, 'How about that half-dollar you owe me?' But this was different. Ten pounds was real money. He was pleased to see Jake keeping up with his flippancy. It helped him to steel himself against the misery of the thought of asking for money. He knew that Jake would give him the money and ask no questions. He also knew that he didn't mind being under an obligation to Jake. It was just that all his prejudices were against it – when he was living in that room and kitchen he knew that to be in debt was to be tilted that wee bit nearer disaster.

'No, as a matter of fact I've had a couple of unexpected items of expenditure . . .'

'Tch! Tch! And you a married man.'

'Oh, get knotted. Look, I won't need it till the end of the week.'

'Just as well, laddie. I haven't heard how the dividends are doing this quarter.' Jake laughed, putting his feet up on the table, clasping his hands round an imaginary stomach, eyeing it, winking, then doffing an imaginary hat to Mat. 'Ha! Ha! Struth though. I'll have to get weaving.'

''S all right then, boy?'

'It so happens,' said Jake solemnly, 'that the pocket book is in the pink of condition.' Then he went out of the door and into the lobby, still talking. 'It's only natural that a clean living, upright young fellow like yours truly, scraping a little nest egg together for his old age, would have something to spare to help out a brother in need.' He had reappeared at the door of the room wearing a warm belted jacket and a cloth cap. He was always neat and dapper, even when going to work in the slaughter-house. 'The rate of interest is pretty stiff though.'

Mat felt thankful to Jake for the persiflage. 'I won't forget this, laddie. And if you're ever in need of anything – anything at all – then you know who not to ask.'

'You're too, too kind.'

A little while later when Helen came Jake was about to go but not before he had slapped her on the buttocks. She had come into the room with a slight worried frown on her face, having fallen asleep then awoken to find Mat still up. She was tying the cord on her dressing-gown, still sleepy, her lips full and relaxed, her eyes blank and very big.

'You nut.' She came across the room avoiding Jake. She was too sleepy for horse-play. 'Honest, I wonder if I'm safe with that half-witted maniac about the house.'

Jake and Mat grinned. 'He's just a healthy red-blooded boy.'

'I must go,' Jake said. 'Better clear that table of your magnum opus. You don't want the old wife to know that you've been consuming the candles.' He jerked his thumb in the direction of the lobby. 'Or the dig money'll go up. See you at the end of the week. Ta! Ta!'

He left, closing the door. Helen and Mat looked after him waiting expectantly, then there came a loud crash as he slammed the front door shut. They both laughed. 'That'll be the whole building wakened up,' Mat said. 'Help me clear up.'

Helen lifted Jake's plate and the coffee pot. 'Put your papers by. I'll lay the table for breakfast. Your mother and father will be coming through soon. Did you manage all right?'

'Sure.'

She came over to Mat and felt his chin. 'You'd better get cleaned up, you look terrible. And you need a shave.'

Mat was collecting his papers together, putting them into the cardboard box. 'Just a minute till I get this junk put away.'

'Your magnum opus?'

'Aye. That's what Jake calls it. I suppose . . .' Mat dismissed the subject with a shrug. 'I don't know. It just seems like a week or two since the beginning of last spring. Every year gets shorter.' Mat stood for a moment sawing his hand in the air. He wasn't frustrated by an inability to formulate ideas so much as by the inability to speak out what he was thinking. It seemed to him to be too extravagant. Especially in the morning when everybody was getting ready for work, shaving in bathrooms, putting on clothes, gulping breakfasts, shivering in the cold, getting ready to run out to catch buses and trams. But he still stood looking at Helen, sawing his hand in the air, opening his mouth to speak, changing his mind. Then he burst out, 'I mean you have a kind of crazy idea that you are exempt. That you have some kind of purpose. Something which you've forgotten but will remember some day. Then you look out of the window and you see that the light mornings are drawing in again. And you think – another year gone – and faster every time.'

Helen demurred. 'Mmm?'

'Oh, you know what I mean.' Mat tried to reduce it to a mundane level. 'It's what everybody thinks. I mean, we're all unique. And we all think that we've got something special in us. It's true, too. We should believe in that – for everybody. It's ridiculous. We're trained to humility. I always think that kids at school are taught to be a little more polite, a little more humble than is really necessary. You know, clasp your hands behind your backs, good morning, teacher, all that. But it makes good factory fodder for people to know their place and not to live in hope – or expectation. Then you say to yourself – it *can't* happen to me. Mediocrity. But we know damned well what we are born to.' Mat suddenly was illuminated by an idea. 'Do you know something? Alec told me I'm ambitious. And he's right. I *am* ambitious. I don't mean the young Scotsman on the make type of ambition. That's just servility. I mean real arrogant ambition. To do something. I was reading Yeats' "Byzantium" last night. To emulate that sheer – sheer –' Mat gazed slowly round the room, then shivered. 'Eh, I'm a nut.' He exhaled his breath slowly through fastidiously pursed lips, 'Eh – eh – Jesus.'

'Pride goes before a fall.' Helen laughed at Mat.

'It's taking a helluva risk.'

But Helen merely laughed this off. 'C'mon, action,' she said, and she carried the plate and the coffee pot through into the kitchenette. Mat was always trying to come to formal decisions about what he was going to do, but this didn't really matter. Helen took the idea of risk in her stride. They were young, healthy, intelligent, well intentioned and they had expectations, which was as it should be. On the other side of the risk of failure is the expectation of success.

They started to talk of everyday things while Mat cleaned the ashes out of the fireplace and set about making a new fire. It was the middle of the month and Helen was about to make her routine calls to the house-factors' offices and for a while they discussed the possibility of their being successful in managing to get a house to rent. They got on all right living here with Mat's parents but Helen was beginning to feel the disappointment of not being in charge of a household by herself.

Mat went into the bathroom to shave and by the time he came out the quietness of the morning had gone. Somewhere there was a wireless blaring out jaunty orchestral music and there were vague noises of flushing and running water. It was still quiet enough to isolate the separate sounds; the grinding of gears as a bus changed down on the main road, the sound of a woman's voice trying to raise some reluctant sleeper from his bed. Mat went to the door and shouted into the lobby. 'You up?' and the sound of his mother's voice came from one of the bedrooms in answer.

'Aye, aye, aye, aye. Keep your hair on. I'll be through in a minute.' Then there was the sound of her voice wakening Mat's father. 'Doug? You up?' She continued shouting so that the two syllables of 'You up?' sounded together like 'Yup? Yup?'

Helen had started to set the table for breakfast and Mat sat in the chair in front of the fire yawning and nodding. He felt really tired.

Jetta, Mat's mother, came into the room with her hands twisted in her apron, a typical pose. She was smiling. She had just warned Doug not to get stuck in the lavatory pan. Mat and Helen could hear the rumbling chest notes of Doug's reply but couldn't make out what he said.

Jetta held up some envelopes. 'The post.' She went through the bundle. 'The electricity!' With disgust. 'What's this? Soap coupons. Threepence and fourpence off. The way these folk want you to buy soap you'd wonder if they're hinting at anything.' She took a newspaper from under her arm and laid it on the broad arm of one of the imitation leather armchairs. 'That's old misery's paper.' She went through the letters again. 'The pools – and what's this? Matthew Craig, Esquire. Hey, Esquire, a letter for you.' She gave Mat the letter and held up the one remaining envelope which was in her hand. 'I know who this is for – you can tell by the smell.' She sniffed at the scented envelope then squinted at it curiously. 'I don't know what these lassies see in Jake.' But she sounded as if she had a good idea. 'Always a different one.' She spoke with affectionate pride. Then she addressed Mat. 'You're up early. Where's Nell?'

She poked her head through the kitchenette door. 'Put the kettle on, hen.'

'It's on. In fact the tea is made. And there's ham in the frying pan.'

Jetta looked at Mat suspiciously and he tried to hide a yawn. 'It's a right bright fire,' she said. 'It seems funny. Everybody up, breakfast nearly ready. This early. Have you been up all night again?'

'Ach, Ma, I couldn't sleep.'

'You couldn't sleep.'

Helen came in from the kitchenette and put a milk jug on the table. Jetta looked at her with disapproval and Helen stopped short, embarrassed. She put the things on the table and went out of the room. 'I'd better go and get dressed.'

Jetta turned on Mat. 'You ought to have more sense.' But Mat shrugged, only half paying attention to her. He was busy reading his letter. 'Ach, Ma!' as if to say, 'Don't fuss.'

'Don't "Ach Ma!" me. It costs money to keep the light

burning all night. And coal for the fire. And anyhow – how are you going to do your work the day? A young man like you not getting any sleep.'

Mat couldn't suppress another yawn and Jetta inhaled her breath through her open mouth and turned her eyes up towards the ceiling, spreading out her hands. Mat laughed. 'Don't lose your rag, Ma.'

Doug had come into the room and was pottering about looking for the paper. Jetta was still going on. 'It's a' these fancy notions he's got into his heid. These letters addressed to him wi' "Esquire" as if plain mister isn't good enough.'

'It's good enough for me, Ma.'

Doug agreed in principle with burning the midnight oil. He had done it himself in his time. He splayed his big hand out in a patting placatory gesture. 'Now, Jetta. The boy's only trying to improve himself.'

'That's right, Pa. You stick up for me.'

By this time Mat had gone into the kitchenette and come back with a plateful of ham. He sat at the table and started to eat.

'There's nothing wrong with the boy except a wee bit honest ambition.'

'You could dae wi' a bit honest ambition.'

'Now, now. I've always been a hard worker and so's my two sons. There's nothing wrong with a wee bit learning – if a man can make a better mousetrap ...'

Mat had been expecting the last phrase and he repeated it along with his father, then finished it himself. '– the world will make a beaten track to his door.' Mat filled his mouth with bread and spoke with a wad of it filling out one cheek. 'That's what I was doing, Ma. Sitting up inventing mousetraps.'

'If it was something practical like that it wouldn't be so bad. But poems! It's a wonder your brain is not turned.'

'Cross my heart and hope to die, Ma. I never wrote a poem in my life.'

Doug was disgusted at Mat's flippancy. 'Ach, the two of you.'

Mat went on eating. He thought of his father's simple boast.

'We've aye been good workers.' He felt touched by this. And yet it was the attitude deliberately bred into the people who would become factory fodder. Beneath the surface ambiguity of Mat's attitude towards work there was another deeper equivocality. He loved work and this was a simple virtue, yet he felt something of the emotional regressiveness which was what immersing yourself in work amounted to. He thought of a phrase which he had read somewhere. 'The flirtation with indolence.' There was a virtue suggested here which was somewhat more complex. Was this the flaw, his ambiguity, his failure to find any resolution in all the paradox which he felt in life, the circles in which he was always thinking? Or was it that these paradoxes were continually being created by a deeper inner scepticism, a refusal to commit himself, the same regressiveness that forced him to immerse himself in work? It was interesting to see the same principle individualising itself in different ways and being then so critical of itself. But that was another paradox, and there was the flaw.

'You're a cool yin,' Jetta said, 'sitting there stuffing your face as if naebody was talking to ye.'

'I'm a growin' laddie.'

'Aye, and you'll be growing in the opposite direction if you don't get your night's sleep.'

Mat sat laughing and chewing his food.

'You leave him alone. It's not often he does it. Me, I'm having my breakfast.'

'You sit down,' Jetta said, 'I'll get it for you. But I'm not forgetting. Nothing good'll come of not behaving like normal people.'

Doug grinned at Mat when she went into the kitchenette. 'Listen,' said Doug, 'I'll tell you something. Karl Marx wrote with carbuncles on his behind. Have you ever had a carbuncle?'

'No.'

'No. I didn't think so. Had one myself on my arm. Here.' Doug pulled up his sleeve and showed Mat a scar on his wrist.

'Grim. But imagine something even worse than a boil on your behind. And you sitting on a hard bench in the British Museum Reading Room with the whole of *Das Kapital* unwritten before you. Just imagine the first time you sit down and all the boils on your behind all loup like hell.' Doug eased his backside on the chair in sympathy with Marx and with an expression of distaste on his face. 'And you think. What'll I write? Yes, a critical analysis of the Capitalist system. You feel another twinge. A marathon sitting match. You've got to *concentrate* just to sit. And, incidentally, while you're sitting there you have to rack your brains and tease out of them a lot of dusty ideas like relative and equivalent value, the labour process, you know, et cetera, and read up hundreds of volumes of statistics all crying out with misery and pain. Wee weans climbing up chimneys and pregnant women pulling wagons of coal and seamstresses dosing themself wi' brandy to keep awake. Then your boils gi' another twinge. What kind of lighting did they have those days in the British Museum? Did your eyes get tired? Did your arm get sore propping up all the Blue Books? Did your hand get cramped with writing? Then – oh!' Doug raised himself from the chair suddenly twisting his face as if in pain. Then he grinned. 'That's one burst.'

'Carbuncles!' Mat was shaking with silent laughter, then repeating to himself with satisfaction. 'Carbuncles! Ha! Ha! Carbuncles! Nae wonder he got belted into the Capitalists.'

Doug stood with one finger in the air and cried. 'Capitalism will have cause to remember the carbuncles on my behind.' They both started to giggle.

Jetta heard them giggling together and became annoyed and came through from the kitchen. 'Don't you be giving him any of your high-falutin' notions, now. There's naebody in the world gets anything without working for it.' She thought about her remark for a second, then added in order to be honest. 'Unless it's on the pools.'

'Don't be daft, woman. Have you never heard of unearned

income? The hardest work some folk do is sitting counting the stuff.'

'Aye. But that's a different kind of folk. It's not us. We're never that fly. Anyway, they're not for us, these high-falutin' notions.'

'I suppose you're right, Ma.' Mat made his hopeless gesture. 'Writers are always other people.'

'Why for that?' asked Doug, 'I always told you there was value in learning, didn't I? We've always had good heids on us, we Craigs. Your grandfather was a gey well-educated man. Myself –' Doug started to tell him that when he was young he had thought of writing as well. Mat had never heard of this before, but in a way he wasn't surprised. Everybody's at it, he thought, but everybody. Then after a while as Doug went on talking Mat realised that he had made a mistake. He remembered the old fellow he had once met in the library. The old chap had been slightly tipsy and had tried to buttonhole everyone in the library and the librarian had been too embarrassed to do anything about it. Mat had been too mild to resist the old fellow's advances and he had to accept the books that the old fellow had insisted on choosing for him. But the old fellow's taste had surprised him – W. H. Hudson's *The Green Mansions* (this was Mat's discovery of Hudson) – and after Mat's refusal to accept a novel by Jack London, whose writing he disliked heartily, he accepted the old man's choice of a book of Flaubert's short stories. It turned out that the old man read Flaubert and Stendahl in the original French. Now here was his father telling him of the plans he once had of retelling the tales from Chaucer, Daudet, Balzac, Rabelais, Burton's *Thousand and One Nights* in Scottish settings. Doug's idea didn't sound all that bad – and yet. There was something sad about the whole thing. Like that old man reading the work of Hudson and the French novels. He must have found in Hudson some vicarious, sensuous world of activity and adventure away from the grey tenement sprouted world of Glasgow. The choice of foreign writers by Doug came from the same sense of deprivation. A whole background against which the drama and the seriousness of life could be played out was missing from their lives. All the background against which a novelist might set his scene, the aberrant attempts of human beings and societies to respond to circumstances, all that was bizarre, grotesque and extravagant in human life, all that whole background of violence, activity, intellectual and imaginative ardour, political daring. All that was somehow missing from Scottish life. In lieu of all this artistic and human extravagance, all the menace, violence and horror which had been the experience of so many European writers, in Scottish life there was only a null blot, a cessation of life, a dull absence, a blankness and the diminution and weakening of all the fibres of being, of buildings not blown up but crumbling and rotten, of streets not running with blood or rivers of fists but with wan puddles, a withering of existence, no agony of living, no cry of warning which extravagance and outrageousness sets up.

It was a country which seemed wrapped in a Scotch mist of understatement, where the edges are blurred, shapes and colours take on the neutrality of spiritual deprivation – a lack of definition, phlegmatic, timorous, apologetic, diffident, hesitant. The canny Scot with his deathly stultifying safety.

Mat looked at his father. He would have liked to tell him what he was thinking. That what a writer should do is wrench his whole world up and put the mark of his thumb on it. Shove it into the violent torrent of events. Make things happen. Disturb the peace.

Yet they were gentle humble people, as he was himself. How could he tell them, or make himself speak of the arrogance with which he loved his trade.

'Oh, I wish I could explain it all to you, Pa. The main thing is . . .' Mat made his gesture of frustration. 'I don't want to get on. I'm too ambitious. Look, Pa, to you a writer is someone who has got on, isn't he?'

'Aye.'

'Well, I want to be a writer who hasn't got on, see?'

Doug was blank but kindly. 'Aye. I see what you mean, son.'

'Ah see what he means all right. He's getting highbrow again. A cut above himself.'

'Oh, Lord.'

'Never mind "Oh, Lord", a clever boy like yourself shouldn't be reading a lot of daft books if it isn't going to get him anywhere.'

'Oh, for godsake. I might never even write anything worthwhile in my life . . .'

'You might not even write? Son, this is not the time to be putting the hems on yourself.'

'You mean to tell me that you waste all that time reading classics, philosophy, all that stuff?'

'Well, I wouldn't put it like that,' said Doug. 'Learning never did anybody any harm.'

'Don't encourage him or he'll go all high falutin' again. And anyway, whit good did it ever do you, wi' all your Socialism and Karl Marx?'

Doug was hurt. 'I was working for my fellow man.'

'Well you should have been working for your fellow family, maybe they'd amount to something.'

'Whit's wrang wi' them? I've always taught them . . .'

'Aye. The value of learning.' Jetta interrupted. 'If I wasn't here to keep an eye on ye ye'd be givin' yer wages away at the end of the week. And noo this yin wants to be writing for his fellow man.'

'Ach, people just gang their ain gait.'

Mat was laughing. 'Look, I'd better get to work.' He finished drinking his tea. He was suddenly on his feet and out into the lobby. While he was putting on his coat he could hear them still arguing in the living-room.

'That was quick,' Jetta was saying. 'It's not that early.'

'He was just trying to get away from your nagging.'

'Me? Nagging? Well, if ah was, I have to nag you lot into staying respectable.'

'Och, Jetta. We've aye been respectable enough, and we've aye been hard workers, even if we dae get fancy notions. He's a decent respectable boy.'

'I'm not saying no to that. They have aye been hard workers. But there's something in all this writing business I don't like. It's not for the likes of us.'

'Ach, Ma, shut your auld gitter. The boy's just got ideals.'

'Ideals? Ideals?' Jetta's voice sounded now genuinely anxious and irritated and Mat could hear his father's paper rustle as he took refuge behind it. 'Much guid he'll get from ideals.'

It was raining a thin soaking haar when Mat got outside into the street. He turned up his collar and headed for the tram stop. There were two kinds of temptation offering themselves to him. One was to avoid the explanation which going to his work would mean, the other was to spend the day writing. It was very early but he could go for a ride in the tram until the libraries opened. He had been sitting writing all night and talking and thinking about it all morning and now he had the curious feeling that it was another person entirely who went to work in the regular office. The feeling disturbed him for it had a tendency to reverse itself so that he would begin to think of himself as the person who went to work in the office and then he would look on the person who sat up writing as absurd and ridiculous. When this happened he had to pay the price in disgust with himself. He decided that he would be best to go into work and think up a good excuse as to why he had stayed off. His decision was firmly made when the first tram came going in a writing direction and not in the direction of his work. He crossed the road and waited for it at the stop.

When he mounted the tram he felt guilty and had the feeling that everybody was looking at him and wondering where he was going. They were local people in the tram who knew him, and knew where he worked, so that they'd know that he was going in the opposite direction. He huddled himself up in his seat and gave himself over to his thoughts. He would buy a ball-point pen and a notebook and go into the library and sit and write. The thought of the ball-point pen and the notebook warmed him. He was fascinated by the apparatus of writing. He couldn't go past a stationery shop window without stopping to gaze fondly at the files and folders and pens and paper clips. He would imagine all the thick chapters of manuscript tucked away in the folders, the satisfaction of finished work, all the lovely pages of foolscap covered thickly with the up and down markings of his illegible script, the bulky manuscript of a finished novel being weighed in the little brass scales and being packed and parcelled and waxed and sent off to the publishers; and the desk he would have liked, a big flat wooden surface all covered with papers and cigarette ash and a big office typewriter with a clangy bell that would resound in triumph at the end of every line. Then he thought of his own confusion of paper, the hurried confused notes scribbled on sixpenny jotters, the welter of material which he had collected without giving it any shape or form. It was probably characteristic of a writer to have this urge to collect, to scour through streets and books collecting data, taking inventory. It was the richness of variety that he loved, within a certain scope, when it did not quite amount to chaos. He loved profusion and jumble, and he imagined again the desk that he would like with hooks round the side on which he would hang clips of paper full of information on old Glasgow, histories of streets, names, houses, institutions, events, and which one day he would put into his magnum opus, his great work.

Inside the tram people were smoking and the atmosphere was thick with fog. The windows were all steamed up and Mat wiped the pane next to him with his hand so that he could see out. As the tram passed the curve at the bottom of the park he could see the trees all dripping with the light rain that was falling. Trees! Stripped of their summer garments he'd seen many a lovelier poem. The writhing, battling laborious growth, the heavy limbs, sinking down under their own weight, the gnarled twisted trunks, the fissured bark, the eerie winter shapes twisted like modern wire sculptures – all entitled 'Agony'. He had tried to write a poem once to these trees. Or rather, he remembered, to a particular tree which he had seen once elsewhere which had held these same shapes. He wondered if it had been a good poem. He had got the rhythm right, and the length of the line, as long as a limb. And the feeling of the thing, too, the rippling grain running up the trunk through which the sap rose to nourish the tender buds, and the silver grey glossy bark on to which lovers had carved their names. Lovers of long ago, now proved faithful to the grave, the scars of their names growing up with the tree and becoming slowly obliterated with time, the scored graffiti which had stretched into long unreadable strips of roughened bark.

'The blank impervious hide wraps earth's rising
   nurture.'

'Blank impervious' were words put in to make the length of the line right. But were they right for meaning? Never mind. A wee bit weakness in the line would do no harm, we accept them so that the line doesn't become all clotted with syllables and meanings. One hundred and seven types of ambiguity.

'The blank impervious hide wraps earth's rising nurture
Which seeping through the limbs drives out the bud.'

Echoes of something or other, something quite familiar which he couldn't remember. But the images of the roots clutching at the earth – sucking victuals, nourishment, food, sap and the slow rise of the sap, fullness. The earth round the trees was grey and trodden hard without that fat, fecund, fertile – eatable look of loam or ploughed earth. Was that what gave the roots their twisted searching shape? Thrusting their tender tips into the dearth of stone or gravel or sand or clay or whatever it was. Clinging roots sucking voraciously at the dry earth. Was that what happened? Was there a great plunging movement inside the dry limbs of the tree which sucked into itself all the juices of the earth?

Sucking victuals voraciously.

A great baby at the earth's teat. One could seriously attribute a kind of intention without danger of the pathetic fallacy. The actual tree had been alive and some of its greedy limbs had, like some monster of overgrowth in science fiction, sunk themselves back into the earth to make a circle of smaller beech trees round the great parent in the middle. Somehow, through hundreds of years, the dissolved minerals, gases, chemicals, had forced themselves in a weak solution up from the earth and had crystallised and solidified by some process of chemical change, drying off into millions of minute fibres which made up the great solid bulk of the tree. Nature's illustration of Samuel Smiles. Mat enjoyed thinking of the tree and its patient timeless plodding accumulative nature.

'There is patience there; patience to labour and to
    wait.'

Like a great numbskull! Mat had never finished the poem.

Now the tram was passing over a crossing and the jolt of the wheels shocked Mat back into awareness of his surroundings. He felt the usual feeling which he had when he became lost in thought and he was shocked back into consciousness of his surroundings. Like that he should be at his work instead of sitting on trams writing weak poetry about trees. He felt guilty because he had leisure and irritated at the thought of having to come to grips with life even if it only meant having to get off the tram before his fare was up. It was still fairly early and as the tram passed between rows of tenements Mat thought of all the people ensconced in their homes with a regular day's routine before them. He envied them and started to wish that he'd gone into work. In another half hour he could be sitting comfortably at a high desk immersed in all the safety of calculation. But eventually he would find the desk become irksome, too. It occurred to him that he would be far better off if he had become something like a farmer, or an engineer. Someone who, like the poet chopping wood, was happy with the singleness of his vocation and avocation.

When he got off the tram he went down a side street towards where he knew there was a workman's tearoom. It was one of those places with brown painted walls and with letters in whitewash on the windows saying, 'Breakfast' and 'Special Lunch Today'. It had a big copper urn on the counter for tea that Mat called the samovar, and he began to feel like literature with that thought, like a Dostoevskian character with his strange ingrown walk. Walking as sheer movement gave salve to his thought. It prevented the peculiar sensation which he got sometimes when a new idea came to him, or when he thought of writing or trying to explain to Mr McDaid why he had already been two days off his work. This sensation was of tingling in his fingers and toes and an awful shock as the anxiety in his mind would send the adrenalin surging through his limbs. When he got into the tearoom he went over to the counter and asked the woman behind it for a glass of tea.

'You mean a *cup*, son. Think you were in the pub? Ha! Ha! Wishful thinking!'

'Just a habit wi' us hard drinkers, you know!' He felt silly having projected his whimsies outside himself like that. But as he sat and sipped his tea he thought of Russian literature, then of Alec's description of *Oblomov* that time he had first talked about the book when they had been sitting in the park. He remembered what Alec had called Oblomov – a layabout.

6

IT WAS A Friday afternoon a few days later when Mat and Jake scuffled up the stairs making their usual Friday racket. When they came in Doug was sitting on the arm of his chair and flipping through the paper. Jake poked his head round the door and held out a paper bag towards Helen. 'Here. We brought the necessary for a wee libation. Stick that in the cocktail cabinet.' Helen took the bottles of beer from Jake and put them on top of the sideboard, folding a tea cloth under them so that they wouldn't mark the polished surface. Mat came in and grabbed the paper from Doug. 'Gimme that.' He riffled through the pages, then as he held a page open his head would move from one side to the other, then he'd riffle through the pages again.

'Huh!' said Doug. 'You can keep it for me.'

'It's all right. It's not a bad rag.'

'Aye, rag's right. Nae Radical paper should be like that.'

'Away! Ye cannae be fire-eating all the time. There's some good things in it.'

'That's not what I'm talking about. Look, I'll show you what I mean. Here, haud it up.' Mat held the paper and Doug smacked it with the back of his hand. 'There, you can read it all right?'

'Aye.'

'Well, the way you're holding it up towards the light?'

'So what?' asked Mat.

'In my days you couldn't do that with any Radical paper. You had to fold it up' – Doug took the paper and folded it up and peered at it – 'like this, afore you could read it. Or the light would shine through the back. Nae left-wing newspaper should be printed on such good paper as that.'

'You're nothing but an auld Calvinist. I suppose you think the devil should have all the best tunes?'

'Naw. But I know he runs all the best printing presses. Forbye that, I'll show you something else.' Doug looked through the pages. 'I'm just guessing that it'll be there. No, they've missed it out this week. It was all about the birds and the bees, and buds on the trees and how the editor's garden was doin'. Ah was aye awful interested.' He went on turning the pages. 'Ah, here's something. Travel advertisements. Holiday travel. Trips to the Continent.' Doug read on a bit. 'W'd ye *hark* at it? Pffft! When they should be giving you instruction on how to leave the country without a passport. That's not for the working classes.'

'Naebody said it was. It's for the middle classes. The intelligentsia. That's who it's for.'

This made Doug angry. 'Is that a fact! And we could not understand it? It's way above our heads?'

'I didnae say that.'

'Naw. So the intellectuals wouldn't read it if it wasn't printed on nice paper wi' bits about the editor's garden and Holiday Travel?'

'Ach,' said Mat, 'all work and no play.'

'Aye, you're right. Some folk all work. And some folk all play. Your intellectuals can all afford a month off from the struggle.'

'You're just jealous.'

'Jealous! Of course I'm jealous. Why should I not be? It's bad enough less fortunate folk feeling jealous without having it aggravated by a display of opulence from better off folk, especially if they're supposed to be Socialists. Oh, I don't begrudge the bloke his wee plot of ground. Guid luck to him if he would only suffer his good luck in silence.'

'You've got to learn to move with the times.'

'Whit you young yins had better learn is not to teach your

faithers to suck eggs. Maybe things is changing. But the old things still hold. There's still good and there's still bad.'

'Aye,' said Mat, 'and there's a time and place for everything.'

'Is there? I don't know. Plenty time? When some of us might never see our natural ends. Aside from that –' Doug shrugged. 'There's plenty time when you're young. You'll see in another few years.'

Mat knew what he meant. He could remember his father's advice to him about marriage. Then he wondered about this Socialist society which his father had dreamed about all his life, which he must have even thought of at one time during the twenties as a material possibility. It had been the only aspiration he ever had which was outside the mere ruck of living. And now he guessed that he would never see it. Supposing it happened? Would these men and women of the future with all their perfection and liberation ever be wholly blithe knowing their history? Knowing of the long roll of martyrs or of the slaves and sweeps and seamstresses, the crucified, incarcerated and exiled of all lands and of all times. Mat had often been surprised at the terrific richness of aspiration of people he knew in comparison with what they had achieved or had the luck to gain. Inside the deaf old man or woman would lurk the seventeen-year-old boy or girl who wanted – nothing in particular, yet everything – scope, release, possibility, a chance. Knowing this, would these people of the future not have something in them of guilt, or sadness; a melancholic harking back to the suffering past which would point the value of everything they possessed; would they have a streak of tragic conservatism, a love for and a desire to conserve everything of value which men had built or had suffered for? There was already something of this in himself. Was it a contradiction in the radical nature – or its real beauty? Like the pessimism in art with all its reactive values? To yearn for what is lost and gone and irrecoverable. The regret for the irrecoverable past. Shakespeare's great sonnet. Proust's madeleine. His own infatuation with his memory.

'Aye,' said Doug. 'You'll ken in another few years.'

'Listen to him,' said Jake. 'Old Elijah.' He was shouting into the kitchenette. 'Hey, Ma. D'ye hear him, Ma? Old Douglas is doin' a bit of prophesying.'

Jetta came out of the scullery holding her palm upwards. 'Aye. And I'm prophesying that there'll be nae tea for anybody that doesn't remember what day this is.'

'The greengages! I wouldn't disappoint my wee mammy.' Doug handed Jetta his wage packet.

'And how about you?' she asked Mat.

'Sure, Ma,' he said and followed her into the kitchenette. Nell had filled up some glasses with beer and Jake and Doug helped themselves. Doug drank the beer in small sips but Jake put his head back and drank the whole glass in one swallow. Doug watched him, fascinated. When he had finished Jake handed the glass to Doug with a casual sultanish air. They were standing before the fireplace and Doug had to carry the glass over to the sideboard to put it down. When he had returned the glass to the sideboard he turned, realising that Jake had caught him.

'Am I your servant? Just whistle and I'll dance.'

Jake held his hand out and flapped it palm down. 'The old reflexes, Pa. They're slowing down.'

Doug appealed to Helen for sympathy. 'The number of times he's tested my reflexes.' Then he turned on Jake. 'What the hell do you think I am? Pavlov's dug?'

Jake didn't answer but instead he started to move his arm up and down as if ringing a bell.

'Christ!' said Doug. 'I'm salivatin'.' Jake and Helen were giggling at him. 'I don't know how you play these tricks on folk.'

'It's just the old –' Jake flicked his sleeves up and chanted like a circus barker. 'Watch the five fingers, they never leave the left hand.'

Mat was watching from the door of the kitchenette. He came over and started to recite dramatically in front of Jake.

> 'Beware, beware!
> His flashing eyes, his floating hair!
> Weave a circle round him thrice,
> And close your eyes with holy dread,
> For he on honey dew hath fed,
> And drunk the milk of Paradise.'

Jake reacted to this by ruffling his hair up, crossing his eyes and grimacing with his bottom lip hanging loose.

'Ach,' said Doug. 'You havenae got a' your onions.'

Mat lifted his glass of beer and drank it in three gulps, then offered Doug the empty glass. 'I wouldn't say that, Pa. It's a couple of bright boys you've reared.' Doug was looking at the glass in his hand and laughing ruefully.

'Would you believe it? Once bitten twice shy. If you start ringing bells I'll spit in your eye.' Jake was making sarcastic gestures round Mat with his forefinger. Doug flapped his hand at them in disgust. 'If you want a wee collie dug why do you not buy one wi' four legs and better lookin' than me? The trouble wi' you young folk is that you've no respect for your elders. Remember the fifth Commandment if you don't want the back of ma hand drawn o'er your lugs. The pair of ye.'

Jake and Mat linked arms and were swaying back and forward singing mockingly, 'We're a couple of swells —'

'It's just a lot of kiddin' and swankin!' said Jake. 'The old Friday spirit. Don't get curly-hieded.'

'Some o' these days I'll show you two something about kiddin' and swankin' ye didnae know. I think the two of ye has the evil eye.'

Jetta poked her head through the kitchenette door, 'I think the two of ye would be better occupied if you werenae takin' a lend o' your old faither. Anyway the tea's ready if the lot of ye would sit down.' Jetta carried out some plates to the table and Mat and Jake fetched chairs and put them round the table. They all sat down.

'This is the time when somebody always knocks at the door.' As Doug said this there came the sound of someone knocking at the front door.

'Talk of the devil,' said Jetta. 'What did ye not keep your big mouth shut for?

'Ha!' Doug made some circles round his own head. 'You're not the only magicians in the house.'

'Whatever spirits you sum up'll not be wanted. Jake, son. Seein' you're on your feet' – Jake wasn't on his feet, but he jumped up – 'away and answer the door.'

'If it's Fate don't let him in. See's o'er the pepper. I wonder who it can be?'

'It'll probably be somebody wantin' the lend of the mangle,' said Jetta. 'Anything to prevent us getting our tea in peace.'

'We can charge them for watching the animals eating.'

Jake came back into the room. 'It's just one of your fellow penpushers to see you, Mat.'

It was Bill from the office. He was embarrassed to see Mat hale and fit and he put his hand up to his spectacles and pulled them down over his nose and squinted and grinned. 'Hello there,' he said. 'You're looking well. Have ye been ill? Ha! Ha! I just dropped in to see how you were. Mr McDaid asked me, like. Seeing you hadn't phoned or anything.'

Jetta got excited. 'What do ye mean he hasn't phoned? Mat's been at his work, haven't you?'

'Haud your wheesht, woman,' said Doug. 'Maybe Bill would like a cup of tea or something to eat.'

'No thanks, Mr Craig. I'm on my way home. I just thought I'd come over and see how Mat was doing.'

'Right, Bill,' said Mat. 'I'll see you to the door if you're in a hurry.'

Bill was only too glad to go and Mat and Helen both saw him out into the lobby. Jetta watched them suspiciously as they went. 'Whit was the gist o' all that?' she asked.

'Now look, Jetta. Don't you be interfering,' said Doug.

Jake spoke. 'He hadn't been to his work all week. Instead he's been rampagin' about the public library. He's under the illusion that the novel's mightier than the cash ledger.'

'Whit are you being sae cutting about?' asked Doug. 'You're aye perfect?'

'I slaughter beef. Ye can eat it. Ye get money for daein' it. Ye cannae eat stories. Ye get nae money for writin' them.'

Jetta was upset. 'Ah just knew that something would happen. He would get those silly notions into his head. Supposin' he loses his job?'

'We'll see. Don't always be imagining the worst.'

'He's been off all week,' said Jake, 'which is why Bill came up to see him. He's nae doctor's line. Nae excuse. Whit's he supposed to say? Ah was too busy on my magnum opus to come in? Huh! Ah can imagine auld McDaid!' Jake mimicked a posh voice. 'It's all right, Matthew, don't worry. I've always been a great lover of literature myself. Oh, and here's your wages, Matthew, in case you're needin' them.' Jake screwed up his nose. 'Ah can imagine! Books! It's his books he'll be getting.' He mimicked a posh voice again. 'Just you run away down to the Labour Exchange and sign on. This is a works office – not the Young Writers Benevolent Society.'

At this Mat came back into the room. He had found the job of explaining to Bill why he had been off all week very difficult. He felt under an obligation to him, that Bill was due an explanation on the grounds of their friendship. But he couldn't say that he'd stayed off work because he had just wanted to write and that it had seemed a good idea at the time. So his explanation was inadequate, nothing more than that he was fed up, the office was beginning to get on his nerves, Mr McDaid's fussiness was getting too much for him and he hadn't been feeling too well lately. All of these reasons spoken in a hesitant, gauche, unconvincing manner. Bill had said, 'Be seeing you,' and Mat had said, 'All right.' But he also told him that he wasn't coming back to the office. Strangely, he felt remorse at this. He thought of all the familiar things in the office, the big sloping desks, the old clock which ticked so sonorously, the calculating machines with which he would get so absorbed, Bill's familiar presence every day. He felt a little pang about the whole thing.

'You werena' at your work, son?'

Now another explanation was due. He thanked God for Helen. She wouldn't have to ask him and he didn't have to tell her anything. She just seemed to know. Mat shrugged his shoulders at his father's question. 'Naw.' It wasn't the short English 'No' which he used but the long drawling nasal Glasgow sound which could contain such a wealth of feeling. Disgust, dismissal, defiance.

'What happened?'

'If you're worried I'll tell you. I told Bill that I wasn't coming back to the office. For the boss to send me my books.'

Jetta rose out of her chair. She was very angry. While she was speaking Helen stood at the door quite composed.

'What! You silly lukkin' . . .'

'Stop it!' Mat said. 'Stop it! Now just listen. I'm not going back to work in the office. I've stayed off that often in the last month that they're beginning to lose patience with me. They keep asking me, what's wrong – and I keep telling them the truth – nothing. I just say – nothing. I'm not going to tell lies just to ease everybody's conscience.'

'Everybody's conscience?' asked Jake.

'It's what I said. *Everybody's* conscience.' For some reason Mat thought of that emendation which he had made in the front page of his manuscript last year. 'Let Glasgow flourish.' – 'Lord, let Glasgow flourish by the preaching of the word.'

'Anyway,' he went on, 'the long and the short of it is this. They were beginning to look kind of queer at me. Not quite buttoned up. You know? The whole position was quite untenable for me. I can't go back. They definitely think that I'm a case for the bammy kane.'

'And they're not far wrong. I've never heard of such a thing in all my born days!' Jetta's voice rose again in sarcastic protest. 'What are you goin' to dae noo? Live on your interest?'

'I'll get another job altogether. I never felt like a real body in an office anyway. I'll get a job labouring.'

'Labouring?' Jetta was indignant. 'Is that where a' your classics get ye? Labouring?'

Doug tried to placate her. 'Now, Jetta. A lot of good men were labourers.'

'A' guid men,' said Mat. 'They were all labourers of one kind or another. But office work. It's not labouring. It's connivin'. Imagine an office full of clerks, a' checking up on other offices full of other clerks, who are checking up on still another office full of still mair clerks – a' this so that naebody gets diddled. Hundreds of suspicious wee bodies a' takin' tent o' one another and imagining themselves big dealers when all they are dealing in is a heap of petty suspicion and lack of trust. It would give you the jaundice.'

'It's a guid respectable job with a collar and tie.'

'Aye. It's respectable. And I'm fed up to the teeth with respectability. As soon as anyone shows any sign of gumption you want him to become respectable. Put a collar and tie on him. It's in case they'll bite. They're frightened they'll bite. And so they will. The ones that don't get collared.' For a minute Mat was enticed with that, the idea that he should make a great demonstration of courage and go right now and sit on his arse in front of some paper with a pen in his hand and refuse to budge. If I wasn't a writer, he thought, I would be capable of that kind of simplicity. He would always have to make concessions to others just because he loved them. It was exactly thus that conscience makes cowards of us all.

'I don't know what kind of nonsense you're talking,' said Jetta, 'but I'm telling you this. You'd better put the hems on your ideas, m'lad. Or there's nae telling where ye'll end up.'

'Never mind about that,' Jake bit the nail on his thumb and looked up at Mat. 'We were talking about clear consciences. What a' want to know is – can you eat it?'

'Unfortunately, no.' Mat spoke politely, then he leaned over with his hands on the table and bawled at them. 'But I can aye show it around as a freak.'

Jake jumped to his feet. 'Now, Mat. Listen. I didn't mean it that way.'

'Naw.' Mat used the long drawling Glasgow sound again.

'Well, maybe. Look, we never fight in this family. If we say things it's because we're worried. C'mon.' Jake came over to Mat and shook his arm. Mat was contrite and Jake went on. 'C'mon. Practical, eh? I could maybe get you a job in the slaughter-house. Speak to some of the lads. Eh? If you think you could stand it. The blood and everything.'

The idea appealed to Mat, the idea of working with his hands and his body. As for everything else, 'I suppose it's just good clean shit.'

Jake grinned. 'Aye. Which you can wash off at the end of the day.'

'Aye, you're right enough.' Mat smiled at Jake. 'I've got to be practical I suppose.'

Jake grinned back at him. 'The old spondulicks – the corporate body – you do that. At least it'll be honest work.'

'Mat's not feart of work, Jetta,' Doug said. 'He's quite willing to go in with Jake. I wouldn't have fancied office work myself. All cooped up . . .'

Mat caught on to his father's sympathy and now that he had quietened a bit felt he could explain himself. 'It was beginning to drive me nuts, Pa. It's not a clean job. It isnae even easy. You come out of the office at night feeling like a manky auld bit of blotting paper. Addin' and subtracting. Counting the cost. I'm asking ye? And ye'd get some henpecked nyaff that couldn't punch his way oot o' a wet poke writing strong letters to clients. Further to our demand of the 17th inst., etcetera, and further action will be taken, etcetera. And whit is the strong action. Get the polis. If ye'd any respect for language or morals or decency ye'd write just plain – come up wi' the dough or else. And if your client was bigger than you you'd end up wi' a keeker and your self-respect. I mean that's the whole thing about office work. It's unreal. The whole thing would really sicken the chops off ye.'

Mat knew that he really believed all this. But at the same time he knew that it was a built-up justification of his conduct. He couldn't really explain to himself why he had stayed off his work and gone to the library. He had just wanted to write and it had seemed a good idea at the time. All the time he had been off work he had tried to evade thinking of the consequences of his irresponsibility.

Doug was all for letting him off lightly. 'Well, if you feel that strongly about it you'd be better at something else.'

'As long as you don't get any more fancy notions.'

'Look. I'll not get any fancy notions. I'll go and work in the slaughter-house if Jake can get me in.'

'I think it's pretty sure, Mat. We're pretty busy.'

'It's a good job really,' said Doug. 'The money's good enough and it's steady. Ye can carry on your writing at night – as a hobby.'

'As a what? A *hobby*? Look, you'd better get a haud o' this – maybe I've not explained it to you before. I'm not writing to pass my time in the evenings, or to kid myself I'm cultured . . .'

'Aye, all right, son.'

'. . . or because of any fancy notions, or to show people what a lovely deep soul I've got . . .'

'Aye, all right, son.'

'. . . or to get my worries off my chest, or relieve some neurotic compulsion . . .'

'Aye, all right, son.'

'. . . or to indulge a whim, or gratify my ego . . .'

'Aye, all right, son.'

'. . . or because of some daft social aspiration. What I have to say has to be said aside from a' that aforementioned guff . . .'

'Aye, all right. All right.' Doug rose with his hands protesting in front of him. 'I'm sorry I said it. Now let's not get started all over again.'

Yet this outburst was still no explanation. Mat had been thinking about something which was, he felt, essentially serious, something which he knew as 'literary values'. Consciously in his mind he even referred to Eliot's idea of poetry as an escape from the personality and emotion. Yet the very sophistication of these ideas seemed to him, in his circumstances, to be over-wheening. These ideas had no equivalence in his actual experience. They were serious matters for the practising writer, but they had no reference to the outward facts of his life. Privately they were to him exciting and serious, but in his actual life as lived they were just as Jetta would describe them. Fancy notions. He had no language in which to say these things. The emotions which he experienced inwardly in relation to his writing were as foreign to his mundane life as Hudson's Argentinian pampas, or Flaubert's original French.

'You sound awful sure of yourself wi' all your clear consciences and your got-to-be-saids . . .'

'Aye. There's thousands of people thought like that and they wound up wearing wee canvas jackets.'

'I think what I said is important. If not . . .' Mat shrugged. He might go on as long as he lived thinking about these matters which would in the end be trivialities if he couldn't actually create a world for himself in which they would be real and applicable. He would go on to the end of his days thinking that literature was important, but never feeling it so. 'If I'm right?' Mat left this question unanswered. Life would be glad then. It is best not to tempt fate by naming names. 'I don't know. But if I've nae convictions, I'm nothing. That's what we always try to dodge in the end.'

'Well, what about the noo?'

Jake and Doug turned towards Jetta with their fingers to their lips. 'Wheesht!'

'Don't start again.'

'Or we'll be arguing all night.'

'Well, he's got a wife to think of,' said Jetta.

Helen had been standing all this time away from the others

at the door. Now she came forward. She leaned her hands on the table and stood over them. Mat had sat down and was sprawled out on his chair.

'No! No!' Helen said. It was the first time she had ever said anything with such definiteness since she had come to live in the house. They were all surprised except Mat. 'Don't bring me into it. I'm out. I didn't think when I married Mat that I was marrying him for money or security.' She laughed. 'He isn't exactly what I would call the gentry. And I didn't ask him to be responsible to me . . .'

Jetta was offended. 'And whit, might I ask, did you marry him for?'

'For his fancy notions. Aside from a few – unmentionable things. You know, living in this house has made me realise one very curious thing. You people don't feel any entitlement to anything; not even Mat. You seem to be in a perpetual state of apology for your very existence. Well I'm not in that frame of mind and' – Helen suddenly broke into broad Glasgow speech – 'if ma man wants to acquire any fancy notions he needn't look to me to reprove him for them. You're a' entitled to a bit mair than a mess o' pottage.'

They were all a bit taken aback, first because of the sentiments, then by her speech when she broke into the broad Glasgow sound. But there was a dawning light on Doug's face.

'Nell, hen! I always thought you were a wee bit of a Tory.'

'It's got nothing to do with politics, it's just the way I feel. Blessed are the meek as long as they don't have any high falutin' ideas. That's your whole philosophy. Even you with your Marx. My God! If you people ever got the dictatorship of the proletariat it would be the mildest tyranny in history. If you took any property from anybody you'd give them it back if they gret too loud. As a matter of fact that's what you did.'

The three men, Mat, Doug and Jake all burst out laughing. 'You're absolutely right, hen!' Doug was grinning ruefully. 'You're absolutely right. My God! I didn't think you had it in you.'

7

WHEN MAT STARTED work in the slaughter-house he stopped writing altogether. In the first place he had so many obligations throughout the day – his work, his family, so many of the things which one does when one is alive – that he had no time to write. He found that writing in the direct glare of the day was inimical to him, and nobody can stay up late at night when they have to rise at five in the morning to go to work. Besides, the hard physical work made him all the time so sleepy. He decided during the first few weeks when he started his new job that he would defer any schemes he had, and he got into the habit of procrastinating. In the second place, he felt quite happy in his new job and he had so many things to occupy his mind – new events, new experiences, new people, a new world full of physical activity. The habit of writing dropped away slowly and easily. If writing was a kind of illicit need, then a cold bath and a run round the block were the best cure. Mat started to take the cure.

The slaughter-house was inside a huge area, surrounded by buff coloured walls. This area, which was all roofed-in, comprised the cattle market where the pigs, sheep and cattle awaited sale and slaughter, the slaughter-house, where the animals were killed and dressed, and the meat market where the animals, now transformed into beef, pork and mutton, were sold to the butchers. Inside this place on a Wednesday afternoon, which was market day, there was always a welter of activity; big livestock trucks backing into the various entrances and disgorging their loads of cattle or sheep, butchers' lorries and vans everywhere, farmers with their big boots, labourers with the dungarees beginning to shine and darken with grease and coagulated blood, white-coated salesmen who were cutting, pinching and slapping at the hanging meat; there were swinging slabs of meat which hung from cambrels fixed to an overhead trolley and which were sliding down from the slaughter-house to be lost in the rows of meat hanging in the various stalls and stances; the red gape of cut meat, the yellow-marbled sides of beef, the sawdust that soaked up the dripping blood from the necks of the carcases, barrowfuls of day-old calves with slacked limbs and lolling heads, the pink schoolgirl complexions of the scalded pigs, droplets of red blood on the cobbles. This was the meat market.

You went up to the slaughter-house through a big lorry-filled entrance gate and underneath a tangle of lights and girders which supported the system of rails on which the cambrels hung, then right through and up a wide pass, tarmacadamed and with red glazed brick walls. In the slaughter-house itself were rows of big cubicles where the animals were dressed and flayed. Outside these rooms hung the freshly killed steaming carcases awaiting the porters who would stick a meat hook into the spaul and slide them away. There were heaps of feet being cleaned up by labourers into barrows, heaps of round manyplies, the fat stuffed fourth stomach of the ox, which the killers would skite out of their rooms like curling stones, slipping on the blood soaked floor, and limp hides with the hair all soaked with water and blood lying in folds amongst the other stuff. The men, all rubber booted, walked carefully with an odd mincing gait among the pools of blood and water, among the slippery refuse, the feet, manyplies, pieces of fat and lumps of jelly-like lappered blood. In the middle of the pass barrows were being pushed up and down as the labourers collected the offal – tripes, livers, hearts, lungs, heads. And all the time the grinding of machinery, the cries of men, the clatter of iron-felloed wheels, the crack of the guns, the lowing and bellowing of the cattle and the crunch of big heavy bodies being felled on to the concrete floor.

Mat worked in one of these slaughter-rooms. At first he had felt slight revulsion, though perhaps less so than most who started work there. It was not the shambles that caused this, however. He found it quite easy to have his arms covered up to the elbows in reeking blood, and he handled the dripping gobbets of offal and fat with no qualms. What he did dislike was the moment when the animals, the frisky wee bullocks, the quiet maternal cows, the placid indifferent bulls, had their heads tied to the stunning post, and the gun, the bolt pistol, was fired into their foreheads between the eyes. The gun cracked and the animals went down on to the floor in the same sudden moment. Like a felled ox, Mat would think. For nothing, other than the thing itself, could convey that quick loosening of the limbs as they slackened and folded under the animal and it would drop on its knees, its stomach, and its chin, all together, making an odd sound combining the slap of soft flesh and the solid but dull crunch of the padded bone as the chin bounced loosely on the concrete floor. Then the shuddering sigh and the spasm of the muscles as the animal tensed them to grip at the soft elusive life which suspired from the tiny hole in its forehead. Mat found this difficult to get used to, and with every crack and thud of a beast dropping he would ponder on the fragility of bone.

Even worse than this was the killing of the kosher beasts. From a commonsense view it was as humane as the bolt pistol. The animal was turned on its back inside a huge drum and its neck was stretched with a halter which was tied round its lower jaw. Then the Jewish killer, wearing his little black cap, would come and with his long gleaming knife would stroke the blade from the curve at the jaw, back through the muscles lapped around the gullet, windpipe and arteries of the neck, right through to the backbone. All in one stroke loosening the head and laying bare the big pad of muscle which stretched from the breast right up to under the chin, and the quivering arteries would spout rich frothy blood in spasms and the windpipe would rasp as the animal let out a great spasmodic breath. It was the possible moment of consciousness, when the head loosened and the animal took that last great breath through the chittering windpipe, that Mat thought about. The horror of a possible combination of consciousness and the irrevocable state of death. It was a kind of metaphysical horror that Mat felt at the idea of consciousness, if even only for a second, knowing that it was cut off from its animal source, a horror even worse than the ineluctable obliteration of the gun.

In Scotland, an ox when it is killed by a bolt pistol, is pithed; that is, a long cane is passed through the hole in the skull down through the canal in the spine through which the spinal cord runs. The effect of this pithing, or caning, is to scramble the brain and prevent the nervous system of the animal from passing gratuitous and unnecessary messages to the muscles of the body, to destroy the organisation on which the animal depends for its life. In other words, caning kills the animal completely so that it ceases to kick and the muscles cease to flutter and it becomes safe to work on the carcase with a knife. When the beasts were killed with the kosher method, Mat would always, as soon as it was on the floor, draw back the skull and insert his knife between the last vertebrae and the skull to sever the white pulsing mass that was the spinal cord. He was hoping to obliterate the last possible gleam of consciousness which might lurk inside the narrow sloping skull.

Mat now got up in the mornings along with Jake. They got themselves ready in the morning quiet, absolutely silent themselves, communicating only by grunts, each still wrapped in his thoughts of sleep. They drank tea in the kitchenette, more often than not standing up in the cold room. Then they'd put on their jackets and hitch over their shoulders the little ex-W.D. haversacks in which they kept their knives and stones. Then they would go out – slapping at their pockets to see that they had remembered everything, their tea, sugar, money, keys, fags, matches. Every morning they caught the same tram at the same time. When they got into the market they would walk up the long pass into the slaughter-house where everything was quiet except for the occasional bellow from some beast or the bleat of a sheep. The wide tarmacadam pass was a matt grey colour at this time in the morning. The night before it would have been hosed down and now it was all dry without a trace of refuse or blood. The concrete floors of the slaughter-rooms were the same, dry and light-coloured.

They would switch on the lights that shone directly on to the floor beside the stunning post where the beasts would fall. They then switched on the overhead cranes and lowered the hooks on to which were suspended bags, aprons, rubber boots, cleavers and ropes, all the equipment needed for their work. The men carried on meaningless bantering conversations between the rooms. Occasionally some of the young blood-boys would vent a whoop, and from the back of the slaughter-rooms among the pens there would come a flurrying scuffling sound as an impatient or cross beast would butt another animal with its head. During this time they would dress in their bloodied dungarees, put on their stiff aprons and hitch on the belt which held the steel and the narrow wooden box for their knives. After that they would go into the cattle pens and push among the press of cattle looking for the marks on the hide and picking out the cattle which they would be slaughtering. If possible they would try to put their allocation of cattle for the day into a pen as near to their own room as possible. By the time six o'clock came and the whistle blew there would be two beasts tied up to the stunning posts in each room. Then the gunners would come along with their bolt pistols and the crack of the guns would start and the beasts thud on to the floor.

Jake actually worked for himself. The system was that he hired a room from the market authorities and along with a mate he offered his services to butchers or dealers who had cattle which they wanted slaughtered. Payment was at so much a head so that the harder the killers worked the more they were paid. Mat's job was to collect the offals from the room on behalf of a firm of offal merchants who paid him a weekly wage. His duties in the room were laid down precisely; he skinned the heads of the two felled beasts, cut the heads from the carcase, separated and emptied the tripes, trimmed them of fat, washed them and hung them on hooks for the barrowmen to collect. Then the same with the buffs, or cluster of lungs and heart, which were washed and trimmed and the pericardium or fatty sac round the heart cut off and the heart itself slit to release the lappering gobbets of blood from the auricular and ventricle cavities. His job was known as 'benefit lifting' and he was known as 'a benefit man'. In fact the benefit man helped the killers in every way he could and for this he was paid at the end of every week what was called a 'bung', an unofficial tip.

Mat had in his time come across horrified descriptions of shambles and he had shared in the horror of the writers, recoiling from what appeared to be the awfulness of the experience. He had only worked in the slaughter-house for a few weeks before he learned to despise this point of view. It began to seem to him that the morbidness was a projection by the writer on to the shambles that he viewed and that the recoil was a luxury which could be afforded by the writer in not being involved or responsible for the shambles.

A man, Mat thought, need not be insensitive because he was not squeamish, nor devoid of pity – it was a point of professional pride to the slaughterman that he would kill an animal neatly and quickly without causing it unnecessary suffering. Mat noticed too that any visitors to the slaughter-house were more concerned with their own feelings, their own disgust, than they were with pity for the animals. In fact Mat was attracted to the work although he had difficulty in explaining to himself the nature of this attraction. But he had seen something in art which confirmed to him the sanity and health of his viewpoint. Once the slaughtering had got under way in the morning, the slaughtering floor would turn pink with watery blood, the electric light would begin to glare on the fleshy slabs which hung glistening and palpitating from the rails, the steam from the hot pipes and the gutted carcases cast a haze which was suffused with red reflected from the bloody floors, the meat, and the pans of steaming blood. All this caused the same effect of morbidezza which Rembrandt had caught so calmly in his painting of a flayed carcase which hung in the Glasgow Art Galleries. The ultimate wisdom of art, a healthy liveliness and acceptance of sensuous life. It was this that attracted him about the place – the liveliness, the tremendous sense of physical vitality which came from the hard work, the men, the cattle, the movement, even from the dead slabs of meat.

Once the whistle blew at six the place began to resound, the cattle would become restive at being continually disturbed and would bellow violently, or the bulls which were chained in stalls would trumpet at the cows and cause them to mill and plunge round the pens, the overhead cranes would begin to whine, the killers bawl for the benefit men who would be standing smoking in the middle of the pass with their bare arms tucked into the tops of their aprons, the guns would start to crack and the cleavers begin to thwack into bone and flesh.

When a beast was felled it was quickly pithed, the killer feeling for the hole in the skull and inserting the cane, pushing it down the spinal canal for about four feet, then working it in and out until the animal would thrash its legs about and its muscles would twitch and shudder. After he had pumped the cane in and out a few times the animal would be left lying absolutely slack and the killer would stand up between the animal's forelegs, kicking the top leg back with his heel so that the skin about the throat would be stretched tight. Then casually, usually while bantering away with his mate, he'd stroke the eight-inch sticking knife on his steel then bend down and, inserting the knife's point under the hide just above the dewlap, he'd bare the flesh in a long forward stroke to beneath the chin. The flesh would then be stroked lightly with the edge of the blade until the killer could feel the warm pulse of the carotid; again he'd insert the point of his knife and slit the artery longitudinally, releasing the rich purple frothy blood into the waiting pan. After this the beast was hung for a while by a rope, hitched round a hind foot and slung on to the crane. When the blood had drained from the carcase it was lowered back down on to the floor and turned on its back with its head twisted round and a loose foot wedged into the ridge of its spine to help prop it up. This was when the killer's job really began. While the head was being skinned by the benefit man the killer would remove the feet with his straight sticking knife. This was done quickly, the killer swiftly laying open the knee with a semi-circular cut and a flick of the knife which folded back the skin pad of over the knee and exposed the white membrane over the joint; then he merely twisted the knee with his left hand and stroked the joint with his knife and the foot was off and flying through the air to join the pile of other feet lying outside the door of the room. Before the last foot had landed the long straight knife was being used to extend a slit in the hide, from the throat, over the dewlap and breast, down the middle of the broad flat belly, and back to the vent. The hide was then flayed with the curved skinning knife, from the forelegs, flank and rump of the animal and spread out leaving the flensed carcase all glistening and fresh with the hide attached now only to the tail, back and shoulders. A six-inch slit was made now in the muscle covering the belly, releasing gas with a gentle suspiration. Then the killer would split the breast-bone with the big seven-pound cleaver; a few controlled drops of the heavy blade and the narrow breast-bone was split in a clean straight line. The cambrels were pulled out from a rack, hooked on to the crane and their ends pushed into the spawl between bone and sinew, then the animal was half lifted from the ground to bring the tail up breast high with the killer and allow him to separate the hide from the tail and to clear the vent.

While this was being done the head was finally severed, the work of a few seconds, the benefit man bending and gripping a cord in the lower part of the beast's jaw, pulling the head back and stroking with his knife through the joint between the skull and the first vertebrae. It was at this point that the animal was gutted, the belly slit to reveal the glaucous mass of entrails all neatly dimpled and coiled to the scalloped edge of the mesentery fat. The intestines were draped over the forearm and cut free from the vent, pulled out from the animal, and the various conduits and canals which connected them to the stomach and liver and spleen – and they were ready to be thrown into the shallow wooden trough which stood outside the room. Then the big ballooning bluish-grey paunch, already beginning to drop of its own weight, would be sliding over the diaphragm and stretching the pink oesophagus. A flick of the knife and the mass of stomachs would flop on the floor. The benefit man would separate the stomachs, sling the tight round manyplies out of the room, trim the warm globules of fat from the surface of the paunch, then drag the gagging blue mass to a hole in the floor in the corner of the room. He would slit the bag in a swift curving flash of the knife and release the feculent contents of the stomach down the chute. The spleen and liver were now removed from where they were tucked in their corners of the abdominal cavity, the tissue connecting them to the wall of the beast's flank being torn away by the fingers and the edible valuable liver being placed on a clean wooden shelf. Two quick semi-circular cuts were made in the diaphragm from the backbone round close to the ribs, the lungs, heart and loose flaps of the diaphragm were cut from the backbone and carried away, and the whole cluster suspended by the gullet was hung on to a hook on the wall.

The beast was now an empty shell of bone and muscle and fat, except for the kidneys which remained embedded in the thick fat attached to the backbone and ribs. While the beast was being gutted the hide was torn away from the back and now lay suspended from the shoulders, its lower part lying in folds on the wet bloody floor. Now the backbone was split through, the most skilled and difficult part of all the killer's work. He started slitting with his heavy cleaver from the flat bone at the base of the tail right down to the neck stump, and in spite of the clumsiness and weight of the big cleaver the vertebrae were split neat and clean. It was a delicate and arduous operation which required both strength and skill so as not to leave broken shards of bone which would spoil the roast cuts, or the appearance of the carcase to the butcher. This done the carcase was now two separate sides of beef, opened out like a book and joined together with muscle only at the rump and the shoulder. While the benefit man was drying off the carcase with a cloth the killer would, with soft strokes of his knife, part the fell between the last piece of attached hide and the bluish lump of muscle on the beast's shoulder. Then he'd drag the mucky sodden hide out of the room.

The carcase was now ready for the butcher. Only twenty-five minutes ago the animal had walked into the room. The irrevocable transformation never ceased to astonish Mat. Even in foresight he would find it difficult to imagine the placid chewing animal brought into the room transformed so quickly into a carcase.

Yet after all, the whole process was routine, it never varied, and in the end the result was beef. This could only add to the satisfaction of the work. In the morning, when Mat had worked hard for an hour or two, and he was beginning to work up an appetite for breakfast, he would notice the smell of the meat and the rich bloom of the flesh as he sliced through it with his knife and this would make him salivate. It was simply that a vigorous and healthy appetite resulted in the disappearance, the absence, of fastidiousness. In the same way Mat enjoyed the warmth of blood on his hands, the smooth bland sheets of fat which were trimmed from the paunch, the silken slightly tacky feel of the intestines, the dry flaky texture of the lung, or the slabby firm feeling of a haunch or a shoulder. It was a world of simple and strong sensuousness, with a lot in it which would appeal to anyone starved of bodily activity and sensuous stimulation – the agility and skill needed to watch against flying hoofs or a subtle dig with a horn, to subdue a restive beast, lassooing it and coaxing or fooling it on to the stunning post, the heaving and pulling to get a ton of bull flesh on to a resupine position on the floor, the alertness and skill needed to handle a razor-sharp knife with safety.

Above all this there was something which Mat counted as important and which he had tried to formulate clearly to himself; it was the need to be intimately involved in a material process. It was one of his favourite ideas, originating from long tedious hours spent adding columns of figures, that it was essential for a man to have a connection with his bodily and economic needs other than in a mere abstract way. Whether this could be elevated into a social idea he was doubtful, somebody had to do the abstract thing. But for Mat there was this newly discovered enjoyment, and he took delight in the unctuousness of the fat, the soft maternity of the udders which he stripped from a flank, or the heaving at a massive bull's head as he gripped it through the slit nostril.

In a few months he became completely immersed in this new life. There was the regular cycle of each week, beginning on Monday with fairly hard work, mounting up towards Wednesday which would be hectic, everybody working at full pitch the whole time. Then there was the breathing space towards the end of the week, along with the Friday opulence. Even getting up on the bitterest mornings had its solace. In the cold mornings they would send out for tea and drink pints of the scalding liquid during pauses in the work and smoke cigarette after cigarette or eat fried sausages or eggs between rolls, two bites to each roll, and the body would become warm from activity and full of its own warmth and the enjoyment of itself and its appetites.

The men in the slaughter-house showed good personal

feeling towards one another and there was an atmosphere of camaraderie. As the killers worked for themselves there was never any intervention by bosses and all authority came from the demands of the job. Along with this there was the richness and variety of personalities and opinions, with much teasing and physical fun. On a Thursday or a Friday if the work was slack there would be hilarious ball games with perhaps thirty men sliding and slipping about on the wet tarmac after a tiny rubber ball, or hectic comical fights going on with buckets of water or hoses. There would be tremendous cheering when a hefty swipe at the ball would go amiss and someone would slither down on the wet floor. One time when Mat got unusually excited and was chasing after a ball this happened to him. He hit the ball a terrific kick and scored a goal but on so doing he fell to the floor on the base of his spine and the point of his elbow. He lay there unable to move because of the nauseating shock which jarred through his bones. A wave of pain and sickness began to spread through his body while at the same time his diaphragm was jerking with giggles. He was carried off the 'field' with great ceremony, everybody cheering and whistling, and he was unable to suppress the tears of laughter and pain which rolled down his cheeks. As they laid him down on a bench he was letting out genuine groans of pain which under the infection of everybody's laughter would turn into spasmodic whoops and giggles. It was the kind of fall which might have laid a man up for a day or two, but under the influence of the sheer bounce and vigour of the football game he had thrown off the shock in about ten minutes and was up on his feet chasing after the ball again.

While the men were actually working all this turned into good-natured yelling and shouting, the telling of jokes, the recounting of tales. Many silly useless arguments would start just for the sake of the noise and the exuberance and ferocity of the language, the whole thing becoming formal, almost stylised.

The months passed in this way in a regular peaceful routine. Only during rare moments would Mat reflect on how commonplace he had become. Not that he had any contempt for the commonplace. There was too much about it that was valuable and healthy. He often thought, for instance, about the interesting effect which living in a commonplace manner had upon his sense of time. Without any nagging compulsion to strive after some kind of achievement, he found himself able to concentrate upon and enjoy the content of his everyday life. Somehow, before, when he had been feeling all the time the obsession to write, everything about the mundane part of his life, taking a tram, eating a meal, visiting, the ordinary duties of life, the day itself, all had to be got past for the sake of the next moment when he would sit under the circle of light and start again on his novel. This had seemed to make his time fly. When every part of the day seemed to be spent waiting, every act was a mere provisional gesture to atone or dismiss what to a normal man would be the content and reality of his life. Now he could enjoy the commonplace for its own sake and without the nagging anxiety of having something waiting which made every moment when he was not writing seem trivial and absurd.

The content of life, too, the commonplace, was well worth attention. He began to indulge his appetites and senses. At weekends he would go home with a couple of whiskies under his belt and the pleasant sense of looking forward to a weekend of relaxation. He began to buy literary magazines and weekend reviews and pay attention to the current literary scene. He read all the time with a kind of voluptuousness. He bought himself a beautiful book of reproductions of Vermeer's paintings. His interests were not exactly commonplace, but his attitude was; in distinction to his former excitement about art, which came from his need to use experience, now he merely enjoyed it. Sometimes, when the slaughter-house was busy and he had to work very hard, he would lose himself in the physical cycle of working, sleeping and eating. He would come home and sit the whole evening just waiting to go to bed, enjoying the comfort of his relaxed limbs. His hands would be stiff from holding the knife and he would place them on the arm of the chair and sit back staring at the fire and dozing. At these times he felt no anxiety, not a sense of being flawed, but whole and complete and unable to remember what it was like to be anything else but relaxed and nerveless.

8

WITH HIS INTERESTS directed outwards Mat began to make some discoveries. The great idea which he had shelved came to the forefront of his mind in an ironic way. He had been visiting the library, on a legitimate occasion this time, and had been browsing around the shelves. For some reason he had taken a copy of Thomas Mann's *Buddenbrooks* from the shelves and had idly started to read it. He had experienced the shock of complete recognition. What he had recognised when he read of the house of Buddenbrooks – the family, the trading house, the magnificent meals, the family heirlooms and records, the traditional life – was his own concern with the Royal Burghers of Rutherglen. Yet there was a difference. It seemed clear to Mat that the author's love of this traditional, conservative way of life, was the same as his own – yet there was something else there. It was like the thing that happens when, as the expression goes, 'It rings a bell' and you are vaguely reminded of something. Mat read the book at home and it prompted him to go back and look over the material which he had collected for his own novel. He felt on re-reading it all that the whole thing was almost comical. It was a kind of antiquarianism. He was reminded of those folk who go about collecting old objects – pieces of bric-a-brac, old swords, pieces of Victorian furniture, wally dugs, wag-at-the-wa' clocks; it was indeed what he himself had been doing. There were long accounts of the details of the domestic life of his people; he had collected old recipes, maps of the streets, copies of old prints, records of exchanges and purchases of lands and properties, copies of the accounts and minutes of societies and lodges, reports of various acts of charity and social provision; he knew exactly the style of clothes and materials which were worn, where they were woven and made, and the manner in which the women embroidered, crocheted, crimped and ironed their dresses, bonnets, ribbons and inkles, what artefacts the men carried in their pockets and hung from their fobs or collected in drawers and desks and shelves and what-nots; there were long copies of minutes of learned societies, pocket histories of business houses, of theatres, of books published; the doings of Presbyters and congregations; benefactions and municipal acts and provisions. A great conglomeration of material whose sole object seemed to be the social and civil acts of men of a past era. He noted that the word which he used most often and in a characteristic way was the word 'provision'. It seemed to him strange that he, who outwardly and explicitly paid service to progressive and forward-looking ideas, should have this strong feeling and sympathy for an old capitalistic way of life, and that he should be attracted most strongly not to any individual or personal side, but to that social or workaday side whose concern was totally with provision and conservation in the material world. In Mann's work there was something else, some energetic attitude towards his material which allowed him to people and manifest his world with individuals and events. This gave Mat a sense of unease, the same which he sometimes felt when he realised that the same tobacco lords whom he admired for their conservatism had shown a radical resilience in helping to create the Industrial Revolution. When Mann inexorably allowed the facts of European history, the crisis of Capitalism, to ride rough shod over the Buddenbrooks and finally extinguish them, he had done something essentially modern and progressive which his love for his characters and their way of life must have made difficult. It was too difficult for Mat, and he put away his big dossier of papers, the richly varied but intractable material which he sensed now he would never shape; he put them away with the reflection which gave him grim satisfaction, that the only difference between himself

119

and this wonderful German was his own inferior talent. He put his failure to shape his material down to a simple intellectual lack, a lack of the novelist's ability. He didn't see the lack of ability might consist simply of his refusal to stand in an active and energetic relation to his work. Besides, he was genuinely confused.

Into this confusion came a sudden clarity when he read *Tonio Kröger*. The idea of the artist as a bourgeois manqué came to him as laughably and crudely true in his own case. At last he had come to realise the nature of his artistic impulse; a mere need to become vicariously immersed in something from which he had been isolated. A traditional, solid security in life. He began to understand the nature of the attraction which everything solid and substantial had for him in that they would lend gravity and stillness to the flimsy, vibrating amorphousness of his life. The solid burghers had a clear and solid footing beneath them and their floors did not slope towards the street. That history had put the skids under the Buddenbrooks was enough for him to realise, or to pretend to realise, that he could avoid the precariousness of life by drawing in a regular weekly wage, and the other moral precariousness he could hide away from, exhaust his knowledge of it in the rich and banal life of the slaughter-house. He could have realised more than this but it would have meant recasting himself, reassessing himself, and becoming involved with literature again. It was easier to explain his aberration, his flaw, his artistic side, as a mere reflex from his fear-ridden and poverty-stricken childhood. This dismissal of literature was made doubly easy for him by his sense of urgency of the questions of the day. He read further in Mann, in a way repelled by the kind of subject which Mann treated, and which Mat saw as a morbid interest in disease. On reading *Death in Venice* he took in a straightforward way Mann's questioning of the nature of art. Furthermore, with the understanding of his own relationship with his work he felt a growing sense of fastidiousness, descending into disgust with the whole business of art. He felt unprepared to take part in the kind of excessiveness which art demanded, a kind of inflammation and heatedness of the mind, a shameful exposure of the self. What his mother and Jake had said to him – 'High falutin' nonsense' and 'Look after the old corporate body' – took on the dignity of serious argument. It was easy to go on from there to the moral view that art was essentially too frivolous and irrelevant a matter in a serious and precarious world. The old corporate body was being seriously threatened by this very high falutin' nonsense – the scientists and their hubris, and here he was playing around with the same dangerous toy. He wondered how he had become entitled to play around with art, a thing that was an excess, an excrescence upon life, a luxuriant and diseased growth. All the Calvinist beliefs came to the fore here – when people were suffering all over the world – for real!

If he had previously side-slipped into living the common-place life, developing an aptitude and a taste for what he called 'real living,' he had now found a rationale, a good substantial reason why he should continue in this way.

He began to look upon the act of writing with the realisation of the presumptuousness of the thing and he felt towards it that mixture of embarrassment and disgust which he would have felt in having to take part in an everyday role dressed in a top hat and tails. Although this disgust was of a moral nature it began to find expression every time he thought of writing, as a nose-wrinkling grue, a flutter of the fingertips, a soured grimace, a clearing of the tongue, a long fastidious exhalation of the breath through pursed lips. Sometimes it went as far as real physical nausea, sometimes he would cause himself a real physical blush when he thought of his presumption and his complete incapacity to live up to it.

Early in the year, at the same time that Mat had started work in the slaughter-house, Helen had become pregnant. The baby was due in September, so Mat and Helen redoubled their efforts to find a house for themselves. In April they succeeded in renting a very small room and kitchen on the south side of the city.

The day that Mat had come home from work and found that Helen had managed to persuade a house factor to rent a house to them – at long last, after waiting around for weeks and months in various waiting rooms, putting their names down on lists, calling every month on a dozen different offices – that day Mat was inspired by the hope that at last he would be able to consolidate, at last make something permanent, have something solid and absolutely lasting in his life, and he thought of the life ahead of him with a home of his own and a family and the quiet day-to-day pleasures that would be his. A door of his own which he could lock against the world, and the life of his family which would be good from the beginning. He would find in making a home with Helen a resolution to all those tensions which he had sought before in writing, and they would be resolved in actuality and not in the false and insubstantial way of art.

All this was bound up in some way with Mat's view of Helen as she had stood before him as she always did with that significant open-handed gesture, her body towards him and her hands turned out. In her early pregnancy her whole body took on a soft amplitude and Mat felt continually drenched in an atmosphere of love and womanly generosity.

On very rare occasions Mat would remember how he had created an image out of the actual reality that surrounded him, and how this had given him a release from fear and anxiety; when he had sat in the office and listened to the clock ticking, posting up the big heavy bound ledgers and enjoying the half somnolent tedium of the inflexible routine. That had come to an end out of something in him, perhaps no more than a primitive energy of will, which recognised that even tedium and boredom does not put a stop to the processes of life or the passing of days, that his mortality was just as sure, his life just as precarious whether he immersed himself in routine work or whether he threw open all doors and dared to presume. But he dismissed these thoughts on the authority of the works of one of the greatest writers of the century and persisted in his profound and deliberate misunderstanding of Mann's work and of his own nature, ignoring the irony that what he was experiencing in himself as a dismissal of art was in fact that very doubt which is at the centre of the experience of art itself.

Mat and Helen sat in the tramcar in the third seat from the front on the left-hand side. Whenever this particular seat was empty, and they were together, they always took it. Mat did this out of nostalgia, Helen out of sentiment. Once they had sat on this seat on an empty tram and steeped in the roseate glow of young love they had made shy confession. They had been travelling home after being out together the whole day, having been to see a French film – a whimsical and touching film about youth and memory in which a haunting little musical theme had been played which they whistled as they waited for the tram. Before seeing the film Mat had stood waiting in the foyer while Helen went to hang her wet raincoat in the cloakroom. When she came back she had stood at the entrance to the foyer in her characteristic stance – peering about her short-sightedly yet without the slight stoop that is usual among short-sighted people. Instead she stood erect and supple and with a little smile on her face as she looked for Mat among the crowd in the foyer. Mat did nothing to attract her attention, for it amused and touched him to see her little smile of expectation as she peered in quite another direction from the one in which he was standing. Then as she had noticed him she had come forward and he had noticed her body and her movements which had an amplitude not so much sexual as purely human, an attractiveness entirely personal and out of which sex was compounded rather than an attractiveness having its basis on sex. Then they had gone upstairs to see the film, Helen running, Mat following behind smiling quietly and comfortably as Helen stood at the top of the stairs waiting for him and holding the door of the balcony open and looking back down towards him. Mat remembered that day; a day when the wind had whipped sheets of rain up and down the streets, but which they had spent in warm carpeted restaurants and lighted rooms, gazing outwardly from the gay interiors to the grey city outside.

So it added to Mat's sense of expectation that they should sit together in this seat. It was a lucky sign. Mat had the quaint habit of holding to these things. If he was going somewhere which involved a choice of routes he would consciously take that one which he remembered as having taken at a special happy moment in his life. Moments like sitting on the third seat from the front on the left-hand side were too rare not to be partaken of again when possible – if only in memory. And so they sat together, Helen clinging to Mat's arm, Mat pressing her arm against his side. They were going to see their new house together.

As the tram went through the streets Mat gazed out at the lit-up windows of the houses. The tram slid through the bright streets into the town. They changed in the town to another tram which would take them over the Clyde to the south side of the city, across the bridge, where they looked over the light-streaked river to the gay upside-down reflections in the water, and on out through the Gorbals to the quiet streets beyond. They found the street they were looking for in a recess between a sunken railway shunting yard and a bus garage. Before finding it they had walked through several streets in the wrong direction, quiet streets with big sandstone tenements or smaller two-storey houses with stretches of worn garden in front. The streets seemed peaceful with the gas-lamps casting their individual quiet pools of light around them; they passed a little square with a railed-in children's playground in the centre and with trees planted close to the railings, overhanging the pavement. The trees hissed slightly from the wind and the light smirr that was falling. After that they found themselves in what was to be their own street and they walked down it looking for the number of their close.

When they had found the close they walked inside and found

the vacant house they were to look at, a door at the back of the close. Mat had the keys in his pocket and they opened the door and groped their way into the darkness of the house. Mat found the electric switch and turned it on, but they had forgotten that the electricity had been turned off and there was no light.

They spent the next half-hour wandering up and down the adjacent streets looking for a shop that was open. The rain had begun to fall heavily but they were so eager to see the house that they kept on looking until they found a shop open. It was a tiny cluttered shop full of cheap kiddies' sweets, cards of hair pins, tin mugs and coarse china cups lying in cardboard boxes among dry straw. The old woman who looked after the shop insisted on parcelling the two candles with her twisted arthritic hands, wrapping them up tightly in a piece of newspaper and giving the end of the little parcel a twist so that it would not come apart. Then they went back to their new house.

It was very quiet when they got back and they stood in the close, Mat fumbling for the keys and unwrapping the old woman's parcel to get at the candles. They could hear the splutter and slap of water falling from a gutter in the roof on to the back yard. Mat opened the door and went inside to the dark lobby and shut the door behind them so they could light the candles out of the bitter wet draught which was blowing through the close. They found themselves standing in a small irregularly shaped lobby. There were two doors to the right-hand side, one opening into a cramped privy, the other into a small square room. As they walked into the room on tiptoe, so as to avoid the empty exaggerated sound which their feet made on the bare wooden floor, they passed the candles slowly round the walls of the room so that each feature of the room moved before their eyes like a film. To the left of the door through which they had entered, in the same wall, was the bed recess about four feet deep into the wall and about six feet long. Then in the left-hand wall there was a gap and some loose exposed bricks where the previous tenants had removed the fireplace, then a cupboard the door and shelves of which had been removed and the back all roughly tiled. Running along the door frame of this cupboard was a lead gas pipe, the end of which had been sawn off and crushed with a hammer and which had obviously connected with a gas cooker in the cupboard. Opposite the doorway were the double windows, tall and narrow, and below them the sink and draining board. Mat was able to pull the crumbling damp wood round the sink apart with his fingers. The sink itself was of cast iron and brown with rust. In the right-hand wall at the window end of the room was another door which led into another room even smaller than the kitchen.

Back in the kitchen Mat held up the candle and looked at Helen's face. There were still drops of rain on her cheeks and the fringe of hair on her brow was damp. She was looking around, her eyes shining in the candlelight, her face composed and serious with that look of being disconnected with her surroundings that people often have in a strange place.

'It's a bit of a mess,' said Mat.

'Och!' Helen shrugged. She didn't seem to expect, anything else. 'A wee bit scrubbing out. Some wallpaper.'

They went over together and looked at the hole in the wall where the fireplace had been. 'We'd need a fireplace and a cooker – and a new sink – and all that woodwork round the sink.'

They went out leaving the candles lying on the floor of the lobby. Mat locked the door and they went to the front of the close and looked out into the wet street.

'I suppose we'll take it.'

'We must.'

There was really no question about it. Houses were scarce and any house, *any* house at all was a blessing. On the way home they sat in the tram counting up the probable cost of the things they would need. Mat sat with a piece of paper on his knee and a pen in his hand and jotted down the figures. The seat third from the front on the left-hand side had already been taken.

* * *

During all the time following, while getting the house ready and buying things for the expected baby, Mat's mind became preoccupied again with the art experience. He felt this time precipitated into thinking about writing by the experience of actuality rather than through the direct experience of literature. For these first few months when he had been working in the slaughter-house and living in his parents' house, when Helen's pregnancy had been a half realised thing, a mere twinkle in the eye, as the saying goes, a mere abstract speculation – these few months had been comparatively safe. The circumstances of his life had wrapped him round with protections. The routine of work and domesticity and enjoyment. Now his preoccupation with the need to find and make shelter for his family, Helen and the expected baby, began to grow into an enormous symbol in his mind.

Mat had signed the missive in the factor's office and paid over the month's rent on the day after Helen and he had paid their first visit to the house. After that there were a million things to attend to. Jake and Mat had gone over to the house in their working clothes and redd the place out of rubbish. Then they had taken stock of everything that would have to be done. A simple thing had caught Mat's imagination that day and became later an obsession with him. The skirting board in the house was in bad condition, the wood was warped and old and crumbling. The sink, which was old and rusted through was boxed in with damp mouldy wood. Mat and Jake tore all this rotten woodwork away and left exposed the black stones which were at the back of the outer wall of the building. When they took off the skirting board round the bottom of the wall and left the crumbling plaster exposed, Mat had the impression of the lack of definition in the room. It was not precisely a room any more, what with the broken plaster, the exposed blackened and mildewed stone, the gaping hole with the loose bricks round it which was the chimney place, the raw irregular line of the floor boards where they butted against the wall and were not nicely trimmed by the skirting – not so much a room as a scrabbled-out hole in the building.

Although it was now April the weather was still raw and damp and this gave point to Mat's search for a fireplace. He wandered round the Gorbals one day in a bitter cold wind looking for a tradesman from whom he could buy a fireplace and order it to be built in. They weren't entirely satisfied with the fire they bought, but there was so much to do to the house and they had to buy as cheaply as possible. The fireplace which he bought was of cheap highly glazed tile, with an ugly stippled finish. He managed to scrounge a very good porcelain sink from a demolisher's yard and some good timber which he used to replace the rotten woodwork which had been torn out. Then there was a gas cooker to get from the Gas Board, and paint and wallpaper, various items of furniture and household necessities – pots and pans, brushes and scrubbers, cloths, paraffin. turpentine, linoleum, hooks, hangers, pegs, ropes, towels, basins, trays, covers, varnishes, soap receptacles, pails, mops – all the paraphernalia needed to set up a household.

What struck Mat about all this, what struck his imagination in a kind of perverse way, was the provisional nature of all the various accoutrements which they had to buy. When Mat had written of his Burghers, of the old fellow who sat at his escritoire and clipped his lighted taper on to the little stand, or the maid in the kitchen who popped the heated bolt into the goffering iron in order to crease her linen, he had been obsessed by the role which the ordinary household artefact or working tool has to play in the life of men. Giving men a place in which they could live their lives and shutting out what was alien and inhospitable, or chilling, or brief. As if the warm fires, the workaday routine, the traditional family effects, the Bibles and diaries, had something in them which fronted against what was contingent or provisional, created that order and definition in the material world which the little house lacked and which was so necessary for men's peace of mind, containing in their craftsmanship and substantialness a little glow of permanence, being handed down through the generations to temper a little of men's sense of the brevity of their lives.

And so Mat and Helen wandered among the shops, buying and counting their money; or they sawed and painted and constructed and measured; they arranged for plumbers and electricians and plasterers. Six weeks passed and the summer had come when they moved in. By this time all their ready money had gone and they were left with hire purchase debts which stretched a good two years ahead.

Mat felt it was great nevertheless, when they were able to come home to their own house and be by themselves. Helen sat contentedly knitting for the baby. They fitted up the tiny little room with its long narrow window with a cot and a little chest of drawers for the baby's things and put the big expensive pram, which had been their only extravagance, in it. Mat loved the journey home from his work which took him through the Gorbals with all its movement and excitement, its big broad streets and Jewish shops and Irishmen with their wide floppy trousers standing outside the pubs. Living here they could buy Jewish bread and properly roasted coffee and exotic fruits and vegetables from the Jewish and Indian shops. The summer was long and hot once it had started so that work in the slaughter-house was slack and money became a worry to them. But they could still afford to take a tram or a bus out to the south of the city and walk up to Cathkin Braes and look down on the spires and chimneys and the hazy pall that was Glasgow. Or they'd spend a whole day in a quiet corner of the park with sandwiches and a flask of coffee. When they stayed in at night Mat pottered about the house while Helen knitted. Occasionally Mat would get some books from the library, but now they would lie unread until he had to take them back and pay a fine for keeping them too long.

But beneath all this Mat began to feel uneasy again. He would be surprised occasionally when thoughts and ideas would spring to the surface of his mind completely fledged and new as if they had developed of their own accord. He would catch himself at the old dangerous habit of writing in his head. Becoming conscious of it he would sometimes wonder if he weren't in fact doing it all the time. Sometimes he would be aware of a mixture of unease and exhilaration at the growth going on inside himself, of a crystallisation taking place. It had something to do with his putting aside the great novel, with his dismissal of art, as if this act of rejection had left inside him a new maturity. But it was a maturity which was going to get him involved. Then again the new house was completely unsatisfactory really. It wasn't that he was avaricious for more than his share, more that a cool knowledge of what life had to offer made him realise that all his arrangements were a pretty weak bulwark against the possibility of accident, that the putting up of a structure between himself and life could never guarantee safety.

But he resisted thinking about writing. True, he was really discontented with his lot. Living in the small house on a small wage and having to count and scrape the money all the time – this made him dream sometimes of the kind of freedom and comparative opulence which was the life of a writer. But that was no real reason to write, it was in fact the most frivolous of reasons. Mat's moral sense told him that the only real or valid artistic impulse came through the creative need itself and not from something extraneous to it like ambition, or the lack of money. Something in him, a moral fastidiousness, made him feel concerned that his impulse to write should not rest on a mere contingency. But as the days and weeks went by Mat became aware of something growing within himself, the strengthening of an impulse which however much it was generated by the particular or circumstantial side of his life had a general relevance which satisfied and quietened that moral aspect of his nature.

9

IT WAS ABOUT eleven o'clock on a Tuesday morning. Work was slack in the slaughter-house. Already half the slaughter-rooms were empty and Mat himself was finished. The last two beasts were hung up on their cambrels and the offals had been cleared from the room. Mat had taken off his apron, his belt, and his bloody dungarees, had washed the grease from his knives and was now busy honing them. They had worked hard that morning, missing breakfast so that they would be finished all the earlier. Now Mat was clear of the constricting apron and belt which hampered his movements and free of any obligation to work he was enjoying the leisurely task of honing his knives and the earliness of the day. When the knives had been honed down to a fresh bright razor edge he wrapped them carefully in a thick wad of muslin and put them away in his haversack. After he had put away his blood-stiffened dungarees, taken off his rubber boots and put on his shoes, he washed himself from the hot water tap in the room, combed his hair, put on his pullover and jacket so that he looked quite tidy. The place was now quiet. There were few cattle left in the pens and all that could be heard was the swish of hoses and the scraping of a coarse brush on concrete. He smoked for a while, sitting on the side of a bogey with a piece of newspaper under him. Jake was busy in the room loading into a bogey some sheets of clean fat which had cooled and stiffened.

'Have you not got a home to go tae?' Jake said.

Mat sat and kept on smoking. He looked forward all day to finishing work, then when the time came he'd linger about, sharpening his knives, or if there was anyone still working he'd stand at the door of the room and talk.

'I'll just finish my fag.'

'Me,' said Jake, 'I'm for out of here as quick as I can go.'

'It's early,' said Mat. 'Are ye for anywhere in particular?'

'Something to eat in the town,' said Jake, 'then the pictures.'

'Wait a minute,' said Mat. He put his hand in his pocket and took his money out and counted it. Helen would be out the whole afternoon until teatime so he needn't be home until then. 'I'm flush. I'll come with you.'

When Jake had got ready and cleaned himself up he looked quite spruce. Soft shirt, expensive woollen tie. He always came to work well dressed for he kept his clothes in a locker while working. Mat felt untidy beside him, although he didn't look any more untidy than someone who had been working in a shop say, or a warehouse.

'We'll go down to the market first,' said Jake. 'I've got to collect Jimmy Aitken.'

They walked down the long tarmacadam pass to the meat market. The sheepery was still working and there were loads of mutton being pushed down into the market. The pass was still unwashed and they had to watch that their shoes didn't get dirty. When they got into the meat market there were just a few odd lorries and vans in the place. Business at this time on a Tuesday had come to a standstill and with the exception of a few porters sweeping up sawdust most of the men were standing about in groups, talking, laughing and shifting their feet restlessly. It was half day in the market and it would soon be time for them to be finishing. Jimmy Aitken was standing among a group of men and when he saw Mat and Jake coming he waved his hand to them and turned away from the men. He looked back, said something and there was a burst of laughter, then he turned and came towards Jake and Mat. It was characteristic of Jimmy that he always left laughter behind him; it was also strange that the quality of the laughter always disturbed Mat with its ugly derisive note. Yet he felt drawn towards Jimmy for the deprecating grin which would come over his face after he had caused such laughter. Just now as he came towards them he was shaking his head back at the men he had left and with this sour smile still on his face.

'I'm starving,' he said. 'Where shall we eat?' His face took on an anxious speculative look as it always did when he talked about food.

'We'll eat,' said Jake, 'don't worry.'

Outside the market as they waited for a tram the sun was very hot and Mat felt the stiffness and dampness dry out of his shoulders as he felt the heat through his jacket.

'Not be long now,' said Mat.

Jimmy sighed and turned up his eyes with a comic ecstatic expression. He hated his work and lived for his holidays every year when he went off to Paris and lived the gay life for a fortnight. He was a small man, dark, with a round chubby face and moist brown eyes. He was a good tradesman, so good in fact that he did all the cleaver work for his own squad. Doing this for years he had developed powerful arms and shoulders, yet when he was dressed he looked oddly slight.

'Wake up and live,' Jimmy said.

There were girls in summer dresses walking about and the few porters still carrying beef through the market entrance were sweating. The street was dry and each vehicle that passed threw up a cloud of dust and chaff into their faces. It was going to be a really hot day.

'You're a natural son of the south.'

Jimmy started mimicking one of his stock characters, a French taxi driver slopping wine through his moustache with a spoon. It was a character from a French film, however, and not observed from life. Jimmy gesticulated in a comic-French way and talked with a French accent, but all the time with a poker-faced irony as if he was watching himself and deprecating his own obsession. It was the same with his other obsession – the theatre. He had a passionate love for the theatre, but on the few times when Mat had tried to draw him into conversation about a play he had seen it had been as if he had committed a clumsy faux pas, for Jimmy had fobbed him off with a riotous burlesque of the play. It was as if he felt that this interest was somehow illicit and that he could only defend himself by pretending to a destructive and ironic attitude towards it. On the other hand when he talked about anything which had to do with everyday life he always seemed anxious and sad.

When the tram came Mat sat in a seat away from Jake and Jimmy and began to feel glum. He had thought of going to the pictures because he felt the need to do something. The trouble was he hadn't worked for long enough that day to feel really tired and enjoy the mere act of stopping work, but still felt the need for activity in himself. He wanted something to happen, something to disturb the regular course of his life. On the other hand Jake and Jimmy seemed quite content to be finished and nothing else. They were sitting at his back talking in their usual cryptic, allusive way.

Jimmy was a fastidious eater so they went to an expensive restaurant which was full of businessmen in dark suits. Mat felt ill at ease among the waitresses and the paper napkins. He preferred to eat in the market restaurant among the men in dungarees where he could eat his food as if he was hungry. Jake and Jimmy were enjoying themselves, talking away about nothing in particular. When Jimmy had finished his soup he sat picking absently at pieces of dry roll on his plate, then he turned suddenly to Mat.

'How's things in the literary world?'

Mat waved his hand in dismissal of the subject. Jimmy started to talk about books. He had just been reading Negley Farson's book about his life and he retailed with great zest some of the stories which Farson had told. This was the kind of thing that Jimmy was fond of – books like Axel Munthe's *Story of San Michele* or Curzio Malaparte's *Kaputt.*

Mat started to tell them the story told in Kelvin Lindemann's book *The Red Umbrellas* of Lady Anne Lindsay, the author of the Scots ballad 'Auld Robin Gray', who had encountered a goose amid the snows outside her castle in Scotland, and how she owned a necklace of pearls which was celebrated for its lustre, and how she had fed these pearls to the same goose, and how the celebrated lustre of the pearls, which was attributed by all European society to the personal radiance of the lady, was in fact got by their being polished in the craw and bowels of the goose.

'Good, eh?' Mat asked them.

To Jake the point of the story was that society had been 'had' and he was much amused, but the story seemed to make Jimmy sad and anxious.

'The earthy basis of our aspirations.' Mat quoted.

> 'Ye labour soon, ye labour late,
> To feed the titled knave, man.'

Jimmy broke off quoting Burns to say, 'One fortnight in the year. It's ridiculous.'

'What are you binding about?' asked Jake. 'You're going to the pictures this afternoon.'

In fact Jimmy's eyes were red rimmed and occasionally he was rubbing his eyes and yawning. 'I was a bit late last night.' He rubbed his face and gave his usual rueful grin.

Jake had a newspaper spread out and was looking down columns of adverts to find out the time when the pictures started. 'Order a cup of black coffee.'

When the waitress came to the table Jimmy looked up at her anxiously. 'Black coffee – and have you any Danish blue cheese?'

After they had drunk their black coffee they smoked a bit. Special cigarettes with a thick toasted flavour which Jake liked and which he bought in a big fancy tobacconist shop whenever he was in town. When they went out into the street afterwards, out of the dim restaurant, they had to screw their eyes up against the light. The city streets were resplendent with sunlight and colour. It was lunch time and the streets were full of girls in summer frocks and bare shoulders. Jake walked in front of Mat and Jimmy, for the street was crowded, and he stared arrogantly at all the good-looking girls. As he passed them he would give a little quiet whistle, then walk on all casual and debonair in his good sports jacket and flannels, and the girls would either giggle, give a little quiet smile or, more often, stare stonily ahead as if they hadn't heard him. Mat and Jimmy amused themselves with watching the girls' reactions.

Jimmy shook his head. 'He's a heid case.'

When they had just turned up the side street that led to the cinema Mat changed his mind. 'Look, I don't think I'll bother.'

They both looked at him solicitously. Mat spread his arms out and put his face up. 'It's the sun. It puts you out of the mood.' He felt that he didn't want to go to the cinema, which would be dark and empty in the afternoon.

'Ach, c'mon,' said Jimmy coaxingly.

'No, I'll just wander around and see what they have in the bookshops.'

'O.K. See you in the morning.' They both waved and walked up the street, Jake with his hands in his pockets and Jimmy just one step behind, carrying the little wooden case in which he kept his knives.

Mat walked on slowly. He felt slightly exhilarated by the sunlight and the colour in the streets, and unusually relaxed with the heat. It was the first hot day they had had that year. He was strolling idly looking at the shops and wondering how all the people in the street had known that it was going to be hot, for they all seemed to be dressed in light clothes.

Outside the Municipal Gallery, glaring in the strong sunlight, was a poster announcing an exhibition of paintings. Mat stood and looked at the poster for a while. It had been mechanically reproduced but it looked as if it had been just written with a large dripping brush. Inside the gallery was another poster taped against the wall with sticky transparent tape and it looked incongruous against the marbled tidiness of the hall and the broad curve of the stairs. He went up the stairs, cool from the marble and comparatively dim from the glare in the street. At the top of the stairs one of the large galleries was open and hung with big paintings all painted in red, orange or ochre colours. There were three or four people wandering round the hall. It was very quiet, just the scuffling of feet and occasionally the tap of heels on the floor as someone shifted self-consciously to a spot in front of the next picture. Near the entrance a man was sitting reading beside a green baize table on which were lying some newspaper clippings, a ball-point pen and an open jotter which was being used as a visitors' book.

Mat walked round looking at the paintings. They were mostly landscapes drawn in a crude way rather like a conscious stylisation of the kind of marks a child would make when representing rather than drawing an object. The paint had accommodated itself to the style of the drawing by being massed in the spaces between the lines and was all of a violent and glaring quality of colour. Mat had seen this kind of painting before, in fact he knew of a particular French painter who painted like this and whose work repelled him utterly. As he stood staring at the first picture in the gallery he tried to remember the name of the French painter. He moved on round the walls until he noticed that he was catching up with the other people who had come in before him, so he walked back along the row of pictures and started to examine them closely. On closer inspection he noticed that the big swathes of colour had been filled in by the painter with curious little swirls and convolutions and criss-cross marks, which gave the surface of the picture a peculiarly heavy and glutinous look. The artist seemed to have been pursuing some abstract theme entirely separate from the landscape in these minute strokes of the brush. Mat stepped back from the paintings until the separate brush marks merged into a flat textureless colour again. The conscious naïveté, the deliberate atavistic simplicity of the pictures irritated him. He looked along the paintings and noted that in each of them there were curious coloured holes; perhaps at the bottom of a painting, or in the triangular shape of a yacht's sail, or the irregular shape of a house, or cutting off the corner of the canvas, were great areas of flat colour which were not recognisably anything; like the great tract of chrome yellow lapping over in a bulbous curve from the left-hand edge to the bottom of the picture, which could have been a sunlit rock or the edge of a pond or the petal of a flower in close perspective. Mat felt uncomfortably embarrassed by these holes. He had the feeling they meant no more than the lack of visual purpose in the artist, that groping tentative undecidedness which often falls upon waywardness, or uses the arbitrary as a last resource. He wondered idly about the colour, whether its own violence came from the painter's sense of his own inadequacy, and about those brush marks which searched and probed desperately all over the canvas after some kind of form. It reminded Mat strongly of something he knew and although he didn't like the paintings he felt a sort of fellow feeling for the artist, for there behind the flat ineptitude of the pictures were the violent marks of the artist's struggle against the meagreness of his talent, the signature of failure. He looked around the hall and counted the pictures, about forty in all. Mat knew nothing about painting but he tried to imagine it. Assuming that these were the painter's best pictures and that the total number of pictures painted in order to show this lot was very much larger; assuming also that the artist's method of work was as desultory as the feeling suggested by them, then the collection of pictures shown represented a good year or two of work.

Mat sat down on a bench opposite one of the bigger paintings staring at it scrupulously, in the hope that with some act of sympathy on his own part the painting would fire into life. But it kept its orange and green futility. He closed his eyes and was surprised by the vision still retained on his retina of the glaring street which he had left outside with all its flurry and scatter and trafficking; moving people, fluttering dresses, sunlight on the prismatic row of shop fronts, high buildings with the cotton-wool clouds soaring above in the childish blue sky. In the stillness he could hear from outside, as if from very far away the grinding of gears, the whine of accelerating engines and the thin toot of horns. He could almost imagine the laughter of the girls as they strode along.

A sudden thought made him blush, but he got up nevertheless and walked back to the first painting, then followed the course of the wall right round the room. He wasn't looking at the pictures any more, but for something else – the little red sticker which proclaimed a sale. There wasn't a single one in the whole exhibition. 'What a poor bloody fool,' he thought, and felt that strange feeling which we have when we see someone doing something ridiculous or absurd or gauche and feel embarrassed for them. He couldn't have looked at another painting and he made to leave, passing the green baize table by the door.

The man sitting at the table looked up from his book. 'Could you sign the visitors' book, please?'

Mat stopped in his rush and walked back to the table and took up the pen. The book was divided into headings Name – Address – Comments. Mat wrote his name and address and put a dash in the comments column. He noticed several of the comments, most of them mentioning colour and one remark written in a large flamboyant hand. The writer had used her (it was a woman's signature in the 'Name' column) own pen, with a broad nib, and had written 'brave and original work'.

'Do you like the paintings?'

The young man was looking at Mat with an absent curiosity. He seemed to be asking the question not out of any real interest but in order to note dutifully the reactions of the philistine.

Mat shook his head as if to show bewilderment.

'Why?' The young man smiled knowingly. 'Are they too' – he hesitated for the word – 'modern for you?'

Inside himself Mat gave a contemptuous 'Huh!' and stared at

the man. He was sitting fastidiously straight in the seat holding the book with his finger in his place. He was very dark with a funny narrow beard, which looked as if his sideburns had grown down and hooked themselves under his chin. He was wearing a loose crew-necked jersey and bedford cords. Mat was able to read the name of the author of the book he was reading though it was upside down. O-Z-E-N. Ozenfant. I hope he's reading it, he thought.

'It's not that . . .' Mat said, then was silent. He didn't know how he could go into what he felt, and was hesitant about using the artist's pathetic failure as the occasion for a bit of art chatter. 'It seems to me that what we mean by modern art was, at first anyway, a rejection, it was all meant to be shocking and wild, like with the Fauvists . . .' Mat spoke deferentially from his usual feeling of the inadequacy of saying anything. 'I suppose that's all right. But the whole style of modern art comes from rejection. That's all right. At the first blows – you know – from science, politics, industrialisation and the depreciation of the artist's resources – it, I mean Art, puts on its bitter ironic smile. Then we have two world wars and the hydrogen bomb and we're not laughing any more – anyway, who can we shock?' Mat stopped abruptly, then he blurted out in explanation, 'You see, I'm against art.'

'*Against* art!' The young man put his head back and laughed heartily. 'It's the first time I've heard anyone admit it. *Against* it!' He laughed again. 'Usually what they say is that they've a wean at hame who could draw better than this, or that a blind man with a wooden arm could paint better. Or they want to know if the artist would like a job as a plumber. But they don't usually come right out and say that they are against it – and we get all kinds.' He spoke as if he was addressing not Mat but some third party.

'Perhaps you've misunderstood me,' Mat said. He felt a vague hostility towards the man which was aggravated by his contemptuous dismissal of him as being just another brand of philistine. 'Aside from the fact that it is dangerous to have these stock responses to people's remarks – don't you think that it might make for – complacency? Aside from that, I think my own attitude is a bit different. I mean social problems . . .' His voice trailed off. He was about to talk of the social problem as being something over and against art, as something more important than art, or at any rate more urgent than any artistic question. But when the sudden image had come to him of the flowing bustling street outside and he had blushed with shame on the artist's behalf he had felt that the absence of little red stickers was an awful confirmation in actuality of some mistake, omission or absence on the purely artistic side. He gave a name or a category to this feeling – 'the relation of art to actuality' – but the phrase was a mere indication of a whole rich complex of confusion and ideas and feeling. From under his feet he felt a slight vibration from the floor caused by the rumbling of the traffic outside, and he had a peculiar sense of the heavy weight of the building, of the physical presence of the city, the masses of stone, the tangled complex of wire and piping, the crowds, the smoke and steam and electricity, the traffic, the river, the ships, the warehouses and yards and factories and calloused grimy tradesmen, the housewives and activity and pubs and slums – the whole untidy ruck which was Glasgow. Social problem! He looked round the wall at the paintings and replaced them in his mind with some beautiful bitter canvases which would attract the crowds with an insidious irony and snare them in a delusion. Even that would be better. He waved his hand at the young man.

'Och, never mind . . .'

The young man stretched himself then yawned delicately with the back of his hand to his mouth. 'The social problem.' He paused for a second or two. 'But to get back to your idea of painting being all – what was it you said? – rejection?'

'And mockery – it adds a new dimension.'

'Quite. It does indeed. Surely that's exemplified in Picasso's parodies. You know them?'

Mat nodded. 'I agree that they lack seriousness.'

The young man gave Mat a gley look. 'But anyway, you're missing out half, no, nine-tenths of modern art – cubism, expressionism,' he glanced at his book, 'constructivism, which have all tried to come to terms in some way with the twentieth century, whether through expressing modern feeling, or the scientific viewpoint, or coming into line with the shape of modern life, becoming interested in technology-design. The account which they have taken of modern things implies more than mere rejection. In cubism for instance – the creation of a genuinely new form.'

During the whole of the conversation Mat had been half backing out of the door. Then he realised that the man was bored sitting there all by himself in the quiet hall and was now quite enjoying talking to him. Mat stepped forward a little, remembering the book which the man was reading.

'In that book which you are reading, it says . . .'

'In *this* book?'

'Yes.'

The young man opened a packet of cigarettes and pushed them towards him, then leant backwards and took a folding chair that was propped against the wall and, unfolding it, shoved it towards Mat. Mat took the chair, sat down and lit a match. While he was holding the match towards the young man he felt a strange pausing sensation. There was nobody left in the hall and the noises drifting in from the street seemed much further away. A feeling of calm and quiet took over from his previous restlessness. The young man wanted to know who he was and Mat told him his name. Then the young man introduced himself as Sam Richards. He was a writer who had published some poetry, some short stories in the literary magazines, had written occasional features and short plays for the B.B.C. He had also been a student of literature at Edinburgh University but had left of his own accord after finishing his second year. This struck Mat as bizarre, the idea of anyone leaving university. But Sam gave Mat a plausible account of the indifference and stuffiness of the English lecturers and of the other students. Mat didn't quite believe all this but he didn't demur. Sam, however, was interested in Mat. He wasn't at Art School, nor was he a student. What did he do?

'I work in the slaughter-house.'

'In the what?'

'In the slaughter-house.'

'You mean you – tchkk!' Sam drew his finger across his throat and made a face expressive of disgust.

Mat laughed. 'More or less.'

'And you've read Ozenfant and you know Picasso's parodies and you have ideas about modern art?'

For some reason Mat thought of Jimmy Aitken and his remark about a rather stupid young man whom they both knew. 'But he must be clever, he's got his Highers.' There was a lack of integrity, something patronising in Sam Richards' tone as if he had decided to view Mat as some kind of rough diamond. Mat knew that in fact there was nothing in his background to prevent him from having read Ozenfant, or even to prevent him from falling into the habit of sophisticated discursiveness. He thought of the long evening he had spent as a boy reading Schopenhauer and it all seemed fitting, coming as it did from his need to pacify and explore the world. And he thought of all the violence and absurdity and fear and precariousness which had precipitated him into this exploration and which he still had in him preventing him from ever being anything else but – sophisticated. Mat, however, dismissed Sam's question.

'What I meant to say was that in your book it mentions somewhere that the thing about Picasso was the drama of his inventiveness, the drama of fertility and ease so much encouraged in him by Cocteau.'

'Where?' Sam opened the book, he hadn't come to that bit yet. Mat took it and turned the pages until he found the part he was looking for. He read it out to Sam. '"But actually, what matters to the writers in question is less Picasso's *oeuvre* than Picasso the phenomenon. We will not enlarge further on the 'drama' of the painter" – but Ozenfant's comment is interesting.' Mat read further from the book. '"Indubitably his influence on Picasso was not all for the best, for by giving particular appreciation for his inventive qualities, the possession of so much invention at last came to seem altogether too much."'

Sam agreed delightedly. He seemed altogether taken by the idea.

'I should imagine,' Mat said, 'that this refers to the process which goes on between Picasso and the picture; inventiveness itself cannot be the character of an individual work but exists between one picture and another in the relationship between them and the change which takes place. As if the distinguishing artistic-ness of the man was something which took place outside his work. Take the Da-daists with their insistence on the wayward, contingent and accidental arrangement of things. All this bizarre juxtaposition and construction is like an analogue of nature, for accidents occur in the natural world and have nothing to do with the world of art. Attention is turned away from the work itself towards the processes that we call actuality, by exposing them to chance, by denying intention and purpose. You have a similar situation in atonal music, in serial composition and in the whimsicality of certain kinds of modern writing.'

'My God!' said Sam. 'You're a real *horror*. You really are against art. I think you bloody well *mean* it.' He seemed excited and incredulous. 'You mean you'd really throw out the lot – lock, stock and barrel?'

Mat decided that he would in a way – Picasso, Schoenberg, Ionesco, Ernst, Webern, Stravinsky – definitely Stravinsky, Kafka, Joyce, Kandinsky, Pound, Virginia Woolf – the lot. Then he laughed. 'What am I saying?' He knew that with the first cheap jibe at Picasso, the usual, a wean could draw better, or Schoenberg, Christ! what's that noise? and his fingers would itch to strangle the joker. He was always rejecting art and yet at the first sneer he would fly into a consuming rage to defend it. 'Oh, Lord, no!' he said to Sam. 'I'm attacking you. I'm sorry.'

Sam waved the apology aside and sat puffing at his cigarette, waiting for Mat to continue, but as Mat kept silent he eventually leaned forward and raised his eyebrows in inquiry. 'Well?'

Mat went on then to try to explain his feelings, repeating his list to Sam – 'but the point about these people is that they are like – you know, the kind of life you get in the South American jungle – full of parasitism, hermaphroditism, savagery, illusion like those little fish which enter into the cavity of any animal body, or the butterfly with the savage face painted on its wings, or the insect which looks like a twig or has a foul repellent odour or a virulent poisonous colouration – all this aberrant protectiveness, evolutionary cunning and tour de force shows a kind of vitality, a wish to exist at all costs. And yet, consider the rigid formalism of these organisms. All the adaptive energy which goes into the evolutionary process is denied, in fact is positively taken away from the individual animal. Art, too, is like this in that viewing it historically is often more interesting than seeing its individual works. Nevertheless, if art as a last resource, in order to exist at all, has to become unlike itself, to protect itself by taking on the appearance of actuality, then,' – Mat flapped his hand about, then rubbed his brow with his knuckles – 'then, I admire it. Just as I admire Duchamp's silence.' He pronounced this last with an air of fiat and looked aggressively at Richards.

'I'll bet you're a writer.' Richards was wagging his foot up and down over his crossed legs and scrutinising Mat with a sarcastic smile on his face.

'It surely follows,' Mat said stiffly, pursing his lips. 'No.'

'A failure then,' Richards said. 'You can always tell a frustrated writer by the way he talks – too much.'

'All right.' Mat blushed, he could feel his face turning hot. He turned away from Richards, crossed his hands over his chest and started to rock back and forward. He could feel the anxiety and the sharp tingle in his limbs again. Then he straightened up. 'As long as it is understood that my failure is not a question of talent.' His lips were pursed again.

'Wow! You're a *honey*!' Richards put his head back and laughed. His whole body shook. 'However, I can't say I didn't ask you.'

'You did ask me, right enough. But I didn't answer you. You wanted to know what I thought of the paintings. But that's useless unless I set my reactions to them into a context.'

'Well, you've given me the context. What about the reaction? Do you see these' – he waved his hand towards the pictures – 'as – eh! – aberrations?'

'One of the reactions I haven't fully mentioned, it's not properly a reaction – more a mere result of the sufferings of modern art . . .'

'Whoops, he's off again.' Richards spoke with mock admiration. Mat ignored him and went on.

'. . . is exhaustion, devitalisation.' He waved his hand about to indicate the pictures on the walls. 'Not conscious silence, which has dignity, not exoticism, which has life, nor whimsicality, which may have irony, but banality, meagreness, a thin, screaming, hysterical void.'

'Steady on, lad. He's a pal of mine.'

Mat still went on. 'The worst, the most painful judgement we can make of an artist's work.' Then he grinned at Richards.

Richards shrugged then sat in silence. Mat threw him a cigarette. They lit up and Mat asked him for the time. Richards looked at his watch then showed it to Mat. 'Are you in a hurry?'

'Not particularly.'

There was another silence. When Richards spoke again he used a deliberate light tone to show that the weight of the discussion had now been dropped.

'What do you think he should do? Get a job?'

'No.'

'Give up painting?'

'Oh, look, if his failure is a question of talent there isn't very much either you or I can say or do about it, except to look at the whole thing with a wee bit humanity.'

Richards stuck out his lower lip and considered, then nodded his head. 'All right. I agree with you. As a matter of fact it's all a question of loyalty. You commit yourself to a certain way of life – so – you have to accept it in all its manifestations. Like these . . .'

'It seems to me that you could find yourself too often in a false position. I mean commit yourself to being – overtly – an artist. To belong to the art world socially. To wear its badges. I couldn't – I don't think I could commit myself to anything – perhaps I'm a coward – except doubt.'

'Ah, well,' said Sam, 'at least this one's a worker, he really beasts into it, churns the stuff out. And incidentally' – Richards pushed some of the newspaper clippings towards Mat – 'this is quite ironic. The critics don't agree with you.'

Mat was struck as he read through the clippings by the kind of language that was used. A formal jargon which was supposed to describe the paintings, yet there was no connection between what was written and what Mat saw on the walls. What most of the writers had tried to do was write about their feelings and make evaluations as if they were in fact describing the paintings themselves, so that their writing was full of heightened-up phrases which really only denoted a whole set of hidden assumptions. In one article there was a homily on the neglect which this local and very talented artist had suffered in his own city. It was probably true, as the man said, that a Scottish artist, whether painter or writer, would have difficulty in finding somewhere to sell his work. What was more important to Mat were the difficulties native to Scottish art itself, the pure creative difficulties which made it so nearly impossible to produce anything at all.

While Mat was reading the clippings there were footsteps on the stairs, then a wee man came bustling into the exhibition hall. He was dressed all in one colour – brown shoes, chocolate-brown slacks, fawn pullover, khaki shirt, light-brown tweed jacket with reddish tints in it, and a dark orange tie. He was small, stockily built, and his clothes looked baggy and bulky, particularly his heavy tweed jacket which, being unbuttoned, stuck out in front of him like an unshut double door exposing the stretch of fawn wool on his chest. His complexion was brick coloured, coarsened by the network of capillaries which could be seen beneath the skin of his jowls and cheeks. Mat thought he saw a family resemblance between the wee man and the paintings on the wall.

'Sorry I'm late,' the wee man said, and looked anxiously around the room. 'Has anybody been in?'

Richards shook his head and the man stood breathing heavily from his hurried flight up the stairs and looking expectantly from Richards to Mat. Richards sat for a while looking at him then he slowly introduced Mat.

'Mat.' He waved a hand in Mat's direction. 'This is Charlie.' He glanced at Mat then meaningfully round the hall at the paintings. 'Mat has ideas about painting – he even had some interesting things to say about *your* paintings.'

Mat had guessed right. This was Charles Dick, the man of whom Mat had thought 'poor bloody fool', but he had the disconcerting sense that the wee man's anxious bustle precluded any scruples about his own work. He was right again for Dick completely missed the malicious sarcasm in Richards' voice. Instead he immediately turned towards Mat, taking him for an admirer.

'It isn't worth it,' he said, 'you can't get people interested.' Then he started to talk. He was, it seemed, a 'political artist'. That is, he held to the conventional left-wing sympathies with the proletariat. But unfortunately the proletariat were not interested in his work. Neither were 'these people'. These people, for whom he held the most hatred, were the academics, the men associated with the various art bodies – the art schools, the art galleries, the R.S.A. – and who refused to show his work. Because, he implied, it was so shockingly modern. He implied so much, confidentially assuming that Mat not only agreed with all his attitudes but that he was familiar with all the ramifying complexities of art politics and with the names, habits and prejudices of all those concerned with these. The long and short of it was that he, Dick, as a true and pure artist was a danger to the established social, political, artistic and sexual order. There was therefore a conspiracy against him, a subtle indirect conspiracy. 'These people' were afraid to come out into the open against him, they were tired, dishonest and disappointed men whose work had gone stale, artists manqué who were hotly jealous of his productive energies.

Mat nodded his head in dazed agreement with all this, so amazed was he at the complete certainty out of which Dick spoke. In himself Mat knew that all the energy would go into shame, dissatisfaction and scrupulousness about his own work.

Richards, however, was able to breast the torrent. 'We can't stay and listen to you all day. I'm dying for a cuppa.' He spoke jocularly, but the torrent stopped, and Dick looked at him with anxious eyes, his face shining with sweat.

As they went down the stairs together Richards was laughing quietly. 'Christ!' he said, 'you should have seen your face. Your eyebrows were up into your hairline.'

Mat couldn't help comparing Dick's outbursts with his own solemn and pedantic tirade and he was loth to judge him too harshly lest he judge himself as well. 'Well, he's quite a man. But we've all got our obsessions.'

'Oh!' said Richards. 'You should have seen your face when he said that bit about him being dangerous.' He laughed. 'He doesn't like it too much when the critics praise him.'

Mat shrugged.

Outside, the street was quieter, but in contrast to the mild light in the galleries the sun's glare made them squint. After the stillness the remaining bustle of the street gave a slight feeling of dizziness. Richards indicated with a wave of his arm the direction they were to go and they crossed to the shady part of the street. In the shade it was cool, almost chilly now. For a while they walked in silence, then Richards asked Mat:

'This place you work in interests me. Do you like working there?'

'Of course,' Mat said. He tried to explain what it was he felt about it but Richards kept interrupting him with questions.

'How do they shoot them?' Then he said, 'Of course the cows know that they are going to be shot.'

'Well, you know,' said Mat, 'they're ten times our weight and with big horns. If they knew you'd never get near them.'

'They're paralysed with fear,' Richards told him. 'They smell the blood.'

Mat had seen cows lick wisps of straw from the bloody floor of the slaughtering-rooms, even lick pieces of congealed fat from where it was stuck to the wall. Also he had skinned so many heads that he knew how narrow the skull was and how surprisingly little room there was in it for the brain box. 'They're too stupid,' he said.

Richards was indignant. 'Stupid!' He didn't think that animals were stupid at all. They were in fact in tune to many things which human beings didn't understand. 'You struck me as an intelligent sort of bloke. But that's a really crass remark. Stupid!'

Mat laughed at this. 'All you're saying is that animals lead a rich sensuous life.'

They walked towards the coffee shop with Richards haranguing Mat about the cruelty of his trade and with Mat unable to take Richards at all seriously.

The restaurant was in the basement of a large bakery and cake shop. There were only a few people sitting round a large table in one corner, some of them sitting on a sofa against the wall, the rest in big comfortable armchairs. There was laughter and noise coming from them and their table was littered with coffee cups and trays. Richards took Mat over to the group and they sat down. Then Mat was introduced to them by Richards in the casual way he had. One of the group looked at his watch and said, 'Another hour until the pubs open.'

It turned out that there was a poet, a stage actor whom Mat remembered seeing in small parts, three painters and a B.B.C. Radio producer among the group. Mat was thrilled and curious in talking to them as it was the first time he had ever spoken with a group of artists or intellectuals in his life. They were indulging themselves in a good deal of small talk and banter. One of the painters told a terribly lame story of a man who farted inadvertently in polite company. Then the actor started talking of how, when he had been reading Hemingway and identifying himself with one of the characters, he had begun to feel the pain of the wounds. He was saying the titles of the various novels and writhing and holding himself in the appropriate places. He looked slyly at the waitresses and when they weren't looking he said 'Fiesta' and clutched at himself, his face twisted in agony as if he had been hurt in the crotch. Then when he had finished he looked serious and said, 'You should see my lady friend doing Faulkner's *Sanctuary.*' The producer ad libbed a review which he said he was doing of a biography of Rimbaud, 'I was a teenage poet.' Everybody laughed and a heated but not quite serious discussion took place as to the reasons for Rimbaud's rejection of poetry. Mat felt too shy to take part but the poet who was sitting beside him on the right spoke to him. He was a tiny fragile looking man, large pale blue eyes and fine expressive features which were sadly marred by his teeth, which were badly impacted and which he hid with fastidiously pursed lips as if he had a bad taste in his mouth. He began to question Mat, giving the impression that he had a serious curiosity and concern about people and an acute personal sensitivity. He told Mat about his own poetry which he published under his own name – George R. Duncan – which Mat recognised, having read some of his astringent poems somewhere. The others were busy by this time discussing a get-together they would be having that same night in a pub.

'You'll come of course, Mat!' said Richards swivelling his body round towards Mat. 'We'd love to hear some of your *ideas* over a pint.' Then he turned back to the rest of the company. 'He's a man with ideas. He should come, shouldn't he?'

There were cries from the rest. 'Aha!' 'That's a change.' 'I'd like to hear a few ideas.' 'Bring him along.' George Duncan smiled sarcastically.

Mat excused himself. It was time for him to go home for his tea. No, he couldn't miss it, his wife was expecting him. He might manage to the pub later. Richards spoke to him for a minute, telling which pub they were to meet in and that he hoped he would manage to come. Mat left and the poet Duncan came with him. They walked together to Mat's tram stop and Duncan asked if Mat could visit him at his home. Mat felt flattered at the invitation and said he would be pleased to accept.

'Are you going to meet them tonight?' Duncan asked him.

'Them?'

Duncan merely wrinkled his nose and pursed his lips tighter.

'Och,' said Mat, 'they seem all right.' He knew that Duncan for some reason would have liked to put him off going. Earlier he had noticed that Duncan had not appreciated the banter that had been going on in the restaurant. For that matter Mat had himself felt a little uneasy at the note of bantering levity in their talk. He had felt that there was something humourless in the forced pitch at which they'd create their whimsical and elaborate constructions. But he was curious.

'Ah, well. Curiosity killed the cat. But I don't think I'll come to any harm.'

Duncan by his expression was doubtful.

'I'll see you on Sunday night,' Mat said, and waving back he boarded a tram.

When Mat got to the top of the tram he looked back and saw the little figure, hunched, slightly splay footed, in his neat suit and looking nondescript in the distance, turn sadly and inwardly and walk away.

*   *   *

Mat had got drunk. Not very drunk, just a few beers and a couple of nips of whisky. But he was a bit drunker than everyone else and he was well able by this time to join in the conversation, if not dominate it. He was aware that he was talking too much and the others were laughing at him – Richards who remained almost sober, Dick who now exuded a sort of glistening benevolence, the actor Marquis whose fruity sarcasms were becoming richer, and the three painters whose laughter was now becoming thinner and higher pitched. Richards had egged Mat on and now Mat had started to talk about art again. He had begun by making his comparison between paintings and the gay plumage and exotic colouration of tropical birds, flowers, insects and fishes. There was the vividness of the colouration, and another element, stiff and formal, in fact abstract, in the stiff markings of some of those tropical fish. Picasso's prolific productiveness (Mat's exact and deliberate handling of this alliteration caused much merriment) which, as he had said before, being too much of a good thing, was like the myriads of eggs laid by the turtle. All the little turtles hatching, crawling out of the sand and making for the sea only to be devoured by the sea birds, the crabs, the octopi, the fish, until only one out of the hundreds of eggs survives into full adult turtlehood.

'Was this adult turtle one of Picasso's great paintings?' They kept egging him on, firing questions and giggling all the time. 'Which one?' 'Guernica?' 'Les desmoiselles d'Avignon?' 'What?' 'Which?'

'No! No!' Mat was drunken and solemn. 'It is the man's essence I am trying to show. His real response to the world was not in fact cubism – his essence was in his fertility, in that he invented cubism. Not in what he did, but the way he did it. As if the ease and frenzy and speed of his inspiration were the whole quality and mark of his work. And in his work there is the same sadness and waste and mechanism that you find in the biological prodigality of the turtle.'

But they wanted to know of other cases. 'Cézanne?'

'The oyster. All the formalism was characterised by the habit of shutting out experience.'

'Hugh MacDiarmid?'

'Nothing exotic there. A magpie. A collectomaniac in whom an inventorial passion was substituted for energy.'

'Kandinsky?'

'Of course, the striped fish.'

'Moore.'

'The dung beetle.'

'Eliot?'

'The hermit crab.'

And then there were the innumerable peacocks, the humming birds, orchids, parrots, chameleons, vultures and that strange race of American poets, musicians and jazz singers who were like the lemmings.

'Who's the parrot?'

'Nae names, nae pack drill,' Mat said.

But they went on teasing him and laughing at his garrulousness.

Lautréamont was the butterfly with the horribly painted wings, though after all only a butterfly, but someone demurred at this. Mat suddenly felt resentful at their laughter, not because they were laughing but because they didn't realise that his drunken solemnity wasn't as serious as they thought. He laughed and wagged his finger at them. 'And you're the little monkeys who are frightened away.' For some reason he thought of George Duncan and his reluctance that Mat should have come to the pub. He had a sense of impending disillusion, for he had not thought that these men lived in the same grey world as himself. Yet he sensed the boredom and disappointed expectancy which was latent in their frivolous banter. 'Ah, well, Lautréamont? And Poe, Byron, Baudelaire, Dostoevsky, De Sade, Nietzsche – they all frightened the little monkeys. Maybe they weren't butterflies. When you think, though, what later poets were to actually see – like Céline, Owen.'

Mat got up and went to the bar to order more drinks, buying half pints all round. When he had paid for them and bought another packet of cigarettes, the ten shilling note which he had got from Helen at teatime was gone, also most of the fifteen shillings which he had that morning was nearly spent. For a while he was almost sobered by a feeling of guilt. Twenty-five bob gone in one day. It was equal to a fortnight's pocket money for him. The conversation had abated with Mat's silence and he began to notice the pub round about him. Being a Tuesday night the pub wasn't very busy and the few other people in the place seemed to be just sitting drinking glumly without talking. The waitresses behind the bar were idly busy, wiping the bar and polishing glasses. The glass topped table round which they were sitting had several rings of beer on it from the bottom of glasses. The mirrors on the walls reflected back the harsh aqueous light from the glaring electric lamps in their modern frosted bulbs. He began to feel the beer slapping in his stomach and it made him feel cold; there seemed to be a damp coldness exuding from the mirrors and the glass topped table. When Richards ordered another round of drinks Mat couldn't face beer and asked for a half of whisky. When he swallowed it he felt himself grow warmer again, but also dizzier and his stomach heaved a little. He tried to remember what it was they had been talking about but could not. His head was full of ideas he wanted to express which seemed clear and at the same time incoherent. It was the feeling which he often had of thinking in images and then turning them into words, except that the images seemed unusually clear and forceful and the words unusually garbled and inadequate. Then he gradually got drunker until he became aware only of the extreme clarity and simplicity and profundity of his thoughts. He started to chatter again hardly knowing whether anyone was listening to him or not. Through the thick fog round his senses he could hear an occasional giggle and see an occasional face grinning at him. He had the feeling that his garrulous tongue was like a heavy steel ball rolling away before him down a long slope.

It was very late when Mat got home that night. They had all gone up to Charlie Dick's studio and drunk coffee and talked again. Or rather they had argued – a fierce, wild and stupid argument about solipsism which went round and round in logical circles. Everyone spoke with angry indignant voices as if they were forced into the argument by the stupidity of the others. Then as they had grown sober they had all become bored. Mat left at midnight and had to walk home. It took him a good hour and a half to walk through the lamp-lit streets. When he arrived home he was very sober and very tired.

Helen was asleep when he got into the house. He didn't bother to put on the light but undressed in the dark. He could see Helen's form lying in the inshot bed and her hair spread all over the pillow. It had been chilly in the evening after the heat of the day and Helen had left a tiny fire in the grate. Mat poked the fire until it blew up and a flame grew, lighting up the room. Then he noticed something lying on the couch. He went over and looked. There was a little knitted woollen jacket, a pair of matching pantaloons and placed at the ends of the outstretched jacket's sleeves a pair of tiny mittens. Helen must have finished them when he was out and placed them out for him to see.

10

WHEN MAT WOKE the next morning with an awful jerk he knew that he had slept in. He had been dreaming that he had got up, dressed and gone to work, then he had realised suddenly in his dream that he *was* dreaming and had woken with a start. It was now seven-thirty; too late for him to go to work; he remembered that it was Wednesday, market day, that it would be very busy, that beasts would be felled right up until four o'clock in the afternoon and that he would be missed. Right now he would be getting cursed right, left and centre. The shock of that thought made him feel the old coursing of adrenalin and he covered his face in self disgust. When he wondered why Helen hadn't heard the alarm he remembered that he had woken himself, put it off, and had lain back in bed and started to dream that he had got up. It was as if his unconscious had played a dirty psychological trick on him. Now the recollection of the whole previous night came to him, that he hadn't slept properly, that he had lain in that state on the verge of sleep when his dreams had part of the quality of real dreaming and partly had been shaped by some conscious theme. He could remember certain parts of the night, a kinaesthetic memory of the positions in which he had been lying and how he had come occasionally to wakefulness just enough to shift his cramped limbs. Mat still felt tired with his head thick from the drink and he lay back for a minute or two on the pillow and closed his eyes. The effect of this was to remind him of the theme which had so possessed his sleep.

When he had been coming home the previous night his

head had been full of a whirling frivolity, an inflamed exacerbated activity. He had begun to see strange connections and interrelations between things apparently opposite and to make unusual juxtapositions of ideas which usually didn't seem to belong together; at the same time he was aware of a sense of disjointment, a kind of conflict of similarities as if the calm surface of life was being ruffled and broken. He felt at once attracted and repelled by his mood, at one moment delighting in the grotesque disintegrating ideas which he had, his mind like a flywheel running on and on of its own accord; and in the next moment feeling the urge to stop this impetus, as if he felt a sudden eccentric motion of the wheel and his mind seemed to move in a series of bumps and rattles.

The sight of the small knitted garments lying on the couch had the effect of a quick drench. During all the time that he had spent in silly chit-chat Helen had been finishing off the baby clothes. He had gone to bed shamed by this simple bit of actuality. Yet his mind had gone on working. All that chatter had been silly yet in spite of that Mat felt that the evening he had spent had been on the surface of something important. It was as if his interest in the people he had met, in their conventional irresponsible chit-chat, in talking of other people's work, was a pale reflection of something else; a deeper, primal creative passion which was concerned solely with his response to the immediacy and directness of his own personal life. He supposed that the chatter was not entirely reprehensible, however wry and twisted and bitter it might be, in that it was wrung out of each person's separate and unstated concern with his own creativity. Mat went on thinking and remembered that having fallen asleep he had started writing in his dreams. It appeared that he was writing yet the words had all leapt to the page as if by themselves and he had the experience of reading his own work as he wrote it. And it was writing of such ease, such fluency, such richness, such coherency, such significance that he was awed, exhilarated, amazed at his own prodigious talent. At one moment when he had come half to consciousness he thought that when he was awake he would be able to write it all down, like Coleridge and his Khubla Khan. There were times before when he had had this dream and had either been able to remember nothing when he was awake, or that his writing had been nothing but the monotonous repetition of meaningless phrases. But this time he could remember what it was he had been writing. Aside from the few scraps of nonsense he *had* written something which had as much significance and richness as he had dreamt.

> 'The unpurged images of day recede;
> The Emperor's drunken soldiery are abed.'

If he hadn't slept in it would have been funny, but the dirty psychological trick seemed no less dirty for its irony.

He rolled over and shook Helen by the shoulder. 'Helen,' he said, 'Helen.'

Helen woke up. She was lying on her side with her back to him and as she sat up and turned her face towards him she looked slow and drowsy with her lips in a swollen sensuous pout from her sleep and her wide set eyes blank and peering. She was smiling. Mat could have lain down with her in his arms under the warm covers had it not been for the de-sexing effect of his anxiety and coursing of the adrenalin in his blood. Suddenly Helen gave a little cry. 'Oh!' She put her hand to her mouth. 'You've slept in.'

'I've not half.'

Helen peered at the clock. 'What time *is* it?'

'Eight o'clock.' It was amazing how he had put his head back on to the pillow to think for a couple of minutes and when he looked at the clock again another half-hour had passed. He thought of the slaughter-house and wished that right now he was there with his knife kit on and working away with everyone else. 'Right now they'll all be getting steamed into it.'

Later on when they got up Mat began to feel a little less

guilty. Helen sent him round to the bakery to buy a twisted loaf with the poppy seeds sprinkled over the crust. It was a lovely clear morning, though still a little chilly. The streets were quiet with only the schoolchildren going to school and when Mat went into the baker's shop the smell of the baking, seeing the variety of toasted and brown crusts on the baker's boards and the old-fashioned sprawl of cheeses, rolls, sausage, butter in the shop had a soothing effect on him. As usual when he went into this shop he couldn't resist buying half-a-dozen of those hard doughnut-shaped rolls which the Jews call bagels. When he got back to the house there was the rich mixed smell of coffee and ham and eggs.

While eating breakfast Mat became full of optimism. 'There's no use crying over spilt milk. You know what I'm going to do?' he asked. 'I'm going to sit all day and write. In fact I'm going to finish a story.'

'Good!'

They cleared away the breakfast and washed the dishes, then Mat helped Helen to make the bed. On a normal day Helen would do these domestic chores in a leisurely way, but today Mat hurried her on, being anxious to get them done and past so that he could have more time to work. But on finishing the chores and with the house all tidy he sat for an hour or so just smoking and staring in front of him. He was sitting idly thinking and dreaming. The surfeit of words which he had suffered the day before had left him dry and exhausted. He felt that he wanted to write but it was out of a feeling of obligation and duty and not through the pressure of his imagination. Rather the imaginative excitement which usually forced him to write was completely absent. He should be writing yet the thought of getting up from his seat and putting pen to paper was too much for him. Instead his mind seemed to be absent and he was merely a cold recipient of sensation; just sitting staring at the empty cleaned out fireplace and listening to the clock ticking. He stared at the blank wall, at the patterns on the wallpaper or out through the cold window

frame to the colourless sky outside and the yellow tops of the
buses which were parked in the garage on the other side of
the brick wall which bounded the bleak backyard outside. He
felt bored and his boredom was confirmed by the clattering
emptiness of the sound of trucks shunting in the railway yard.
The sound recalled to his mind the railway line which had been
at the bottom of the street he had lived in as a child. What he
thought of in particular, and the memory seemed to spring
from his dry mood, was how this monotonous clanking had
been the background to so much of his life, had set the mood in
which took place this curious absence of feeling which he had
experienced so often. He remembered how he used to stand at
the close mouth, leaning against the wall, with all the weight
of his body on one leg until his hip became sore. Sometimes
as he stood there an engine would pass with its train of goods
trucks and Mat would watch the trucks. He would be bored,
perhaps a little chilled through standing dreaming at the close
mouth with nothing to do. And he would count the trucks;
count them in that same monotonous automatic way which
one reads the writing on the tomato sauce bottle or the jam pot
when rising too early in the morning. As each truck appeared to
his view from behind the corner of a high tenement Mat would
count and say to himself, 'The next one will be the last', in the
hope that he'd be released from the obsessive addition. Yet this
trivial experience was the mark of a severe dissociation which
he felt between himself and the world in which he lived.

He used to read books like Ernest Thomson Seton's *Two
Little Savages* in which the world of 'nature' was described. To
Mat then the world of 'nature' was the Canadian backwoods
of Ernest Thomson Seton's; a world which was malleable and
responsive to human activity, a world in which his skills and
resiliences could be tested, a world in which owls and rabbits
could be caught and stuffed, arrows fletched, wigwams and
tepees erected, campfires built, food hunted and caught and
eaten. And the vicarious experience of all these things in reading a book was not enough. He wandered about the closes and

backyards in which there were no coons or feathers or tracks or bushes but only the lucid plumb lines of human building; gables, brick walls, iron railings, cobbled streets; then he ended up mooning at the close mouth and counting trucks. In his frustrated passion for making he did in the end try wildly to emulate the backwoodsman. He got a pair of rabbit skins from the fishmonger and decided that he'd tan the skins himself and make a pair of Indian moccasins. After he'd bought the skins he started to look around for some oak bark, bone and deer sinews and the rest of the things needed for curing, tanning, cutting and sewing the hides. He couldn't find any oak bark anywhere, still less the deer's sinews. When he asked around nobody could suggest any place where he might find some, and he wasn't all that fussy as an elk's sinews would have done just as well. He nearly got caught by a park-keeper for stripping the bark from a twisted old hawthorn. The hawthorn's leaves had the same twisted curly look as the pictures of oak leaves which he had seen in a book and he thought that it might do just as well for tanning. Meanwhile the rabbit skins were wrapped up in a newspaper in his drawer. Now Mat smiled to himself as he recalled how the skins had given their presence away. He hadn't thought that the smell was so bad, but he got a severe licking for it all the same.

Mat was sitting smiling to himself, remembering the hard, stinking smell which had seemed to rise out of the drawer in slabs, and the satisfaction which he had felt from it, as if some of the 'nature' which he had so hankered after had entered into the refractory reality with which he was surrounded. Then the thought came to him that all this would make a good story. He got up from his chair and found pen and paper.

It was late in the evening when Mat finished the story. He had sat writing while he was having lunch, then while having tea. There were exciting possibilities in the story. For one thing, in his vivid remembrance of the appearance of the place where it had happened. The front of the tenement where he had lived was a rich red-brown sandstone but it was all scuffed with rubbings, covered with chalked graffiti and spotted with muddy ball marks; there were the neat scrubbed closes from which you were chased when you played, the funny drystane dyke which had been built at the end of the row of macadamised courtyards and on the other side of which was a piece of waste land full of grass and dockens. He remembered how the hard grey stone of the dyke warmed from the sun, how in a particular bit of the waste ground the grass under a wall grew luxuriant with a pale waxy green colour, how underneath the sandy soil there were layers of pure creamy clay which could be worked into shapes like plasticine. He deliberately worked all this into the story. The child's vivid and sensuous apprehension of the world was contrasted with the meagreness of the world's offering to him; the creative excitement of the child and his pathetic attempts at creation with all the lack of apparatus and resource. And, of course, the severe beating which he received for all his efforts in attempting to do something which, besides being dirty, was impossible and unnecessary.

When he was finished Mat put the pieces of paper together and made a rough calculation of the number of words in the story. It was somewhere between two and three thousand words. This surprised him as he seemed to have been writing intensely and quickly the whole day. In his weariness he thought of those prolific people who could churn out that number of words every day and he wondered how they did it. However, he had written the story and he thought that it wasn't too bad. He took a piece of blank paper, clipped it over the rest of the sheets and wrote the title with some satisfaction, *The Realist*.

As they went to bed after supper Mat wound the clock and made a firm resolution to hear the alarm in the morning. During the last couple of days he had had a surfeit of words, also he had lost a good deal of money. There was the day's wages lost and the money he spent while out drinking. He fell asleep thinking about both the story and the alarm. The feeling of pleasure about the story began to diminish and the thought of the alarm took precedence. One of the worst things you could do when you always had to get up early was to break the habit, even if only for one morning, and Mat knew he would feel uncomfortable for a few days until this breach in his habit would heal. Although his sleep that night was dreamless he did waken several times to look at the clock until he finally woke to see that it was only a few minutes before the alarm would ring. For a minute or two he lay there thankful that he was awake then he got up and pressed the button down on the alarm so that it would not go off and awaken Helen.

After the morning halt for breakfast Mat was working in a room beside two killers with whom he didn't usually work. The benefit man who usually did their room had cut himself and as Mat's own rooms weren't too busy he took his place. One of the killers in the room was a big, coarse-built man with a slow sarcastic manner who was in the habit of baiting any benefit man who came into the room to work. He would take a gratuitous dislike to somebody and then he'd try to make their lives miserable with his malicious sadistic remarks. He had the knack of finding out the sore spots in people and the gift of probing them with his wheedling jocular manner. He started on Mat.

'I see you had a day off yesterday.'

Mat had lost a day's wages and the boss had bawled him out, so he didn't want to talk about it. 'Aye, Wullie.'

'You'll have lost a day's wages. You'll be feeling that on Friday wull ye not?'

'Ach, not so bad,' Mat said.

'Whit? Are you rich then?'

'I'm no' rich. Just nut worried. There's other things than money.'

'Of course,' Wullie said, 'I forgot you don't worry about money. You just worry about higher things.' He gloated to people often about money because he himself was invulnerable on that point. Apart from his work as a killer he also dealt in cattle, buying beef on the hoof and selling it in the market to the butchers. 'You wait till the bairnies start coming. Then you'll worry all right.'

'Right, Wullie,' Mat said. '*I'll* do the worrying.' Mat didn't want to needle with Wullie. In spite of the fact that he could be so aggravating Mat felt sympathy towards him. There was a feeling of intelligence which came from the man and Mat guessed that his awareness of other people's vulnerability came from a genuine sensitivity towards them. Also there was this contradiction in the man's make-up in that his bigness, his bulky powerfulness, exuded that kind of gentleness which is so often found in physically strong men and gave a feeling from him that belied his maliciousness.

Mat started to skin the head on Wullie's beast. He cleared the thrapple up to the breast, cut the hide away from the cheeks, slit the nostrils and was about to skin down the last strip of hide from the nose to between the horns. He was bending down over the head when Wullie, who was clearing the hide from the breast, backed into him.

'Oops! Sorry!' Wullie said, and he stood up straight, stroking his knife and looking over his shoulder at Mat. 'Are you nut finished that heid yet?'

Mat muttered at him. 'How in the hell can I skin the heid when your big fat arse is in the road!' He was sure that Wullie had backed into him to annoy him.

Wullie just grinned. 'Temper, temper.'

'Oot the road,' Mat said, and he bent down and skinned the head.

Wullie stood back, ostentatiously giving Mat room. Mat's knife had just been set and he had a good edge to it so that he cleared the last strip of hide in one stroke.

'My, my!' Wullie said. 'Look at the knife flying. It's a pity ye cannae keep up wi' it.'

Mat felt his temper going, but he suppressed it and went on working. He looked at Wullie while he was working and began to think that his dryness and dourness was an affectation in the man – and Mat guessed that he held an image of himself as being like this – slow, indifferent, invulnerable, contained. There was a period of silence while the beasts were being hung on the cambrels. As the carcases started to lift from the ground Mat slit the belly in Wullie's beast, cleared the fat, removed the intestine, punched down the swelling paunch to expose the gullet, deftly slitting the little pink tube and pulling the stomachs on to the floor. Then he went over to the other killer's beast and did the same, working fast in order to keep himself ahead of the killer. Wullie had started to make a running commentary on Mat's work. He was standing grinning behind the beast, clearing the vent and shouting in mock admiration. 'Oh, look at him go. Mind yersel. Watch his knife.' When Mat ran out of the room with the intestines draped over his arm he had to use that characteristic mincing gait as his feet slid over the greasy floor and among the piled-up hooves. Wullie shouted. 'Oh! You'll heat your watter.'

When Mat came into the room again he moved ponderously and slowly, keeping his face dour and in fact half-mimicking all Wullie's mannerisms. He stroked his knife slowly on the steel, put it into its wooden sheath, then stuck his arms akimbo. He spoke in a friendly tone of voice.

'Wullie, lad. You're nattering away there like some auld sweetie wife.' The other killer in the room looked up and grinned as Mat addressed him. 'Tut, tut. What a chatter-box. His tongue's goin' like the clapper of a bell.' He turned his back on Wullie and started to separate the stomachs on the floor. He affected an air of indifference. Wullie didn't like the garrulous role which Mat had cast him in and his face only half hid his annoyance as he pulled viciously at the hide under the tail.

Wullie didn't speak again until the next two beasts had been felled and he had just about finished. Mat had cleared the room, hung up the offals and was standing watching Wullie splitting the beast's backbone. Both Wullie and the other killer were taking great care with the splitting as both the beasts belonged to Wullie himself. The carcases were from young bullocks and the bones were soft and easy to split. Wullie got back into his jocular mood again for he turned and smiled sarcastically at Mat.

'You've got time to go down and get a haircut before the next felling.'

'Go and get stuffed,' Mat said. He turned and walked away to the door of the room and Wullie shouted after him 'Look at the intellectual cheating the barber.' Mat stood at the door of the room looking into the pass. He wished that the next felling was past so that he could get away from Wullie to another room. Wullie was still shouting at him 'He's saving up for a fiddle. He cannae get his hair cut till he gets an estimate from the barber.'

'I thought,' Mat asked, 'that you had enough big deals of your own without worrying about other people's business.'

'It is my business.' Wullie spoke with his voice full of moralistic viciousness. 'You shouldnae be allowed to work wi' food wi' your hair that length.' Wullie had stopped splitting the beast and was now stripping the pleural membrane from the inside of the ribs. Mat watched. There were two diffuse pink spots on the inner side of each rib cage and as Wullie removed the pleural membrane he was also removing these pink spots along with some little brown oval-shaped tubers. Adhesions and tubers.

'Why?' Mat asked.

'Because people have to eat the beef,' Wullie said, still moralising.

Mat looked at Wullie incredulously. He felt goose-pimples crawl all over him as he realised that as Wullie was reproving him with all the fervour of his moral indignation he could also remove this slight trace of tuberculosis from the carcase so that the meat inspector wouldn't see it, and so that he wouldn't lose the price of the carcase.

'So they have, Wullie,' Mat said and went over to where

the lungs were hanging. He trimmed some fat away and cut through the lymph nodes attached to the trachea. In the centre of each gland there was a focus of yellow pus. Mat started to shout. 'Inspector! IN-SPECTOR!'

'Shurrup,' Wullie said.

Mat went on shouting. When you are used to working amongst the clatter of bogey wheels, the crack of pistols, the grinding of gears, the bawling of cattle, you have to learn to make yourself heard and Mat had cultivated a clear mountaineer's yell which pierced through the other sounds and could be heard in every part of the slaughter-house. Wullie came out from behind the hanging carcase with an expression of pain and disgust on his face. Mat started to shout again using his hands against his mouth like a trumpet.

'Inspector! Inspector!'

When the meat inspector came in his white coat he glanced casually at the suppurating glands and gestured towards the door and Mat took the offals and dumped them on the floor outside. The rest of the carcase as well was condemned as unfit for human consumption. Wullie was furious and when the inspector had left the room he turned on Mat. He spoke slowly, and he seemed genuinely hurt. 'Whit did you dae that for?'

'People have to eat that beef,' Mat said, deliberately repeating Wullie's phrase.

'That carcase would maybe have been cleared if you had kept your mouth shut,' Wullie said.

'You're a big firm. You can stand it.'

Wullie shrugged. He wouldn't admit that he could be touched by any financial loss. In fact the loss of the carcase would make no real difference to him. Much less than the loss of a day's wages to Mat. Wullie wouldn't have to do without anything, yet Mat knew that he'd brood and concentrate on his loss, that it really hurt him. He showed his anger at Mat with a huffy silence.

After the next felling Mat was finished in Wullie's room. By this time it had spread around the slaughter-house what had happened and several benefit men had come into the room to gloat at Wullie and give Mat the thumbs up sign. When the two carcases were hung up and the offals cleared, Mat cleaned the fat from his knife under the hot-water tap. Wullie was standing at the top of the rooms steeling his knives and putting on a sad reproachful look. He shook his head and clicked his tongue. 'I didn't think you'd do a thing like that.'

Mat felt the hilarity bubbling up inside him, he put his hands to his mouth and bawled at Wullie. 'You're nothing but an effing big hypocrite.'

Wullie picked up a foot and slung it viciously at Mat who ducked giggling behind the wall of the room. Mat heard the thud of the foot against the wall, then poked his head round the corner of the room and made an obscene gesture at Wullie but Wullie had turned and was poking away at the carcase with his knife.

In the next room where Mat had to work there was only a single killer and Mat gave him a hand to get the cattle out of the pen and tied up in the room. These were the last two beasts to be killed that day as far as concerned Mat. The killer with whom he was working now, Jimmy McGuire, was a slightly built elderly man, a very good tradesman whom Mat liked. He was the kind of man who'd look up from his work and say, 'Gie's a song,' or when he was standing steeling his knives he'd grin at everyone and say, 'Are you all right?' Otherwise he didn't talk much but just whistled and sang all the time. After they had got the beasts tied to the stunning posts Jimmy waved to Mat. 'Don't shout on the gunner. We'll have a smoke first.' They stood facing one another across the room, leaning against the haunches of the beasts and smoking their cigarettes. Mat felt relieved to be away from Wullie's room but the depressing thought came to him that everyone's approval of the trick he'd played on Wullie came from the fact that Wullie was so unpopular and not from the fact that he was right to point out a diseased beast to the inspector. Also he thought of Wullie's remark. 'He's saving up for a fiddle.' This was part of a general feeling of aggressive philistinism that he was always having to put up with. He felt so disgusted with this attitude that it was worse to have the taint of fiddler than it was to try and hide a diseased beast. He had sometimes found himself at the receiving end of contemptuous remarks from people other than Wullie, sometimes from the very ones who were laughing at Wullie now. If he didn't know how to defend himself it would be worse. He thought of the invitation he had received from George Duncan, to visit him the following Sunday. It would be a pleasant change from people like Wullie.

They finished their cigarettes and brought the gunner into the room. Both beasts were dropped to the floor. On one side there was an Aberdeen Angus bullock and on the other a bull. Mat took the rope from the bullock's neck and hung it up; then took the cane down from its hook, pithed the bullock and went over to where Jimmy was loosening the rope from the stunning post next to the bull. It had fallen badly and was lying, its forequarters slumped against the wall, its feet tucked beneath it and its haunches pointing out into the room at an angle. Jimmy was standing inside this angle between the bull and the wall trying to get a purchase with his feet on its shoulders and pushing with his back to the wall. Mat was busy thinking of the violence of the humane killer, the bolt gun with its tiny brass cartridges which could slap the big bulls on to the floor so easily and he was searching in his mind for words that would express the locked spasmodic pose of the bull as it lay shuddering against the wall. He took the bull by the horns and started to pull, trying to help Jimmy roll the beast over on to its other side and away from the wall. It came half way over until its feet were tucked directly under it.

Mat still had a grip of the horns and was still searching in his mind for words. He was tugging hard and only half aware of the bull's growing resistance when he heard Jimmy give a sudden exclamation, three short rising expirations of the breath, 'Ha, huh, *huh*!' and Mat realised that the bull's hindquarters were up and that its forelegs were scrabbling for purchase on the floor. He gripped the horns tighter, tugged violently at the head and tried to kick the forelegs away from under the beast, but the laxness had gone from its neck and Mat might as well have been tugging at a wall. There was a blur of impressions, the bull's glaucous rolling eye, Jimmy's surprised face, the vicious lowering of the bull's head.

Mat threw himself on to the bull's head right between the horns just as it hooked at him, then was surprised by the soft ease with which his body flew through the air. He went flying backwards out through the door of the room just missing the wall. His steel described an arc in the air and hit him on the shoulder and he heard the slither of his razor-edged knives as they fell out of the wooden box. The thing happened so quickly that Mat's reflexes took over and he twisted in the air to land crouched among a pile of feet and manyplies. He rolled over to break his fall and was up on his feet to face the bull all in one movement. His knives had fallen safely away from him and the bull had fallen again on to its side. It was lying further away from the wall now and thrashing its head up and down. The tip of its right horn had impaled Jimmy's foot and he was standing on one leg holding on to the stunning post and working his impaled foot up and down with the thrashing of the bull's head. His face was twisted in pain.

Mat threw himself again at the bull, grabbing a horn as the head came up. He put as much strength as he could into taking the weight of the head and for a second or two held it twisted away from the floor. Jimmy jerked his caught foot from the horn and hopped away. Mat grabbed the pithing cane from the floor and jumped on the head kneeling on the animal's face. He was shocked by the animal's distress for he could see the little round hole edged with pink froth where it had been shot. As he went up and down with the motion of the bull's head, he held on to a horn with one hand and felt for the little round hole with the other. He went up and down a couple of times before he felt the cane slip in and the head jerk throwing Mat off again. As the animal's head went down again both Mat and Jimmy threw themselves on to it and Jimmy pushed the cane right in for its full length. The legs thrashed while Jimmy worked the cane in and out, then suddenly the animal went lax.

Jimmy hopped over to the wall, propped his back against it and pulled off his boot and sock. The horn had gone in through the upper of his boot, scraped the side of his foot then stuck into the sole. There was a pink splotch on the side of his foot where a bruise was starting and he had lost some skin. Mat picked up the wellington boot and examined it. Jimmy was rueful.

'A brand new pair of wellingtons.'

Mat stood silent for a moment with his finger poked through the tear in the wellington, then said, 'How the hell did that happen?'

Jimmy looked down at the bull, pursed his lips and blew, 'God knows. I thought you were away for it. *You're* going to be sore wi' that bump you took.'

Mat laughed. He pulled his shirt away from his ribs and they both looked down. Over a large part of the front of his chest the skin had all flaked away and underneath the flakes of skin were tiny little spots of blood. He laughed again. 'I never even felt that.' Then he felt shaky and he went away to look for his knives. Usually when an animal is shot it is dead. He supposed that with the bull having an inch-thick hide covering its forehead and with its tough thick skull, the bolt had just penetrated the skull and had temporarily stunned it without damaging the brain. If the animal had not fallen over on to the wrong side, if it had been pithed quick enough, then the thing would never have happened. Mat felt that he himself had been at fault for if instead of brooding about Wullie and thinking about bloody literature he had been paying attention, noticed that it was a bull that was being felled, he would have shoved the hindquarters against the wall and given the tail a pull as the pistol was fired. Then it would have fallen away from the wall in a position where it could have been pithed right away.

To think that he had pretensions to being an artist. He blethered away to Jimmy Aitken about writing whenever he had the chance. Yesterday he had written a story and Helen had believed in him. The day before he had spent spouting about art to Sam Richards and his friends. If he really was an artist then surely one of the things he should be more sensitive to and more responsible for was the suffering of others, especially the innocent. Instead of mauling words about inside his head he should be paying attention. This attentive explicit attitude towards his surroundings and others should be part of his nature as an artist, part of his duty. It was surely enough that the animal had to be slaughtered for men's sake without having to suffer this messy painful end as well. And besides, there was the innocence of the animal. It shouldn't have suffered through any defection on his part.

The edges of Mat's knives had been turned when they fell on the floor and Mat started to put a new edge on them as quickly as he could. He held the hone at the end and used the ball of his thumb as a stop for the knife. He got a certain grim satisfaction out of the thought that if he didn't pay attention while he was doing *this* that he'd take the fingers off himself. While he was honing the knives Jimmy had stuck both the beasts and was now working the crane lifting up the carcasses to bleed. He was looking at Mat and smiling, making rueful grimaces and clicking with his tongue.

'Tch! Tch! Matthew Craig! I thought you were a goner.'

They looked at one another and shook their heads commiseratingly. Jimmy laughed.

'These things can happen.'

11

WHEN SEPTEMBER CAME Helen gave birth to a boy. The birth took place a few days after the date on which the doctor said the baby was due. In spite of the fact that the boy was very big Helen had no trouble with the birth. Mat had gone with her in the ambulance to the hospital, had been given her clothes to take home and then had been more or less thrown out. He had walked all the way home. By the time he had arrived home, left Helen's clothes in the house, and gone out again to phone the hospital, the baby had been born. 'A remarkably easy birth,' the ward sister had said on the phone and he wasn't to worry as Mrs Craig was all right. 'Mother and child are both quite comfortable.' Mat accepted the comforting words with relief and went home to the empty house. Up until now he had thought only of the possible dangers of childbirth. While he was standing in the corridors of the hospital with its glazed tiles and its disinfectant smell he had felt anxious and afraid. It was the same hospital which the men from the slaughter-house went to when they had to have their fingers stitched and he had stood in the same corridor often before when he had taken men up to have their cuts repaired. He couldn't help associating the place with injury. It seemed to him a focus, a kind of clearing house for all the accidents, the contingencies, the gratuitousness of life. All the cut, crushed and mutilated people who came in through the gates moaning, shocked and nauseated with bloodied clothes, or in white bandages with white shocked faces. The children struck with disease and fevers, the men dropping in the streets with strokes or heart attacks, the anxious frightened relatives. The clean surgical atmosphere which was suggestive of the soft vulnerability of flesh. The thought of all those shiny gripping, pinching and cutting instruments depressed Mat and all the way home he could only think of the danger of living. When he had gone to the phone box there was somebody in it already and he had had to stand outside and wait.

Standing there in the bright lit street he was reminded of another incident which had happened once a long, long time ago. He had been standing like that night beside a phone box but not waiting to phone. He couldn't remember when it was or why he had been waiting at that particular place, except that he had been sent on some errand by a neighbour. Vaguely he remembered that he had carried an envelope and that the faces of the adults concerned had been grave. He had sensed behind the gravity of the errand one of those serious, but mysterious cataclysms, which occurred in the adult world. Anyway, he had felt that evening a menacing sense of the awful possibilities of life. It must have been another September evening for there had been the same smoky chilly atmosphere, with the dusty air and the dusk light all grimy and diffuse. He had stood shivering at the tram stop looking down the long slope of the street towards the bend where the tram would appear. At the bend there were clusters of street lights, each one surrounded by tiny spikes which seemed to shimmer and move. Two women came up out of the dusk and one of them went into the phone booth. As he stood looking for the tram and shifting his feet impatiently he was only half aware of the women. One of them had come vividly to his attention as she dropped the phone and started to moan in protest. She had used the awful banal words, 'He *can't* be' before she had dropped the phone and started to sob and moan. The accusing incredulous note in her voice had caused Mat to feel the same horror like a sharp grip in his breast where his heart was; then she had run from the booth leaving the phone dangling by its cord and had crossed the road followed by her friend, and disappeared into the dusk again. When a tram had come Mat had boarded it with his limbs still shaking. He had looked out of the window and from the lighted tram the sky appeared as a black void. For a while he thought that perhaps He wasn't there, but he rejected, *repelled* the idea for its horrific nihilism. He couldn't bear to think of that woman's cries against that black nothingness. Instead he clenched his fists and found for the first time in his life a good reason for believing in Him, for He could be blamed. The little boy who was Mat vowed on Judgment Day he would throw it in God's face.

Standing there at the phone booth all these years later Mat still thought of the streets as precarious and menacing. He seemed to associate this certain time of evening with the screeching of brakes, little knots of people clustered round someone dying on the pavement, drunkenness, voices raised in anger, blows, blood, broken glass, women's voices raised in screams. Was it that he himself had too great a sense of his vulnerability or was it that the other people in the street had become merely calloused or vitiated in feeling through a continual assault on their sensibilities so that they no longer felt the alien menace of the world and of circumstance? But after receiving the comforting message on the phone the relief had dismissed his black mood and he thought how ordinary in fact the day had been. Even when Helen had felt her pains coming on and afterwards when they had gone to the hospital he had felt as if he was in an ordinary and interesting world. He had shared Helen's feeling as she wondered what it would be like and they had shared silly jokes with the ambulance men. Being cut off from Helen in the hospital had made Mat feel like this.

In the house he sat by the empty fireplace and smoked. It was by now too late to go out and let anyone know and he felt the sense of anti-climax. He thought that birth ought to be more of a celebration, that he should be connected to it in some way other than through the cold lines of a telephone and he felt the need to do something conventional, like buy people drinks and hand out cigars. It was difficult for him to realise that he was a father and he kept repeating to himself in a mechanical sort of way – 'I've got a son.' But this phrase had no effect of making him feel anything. He thought of a poem he had read once about the birth of a child and he envied the poet, not so much for his ability to write the poem as for his feelings which were accurate enough to write about. His own feelings were so exasperatingly unformed, diffuse, that he was hard put to it to know if he felt anything at all. Nearly indifference. Yet when he said to himself, 'I've got a son,' he had a choking physical sensation as he tried to realise this slippery, elusive fact. 'I've got a son,' and he'd shrug, then get up on his feet and pound about the room.

On top of the bed there was a pile of neat, ironed clothes, shirts, collars, peenies, underclothes, and Mat took them from the bed and put them on top of the wardrobe. Helen would have packed them all away in drawers but when he pulled the drawers they seemed already full. For some reason Mat started to rummage about the house pulling open drawers and cupboards and looking inside them. He found a biscuit tin full of buttons, screw nails, broken electric fittings, candle stumps, pins and coins and he sat for a while searching among the clutter of small objects, picking up a thimble and trying it on, spinning the George II penny, closely examining the tiny coin with the Slav characters stamped on it. When he closed the biscuit tin he pulled a small cardboard box from under the bed and went through all the papers in it. There were letters tied in bundles, pink income tax forms that had never been filled in, receipts and bills, some Christmas cards, letters, one or two sheets of paper which were closely covered in his small cramped handwriting which he held upside down and scrutinised carefully. Inside the food cupboard he picked up all the little round boxes of spice, bottles of essence and colouring, blocks of cooking fat, packets of sugar and other groceries and rearranged them all. Then he absent-mindedly made himself some eggs and a pot of tea. When they were finished he sat musing in front of the fire for such a long time that the eggs got cold and he ate them without enjoyment. He supposed that Helen, would be sleeping by now and he tried to imagine her lying in bed in the hospital and sound asleep, and the baby too would be all wrapped up and lying sound asleep in his cot. They had bought a cot for the baby and it was lying in the lobby still wrapped in sheets of corrugated paper. He took it into the tiny room and set it up, unfolding it and screwing in the long metal rods on which the side of the cot slid up and down. After he had placed the cot mattress on to the springs he didn't know what to do as he wasn't sure how to make up a bed for a baby. By this time it was really late and he went to bed himself. For a long time he lay there smoking in the dark. It was the first time in his life that he had ever slept in a room by himself and he felt lonely and rather as if he was only sleeping there on sufferance and that the house didn't belong to him. Finally he fell asleep with his mind still trying to work out how it was that a baby's cot should be made up.

It seemed to Mat that he had been handed a very rare and fragile thing to hold, and he began to clutch it in that tight inhibited way that is more conducive to dropping it than holding it in an easy relaxed safety. This feeling didn't manifest itself in any intimate physical way. By the time Helen had come home from hospital with the baby – they called him John – he weighed nearly ten pounds. He already had a strong little neck that would strain its head up from the pillow and Mat was able to enjoy handling him, bathing him with almost as much confidence as Helen. It was more like that embarrassment which is akin to the feeling working-class people get when they have to offer hospitality to a stranger and they find that their condition makes embarrassing limitations to their offerings. They become conscious and painfully aware of the meagreness of their lives, feeling that although it may be all right for themselves they ought to be able to offer better for others. As the months passed John grew up into what Helen proudly called 'a great coarse lump' with his big round head, fat cheeks and creases at the wrists and knees. Without noticing their lives became narrower, more involved in routine. The little house with its two tiny rooms seemed to grow smaller with the baby's presence and all the objects with which he had to be surrounded. Mat began to find it irksome to have to squeeze past the pram in the narrow lobby, always having to be moving things – chairs, tables, baths, prams. They had not had the long usage of domestic matters to acquire skilful management.

Mat felt that he had introduced his family, of which he had so often dreamed, into a shoddy and provisional world where every enjoyment was deferred until later, until some physical obstacle had been got over. The innocent enjoyment of everyday commonplace life which Mat so hankered after was prevented by the congestion, the sheer clutter of things which had to be moved around or out of the way. Before bathing John at night they would spread the carpet with a rubber sheet, boil kettles, remove chairs from in front of the bed to get at the baby's bath which was kept there; then they would have to mop up the water which had splashed all over the place, empty the big bath into the tiny sink, wipe off the windows which had become all steamed up from the boiling kettles, dry the bath, remove the chairs from in front of the bed so that it could be put away. For their meals they had to manœuvre the table out into the middle of the floor and as long as it was there it divided the room into two so that they had either to squeeze between it and the big easy chair in front of the fireplace or climb over the divan if they wanted to move from one side of the room to the other.

All this came on top of the physical fatigue which the harsh demands of the slaughter-house made on him, the early rising, the hard physical labour. After a few months Mat felt the horror of congestion, conglomeration and clutter always some place near the surface of his mind. They both began to act as if this period was merely to be existed in until something better happened, when they would have a life in which the simple immediate things could be enjoyed, like having a meal or bathing the baby. Of the provisional nature of their life there could be no doubt. The nature of their expectations was more dubious. Yet out of this dubiety Mat tried to maintain a sense of the possibility of a radical change in their circumstances so that he would be able to offer Helen and John something more than this cramped and cluttered way of living. They could no longer afford to go out so often, even if they could get someone to baby sit for them.

Mat occasionally thought about writing, but aside from the fatigue which he felt in his body his mind had gone numb. He found himself unable to pay attention to other writers, still less write himself. He stopped reading. Slowly they found that the constructive life which they were leading was draining their vitality away, making it harder and harder for them to cope with its menial exhausting demands. They began to accept things as normal which they never would have done before, finding themselves being forced near the edge of squalor and accepting it. The sharp edge of their energy, their youth, was being abraded away. More and more their lives became an arid routine; for Helen a routine of washing, mending, scraping and paring with their finances, washing and cooking and trying to stave off the tide of squalor which threatened them; for Mat, he was lost in a routine of working, eating, sleeping. Friday night, which once had been the peak of existence for them, the great pay-day, was now spent, Helen washing the close or doing the napkins, Mat sitting and dozing. The week-ends when they would dress up in their good clothes became fewer and fewer.

About this time Mat began to think about how he had left the office with its ticking clock and its regular safe routine to work in the slaughter-house. The reason he had done this with so little qualm was, he realised now, that he had lived all his life until the present with some vague expectation. He had as Scott Fitzgerald put it 'a heightened sensitivity to the promises of life'. Now he viewed this 'heightened sensitivity' somewhat sadly as a not very exclusive possession, in a way a mistake, a fault, a chimera, an illusion, a cruel joke. For, of course, what he had expected didn't come; he had expected all life to retain the quality of youth, to be always latent with growth, movement, interest, and he had expected too some particular event, some achievement which would mark, signify that the promises of life were to be kept. In some way John's arrival was significant in that it marked the time when Mat's expectations, the note which he held, had become due. But it was as if life, the payee, had become bankrupt.

Mat thought of other people he knew, people with talent like Alec and Andrew. Although he had lost touch with them he knew that they'd both be away somewhere using their talents and abilities, leading rich active lives. Of course that was the whole nub of the question, for they had attached their expectation to something concrete, they had studied or gone to university, learned a trade, while he had followed this illusive 'idea of art'. He thought at times with horror at how stupid he had been, how stupid and yet how hopeful to have maintained such an illusion. He had not expected anything specific from art. He did not think in terms of earning money by his writing so that he could win his liberty in a physical economic way. It was vaguer than that. He expected that he would get directly from art, be able to take into his being, the quality of lightness and freedom that art had, and that the chain of circumstances would never be able to hold a participant in this morally free world; that the interior freedom, the glamour, the enticements of art would in some necessary way always be reflected in his life. Yet now he found himself chained even with a sense of interior constriction.

Apart from many outward compulsions, physical, financial, he was obsessed by a myriad of moral obligations, obsessions, guilts. One of these frantic scruples, significant of his morally arid outlook, was his being unable to think of writing in a worldly sense, as an activity, a profession with which he would be able to change his life, earn money, live in a bigger house, open up a world of physical freedoms, excitements, stimulations – the kind of life which he and Helen had dreamed of, full of music, eating, conversations, love, creativeness, drinking, companionship, theatre, writing, work. Because the vitality of that life would be contingent upon his success, and Mat dearly dreamed of another thing, something absolute, of a vitality which would come directly from the nature of the art which he would create, of a compensation which would not be strained through the dirty filter of commerce, the world of circumstance. He wanted to discover a source of vitality which would be contingent only upon his existence as a human being and which could be found in the human being even in the dregs of life, when all hope was gone, in the complete absence of anything but the flat tedium of existence in a world thickened by absurdity, and dense with its own exhausting presence.

But out of this same scrupulosity of feeling, this neurotic finickiness, Mat was able to see the equivocations which his over-developed sense of responsibility put him to. His attitude, he realised, could be seen as a mere evasion of the risk and responsibility of success, but on the other hand there was the temptation of this act of discovery, the challenge of the sheer over-wearing arduousness of the task which he might set himself which appealed to the ambitiousness in him, the arrogance. 'Ambition should be in the work' was the motto he made for himself. He made the decision that he should choose the level at which he should work, and he chose for himself that level which was at the same time the highest and the lowest, at which the most exhilarating flights of creativeness should occur and at which the most exhausting demands should be made on him. However wryly he might think of himself as 'just an old Scotch Calvinist', and wonder at times with detached amusement how he, Mat Craig, a labourer in the slaughter-house, would have the effrontery to think of himself as capable of lifting himself by the bootlaces, he still desired, and in the act of desiring believed himself capable of the accomplishment of that kind of task. It was a task which demanded the overweening arrogance and spiritual toughness of those men who are capable of breaking through into major art. Again and again he would think that he mistook his capacity for admiration of those men – Dostoevsky, Eliot, Sartre, Mann, Keller, Goethe, Coleridge, Joyce, Hopkins – that he mistook this admiration and the exhilaration with which he appreciated them for a capacity in him to emulate them. Then he would shrug, grin wryly, and accuse himself of a ridiculous personal arrogance. Yet again, all this arrogance might have its ground in something quite humble. Mat thought of all the things he had tried to write in his magnum opus, 'Rutherglen's wee roon red lums reek briskly', and of the pathetic source of its inspiration, the shuttle-like existence which he had had as a child and which had so broken the continuity of his life that he had begun to search back into the past for traditions, roots, and experience however vicarious of a solid provided life which could be passed on, in which tradition and attachment had a reality symbolised by a smoking chimney. In attempting the task of creating a bridge between his broken world and this old traditional one, part of the pathos lay in the absurd gap between the difficulties of the task and his own inadequate equipment; another part lay in the franticness with which he pursued this commonplace aim – a reeking lum, that it should stand as a token and symbol of his utmost satisfaction.

This conservatist desire which he felt for a rooted and stable world was at the back of his strong emotional attachment to socialism and his loyalty to his class. However much he might want to go away from the miseries of the world he lived in, and he thought of this perpetually with disgust and hatred, the sight of the little girl in calipers from next door, the real little girl who'd clutch at his jacket as he'd pass up the close, or throw her ball to him in the street, this sight would make him pause and stay.

He could easily make his personal quietus – get away from it all – the dull parallel lines of the tenements, the dirty dull closes paved with tilted granite flagstones, the worn and dangerous spiral staircase down which the little girl would clump every day in her calipers. Outside, the backyard was an area of soggy mud when the weather was bad, a dust bowl when it was dry. There was a selvedge of coarse grass round the backyard but the middle of it was a trampled black mess littered with broken bottles, rusty tin cans, mouldering refuse and manured with dog's dirt and cat's piss.

The parents in the street let their children out to play, there being nowhere else except the houses themselves, and they are so small and cramped that parents have been known to strangle or half murder their children for the sake of a few moments of peace or privacy. So the children play in these streets so full of lethal possibilities. Through the day while the fathers are out working the mothers are continually running out of the houses with their hearts fluttering in their throats when some child has had a narrow escape, and they belt their children out of relief that they haven't been mangled under the wheels of a bus, nor become impaled on the spikes which separate the yards, nor fallen from the stair windows or ripped themselves open on broken glass. Except, of course, when these things do happen. And the other lethal possibilities – running noses, coughs, measles, scarlet fever, whooping cough and all the other ailments of congestion.

From all this Mat had no doubt he could make his quietus. Yet it was what he had been used to most of his life; it was his background, his tradition, what roots he had. He thought of the exuberance and dreams and poetry which the children sustained and he thought that he owed his loyalty and his being to the hope that was in them. To break with them, to go his own way was to break with what he was. And in the same way he thought that to turn his back on the absolute claims of art, however exorbitant they might be, was to play a false role, to try to become something other than what he was and in the end to betray art itself.

It was as if the acceptance of his own humble role in life, his not deserving anything other than the arid and empty existence to which he was used, this was the very fact that made him take on the task of the creative artist, obliging him to accept the arrogant task of creating art out of deprivation rather than choose the easy way of leaving deprivation behind him. It was this very humility which obliged him to attempt the difficult, almost impossible task of making art out of his Scottishness rather than turn towards a sophisticated, successful but alien tradition.

However much Mat felt himself to be a welter of oppositions, of tugging scruples, of fastidiousness and doubt, the fact was that this wrestle with himself, as his state of exhaustion became worse, grew sluggish and finally the warring contestants became locked in a strained quivering effort like a tight grip on his brain until he was unable to think about writing and his whole being seemed to become just an unfeeling blank. He felt a desperate anxiety not to write, but to have some feeling out of which writing would become possible; he was left in that singular emotional state when his one emotion was the desire that some time he should feel – feel anything at all, as if his being was without content. He started to read again, but turning more and more to abstract ideas. All art irritated him, exhausted him, at times terrified him. Now he read Kant, Hume, Schopenhauer, Hegel, Nietzsche, Marcel, Sartre, Jaspers, anything which he could read which did not refer directly to the stuff of existence – conflict, ruck, drama, strife, feeling; he read anything which was systematic and orderly and in which he could lose himself without involvement. He found his mind curiously sharp and he was capable of reading at great speed, and concentrating for long periods on the most abstruse and difficult of ideas. Yet he did not try to evaluate these ideas, or make any decisions between them.

The whole winter passed. Later on he was to connect this period with the winter landscape. Travelling in the bus in the mornings the streets were filled with only a few figures standing at bus stops, the big arc lamps filling the vacant streets with purposeless light and the traffic lamps flashing their signals to empty crossings. Once a week he'd seen the same woman scrubbing the steps or the granite facings of a bank. All the familiar faces in the bus would be showing sleep, people talked in undertones and grunted at one another with the democratic familiarity of the early morning regulars.

There was a heavy fall of snow in late January which quickly turned to slush. Then more snow fell through the first week in February and added to the piles of slush heaped at the side of the roads. The slaughter-house was busy as usual in winter so that Mat normally travelled home in the late afternoons. The windows of the buses were always steamed up and Mat would wipe the pane and expose the winter landscape in the street outside. The late afternoon light diffused its way through zinc coloured clouds and spread itself over the wet city streets. Solid objects, people, lamp posts, heaps of hardened sooty snow, buildings, chimneys, all stood silhouetted against the reflected metallic light. The low bagging clouds were like dirty sheets soaking in a tub except where here and there the discrete edge of a cloud would be etched sharply against a fierce argent light. A lurid greyness hung over the whole city, a shiny silvery grey like the colour of a dirty puddle reflecting light. When Mat got home he would curl himself in front of the fire as if to dry out the damp in which he had been working all day.

One weekend at the beginning of March, Mat and Helen went out for a walk with the pram. A Sunday afternoon in the park. The Sunday newspapers these days had begun to reflect an excitement, a sense of something new in the air, but Mat only half-read them, putting them aside with a feeling of unease, guilt, envy that he was not taking part in the excitement. Yet he felt too that the excitement he experienced on reading of other men's good work was turning him away from some vague purpose. On this afternoon as he got himself ready to go out walking the papers lay still unread. They walked up past the little recreation park which they had passed when they had first come to this place to see their house, then further on through a fairly well-kept prosperous district full of good tenement houses, then still further on through some streets where the houses were set back from the road and were fronted with gardens full of bare winter trees like twisted broomsticks. Even in the afternoon there were some windows lit up. As they walked they talked and the breath came from their mouths in clouds. In these back streets the pavements were still made of dirt and Mat took the pram so that he could handle it over the cobbled driveways which led into the gardens. The trees hung from the gardens over the pavements and bare looking privet stuck up over the walls.

In the park there was a broad area where the playing fields were, the goal posts sticking up black against the dazzling expanse of snow which covered the football pitches. They walked over the cleared pathway through the pitches towards the trees, then under the trees they turned along a broad railed path. There beneath the trees there were patches of bareness where the snow had fallen lightly, had thawed and taken on that porous look which half-melted snow has. Some bare patches showed where the grass had been crushed under the weight of the snow. Suspended under the railing at the side of the path were rows of water drops. The path had a slight slope downwards in the direction they were walking and as they went along it Mat pointed out to Helen how the rows of crystal drops were moving down the railings like a little upside down stream. They stood and watched the fanciful display of gaudy lights. As a drop would grow too large its weight would pull it off the railing. It would fall to the rail beneath, causing a delicate coruscation, a tiny spray of fragments to glisten in the pale light, then the whole tinkling cavalcade would move like a diamond abacus down one space to fill up the space the fallen drip had left. When they noticed it happen once they looked up and down the railings on each side of the path and noticed it was happening all the time. A continual procession of trickles and splashes, a mad exuberant game. They stood and laughed at the free show, at the extravagant humour and gaiety of it. It was like a miniature Niagara of splashes and sprays, all a comical variety, the drops jostling and quivering and dancing like children at a treat, a whimsical changing of effect as the drops would fall now here, now there, with a laughable and gay gratuitousness.

They couldn't stop laughing. Mat had tears of laughter in his eyes. 'It's an experience which was very popular among the romantics,' he said, still laughing. 'Kant, I think it was, called it the "dynamic sublime" as it was usually the kind of feeling evoked by raging torrents, tumultuous waves, majestic thunderstorms, lofty mountains, soaring precipices, great denizens of the forest. Well, there you have it. The dynamic sublime. A wee Glesca one. All on a reduced scale.'

12

IT WAS A morning in late May. It was cold standing there at the bus stop. The dawn had just come up, a spring dawn, cool, rosy and blue. In spite of the cold Mat had held the collar of his shirt open to allow the fresh breeze which ruffled his hair to blow freely down his neck. There were a few morning stars left, just diminishing into the blue and as Mat had walked to the bus stop through the mucky backyards he heard the inane liquid chattering of a starling coming from some gutter. He had looked up to the sky and felt a joy which the sluggard and lie-a-bed never knows. When he had woken it had still been dark outside, his head had been full of pieces of dream and his body suddenly full of tensions like an alarm clock waiting to go off. He had turned out, nevertheless, to face the dreary routine. Swallow his toad, as he put it to himself. But he had awakened earlier than he had thought and as he made himself tea and toasted bread the day had lit up. Now, standing in the quiet with his face still tingling from the cold wash and shave, the new day was as fresh as butter from a churn and the wind which blew on him felt like a shower bath. Above the roof of a building across the street some gulls were holding a gay regatta, full of salt and dash, their white wings soaring against the maritime blue of the sky. Apart from the occasional gurgling of pigeons there wasn't a sound. From the multitude of chimneys there came not a wisp of smoke. Nothing disturbed the blithe clear stillness of the morning, except for the faraway sound of the jingling of bottles.

It was that hour when even the raging insomniac's inflamed limbs and heated thoughts would be cooling into slumber. All the busy world asleep and only those intent on men's blessing were awake – the nurse on her vigil over frail men, the milkman bringing the babies their bottles, the lamplighter running upstairs and down, turning off the gas mantles, husbanding his gift of light till nightfall; but the statesmen, accountants, lawyers, executives, businessmen, judges and juries were asleep with their awful forefingers relaxed and dreaming of a kinder life. Early morning, fresh and innocent as a lettuce leaf, with the world settled, provisionally, for peace – a truly lyrical moment.

When the bus came, Mat shrugged off his mood with a grin. He felt slightly embarrassed by his mood. 'Specious lyricism,' he thought. But the cigarette which he lit in the bus, he had to admit, was sweet and fragrant, and sitting there he remembered waking in the night to feel Helen's relaxed gratified limbs round him.

The slaughter-house wasn't very busy. Mat put on his rubber boots but didn't bother to put on his apron or his kit. At the back of the killing rooms the pens were half empty and Mat sat with Jake and some of the other men, talking. They sat on stacked bales of straw, leaning with their backs against the wall. For a while Mat went off to grind his knives, taking a long time over the job, carefully following the curve of the knives and grinding so that the blades pared down evenly towards the edge without any bumps or 'belly'. Then he came back and sat on a bale of straw and honed the edges, bringing them up razor sharp. Amidst the sound of the laughing voices was the sound of the slither of steel as the men refreshed their dull blades on a fine stone, and a heavy rasp as they ground out a notch from the side of a cleaver with a piece of rough carborundum. One of the blood boys lay sound asleep taking up a whole bale of straw to himself. Another blood boy brought back steaming cans of black coffee and hot rolls with egg and sausage. Jake had coaxed the boy into going and now he refused to pay him for the errand and the two of them fought with one another, messing up bales of straw, stuffing the wisps of straw down each other's shirts.

'You didnae offer some o' yir coffee,' the boy said.

'You don't like black coffee.'

'Weel, I didnae get the chance to refuse.'

Jake laughed. 'How much did I say I would give you?'

'Five bob.' The boy exaggerated and everybody laughed.

'Whit? Five bob!' Jake pounced on the boy, wrestled him down on top of the bale and stuffed a bundle of hay under his jersey. 'How much?'

'Four and a tanner.'

Jake stuffed some straw down the side of his wellington boots. 'How much?'

'Four bob.'

Jake put some more straw down his neck. 'How much?'

'Three and six.'

Jimmy McGuire got up and held the boy's kicking legs and Jake pulled his belt and stuffed straw down his trousers. 'How much?' The boy yelled and kicked and giggled as more and more straw went down into his jeans, 'Hauf a dollar! Two bob! A shilling! A tanner! Ow! Nothing!'

After he had picked all the straw from himself they both wrestled weakly for a while then got tired and started a lackadaisical argument. Then Jake threw the money which the boy knew he'd get all along. Mat tested his knives on the hair on the back of his hand and they shaved off the hair as crisply and cleanly as any razor blade, leaving little bald patches among the dark hair of his arms. They ate the rolls and drank the scalding coffee before lighting up cigarettes. Jake got up and decided to walk down to the market and look for his customers.

'If we've got any work to do we'd as well finish it and get hame!'

Nobody answered him as they weren't keen on starting after lounging about all morning. Mat stretched himself. 'I'm feeling lazy.'

While Jake was away Jimmy Aitken came over with his can and his pieces. 'Had your breakfast yet?' he asked. looking anxiously at Mat. 'Aye, fried eggs and fried sausages and rolls.' He had to laugh at Jimmy's comical face as he made a dyspeptic grimace and held his stomach lightly with one hand. 'And black coffee in an auld dirty can,' Mat said. Jimmy sat down and shook his head. 'Ugh!'

They sat together waiting on Jake coming back. Jimmy didn't talk to Mat but sat grumbling miserably over his sandwiches. 'A' that rich feeding. The pâté de foie gras. Ye fairly get fed up wi' it.' He was eating liver paste sandwiches.

'Next thing yir big toe'll a' swell up.'

Jimmy grinned suddenly and stuck his leg up on a bale of straw. 'Ah'll have to lay off the Aylesbury duck.'

'And the port wine.'

'And the pheasant.'

'It's like the servant,' Jimmy said. 'He came running in tae his master, you know, ruffles at the sleeve, embroidered waistcoat, silk trousers, wig – and he says, "Sire, Sire, the peasants are revolting," and the master, he's a big count . . .'

'A whit?' the blood boy asked.

Jimmy emptied the wet tea leaves in the bottom of his can at him. 'Shurrup. Yer spilin' ma story. A big count I said. Anyway, the count turns round and he says – "Aye, so they are."'

'Is that the end?'

'Aye.'

'Well, I don't get it!'

Jimmy looked at the boy with his black eyebrows raised. Mat said, 'Well, you see, the servant said that the peasants were *revolting* you know, out wi' the old pitchforks. Right? Ye get that bit?'

'Aye.'

'And the count thought he meant *revolting*,' Mat held his nose fastidiously. 'You see? You get it?'

'Aye. But it's no' very funny. And anyway, what's it got to do wi' pheasants?'

'Ach!' Mat flapped his hand at him in disgust.

'Did ye not know how the toffs eat pheasant. They hang them up until the maggots are crawling on them,' Jimmy said.

'Ah, I see. And they used to hang the peasants tae. And that's why they were revolting.'

'Don't say nae mair until you've seen your lawyer. He's getting you all tangled up.'

'Aye, that's right.' Jimmy turned to Mat, his palms uppermost, a look of surprised bafflement on his face. He shook his head. 'Oh, what a tangled web we weave . . .'

Jake had come back during this, listening with his head poked through the doors of the killing room and laughing. 'That bugger's a' tangled up to start wi' . . .'

'Hullo there, Jake. Anything doing?'

'We've four beasts to fell. Then finish.' He brought his arm, palm downwards across his body. Everybody groaned, but they got up and went through into the killing room to find their knife kits and their aprons.

The first two beasts were felled and hung up and the second pair down on the floor. Mat was stroking his knife on his steel and taking the last puff of a fag which he had lit between fellings. He bent down and made the first incision in the beast's head, under the chin. There was a kind of commotion which made him look up. He saw the lorry driver from the market, standing talking to Jake. Part of what the man was saying came to him: 'I don't know how badly . . .' Then he noticed Jake. He had his head down and his hands were scrabbling at the buckle of his belt. He seemed to move urgently, tottering on his feet, turning towards the hooks to hang up his belt and scaling his knives on the floor. When he pulled his apron off the flap came up covering his face but Mat caught a glimpse of it, tense and suddenly white. the lorry driver turned and saw Mat. All he said was, 'Mat,' but Mat moved towards him and the urgency of his movement made everyone stop and look up.

'What is it?' Mat asked. But before the man could answer

Jake said, 'It's Dad. An accident.' In the rise and fall of his voice there was a heave of panic, then its sudden control. Mat felt the same movement in himself, a quick reflex of feeling so that he wanted to gasp, then a sudden absence of feeling. As the lorry driver spoke to them Mat felt the continual ebb and flow of panic and numbness.

'It just happened. And I was passing.' They nodded at him. By this time Mat was himself taking off his kit and apron and feeling the fear ease as he did so. 'Just on the bend as you pass round the park. The two lorries went into one another. Doug, your old man, was in the passenger seat. The load went through the cabin.' They had both pulled their pullovers over their bloodied shirts and were putting on their jackets. Mat had left his apron and knife lying on the slaughter-house floor. The lorry driver followed them as they ran down the pass together. Then he shouted. 'Mat, Jake.' When they turned he spoke with difficulty, warning them. 'It looks bad.'

They didn't speak but turned and started to trot down the pass. They ran together, then slowed down and started to walk, very fast, then broke out into a run again as if following the rhythm of their panic. Mat felt unreal, his cheeks puffed and slack as if he'd been crying, and everything going on round about seemed a stupid meaningless jumble – the porters, the beef, the little knots of sheep being herded into the penning area, the lorries, vans, drovers, buyers, barrowmen. Some of the men they knew shouted to them, waved cheerily, and Mat felt a strange thrill as he watched Jake wave back to some of them, his arm in a weird, still pose. Then as they passed by carrying their anxiety with them the usual common activities seemed bizarre and cruel as if everything ought to have stopped. He had the sensation as if he was watching himself and Jake as they ran, then walked down the long pass towards the street. He felt life inside himself only in that hard mechanical centre which watches us as we act and feel, and it seemed to watch him as he was being immersed in his panic and grief. It seemed to see them, both himself and Jake, as they were tugged by their fear like a pair of marionettes on strings. This banal reflex life continued to work in him and as they stood at the bus stop his eye kept reading an advertising hoarding on the other side of the street. They didn't speak but stood right at the edge of the pavement beside the bus sign watching for the bus. Mat looked at Jake and saw only a calm reposed face. A lorry passed, and Jake's eyes held the lorry in their sight until it passed then flickered back to watch the road. Then his gaze seemed to wander idly about in a mechanical search. Their father had been hurt in an accident, maybe very badly, and everything that was going on seemed extra to that thing. Jake lit a cigarette and carefully crumpled the empty packet and put it into the wastepaper basket attached to the bus sign. Mat heard himself repeat over and over again, 'Keep the streets tidy.' He himself was idly kicking his heel against the edge of the pavement and flaking off the blood which had congealed on his boot.

Again he felt the strings pulling them as the bus came and they got on and paid their fares and sat in absence on the top deck. Mat lit a cigarette and bowed over it, cupping it in his hand and drawing it until it burnt his mouth. When the bus came round the long bend at the park it slowed down as it reached the place where the accident had happened. They caught a glimpse from the top of the bus of the lorries slewed half over on to the pavement, the big yellow crane parked beside them, the dark uniforms of the policemen. The bus slowed down to pass round the twisted lorries and Mat and Jake jumped off and ran over to the police sergeant who was standing beside the smashed-in cabin of one of the lorries. Jake spoke to the sergeant and he took out his notebook and read out their father's name and address.

'It's our father,' Jake said. The police sergeant was calm and composed as he told them that the ambulance had just left. He wasn't able to say anything about the accident, except that Doug had been getting a lift home from the night shift. There had been four men involved. One of them, one of the drivers, had only been shocked but had gone in the ambulance. The other three had been injured. He couldn't say anything about the extent of their injuries. They had been severe so far as he understood, a doctor had arrived at the scene almost as soon as it had occurred. Mat looked at the smashed-in cabin, the splintered glass lying over the street, and wondered at the force that could have caused such a wreck. Somehow, as he watched the two constables measuring the street with their tape, he thought that what they were doing was terribly right and fitting. He felt the ease of relief that there was no blood showing in the inside of the cabin, then something tightened in him like a tourniquet and cut off the thought of his father's spilled blood, so that he was able to feel relief at its not being there without thinking the complementary thought that it might have been.

'It'll maybe be all right,' Mat said to Jake. It was the first word they had spoken to one another since before they had left their work. It wasn't necessary that their father should be seriously injured. You could have an accident without getting anything worse than a broken leg. It wasn't necessary – Mat felt the heavy oscillation of hope and despair as he looked again at that ferociously smashed cabin. But they decided what to do. Mat was to go to the infirmary. 'I'll go and get Ma,' Jake said, and Mat wasn't sure if he meant he'd go for her or to her. The sergeant offered Jake a lift and Jake nodded. But when he went to step inside the low raking police car he stepped back and pointed to his mucky dungarees. Then as Jake helped the policeman to spread a newspaper on the seat Mat watched the piteous common spreading movement of his hands, and he found himself counting the black and white squares on the policeman's cap.

The numbness remained with Mat on his journey to the hospital. Later on, he realised that he must have had to change buses to get there, but he never ever remembered doing so. All he remembered of the journey was a collage of shop fronts and windows flying past him as he sat on the top deck of the buses. He was only in the hospital five minutes when he knew that his father was dead. He remembered the face of the young doctor who seemed to have come out of a mist. Mat told him of the accident and the doctor went in through a swinging door into a room full of shiny vessels like tea-urns. There was a murmuring of voices, the young doctor stood in the half open door. He nodded his head saying 'Yes,' each time. Then he turned towards Mat and opened the door fully to allow the other doctor to come out and Mat could see in their faces that his father was dead. In the nurse's face as she stood looking towards the door and fingering the white starched apron that was pinned to her dress, in the decline of the young doctor's resigned head as he held open the door. The older doctor spoke to Mat. 'Mr Craig?'

'Yes.'

'Mr Craig! Your father was dead when he was brought into the hospital. We think that perhaps he was killed instantly in the accident.' The doctor broke the news to Mat quickly and cleanly like pulling off a plaster.

Mat felt a sound rising in his throat but all he did was breathe very deeply. He wanted to wait in the corridor until Jake and his mother came. The doctor gave him permission to wait there and to smoke and Mat sat down on a bench seat hunched over his cigarette and gazing at the square tiles on the floor.

When Jake arrived with his mother Mat stood up to meet them. They came hurrying forward to him along the corridor not as if they were together but like two strangers who happened to be going the same way. In the hurried anxious way they turned into the corridor and walked quickly towards him, in their faces turned towards him, Mat could see the hope, still alive. As if at their sudden arrival at the place where they'd *know*, the realisation of Doug's actual death, the actuality of it was too impossible and they both started to hope. He stepped forward remembering the doctor's humane brutality, thinking to stop them hoping like this, before their hope got any larger, to tell them the worst before they started to expect the best. He meant to speak out directly, trying to force himself, but at the moment when he opened his mouth he felt a sudden reflex like a burnt finger being withdrawn so that he spoke with diffidence, his voice coming out in a whisper. 'Dad's dead.'

They had been standing apart waiting on Mat to speak and now they turned towards one another. Jake simply bared his teeth in a wincing grin and his knee bent up spasmodically. He bowed his head in a ridiculous gauche way and kicked at the floor nervously with the toe of his wellington boot. Jetta raised her hand above her head and kept on repeating, 'Oh, my God!' Mat and Jake managed to get her to sit down and Jake sat beside her. For a brief moment Mat felt a luxurious pity for his mother and Jake well up in him; a pity which was calming and logical and meaningful against the sterile horror with which he had felt this contingency, this slip; these two crashing lorries with their brutal numb inertia. Jetta sat down on the bench with her knees spread awkwardly, showing the bright flowered apron which she wore to do her housework. Round the tops of Jake's boots there were a few wisps of straw still sticking up from when he had been carrying on earlier that morning. Mat thought of the persiflage, the idle warm human banter that had gone on that morning at work. He thought of Helen the night before, of his mother doing the housework, and it suddenly seemed to him that everything in human life – the everyday common tasks, sex, love, contentment, aspiration, ordinary human intercourse, hope, laughter, were like dirty snivelling little secrets being uncovered by this sneering, wicked, expedient, mechanistic force that was the world. Like that feeling we get when someone is hurt during some idle horseplay and laughter; like the children caught in their innocence in the bushes; like laughter being wiped from the face. With the bowing of his head, the quivering of the muscles round his mouth and chin, the aching of his rasping throat, the fierce excluding clench of the muscles round his eyes, Mat felt himself cringe in a complete and final shame and the absolute blush of living flush through his body.

13

DOUG WAS ONLY fifty when he was killed. He had been a youngest son, born when his own mother was thirty-eight and his father, old John Craig, had been in his forties. His mother had died in her eighties only half-a-dozen years before, his father only a year before that at the age of ninety-three. Both of them had been old and frail but alert, with all their faculties and most of their teeth. Their great physical endowments had been passed on to Doug. Mat remembered when he used to strip off to wash at the sink, that his body was so youthful; resilient, beautifully toned and alive. Under the arc of his chest the ribs splayed out with his breathing as flexibly as a baby's. As he dried himself across the white hairless chest the round fatless biceps and muscles of his arms bubbled fluently under the skin. It was this remembrance of his athletic physical life which hurt Mat most. His lovely erect strutting walk in the street, with the controlled swing of the hip and the loose easy jerk of the knee that made his trousers flap around the ankles; the way he'd move about in a confined space – in the house he'd pad about like a big soft cat. From Doug's reminiscences Mat realised that he had never been properly fed as a child, certainly not during many years of his adult life. He seemed to have held his physical toughness, his endurance and energy in a state of pure grace. And what he had been given in grace, together with its promises, had now been taken away from him by accident.

So it was not just piousness that made people say that Doug had been good for another forty years, for it was certain that Doug would have remained a fit and healthy man for many years. Mat found that his intimately physical memory of his father made it impossible for him to consign Doug into that invalid and pathetic realm in which the dead are put, nor could he remember him with a softened and assuaged grief. Jetta's was a volatile grief, fluid and healing. Jake's was stubborn and painful but yielding to time. Mat observed the formalities but inside himself he coldly refused to mourn his father, except for when with a vivid talent for his hurt he would see his father in the quick and lose him as freshly as he did that day at the hospital. In Mat's life there took place for a while the obliteration of any other consideration than his obligation to Jetta and Jake.

All during the summer he, with Helen and young John, visited his mother every Sunday afternoon. Jake would always be there and sometimes other members of the family, some of Jetta's sisters, or one of her useless brothers. None of Doug's family ever came on these visits. Since the death of old 'Faither', Jetta's father, it had to some extent been Doug and Jetta who had made the running in the family, had been the focus around whom they gathered. And now, during these gatherings, it was the family which was talked about and discussed. Mat found his enthusiasm and attention to this gossip as great as anyone else's.

At first, immediately after Doug's death, Jetta had gone down to Rothesay to stay with a sister. She had stayed away for nearly five weeks, then when she came back the Sunday visits started. There was a way in which they were happy months for all of them, as if they were spending their time rounding off the past and Doug's part in it. Jetta's reminiscences were tearful at first, but as the months passed the tears lightened. The remembrances welled up from her as easily as water from a spring. Mat suppressed the acute immediacy of his own memories and remembered through Jetta as he listened to her stories. Sometimes when her sisters were present they all seemed to contribute – someone would smile and say 'Remember when . . . ?' and with patches of story they would put together a whole life, a background, a history. Occasionally Mat encouraged them, for he would often find himself stirred and moved by this repetitive 'when' and he'd feel a child-like thrill of curiosity as one of Jetta's sisters would raise her blonde freckled face and speak. One time he asked:

'I often wonder at that lampshade, the big one, of orange coloured silk with the tasselled frill, remember, that hung round the gas light, ben the room, in Faither's?'

'Everybody had one of those, ben the room. If you didn't have a shade like that you were naebody.'

'Was that right?'

'Aye. I didn't think you would be able to remember it though, Mat.'

'Aye. I remember.'

'That would be the second one. Do you remember what happened to the first one, Jetta?'

'Do I not?'

And the story of the burnt lampshade would be told. But it wove and interwove with other stories, sometimes with things which Mat remembered, sometimes with events which happened before he was born.

'I never liked being in a big family,' Jetta said. 'In fact, I felt ashamed. Doug would take me to his house and everything was that orderly.'

It was too, Mat thought, and remembered with bitterness how that order in Doug's family had clashed with Faither's family, Jetta, and the rest of his sprawling brood of useless children. That was in the times of the tilted slum when Mat and Jake had gravitated towards that useless family and had learned wildness and dirty habits. Not that this had worried Doug. He had been a renegade from the Craigs, like old John Craig, his father, had been before him. But Doug's mother had raised his sisters to such standards of respectability that had tightened the lines about their mouths and burdened them with insincerity. Doug's sisters had been shocked at the casual upbringing of Mat and Jake and had often snooped around with their dripping aquiline noses. They had bothered Jetta at times so much that she had remained in her own eyes an outcast from a big family. It was laughable to Mat when he thought that both Doug and Jetta had come from an equally large family. To Jetta her own family, old Faither's brood, must have just seemed bigger.

'I told him I was the youngest and he came up to see us every Sunday night for a year. Well, I put the four wee yins ben the room every Sunday night and I told them I'd murder them if they made a noise. So nobody was to tell him and nobody was to send out for chips when he came. At the Craigs' you got lettuce and cold meat with side plates and bought cakes. In our house there was always a big pot of soup on the range, and I used to be terrified, *terrified* in case somebody just helped themselves. Everybody was warned and Faither used to laugh at me. My mother was an awful one for puddin' suppers, but she never sent out for a single puddin' supper on a Sunday night for a year. Then one night they all started screaming and Doug ran through the lobby. They had set fire to the lampshade and Doug had put out the fire. Doug said to me, "Who the hell are they?" and I had to tell him they were my younger brother and my three young sisters. I felt that ashamed. All Doug said to me was "Jesus Christ, Jetta."'

Once Jetta said mysteriously to Helen without ever explaining the remark, 'In a' my early years o' marriage I never had a decent bread-knife.' It had something to do with the taunts of the respectable sisters-in-law about her housekeeping. Mat could remember them well, their insincere drawling voices as they would take Jetta down. It had been one thing for which Jetta had never forgiven Doug, that he just hadn't prevented them from coming around. 'In oor young days it was the lassies that went oot tae work for the men couldnae *get* jobs. And I never knew a *thing* about housekeeping when I got married.'

As Mat and Jake grew older these sisters stopped coming around. At first they used to blow raspberries at them in the street. Jake got a terrific hammering from Doug for calling one of them 'an effing old bitch'. Then, as they grew older still, Jake became too much for them altogether. 'Susan was the worst o' them wi' thon questions she'd ask, "That's a lovely drop soup, Jetta, what's in it?" when she knew damn well it was nothing but a bit bacon rind.' In the end Jake was able to match their sly hypocritical speiring. Mat could remember one of the last rounds which Jake and Susan had together.

Susan had come one Sunday to dinner. Jake must have been about sixteen at the time. He had anticipated her every sneering question to Jetta and mocked and mimicked her voice, her style, her very attitude, saying grace at the table, belittling all the dishes so that she hadn't been able to get a word in. After dinner she had said to Jetta, 'Jake and Mat were aye such sturdy boys.' She sighed as if to say, 'With such an upbringing.'

'Well, you see,' Jake said, 'the devil looks after his own.'

A little later she spoke to Jake again. He had been sitting or lounging about the whole day in his old clothes and with more than a day's growth of beard. But at that time it was only a faint shadow on the corners of his jaw. 'I see you've started shaving, Jake.'

'Shaving? Whit fur?'

'Well, you have got a beard,' Susan said.

'Call this a beard. It's only bum fluff. God, I've got mair hair on my belly. Look.' Jake opened up his shirt, pulled up his singlet and exposed the dark line of fell which ran from his pubes up to his chest. 'It's all right. Ma belly's clean. So's ma semmit. And ma drawers. Ma washes them every month whether they need it or not.' For years Susan and the rest of her sisters had defeated Jetta with their sleekit questions which always meant something else. In Jetta they had always been able to provoke anger, but now they were afraid of Jake's hilarious rebuffs and they stayed away.

Mostly, however, the harshness and bitterness in Jetta had been strained away through the sieve of memory. Although Mat remembered the harshness as it was lived – the long end-half of the week when they would fill up on bread and margarine, the cold nights when Jetta would be out scrubbing and Jake and he would await her home coming and shiver from the cold in the dusk – the others Jetta and her sisters, would spin their tales in a different way. In the end it became clear to Mat that what they were remembering was not so much the events, the circumstances, touching, evocative and funny though they were, but that same sense of promise, of youth, that had been lost. And however vague their expectations had been, Doug's and Jetta's, it was certain that life had fulfilled very little of that promise. Mat was sure that they too had felt their lives being worn away all during that time of the tilted tenement floor. There was something else too, something which Jetta's stories, and all those of her red-haired sisters, had in common, something which Doug must have held to. There had been a middle-aged placidity in Doug's and Jetta's life since they had come to live in the council house which suggested in its contentment that they had shelved their expectations, had passed them on elsewhere. The stories pointed more and more to where these expectations had gone.

Every one of the Devlins had tried to spoil Mat. It had come from something he was never aware of until he had nearly left school. There was a schoolteacher, a friendly, warm and decent woman whom Mat had led a life of hell. Yet once when he had done something which had infuriated her she had stopped in the middle of her fury, held his head in her hands and had said wistfully to him, 'And you are such a bonny child.' At that time Mat became aware of a useful winning thing in himself, but he did not care for his teacher's regret that it should be squandered in extravagant childish wilfulness. Somehow, he was always forgiven and Jetta and her sisters related the stories of his childish mischief until they began to take on the size of tokens.

'Eleven full pounds he was the day he was born.'

'He had a black down all over his back.'

'The bluest eyes.'

'And born on a Sunday.'

A Sunday child. Mat laughed at these stories, yet when they showed him the photographs of the fair curly-haired boy – he had been fair, and like Jetta, the only other dark-haired one, his hair had darkened as he had grown – he had felt a disturbing catch in his breath at the clear line of grace, the lovable, forgivable precocity in the child which was himself and which even the stiff clumsily taken snapshots had failed to hide.

'For the child that is born on the Sabbath Day,
Is bonny and blithe and good and gay.'

Such a child must have been a menace and a burden. He remembered how the Craigs had hated him and how the Devlins had, without stint or grudge, given in to him and forgiven his every tantrum and meanness. Jetta's sister Mary told once how he had kicked in the panel of the door because she had refused to give him a half-penny. Yet when it came to punishing him she couldn't and had ended by giving him the money he wanted. She told with pride how he had let down the table leaf under a complete and valuable dinner set, as if it had been an honour to her that he should do such a thing. Another aunt, Lizbeth, let him wipe his nose on the sleeve of her coat until it became a family joke. And now these aunts with families of their own would say with unstinted pride:

'But your Mat was aye our bonniest wean.'

Not just Jetta's bonniest wean, nor Doug's, but ours, the family's, everyone's.

'Doesn't it make your head swell?' Helen once asked Mat, laughing. Mat had examined his face in the mirror. It was lean, a bit hard, with the blue of his eyes flashing against the dark, but the teeth were crooked, his skin male and coarse grained, the head a little heavy against the column of the neck. Ordinary enough, he thought with satisfaction.

'Sometimes,' he said to Helen, 'it's just as hard learning to be awkward.'

Even Jake was not cynical at these times and would add his admiration to the history. 'The bugger would always get himself out of any trouble.'

All this Mat coldly rejected. All during the thirties his father had worked as a fire drawer in a railway-yard. Mat remembered once Doug being burned when he fell on a shovelful of hot coals. He had come home with his hands and face all covered in unwashed blisters, with the coal and the ash still sticking to him. Jetta had washed and cleaned the burns herself and Doug had gone on to his next shift, his hands all bandaged, wearing an old pair of woollen gloves and with his face all smeared with vaseline. He could remember him, too, when he had had toothache, having a big molar extracted without anaesthetic, to save money, then coming home with his jaw torn and bleeding to snatch a few hours' sleep before his next shift. And all this for a comfortless arid life on a tilted tenement floor.

Mat and Jake had inherited some possessions from their father; a gunmetal watch, studs, cuff-links, a silver watch and chain with a nail clipper attached, a pen knife, a wooden flute and his books. Jake asked Mat to take the books but Mat preferred to leave them with Jetta in the council flat. But one book Mat did take for a while. They found it, not in the bookshelves but lying in the drawer, a tiny book bound in a kind of pink suède. It had been well thumbed through and in places there were lines underlined in pencil. It was a copy of Edward Fitzgerald's translation from Omar Khayyám. It was a book which had been well read by Doug's generation, yet Mat wondered how it could have spoken at all to Doug. For himself he read the poem coldly, repelled by its aristocratic air, its refined sated hedonism. There was nothing that Mat could see in it that could have meant anything to Doug, or would mean anything in his world of bitter poverties, of limited choice.

Yet it had been the same with his other books. The underlining of a striking phrase, the annotations and marginal notes were all characterised by the weak, pathetic literariness of the self taught. Even the working books, the ones which had formed the basis of a practical dream, the books by Marx, Shaw, G. D. H. Cole were not in fact used as tools which would help to explore the world, act on it, understand it, but as authorities for an idealistic and impractical dream of socialism, a sentimentalised orthodoxy, a pathetic and futile hope for utopia. In the little pink book Doug had scored under the line,

'Ah, take the Cash in hand and waive the Rest;'

And Mat thought with a direct hard sourness that even Doug's bitterness had been misdirected.

Doug's was no case for grief, or mourning, for in grief and mourning there comes eventual assuagement. Nor was his life capable of redemption by any act, achievements or success on Mat's part. He was dead and could not confirm his expectations any more, not even through his bonny wean. Yet, Mat thought, he'd write a story of this bonny wean, a story of a bonny gifted child who'd scatter his useless gifts about the world; a story of prodigality, of waste, of squandering, which would contain all his sourness, pessimism and accusation; and his love too, for that battered and violated grace which had gone – from Doug and the useless spendthrift family into which he had married.

14

A FULL YEAR passed from the time of Doug's death until the time when Mat seriously thought of writing his new novel. At first there had been the period of recuperation from the single fact of Doug's death, then the long convalescent-like period of stock-taking during which Mat had lived a steady dutiful life attending to the common realities of living without feeling any other compulsion. The seed of the new idea was laid in him round about this time. An ironic, rather bitter idea which could only have been held by a man suffering from an acute sense of loss. Yet as the idea grew in him – the picture of the small elegant life full of the tokens of promise – this picture of the favoured child who had been himself became more and more representative of something other than mere self love. Mat thought of the Devlins, with all their wit, musicality, generosity, energy, their priceless talents, their sheer exuberant being. He felt a contraction of the heart, an overwhelming sadness. It was the element of prodigality in all this, the knowledge that the value of the child's gifts lay simply in his unrestricted capacity for squandering his largesse, gave Mat the grave sense of the inevitability of loss. The idea that it was only the excessive, abundant spending of his gifts, their unsaved use, gave them their value. So the little graceful child became more and more representative of that sprawling useless brood that had come to being amid the smoke and the grime, the tilted tenements, the yards and factories and mills, the sprawling industrial choked-up muddle which was bound by that same loop of the Clyde which Mat had thought of so often in another context.

In the end Mat's resolution broke. He found himself again tempted into that bright lamplit area in the evenings when he would sit casting his mind back and round in his attempt to redeem all that was past, the destructive uselessness, the love, the generosity, Doug's death, the dissolution of his own promise, all that had been formative in the making of this wasted present, in the making of his own defect, his stigma, his failure. And to give the idea flesh Mat cast his memory back to that loop of the Clyde and he wrote of the fresh facile little boy about whose birth and upbringing were scattered these tokens of promise.

The bright summer of the next year had come before Mat had a sudden leaping exaltation, a notion that he was on to something. Along with the idea that had crept up on him to write the novel there was also a revulsion at the sheer physical bulk of the work. But as the months went by and he sat up at night under the circle of light he teased himself into the work, starting it and continuing almost unintentionally. Then one night as he sat working, or rather looking over his work, with his bits and pieces spread around him and the big cardboard box stuffed with his old rejected magnum opus on the floor beside him, he felt this spark inside him, this spark which grew into a warm glow of satisfaction. For he had recognised something, experienced the creative shock, felt the sudden click like a box shutting which the poets say happens when something comes right. The setting of the novel was somewhere in that same place which he had tried writing of before, the place which he only had to think about for him to be driven by this warm lust to make, to shape, to invent, to describe, this loop of the Clyde with its dusty streets and backyards, its crumbling walls and stretches of waste, its factories and chimneys and noise and nooks and people. And yet there was in his new theme something which excited him in its complementary opposition to the old. A glimmering of an idea here, the bonny wean, with his prodigal wilfulness, an idea which had something in it of the same motive, the same end, as his masterpiece of accumulation and acquisition which had never been written. The bonny wean, the facile profligate waster and the burghers, the men of controlled energy and thrift. There was something in the new idea which was an abandonment of the old, of the substitution of a new thing, the acceptance of the vagrant and lavish shapelessness of life, for the old, the order and rigour of an ethical idea.

Yet it was in a sense no abandonment either . . . But here Mat rejected any attempt at the discursive expression of his feelings for his two loves and saw them instead related in a warm and living image, in his felt experience – his remembrance of a need for excess, for recklessness, his love and admiration for the panache and sweetness of his useless family and his remembrance of a need to conserve, to guide, to order, to fear the loss of those things which were of value. It was as if the old idea had been lightened, swiftened by the new and the new idea had been darkened, thickened of meaning, as if its irresponsibility and extravagance had been given a quality of gravity and significance by the old. But what thrilled Mat, what gave him that classic shock of recognition, was that he had started that extraordinary new theme in opposition to the old in a direct creative way, quite unconscious of any later critical significance which he was now able to see in it.

From then on, during those times at night, Mat smiled to himself with satisfaction as he piled on the tokens, as the winds of portent blew hansel in on the bonny wean, and he thought of those shades which he would darken round the growing boy.

In that spring, before the year of the bright summer, Mat also wrote some stories and sent two of them away. They were both stories he had written in a kind of mechanical way, according to the strict economies of the short story which he had read about. He wrote the stories with a certain contempt and with only enough competence to make them work. They were in strict narrative form, stories which one read in order to get to the end, their only real appeal being to the reader's curiosity. They were not in any way involved with the responsibility to experience which Mat felt his work had, even the overweight magnum opus that had fallen in on itself and failed. They had as their moral centre only those vaguely pious sentiments of the love-one-another-or-die kind. They were hard to write because they were boring and routine; and they both brought in money.

For a while now Mat had been paying regular visits to the house of the poet George Duncan, the little man whom he had met that same afternoon when he had strayed into the picture gallery. Duncan lived only a few minutes' ride on the tramcar away and Mat went to see him, sometimes once in a couple of weeks, sometimes more often. Duncan stayed in a tiny room and kitchen in a tenement with his wife and two children. Between Mat and Duncan there had grown an odd relationship. In one way Mat didn't like the man – he felt out of sympathy with him in a direct, almost physical, way. Duncan had a penchant for red colours, his house was decorated with wallpaper patterned with hideous dark red fleur-de-lys against a pale pink background, there were pink plastic curtains on the windows, red linoleum, a crimson carpet, a bedspread of a different shade of pink, the bed curtains were of plushy, dark mahogany coloured material, the woodwork was stained amber colour and was artificially grained.

Sometimes when Mat went to see him they would play with the children's games – draughts, Chinese checkers, but mostly those kinds of games played in tiny glass topped boxes in which little steel balls rolled through complicated mazes, or tiny bagatelle boards, or wire puzzles, or a delicate game played with fragile pieces of coloured stick – games which called for a kind of skill which Mat didn't have. He was so used to play of another kind, which gave expression to the boisterous needs of the body like playing tig up and down the diving board in the swimming baths; in the army he had boxed, played football and rugby; in the slaughter-house he mucked about wrestling; he was used to the releasing skills of the body and limbs. When Duncan got Mat to play these games which called

for skills of the hand, neatness and deftness, Mat would feel
irritated and constrained. But he would join in, out of a kind
of moral belief in games, but he was so clumsy at them that he
couldn't enjoy the fun. When they ate Mat got the same feeling
– Duncan drank his tea very weak, very sweet and milky and
had a terrific passion for sweet cream-filled biscuits. At teatime
they ate cold meat out of tins, or processed cheeses or tinned
fruits. Duncan spoke quite consciously to Mat about his tastes.
He tended towards vegetarianism, not out of principle, but out
of a revulsion of anything organic. He boasted to Mat of his
buying monosodium glutamate, a substance which seemed to
give flavour to food by exciting the taste buds and gingering up
the appetite. It was this quality of fastidiousness which perhaps
put Mat out of sympathy with Duncan, seeming as it did to
come from a desiccated appetite which had to be whetted
artificially. Mat preferred the bland, more direct flavours of
untreated food. He was in a way proud of his palate, and the
harsh chemical bite of the food at the Duncans' offended him
and caused him something of the same feeling he had when
Duncan foisted his games on to him.

Duncan also collected pin-ups and indulged himself in a
mild kind of voyeurism, cutting out pictures of girls from
glossy fashionable magazines and filing them away. In his
physical make-up, with his beautiful boned head, his ethereal
blue eyes, his small deft hands, his daintly pursed lips hiding
the ugly impacted teeth, there was a quality which repelled
Mat in its non-masculinity. It was not that he was effeminate
so much that he was un-male in his beautiful lack of appetite.
These revulsions which Mat felt in an immediate way as an
un-like of the man were added to by his constant harping
about literary integrity. Mat disagreed with him entirely that
integrity was a thing that needed thinking about. Mat had his
own private term for something which he called his 'entelechy'
and he was simply unable, coming to the experience of art the
way he did, to write out of anything other than the private
distinctness of his own experience. He had not the kind of

talent, the kind of cleverness, to write anything without the pressure of experience forcing him; he only wrote with his 'entelechy', with his back up against his material. It was a phrase which Mat often used to Duncan when he was being criticised for flirting with Sam Richards' crowd and indulging himself in intellectual chit-chat. They were all published poets who came to Duncan's house and among them there was a good deal of spite and small literary envies. Duncan would warn Mat about these and flaunt his own purity in such matters. In all his warnings were the implications that Mat was an innocent, open to the blandishments of the literary crowd who came around, weak to their flattery but good material if he could avoid the taint, the corruption. Mat was indifferent to all this, having taints and corruptions of his own to think about. To him, someone else's success was a matter for a shrug of indifference – 'it's no skin off my nose' – he'd say to Duncan. He was often surprised that the last thing anyone noticed in him was his arrogance, his final and utter indifference to anything other than his 'entelechy'. He was surprised that in spite of his own egotism, his dark private obsession, his slow stand with his back to his own material, they should think him in any way malleable. He was surprised that they were so unaware of them. But his real attitudes he kept to himself.

All this on the negative side might have made Mat lose interest in Duncan, but there were the complications of Mat's own kind of fastidiousness. He could not elevate what was a mere feeling of dislike into a moral judgement, he felt it unfair to dislike a man for no reason. Then in another way Duncan won Mat's loyalty from him. The first came when Duncan spoke about writing, about art. Then all of Mat's reservation went overboard, for in spite of Duncan's continual harping about integrity, in his attitude towards art, his own and other men's work, there was a hard-won love and honesty. And when he wrote – there Mat saw something which made him thrill. For he knew the man, knew his sensations, his obsessions and miseries, his difficulties and the day to day affronts which the world put on him, knew his work through the day in the dull office, knew what he hoped for from art, knew his disappointments, something of his fatigue and lack of appetite, knew something of his greyness; he knew his surroundings – the breadcrumbs on his table, the clock on his mantelpiece, his vegetables in the cupboard, his children, his wife, his stairway down into the street, his window-panes, his dust – and out of this inchoate diminishedness he saw his poetry being created. In the astringent, witty order of the poems he saw the obliteration of Duncan's misery and malice. Mat saw in his enjoyment and love of words, a quality, almost technical, in which Duncan's frozen morality of integrity was lost or overridden; his scrupulous craftsmanship, his artifice, in which all his reproach and meanness was purified into a clear hardness. He saw the mess of Duncan's life take shape, he saw his style. It was something which only showed in his poetry, but it gave Mat a rollicking sense of exuberance and satisfaction. Often Mat thought of Duncan as he'd seen him once in the street, with his halo of dull hair frizzing round his delicate skull, his tidy suit, his sad, inward, pathetic walk. He felt a loyalty and love for something in him, the thing from which he took his easy style. It was Duncan's own 'entelechy.'

Duncan had no sense whatever that he could influence Mat through his work. Perhaps in anything to do with his real creativeness there was humility. But he did try to influence Mat through exhortation, continually carping at Mat, suggesting themes, harping on and on at him to write, what to write, how to write, where to send his stuff. In the end, in a kind of reaction of irritation Mat had written several stories and two of them had brought in money.

It was because of one night which Mat was to remember, when he had first started to put down something on the background to the new work about the bonny wean. There had been several people at Duncan's house that night. The conversation had taken on a hectic flush. Mat had spoken tentatively of his idea that he would like to try writing a novel and had found himself at the centre of everyone's attention. He was reproached for not writing. Especially at this particular time, for there was a new something in the air, changes coming about, a new flowering of working-class literature, a new tone. Why shouldn't Mat do something? He had the background, the right kind of humour, the social insight, the sensitivity to change and new directions. Mat had been unable to express his disagreement, but demurred in a dumb kind of way.

The things they talked about were offensive to Mat – keeping pace with life, newness, which was an idea anathema to Mat, the frantic race for modernity. Duncan read only that work which was absolutely fresh from the pen like the American beats, the French experimental novelists. In returning more and more in the evenings to the circle of lamplight in order to ease himself into this extravagantly bulky and ambitious work which Mat was proposing to himself it was the very question of pace, of timing himself, which came uppermost in his mind, of reserving his energies, of the slow easing out of what was fresh in him. By sheer effort of will he had resisted that tingling thrusting adrenalin surge in himself, had by effort, by calm and lucid thought, tried to relax his time sense, making an atmosphere of silence and leisure. He tried not to force himself by getting into the rhythm, the swing of creation, by letting things come. But his calmness at his desk, being the result of a conscious effort of will, was particularly vulnerable to upset.

And now they talked about 'setting the pace' and it made Mat miserable. He thought of his own slow growth and protested that what they were asking of him were the quick day-to-day responses of journalism. He was not out of sympathy with contemporary writing – but what these men meant could not be decided in a day – one day their work was taken as if it had concluded something, the next it was taken as false prophecy – the responsibility for the immediate evaluation of all this change and flux was a false one – all the hectic atmosphere it generated was false – the works themselves were being ignored by the literary journalists in their desperate hurry for meaning – all these tremendous significances were in the end only journalistic copy. 'It's all very decade-ent,' Mat joked, but he felt very much on the defensive.

Going home in the tram later Mat thought of this talk, that it had, in spite of his protestations, awakened a dangerous egotism in him. In spite of his protests he felt that it would be tempting to enter into this world in which ideas were hurled about so excitedly. It was a temptation of power, the enticing glamour of participation. But it was also a threat to his 'entelechy', his right to be slow, to move at his own pace. It exerted a kind of pressure to false change, to adaptation rather than growth. Against all this Mat felt in himself a black reactionary mood, for he could see no redemption or guilt in any of the new styles of architecture, nor in the images of modernity.

The effort to keep calm was too great in the end for Mat to sustain; however inimical he felt the mood of the world to be to real creativeness, he eventually succumbed to it and wrote these stories which had brought him money. Wrote them out of a kind of irritated reaction against the pressures of time and the world.

15

TO MAT THE story of the bonny wean began with Doug, in his real physical existence, standing before the mirror brushing his hair. He would take a brush in each hand and run them in consecutive strokes, backwards, over his thick auburn hair. After that, just as Jetta would put the dinner on the table, he would roll his shirt sleeves down carefully so not to spoil the stiffness of the starched cuffs, adjust his sleeve bands and put his waistcoat on. Then, just before sitting down to dinner, he would stand erect and tug at his clothes, hauling and smoothing at his waistcoat, wriggling and shifting his body under the clothes. When finally he sat down to dinner he would first give his trousers a little deft hitch at the knees.

In those days everything was always in a state of suspense when Doug dressed himself. At any time he was likely to go off into a violent tantrum if the dinner didn't please him or if there wasn't a clean hanky. Sometimes, too, when he'd look into the chest of drawers in his own private drawer where he kept his handkerchiefs, his lighter, tie pin, cuff-links, nail clips, cigarette case, he would imagine that something was missing. At the very least he would grumble away all during the meal, 'You can find nothing in this house.' Then sometimes Jetta would leave a towel hanging over the back of a chair and Doug would yell, with soap in his eyes, clutching around the hook at the door of the press cupboard, 'Where's the bloody towel?' Doug lived then amidst the squalor, on an island of his own neatness and order, defending himself against Jetta's disorder and carelessness with bouts of desperate anger.

Mat sat up late again at night chewing the end of his

ball-point pen, dreaming, musing, recalling with his arm
curled round the sixpenny jotter, trying to make some pattern
out of the conflict of order and mess which had been the
background of his young life. He drew out of that fund of
common remembrance in the family, from talk, from old
photographs, from his own memories.

First he wrote the story of Doug – as a young man, when
he came home from work to the Craig household. Everyone
had their own hook in the lobby to hang up their working
clothes. Doug wasn't allowed to sit down in the house with his
working clothes on but had to wash and change right away, as
soon as he came in. Even washing was routine. First, soaping
and scrubbing the fingers and nails to get rid of the coal dust
which was liable to work its way into the skin of the palms
and round the cuticle of the nails. There was always a piece of
pumice stone lying beside the soap dish for this, and a big hard
nail brush. Then soaping and scrubbing at the arms and chest
with the loofah, then the face, neck and hair. He had to be
sure to rinse himself properly with a big sponge so that there
wouldn't be a bit of soap froth to go on the towel. He wouldn't
have to look for the sponge either, even with soap in his eyes.
He would only have to reach out and find the sponge lying
in its wire rack above the soap dish. Everyone in his family,
brothers and sisters, had good complexions, bright and ruddy.
They all cleaned the insides of their ears with a corner of the
towel and washed their teeth with kitchen salt.

When Doug came back from the Great War he had his toes
crumpled up with frost bite and a slight deafness which came
from an infection or an injury to the eardrums. It made him
seem morose. With his big chest and the way he'd speak out
of his guts when he turned round to one of his family, saying,
'Eh?' they'd think he was annoyed or irritated instead of just
wanting to know what people said. Often he'd get morose and
sulky at other people's touchiness not knowing about his own
apparently offensive mannerism. But when he had met Jetta
she spoke in the distinct musical Devlin voice so different from

the nasal pulpit whine of the Craig sisters, so that he didn't have to say 'Eh?' to her.

However much Jetta was drawn to the Craigs by their circumspect respectability she was never able to emulate it. She was a Devlin, from a big family, wild and careless, plebeian, generous and happy. She lived in a house where there was always cooking, cups of tea and spilled milk. Everything prodigal, shampoos and curlers, broken egg shells and porridge sticking to the cooker. At first everything had been fine. Doug had come home from work to hang his dungarees still on his own hook, to have everything ready for him – loofah, sponge, towel. He still had the good underwear, the poplin shirts, the serge suits which he had inherited from his single life. He would sit reading the paper at night, sitting up stiffly in the armchair in his good clothes but without the studs or collar in his shirt and flicking the ash of his cigarette carefully into the fireplace.

When Jetta became pregnant she grew plump and was often too tired to do the housework properly. She started to go round to the neighbours' houses, gossiping and drinking cups of tea. Often when Doug came home from work his dinner wouldn't be quite ready or else Jetta would be out. He hated coming into the empty house: What was worse, Jetta left dishes lying in the sink, maybe lying in the basin with tea leaves blocking up the plug hole. Doug would have to lift the basin on to the cluttered draining board and clear the sink of tea leaves. Sometimes the dishes would be washed but the face towel would be left soggy and Doug would wash himself, then with dripping arms and chest and wet hair, his face screwed up with soap in his eyes, he'd be forced to look for a clean towel in the chest of drawers. He used an open razor and it made him tired shaving at the mirror in front of the dirty sink, so tired that he'd cut himself and get into a bad mood.

The initial pleasure of building up a home had begun to fade for them. In the first year of their marriage they had gone every third week, when Doug was on day shift, to the

London Road and along to the 'barrows', where they picked up things. It was in this famous street market that they picked up the last to mend the shoes, screwdrivers, a plane, chisels, pliers for odd jobs round the house, huge earthenware plates that were still in use, the egg cups of turned wood that had all disappeared, the same miniature grandfather clock that had ticked in accompaniment to Mat's thoughts as he sat up years later reading and writing. They had picked up so many things – with the strange omission of that bread-knife.

Mat had heard the story of the missing bread-knife perhaps a dozen times in his life, the story which had marked the bitter separation of Doug and Jetta in all the middle years of their marriage. Jetta had told it with a flush on her cheeks, her eyes seemingly focused inside herself as she re-enacted the memory. The thing had wounded her so deeply, had so impressed itself on her memory that she told it as if fresh from the moment. It had happened as the first bloom of their marriage had begun to fade.

'Your father had a bone-handled knife.' She used to start telling the story briskly and unemotionally until she had laid out the details. 'He kept it very sharp. You know your father, how fussy he can be. Very sharp. And it was a good wee knife. I could use it for anything – vegetables, meat, chopping. I mean it was a real wee handy kitchen knife. Well, I used it for cutting bread too ...' At this point she would look directly at her listener, her voice becoming confident, so that Mat, when he heard her tell the story would remember with her, through her weariness, an old aptitude and energy. 'I was only a young lassie and there was a lot of things I couldn't do. But I could cut a loaf.' Here she would rest her elbows on the table, shaking her head to and fro. 'I could cut a loaf. As thin as you like. I've still got it in the cutlery drawer. Though I don't use it.' She was always silent for a minute at this point. Then she'd continue. 'Well, anyway. Rob and Susan. Your uncle Rob. They came. They used to come quite often then and I'd try to get everything nice. A nice tea and everything. This time I was cutting the bread with this wee knife and Susan says, you know her creeping bloody voice. She says, "Jetta, how long have you been married now, Jetta?" A year, says I, and she says, "And you haven't got a bread-knife yet?"'

Jetta could take off the 'creeping' sanctimoniousness of the female Craig voice to perfection. 'As if it was any of her business. Oh, she was aye that perfect. "How long have you been married, Jetta?" The bitch. The vicious bitch. The bloody disturber of the peace. Her man washing every dish for her. Her being aye that *unwell.* "And you haven't got a *bread-knife* yet?" Oh, she knew. She just knew. And him. Doug. A man should *support* his wife. But naw. Naw. He loses his rag wi' me. And supports her. But it was her. She knew how to rub him the wrong way. Thinking she was God's anointed just because she had some fancy china. Just the same. He could have said something to support me. He could have said something like, "Oh, Jetta can dae anything wi' that handy wee knife." But naw. Naw. Blood's thicker than water. He couldnae support me.'

These memories were something of Mat's 'entelechy'; this his material which he teased out and tried to shape under the lamp. Yet it all became strangely resistant to shape. In spite of the idea, the theme of the bonny wean which had seemed to Mat when it came to him to carry a clear lucid line of narrative, his story became too crowded, too eventful. Too often the pleasure of evoking to himself the childish timelessness, of writing of that world which had been given to him at one time, had tempted him and he had felt a strange reluctance to recount the bitterness and the conflict, to lay out the tensions which were later to tear him in two. Instead he'd write slowly with indulgent pleasure of that single time in his life before these family tensions, history and the world became apparent to him. Then he felt the old trouble again.

For week after week the mornings were lovely. Soft mild mornings when Mat would get up and in a half doze get ready to catch the first morning tram. The slaughter-house was slack again and Mat would travel home in the early afternoon in the hot tramcar through the busy Glasgow streets to the little back street which was full of dust and quivering with light from rows of window-panes. In the tiny kitchen Helen would open up the windows as far as they'd go but the air in the backyard would be lifeless, without a stir, and in the kitchen it would always be too hot. Young John was now big enough to sit in the little go-car and they'd dress him up and go out into the streets, or to the park and sit, letting the baby crawl in the grass. Sometimes Mat would fall asleep in the sunlight and wake up feeling as if he'd only just come into the world. They'd go home reluctantly to the tiny rooms.

In the evenings, after John had been bathed and put to bed, often long after Helen had gone to bed and fallen asleep, Mat would sit up. Often he'd smoke cigarette after cigarette then drink cold tea to ease the burning in his throat and tongue. And often his wilful attempt to relax would break down and he'd find himself alternately worrying and flogging at his theme or drifting off into a loose kind of thinking. He'd find himself sitting there without a drop of juice in him, drained, desiccated of feeling. He would sit there squeezing at himself, wringing his imagination to gather some drop when he would suddenly become aware in himself of something, first a generalised hunger which would later specify itself into a hot lust for sex, money, power, freedom, space. A ravenous appetite for experience, feeling, irresponsibility, refreshment, and he would lose himself in dreams of an unrestricted life of ease and enjoyment and leisure and free choice, of meals and women and drink and music and money. But above all he'd dream of two things – sex and money. Of sex and money unrelated to any responsibility of love or earning. Then he'd look round at the tiny cramped room, he'd listen to the breathing of Helen and the baby, he'd look at the sixpenny jotter held within the circle of his left arm and he'd feel arise in him the nausea, the revulsion, the disgust, the flatness, the staleness of the world and he'd gather the papers together, careless of any order, and throw them into the cardboard box. Afterwards, lying in bed smoking with his tongue still burning, he'd find these generalised lusts still raging in him and he'd fall off to sleep exhausted with wild coloured fancies of lust and violence, of power and self-destruction racketing in his head.

He had thought once that he should be able to tackle the job of writing out of nothing but his own moral energy when all other sources had dried up, but now he was becoming aware of the creative process in himself. It was a thing that would only respond to gentling. Somehow, his body, his appetites, his simple worldly needs were pushing themselves between him and the paper. His imagination refused to respond to flogging. He felt he would have to do something to make himself relax. Instead of making that constant wilful effort he would have to do something to make his outward life suitable for writing. It was Helen who proposed the answer.

It was on a Sunday morning that she made the suggestion. They had got up early before the day got hot, so as to enjoy the cool of the morning. After a good breakfast Mat had been sitting smoking and thinking of another Sunday morning many years ago. Sitting happy and relaxed with the first cigarette of the day, replete with food and sipping hot black coffee, he realised that he was working out in his head a passage of his new novel and he felt the delicious feeling of satisfaction, of having a taste for work. As he idly picked up a pen and got his bits and pieces together and opened up a new sixpenny jotter he felt this robust appetite for working without any interfering desires or hungers, with no other emptiness to fill. It was like a mental tumescence and his only desire was the act of writing. Nor when he had finished the act, when he had written out the passage in his head, did he feel any detumescent sadness, only a sense of relaxation and refreshment. It was the Sunday morning feeling, and when Mat had finished writing he sat back with the bits and pieces in front of him and talked to Helen. He was thinking about the word the poet had used – complacencies.

'If only every morning was a Sunday morning. If it was, I'd finish this book in no time.'

The morning was the best time for working. Somehow at night, writing was either an indulgence or a task, but in the mornings Mat felt moved by a lucid shaping mood. His theme came uppermost in his mind, so that his material was distanced, for his conception of the theme was bound up with his own separation of himself as he wrote and the self which he remembered. At night this separation he found impossible through the indulgent uxoriousness of his own self-regard.

But Helen proposed the idea of stopping work altogether and concentrating entirely on finishing his new novel. They had the money from his stories, he could draw his holiday pay and a week's lying time when he stopped work. In the meantime he could take up what material he had for more stories of the same kind, have them typed out and sent away. They would maybe get some money for that. Work in the slaughter-house was slack anyway. They worked it out – one week's wages, one week's lying time, a fortnight's holiday pay – that was enough money to last for a month. Then there was the money from the two stories – thirty pounds – which would be enough for another month. They had some other money put by which would extend the two months into three. If in the meantime, say for the next four weeks, they were to put as much past as possible they could extend the time Mat would have to three months at the least. He had now got well into the novel. Surely in three months' full time work at it he could finish it, or at least get so far that the task of completion would be less heavy even if he had to start work again. The only thing which made Mat unwilling to agree to the idea right away was that it was so tempting. In a kind of euphoria he agreed. They decided to do it.

At first everything was all right. Every morning Mat got up eagerly. He adopted a kind of routine, going round in the morning to the dairy to buy the rolls and milk, then after breakfast bringing out his bits and pieces from the cardboard box and starting work over the first sweet cigarette of the day. Mat had finished the job in his slaughter-house on a Friday and both he and Helen spent the week-end with a kind of holiday feeling, full of a feeling of safety which the money gave them – the three months or more which they had calculated the money to last seemed to stretch out before them as if it had no end. The sun still shone from early morning till late at night, without the obscurity of a single cloud. On the Saturday they wandered about shopping, Mat pushing the pram and standing waiting on Helen outside the grocery stores and fruit shops while she went inside and did the shopping. They bought supplies of black coffee and cigarettes and paper and cheap ball-point pens, with different coloured inks, and rye bread in the Jewish shops and apfelstrudel. On the Sunday they stayed all day in the park just lying on the grass reading, eating lettuce sandwiches or holding wee John by his reins as he took his first tottering steps on his tiny feet on the grass.

On the Monday morning as Mat had gone round to the dairy for the rolls and milk it had rained. It was the first rain for weeks, large heavy drops in a quick shower which seemed to cool the air with its own gentle draught in falling. The shower hardly wet the streets but left dark spots on the summer dust of the pavements. In the time it took Mat to go into the dairy, buy his milk and rolls and come out, the sun was shining brightly again, but the shower gave Mat that same refreshed feeling we get at the first definite sign of seasonal change. While sitting at breakfast Mat felt confident. It was his first day ever which he would spend writing without thought of any omission or compulsion or necessity. He was free and entitled to write fluently and without strain while Helen did her chores about him and John chortled and cried and ate and slept. He worked the whole day until teatime, concentrating not through any wilful effort but through a simple interest in what he was doing.

It was not every day that he was able to write so well. He would have black spots as well. But they were fruitful in drawing his attention to his theme. Often as the weeks went by he would find himself pausing and thinking about the nature of his theme as it had first come to him and he would try to render down in his mind a clear myth out of the opaque mass of experience which he was trying to recall.

When George Duncan had once suggested themes which Mat ought to have used from contemporary life it had made Mat think that his own imaginative conception of a theme was solid. When he had first felt the thrill of recognition, that time when his aunt had spoken to Jetta saying 'Your Mat was aye the bonniest wean', Mat had seen the novel which he was to write, for a flash, as a complete whole, utterly distinct and almost written. It had come to him completely shaped, with a definite line of events, associations, feelings, meanings which had simply to be written along. But in the process of composing it, working it out, when he first began his teasing at it, the idea had become a little blurred, a little vague; and now as he worked, still with confidence, he found himself wandering a little from that clear line, losing track, finding at one time that the line had become unclear, at another that the material he was using became refractory or overweight. Eventually he found it necessary to specify to himself what the meaning of his myth was. At first he was tempted into working out the specifications of his theme in a discursive form, but he had an intuitive reluctance to take this course. In the end he thought that there was something glimmering vaguely, an elusive significance, he didn't know quite what, which caused him to feel this irritating nag at the back of his mind. But the significance which he wanted to catch would only be weakened by being open or specific. Mat thought that he would let the thing emerge. If he worked at the flesh of his story eventually there would be implicit in it this elusive idea. He had an almost self-approving sense of his own patience, his own understanding of the creative process in leaving his idea on the edge of formulation. To relax, to refuse to strain, to balance, to let the thing come.

And so he wrote on. He wrote of the merry Devlins – of his 'Faither' of the fierce hooked nose and the hooded blue eyes, with his easy tolerance, of his silly disorganised grandmother who was 'Faither's wife', who kept pots of soup on the fire and who ruled over her sprawling brood with a rod of nothing. He wrote of the merry brood themselves – of Eric, with his beautiful disciplined tenor voice who could sing in the old bel canto style and who had sung to Mat and played old records of Caruso and McCormick and Schipa, teaching Mat to love and know the human voice, not least Eric's own, or John with his weird collection of musical instruments, dulcimer, mandolin, fiddle, button accordion, who taught Mat to play the penny whistle by ear and who earned himself an occasional bob or two by playing jazz piano at the local gigs. He wrote of the rakish prematurely bald Jimmy with his boxing trophies, who had taught Mat to sing 'The International' and 'Vote, vote, vote for Jimmy Maxton', of the witty Lizbeth who could stand on her hands on the backs of chairs, who wore slacks and who had done her 'acrobatic' turn in every small theatre on the Clyde coast, of Mary who made Lizbeth's spangled tights on the sewing machine and Sissie the raconteur and Bertha who was a breadwinner and Jetta who carried all the guilt for the rest. He wrote on, peopling his novel with the ploys and mistakes and recklessness of these poor penniless Devlins and their cluttered comforting household.

Mat wrote chapter after chapter through the weeks. As he began each chapter he would give it some title, private titles which he meant to keep for himself. One chapter he wrote with particular care. He had felt something problematical in his idea and in this chapter he half expected his notion of emergence to have some success. The scene of the chapter was a coup, an old dump where lorries had once come and emptied their loads of ash. At one time, this many years ago, before the avulsion and alluvium, there had been a green high bank on the inside of the river's curve. But in the years the loop of the Clyde had sprung, had grown and widened out until the river's edge had receded away from the high green bank. Then a little meadow had grown between the bank and the river's edge. Now the little meadow had been filled up again with the accumulation of ash and slag from the nearby steelworks. Then the sediment from the other factories came – cans, drums, slates, oily rags, rope, old bricks, broken pieces of cement and asbestos sheeting – until there had been no more space left for dumping and the earth, left alone, had thrust up the virulent foxglove through the refuse. Then the rat's tails and the long coarse grasses had followed. It was left as a wilderness except for some dovecotes knocked up out of waste wood and soap boxes which were built round the edges of this waste.

To the young Mat and his friend Geordie this unfrequented wilderness of thistle, nettle, docken leaves, dog's flourish, ashes, long grass, broken bottles and old disused railway sleepers was a paradise. As they sat near the edge of the dump overlooking the sluggish water they could look out through the smoke and dirt of the city to the countryside beyond. They could see softly undulating hills fuzzed with trees, straight lines of hedges marking out the fields of corn and wheat, ploughed fields like tiny patches of corduroy cloth, here and there the white sides of a farmhouse. Sometimes, when the air was damp with rain about to fall and the hills were marked brightly against the livid sky, they could see plainly through the clarified air cattle, horses, and sheep grazing in the fields. These were strange unfamiliar things which attracted, looked at through the obscurity of ash dust, wreaths of smoke and Mat's child's eyes. Always, as he sat on top of the man-made ash heap, he wondered at the sight. It was the smooth dissolution of one scene into the other; the dust, smoke, chimneys, fires, locomotives, electric pylons mingling with and slowly changing to the beauty of the hills beyond.

Mat often went out into those hills. At weekends or during the summer holidays he would get sandwiches and a bottle of

milk and with Geordie take the tram to the outskirts of the city
and walk out into the fields beyond. They would stay all day
and at night coming home tired from the fresh air he would
remember the long cool shadows of the trees, the tumultuous
whirling and cawing of the rooks in the branches above. Mat
remembered it in contrast with the light at night over the coup,
reddened and angered through the factory haze when the sky
seemed to burn and the buildings were silhouetted like dead
black embers against the blazing clouds of smoke. Up there the
sun slid down easily like snow falling and seemed to lie among
the trees and on the grass, cool and languorous. Down in the
coup, even at dusk with cool gusts of wind blowing across the
grasses and making him shiver, the setting sun still seemed to
burn like an inflammation.

Often they'd make hideaways, marvellous secret dens out
of sheets of corrugated iron and railway sleepers. Sometimes
they'd sit in them until late, with a fire burning in a drum, and
they'd talk. As the nights got duller they'd talk in mysterious
hushed voices about all the important things in life, like
stars and ghosts and sex and war and from the older boys
there would come strange rumours of that other faraway
world of men and women. Mat and Geordie would stay
there in fascination listening to these stories, feeling strange
incumbencies, vague premonitions, the glamorous awesome
fear of living. It would only be the shivering which would
drive them home. Mat would feel the pricking of cramp in
his limbs from sitting too long and when he'd stand up his
legs would ache to the bone. The evening would have suddenly
come, like a sadness, not dark but grey, and the smooth surface
of the river would shirr suddenly in a gust of wind. There would
be a lonely last-out feeling in the air so that the rattle of the
trucks, the glissando of the distant trains as they crossed the
bridge, the whistle of the wind in the cables above the pylons,
its rustle among the grasses and weeds – all these sounds would
seem to have a lamenting poignant quality like the cry of these
lost ghosts in their stories as all the locks clicked and everyone

moved inwards to the warm lit interiors, leaving the ghosts, the bills, the city streets, to the sky and the night.

Then after Geordie's death, when his friend had fallen from that awful lavatory wall, Mat remembered the other awful premonitions. He remembered the desolation of the long nights afterwards when he would lie awake, cold and sweating, listening to Jake breathe in the bed beside him, to his mother and father turning in their sleep, to the creak of the rotten slum building, the dreary whistle of a locomotive somewhere far off, and he would think of death and hopelessness, of the long weary life leading to his last moment when he would be shut up in a wooden coffin and be no more. His bed sheets would become all clammy and he would lie on his back and imagine himself dead; dead, not in silence, nor rest, nor oblivion, but dead in loneliness, cold, surrounded by waxy white lilies. Then he'd imagine the windy spaces of heaven and eternity. He'd speak to himself, saying, 'I. I. I.' over and over again until the whole question of his identity became utterly strange and fearful and existence itself became an airy void in which his own self, his own life, became thinned out and lost.

It may have been from this that he had turned with such comfort to the rumours of experience. To sing 'The International' with fist clenched along with his Uncle Jimmy was to abrogate these other questions in the cheery activist humanitarianism of the song. From that time Mat remembered black posters in crude type, books with pictures of fierce looking bearded men with great broad foreheads. Later there were words and names in the air – Marx, socialism, strikes, elections. Once he held a tar bucket for a man who wrote in big black letters the word 'scab' beneath one of the neighbours' windows. During the elections, he stood at the school gates and handed out leaflets with a picture of the beloved long haired Jimmy Maxton on them. At that time they all sang 'Vote, vote, vote for Jimmy Maxton'.

There was all this fuss and seriousness, the sense of something being imminent, a great expectation in the air. All this excited and thrilled Mat. He wanted to know what it was about. But more, it helped to fill out that empty fearful void which Mat saw at night in his bed. It gave content and texture to living and out of the background of this talk of socialism Mat began to acquire a crude intellectual apparatus which seemed to help combat his fear of nothingness. He overheard talk from Doug, his father, from his uncles, from men at the street corner and began to learn the logical play with ideas like free-will, God's omnipotence, the dilemmas of creation in which the atheist arguments and syllogisms fitted together like an ingenious Chinese puzzle – if God is perfect and also omnipotent then all the irresolvable dilemmas of grace, free-will, divinity, sin and choice could be moved about in pleasing logical shapes and patterns. These questions which had made him shiver and sweat in his bed would lose their chilling reality and become domesticated into matters for enjoyable argument, excuses for the construction of rebellious and shocking ideas.

Mat put all this into his chapter which he wrote with such care. He called the chapter, with mild irony, 'Ontological Questionings'. Yet he went on writing with this emergence which he had expected still not taking place. Through the weeks the bright summer still held in spite of the shower which fell on Mat's first morning. But in the middle of his section on 'Ontological Questionings' the weather broke. Mat was a slow six weeks into his time by then. There was little rain to mark the change but mostly it was just that in a few days the skies became grey and overcast and the temperature dropped. For a week or two the skies remained cloudy without much rain and the streets remained as dusty as they had been all through the summer. Then as Mat wrote on, still slowly, still waiting, a chill autumn came on. Mat stuck to his task, but with every day his reluctance growing slowly into aversion until gradually his old trouble returned – the old disgust, the old questioning, the old failure of the heart, the old sense of the complete unreality of what he was doing.

He would wake up in the morning thinking about starting.

By this time the money was getting tight. There was no toothpaste and his gums began to bleed and feel sore in the mornings. He stood in front of the mirror, with a sour wind scouring at his bowels, and tried to make a lather to shave with ordinary kitchen soap, then he scraped at his chin with an old razor blade which he had tried to hone inside a glass. He took to smoking butt ends first thing in the morning and then when he drank the weak tea and ate toast the bread was like dough in his mouth. It seemed as if his money and his creative energy were running out concurrently. When they were very near the end of their money the novel was not nearly finished and Mat sold his record player and some books. They didn't get very much for them but it was enough for some toothpaste, some coffee and cigarettes. That same day Mat went into the slaughter-house to see Jake. He stood in the room watching the men work, with a feeling like nostalgia for the safety of employment. All the time he spoke to Jake he was conscious of keeping up appearances, but at the back of his mind was the depressing thought of his lack of money. He thought of the early morning cups of tea and the hot rolls, of egg and sausages. And of his own mornings now of toast and margarine. It was while he was thinking these thoughts that he got this windfall. The last couple of beasts that had been felled were old dry dairy cows, but from both of them had come first-class livers. While Jake and his mate went out to the pens at the back of the killing rooms Mat had idly inspected the livers. On both of them the part that was usually uneatable, because of the thick veins that were piped through it, was soft and tender. It was an impulse that made Mat take a knife and trim both the livers, making it look as if the piped ends had been trimmed off. But the parts that he had trimmed he wrapped quickly in a newspaper and stuck them in his pocket.

But for all this it only meant a few days' respite. For two mornings running they breakfasted gloriously on fried liver and coffee, for another week on toast and butter and coffee, then they were back to toast and tea and margarine again. Again he would get up each morning to a meaningless day and, unable to work, he would re-read what he had written until it went flat. The excitement and lust for work became more and more an insipid duty. The old idea which had excited him, the theme which had given him his title, became more and more a subject for distaste. Before the autumn had properly started he knew that he had lost, that his gamble had not come off.

It was money they had gambled with in the first place, whether or not it would last them out as long as they thought. And as is usually the case with money, it hadn't. It had leaked away in all sorts of unaccountable ways until now Mat realised that his time was up. But his novel was unfinished. In a way he was even more confused about it than he had been when he had started. Other questions arose. He began to avoid meeting people, even the neighbours in the street. His old trouble had grown larger than ever before, this feeling that his writing was merely a shameful self exposure, that it had no meaning, no place in his life, that against reality it was inept and half-hearted. Nor was there any argument against this feeling. It simply existed, that creativeness was something of which he was deeply shamed. And yet he had to go on writing, wilfully sustaining the creative mood against his anxiety, his self disgust, the reductive timorousness which would assail him, his fear of risk. Still wilfully, painfully he went on, writing and writing and writing, with his balance, his swing gone, his creative lust enfeebled to a rigorous duty, swallowing his toad, wrestling every morning to lift his ton of reluctance. Sometimes when he thought of Doug, of the reality of his absence, he would feel again his own ridiculous weakness and inadequacy, the meagreness of his spiritual possessions, his physical poverty, his feeble stumblings and gaucheries, the paucity of this world, the refractory city, the numbing tenements and streets, his crumbling damp rooms, the Scotch sneer on his neighbour's face, the load, the weight, the density, the insistent immediateness of what is called living. His writing would become to him a jeering, ugly travesty. He would feel this sneering disgust which was in itself disgusting, a double disgust. And he was never sure whether his revulsions came from the grim, twisted mockery of life at art, or the inflated, lying mockery of art at life.

16

THE WHOLE IDEA had been a complete mess. All day long he had been wandering around thinking about it. Now he turned into his own street with reluctance, for in the street was that point where his life focused, his tiny house which was the centre to which everything that was bothering him was directed. As long as he was outside, wandering the streets he was anonymous, but once there in that place they could identify him, dun him, send him their bills. It was impossible to work there any more when every click of the letter box or knock at the door meant distraction. So he went outside to work, or merely, as he had been doing recently, to wander about – but to go away and live for a while away from his own reality. As if to justify his reluctance a cold wind buffeted him as he entered the street.

Inside the close the gas lamp had just been lit for the evening. Part of the mantle had broken off and a tongue of flame stuck out and flickered in the intermittent draught that blew through the close. He turned the key and as he stepped into the lobby he heard voices from the kitchen. The sound of the voices made him feel glad at the thought of company. He went inside.

It was his mother and Helen who had been speaking. Helen and Jetta were sitting on the easy-chairs on each side of the fireplace, Jake was half-standing, half-sitting against the draining board. Mat took off his W.D. haversack, which he had once used to carry his knives and which was now stuffed with sixpenny jotters and books. He hung the haversack over the back of a chair and returned to the lobby to hang up his coat and jacket. While he was doing this Helen and Jetta were finishing a conversation about children. When Mat came back into the room he spoke to Helen.

'Is he asleep, the boss?' He jerked his thumb towards the door of the tiny room where the baby had his cot.

'Yes, you're just in time. I'm going to make a cup of coffee.'

Mat went over to Jake and Jake offered him a cigarette. Mat hesitated before he took it, remembering he had only one left in his own packet and no money to buy any.

'How's the market these days?' he asked Jake.

'Bags of work,' Jake said.

Beside Jake, on the draining board, there were some uncooked sausages lying on the grill pan. Mat looked at them and felt the saliva trickle in his mouth but he drew at the cigarette to alleviate the hunger pangs.

'Oot the road,' he said to Jake. 'If you let me in to the sink, I'll fill the kettle for a cuppa.'

After Mat had filled the kettle and lit the gas under it he squeezed past the table and sat down on the divan which was against the wall opposite the fireplace. It was only when he sat down that he realised how tired he was from walking about. He also felt a bit light headed and dizzy from hunger. Helen got up and put the sausages on the grill. All this time Jetta had hardly acknowledged his entry but went on talking to Helen.

'You'll not be havin' to strain things for the wee fella any more.'

'No. I've stopped that for a while now. He's old enough now.'

They went on talking about baby-feeding. Jake moved away from the draining board to flick the long column of ash from his cigarette into the fireplace then he came over and sat on the far edge of the divan from Mat.

'Aye,' he said. 'Things are quite busy. Doin' well. Some of the blokes are asking after you – why don't you come in and see us oftener?'

During the last few weeks when Mat had been particularly worried or hungry he had had vivid images of himself back working in the slaughter-house, with his kit on, early in the mornings, drinking cups of scalding tea from a can and eating rolls and eggs, or skinning down a head, or slitting a tripe, or smoking cigarettes on a full stomach.

'Ah, well. Been busy.'

'Aye.' Jake paused for a moment and Mat could see that he was embarrassed. 'How's it comin' on, I mean, your – writing?'

It was as if, Mat thought, he was asking after some embarrassing secret. It was the first time that Jake had ever asked him this question. Yet Mat shared his embarrassment, and he simply turned his head away and shrugged. 'All right.'

When Helen got up again and went over to the grill she spoke to Jetta saying, 'I think we'll have some supper.' Mat felt a moment of wild panic for he knew that their whole economy was so finely balanced that this would either wreck the whole thing or that there would be nothing in the cupboard to offer them. He got up and squeezed past the table and opened the cupboard himself. The first thing he saw was the fat packet of sugar, then the block of butter, the mince lying in a bowl, the streaky bacon gleaming through the grease-proof paper. Mat turned and looked at Helen then he went back and sat down on the couch. As soon as he had seen the packed cupboard he knew it was Jake and his mother who had brought the things and that it would have been Jake who would have paid for them. With the amount of fasting Mat had done recently his senses had sharpened. He had smelt the contents of the cupboard almost before he had opened the door. The aroma from the grilling sausages made him swallow his saliva in yearning.

The plates were out on the table and Helen and Jetta had supper ready before Jetta spoke to Mat. He and Jake were talking about work when Jetta suddenly broke into the conversation.

'Look,' she said, 'is it not about time you were starting work again?'

Mat stood and looked at her. He had been thinking the same thing himself – his novel had got into such a mess that he couldn't envisage ever finishing it. He was about to agree with Jetta when something stopped him – in all the lines of her body Jetta stood there disapproving of him; even in Jake, as he stood there looking at him, he could feel the disapproval. There were all the things in them which would be left unsaid, but which were there – he had neglected Helen, subjected her to this life, and the baby. He was a layabout, a useless loafer, a lazy good-for-nothing. Even the supper they were about to eat, the cigarette he was smoking, were reproaches. He felt angry, but also he had a desperate need to justify himself. Sometimes he had asked himself why he did this – expose himself to every kind of humiliation and reproach and abuse. Not just from his own family, to all these strangers to whom he owed money, to these neighbours who sneered at him with their sly smiles because he wasn't working. He hated all this, hated and abominated it – that he should be dependent in any way on other people for anything. He had to cower and cringe and fawn when what he wanted to do was to spit in their eye. But this dependency – even this – he was enduring for the sake of something about which he was half-hearted and dubious. It seemed the only sensible thing to do, to start work again, yet even at this point he still wanted time. He didn't think it was worth it – yet he knew he couldn't stop. It was like a kind of tick in himself which he couldn't control. He opened his mouth to speak, sawing at the air with one hand, 'You see . . .' he was going to try and explain himself, but Jetta interrupted him.

'Oh, don't start. You can twist things round until they mean anything. You just can't go on like this. It's disgraceful. Writing! You've nae time to think of things like that. You've got a wife and wean depending on ye.'

'It's not that. Look, I'm quite agreeable. I'm going to start.'

'I should think so. I should damn well think so. Agreeable?

I should think you'd be agreeable. Do you realise that *food* has been brought into the house?'

Mat winced. He looked at Jake sitting in his dapper clothes.

'Facts are chiels that winna ding, laddie,' Jake said. 'You know. I mean what's a half-pound of tea between friends? Especially when they're helping you drink it. It's not that, Mat. Anytime. O.K. Forget it. But, look, Mat, seriously, I mean, look . . .'

'Aye, look indeed,' said Jetta. 'Look, he hasnae got a decent suit to his back.'

'Oh, wheesht, Ma,' Jake came over to Mat. 'We're gey busy. You could start tomorrow. You should be thinking of putting a bit of something by. You can't go on like this forever. Go back to work and wait until you get your stuff published . . .'

'Published.'

How often had he dreamed of that. Of his bonny wean. Dreams of being accepted as a writer – of critics writing of his work – 'Mr Craig has put forward a secular notion of divine grace. Worked through the rich texture of a vividly apprehended life we have the brilliant idea finally emerging' – he had thought of this exhilarating final thing, but never in the real context of his life, only in dreams. Mostly he thought only of his work, of making some kind of breakthrough, of resolving something of the dilemma of his time. 'Published?' Mat thought, when he couldn't even write! He went and took his haversack and took out the bundle of sixpenny jotters. He felt angry. All this ambitiousness in him, all this endeavour reduced to a squabble in a tawdry room with empty cupboards in a crumbling tenement in a back street in this bloody engineering city. All reduced to a few sixpenny jotters.

'Fair enough,' Mat said.

'It's all right for some folk,' Jetta said.

Jake spread his hands out appealingly to Mat. 'I mean. After all, we're just common five eights.'

'Fair enough, nothing,' Jetta shouted at him. 'I don't know what the devil you've been thinking about . . .'

'Naw,' Jake sighed. 'When the baby gets older. I mean, you can't bring him up here.'

'Why not? Other kids get brought up here.'

'Oh, Mat. Be your age. Your ain wean.'

'Oh, all right.' Mat looked at the sixpenny jotters which were the measure of all his achievement, full of his incoherent, confused searching, lying crumpled there on the table. Jetta went to speak again but Jake gestured at her for silence. Mat was filled with rage and hatred and shame as he stood and looked at the jotters. He tore one of them in two, then another, then another. Jake put his hand to his brow and said, 'Aw, Jesus Christ.'

'Well, I said it. Didn't I? I said it. Fair e-bloody-nuff.' Mat took the last two pieces and threw them in Jake's face. He was surprised at the smack they made. Before he went raging out of the room he saw Helen, her face all crumpled, going down on her knees after the sixpenny jotters. 'You've no right to do that,' she said, and as she picked up each piece she held it to her breast.

Mat stood and looked over the dark waters of the river. He shivered, half from the cold and half from something else – from a depressing fearful ague which seemed to live constantly in his limbs, and which felt like thin aerated bubbling in his veins. He gripped the top bar of the wooden fence with one hand, feeling its worn knotted hardness. He looked across the shirred surface of the dark water, dotted here and there with the reflection of lights. From down river a raw wind blew, puckering the running water and swaying the arc lamps which shone outside the big dockside sheds up river. Above him the tall cranes in the shipyard stood filigreed against the sky, their gantries seeming to plunge into the thin running clouds in the air at their back. Mat put his foot up on the bottom rail of the fence and took his last cigarette out. He threw the empty packet into the river and the wind whipped it away into the darkness.

He had spent the last three or four weeks since his theme had gone either probing weakly at the numb dead thing in his mind or searching in his mind for some formulation of this thing which had happened to him. Instead of stopping at home and writing with his imagination he had spent most of the time in libraries, reading and thinking about the imagination – he had followed every possible trail from the dry notions of mechanical behaviourism to the rich symbolic schemes of Freud, from the irrational ravings of frantic religiosity to the subtle irrationality of Boolean logic, every trail of abstraction or criticism. Out of this distrust of the imagination had arisen this desperate hunger for the explicit. And in the end he was left with his imagination throwing two things in his face. He had copied down on a piece of paper a passage from Goethe's autobiography, Goethe's recollections of his beginning in life as a poet, of his pendulous nature, swinging from one extreme to the other, his need to convert his preoccupations into an image, this rectification of his knowledge of exterior things and the interior tranquillity which was his reward. And in opposition he had copied down Kierkegaard's contemptuous question about this very passage in Goethe's book. 'At what point did he ever bring idea to reality?' This inward rectification and tranquillity which never earned pennies for the bairns.

Mat was tired now of following these ramifying intellectual trails – the connection between art and truth, goodness, morality, reality and what-not. It was easy to construct an arguable case which would connect art with actuality or any other thing one cared to name, but the existential feeling of connection became no stronger, it became in fact weakened and diminished. The explicit when it came could satisfy no hunger, nor pay any bills. This was the existential fact – his bills, his petty little debts which did not even dignify themselves in bills or accounts. Even they were abstractions – for he had crouched away from the thought of them, crouched into this circle of light. He had sold his books and his record player and anything else in the house which could be hawked or pawned or flogged in order to go on writing and eating, and he had held at bay by dint of myth-making the thought of those bills – the rent, electricity, gas, food, milk, his hire purchase – all of them lagging and all of them being shoved continually into the back of his mind so that he could concentrate exclusively on his ridiculous illusion that earned no pennies for the bairns.

Yet fed up as he was with these ramifying trails his mind still roved round them. As he stood there and looked up at the giant cranes his mind went on coiling in on itself in a continual inverted movement. He thought of those stories which had brought in the money. The temptation to write like that, in order to earn money, had come over him, but when he had tried he found he couldn't. The necessity to write out of what was present in his experience had been too great, the reluctance to externalise the drama or conflict which was implicit in his life too strong, for to do that was to take away what was most significant about his life – the very inwardness of his whole situation – its overt existence, its explicitness was exactly in the undramatic nature of his misery. Yet his real life – his actual life, his life in which the grocer wanted his bill, the sheriff officer came to collect, the rent man called, the stomach rumbled with hunger and the lungs ached for a draw of smoke – what was present to him, immediately and unavoidably present all worked against his writing, took the pen out of his hand with a literal and physical force. He wondered if there were two kinds of art, two separate distinct things; there was a difference between the retreat into the self-contained order of art and outward imposition of order upon material. Was he really an artist at all, or did this hunger for the explicit which destroyed his work not make him just another bloody engineer? It was an ironic situation that just where he was most vulnerable in his moral equivocations about reality and art, in his disgust with art's passive wisdom – it was here that his present life bore most strongly. That great gulf which separated him as a man with bills, anxieties, poverties, from the experience of art; was it not just the contingency that comes to all men; the toad, which he and Flaubert had to swallow every day? Was this a mere sickly neurosis which afflicted him or was it a deep essential sickness and analogy of some general and primal condition of his world, his city?

All during the last few days he had pursued his theme, his obsession carrying him in a weird turning pilgrimage through the streets. All day he had walked collecting his thoughts, his journeys, his experiences, taking inventory of himself and the two lives he lived in this dour, grey, unkind and sweetest of all cities.

He had walked through the city, ticking it all off in his mind – the pylons, the chimney stacks and peeling hoardings, the shops and bus routes and tramcars. He stood up the close at the door of the little two-roomed house where he had been born and listened to the flaring of the gas mantle which had lit up the stair. He wandered round the streets of his childhood gazing at the great steel chimneys of the power station, listening to the eerie, midnight hoot of the railway engine and the rattle of the shunted trucks. He watched the last lit-up trams and the lonely skulking policemen. He walked among the sooty greenery of the river, through the empty boyhood parks and lots and grey ash football pitches, up the long stretches of windy road. He had looked over the roofs of the great rain-swept city from the tops of braes and up into the cloudy skies from between the walls of great tenements. He climbed stairs and looked at strange names on brass nameplates, he stared through windows and eyes at other lives.

But still he couldn't find his theme.

Where did the failure of his work come from? Was it from some other source? Lack of courage? Fear of risk? Or the hazards of success? Was it in the language he spoke, the gutter patois into which his tongue fell naturally when he was moved by a strong feeling? This gutter patois which had been cast by a mode of life devoid of all hope or tenderness. This self-protective, fobbing off language which was not made to range, or explore, or express; a language cast for sneers and abuse and aggression; a language cast out of the absence of possibility; a language cast out of a certain set of feelings – from poverties, dust, drunkenness, tenements, endurance, hard physical labour; a reductive, cowardly, timid, snivelling language cast out of jeers and violence and diffidence; a language of vulgar keelie scepticism.

Yet all this walking the streets, this insane envy of the protected and shuttered, these mad reluctances, the life killing nostalgia, the indifference, exhaustion, nausea, the peering in at windows, questioning the stars, the peripatetic frenzies, the great fatiguing turning round of obsessions, compulsions, scruples, hesitations – all this was wasted and meaningless, unless . . . here he found himself shrugging in a familiar vulgar sceptical way and at the same time his thoughts rising to an arrogant pitch . . . unless he were to write in a key in which the rapturous, the hopeful, the exploratory, the courageous, were possible. To struggle through the limitations of his talent and language and create for himself that backcloth against which the great opera of human creativeness and possibility could be sung. The unquestioned high C, the bravura, the strut, the wilful cadenza, the unnecessary aria. Sung at concert pitch. 'The bloody euphoric!' Mat thought. 'The lot!'

Then he thought of something which made him laugh. He had got himself into this awful mess on behalf of literature. Something which in the context of his life appeared as an absurdity. It was no excuse for him to say – I am a moral wreck and a mess because I am a writer. It was in fact his own moral failure, his blame, his weakness as a man which had got him into this. The provisional nature of his situation was no excuse either. It was no excuse to say that he was deferring his responsibilities until he had made good. It was, he realised, genuinely no excuse. He knew that if ever he made enough money as a writer to live decently then the integrity of his attitude would be recognised. Everything would be justified and excused. What had seemed an indefensible and weak-minded neglect of his duties would be forgiven by Jetta and Jake and everyone who knew him. But he would not forgive himself. Yet again, this superior moral scrupulousness of his would not enforce him to change his ways.

And again, a vague idea tickled his mind that in all his weakness he had maintained a persistence that almost amounted to courage. The courage to allow himself to live in this state of despair. Surely any other course open to him would end in that kind of moral disaster which happens to people who take care of their duties, when certain kinds of responsibility have been robustly looked after, and a hardening of the moral faculty takes place. This thought tempted him for he knew that he could allow himself a certain amount of easeful self-approbation by believing it. So he rejected the thought on the grounds of its temptingness, its persuasiveness. Then in the moment of rejection the strange thing happened. He felt that now the idea had been rejected he could see in it objectively, without relation to himself, some truth, and he felt suddenly the exhilaration of knowing honestly about oneself something which is good.

He *had* courage. He *wasn't* weak. These qualms which weakened him so disastrously for everyday living were just the qualms experienced by any artist, his choice between perfection in life and work. All he needed to do was to sustain that courage, to crack his nut, to persist in his apparent weakness. Then he'd write the best novel ever to have been written in Glasgow.

When the ferry arrived at the moorings beneath him there were only a few people to get off. From the top of the steps Mat could see the two men who operated the ferry sit down inside the centre housing among the shiny brass levers. They started to drink tea out of cans. Their faces shone red from the blaze of the tiny furnace which glowed up through a hatchway. Mat walked down the stairs, jumped on to the deck and walked through under the covered sides of the ferry to the open front. He looked out from beneath the canopy of the ferry to the glittering black water. Black enamel. Black lacquer. Sheen, shimmer, ripple, wave. A black shape in the water (a matt blackness against the shimmering lacquered liquor. Oh, literature!) came flowing into the circle of light around the ferry. A mauve shape now, palpitating slowly nearer with each lap of the waves. A laxed dog, a drowned dog, a boxer dog, its blunt head beneath the surface and its bloated side high in the water, its paws limp, and a human hand, a glaring crimson hand, curved lovingly round its shoulder; somewhere in their loneliness they had met, the cold drowned dog, its coat all sleeked with wet to be caressed by the red surgical glove. Quelle chance! Mat laughed. He was still in his euphoric mood.

Then he remembered what he had forgotten in the luxury of all this introspection. That his novel, his bonny wean, had been torn and destroyed. Mat understood very well that he was divided against himself. But he was not prepared for what happened. A voice, a shrugging Glesca keelie voice, said to him: 'Ye're nut on, laddie. Ye're on tae nothin'.' Mat looked around the empty ferry, but still the voice spoke. 'Ye're not quoted. A gutless wonder like you, that hasn't got the gumption of a louse. That has to have *food* brought into the house.' A harsh, ugly, contemptuous, slangy voice. This time he didn't look round, for it was his own voice, he had spoken aloud.

Mat's cheeks went cold, a little unfeeling spot right in the middle of each cheek. On his brow and temples he felt the sweat trickling. Right between the shoulder blades he could feel a sharp grip and as he wiped the sweat from his brow he shivered all over from the cold. He felt the nausea arise which seemed to come from the very marrow of his bones, a moiling utter revulsion as if the very physical elements of his body were coiling and recoiling from each other in disgust. In his self, apart from his body, he felt this deep spiritual boke. He started to retch and tried to check it, but the rippling spasms forced itself from the pit of his stomach up along his gullet until he felt himself choking. He felt his tongue flatten, the lower jaw open and stretch and his neck strain in an uncontrollable animal movement. He retched and retched and retched and retched, each time hoping it would be the last and each time retching stronger. Slowly his nausea changed to a fierce cramping pain as his stomach moiled and knotted and his thrapple contracted and twisted. At the last the strongest retching spasm locked itself at its very height until Mat felt a wild panic and he tried to straighten up and pull out the fixed knot at the bottom of his ribs. Then with a sharp cutting pain as if his gut had broken the last spasm unlocked itself and Mat came to himself on his hands and knees on the deck of the ferry, and with the echo in his ears of the animal boking noises he had been making. His nose and upper lip were covered in snot and his mouth full of a bitter watery bile. Beneath him on the deck was a little pool – it was all he had brought up – just a little watery bile which burnt his throat and tasted acid in his mouth.

Later, as Mat made his way home, he passed a public well and he went over to take a drink to wash the taste of vomit from his mouth. He took drink after drink from the iron cup which felt so cool on his lips. Then when he had finished he searched through his pockets for a butt end and found one about an inch long with the tobacco gone slack inside it. He lit the cigarette and had to force himself to draw the sour smoke into his lungs. Then he stood and looked at the symbols cast in iron which decorated the public well. And there he saw it, his escutcheon, the coat-of-arms of his Gles Chu, his dear green place, cast in iron. The tree, the bird, the fish, the bell. Cast in iron. As he made his way home the childish jingle echoed through and through in his mind.

> *'This is the tree that never grew,*
> *This is the bird that never flew,*
> *This is the fish that never swam,*
> *This is the bell that never rang.'*

FUR SADIE

ON WEDNESDAY AFTERNOON a coal lorry stopped in front of Sadie Anderson's close. The front half of the lorry's platform still held a few bags of coal, but on the back half was spread a folded tarpaulin on which a big, light-coloured, upright piano lay upon its back. Two men got out of the cabin, fixed a pair of skids to the rear of the lorry then started easing the piano toward them, but before it reached the skids the tarpaulin rucked and the piano stuck. Andy, who owned the lorry, stopped pulling and said, 'Just a minute.'

'Pull the damned thing,' said his mate Wullie, a bigger, more powerful man still tugging his side of the piano. The tarpaulin rucked up more. A loose corner was caught by the wind and flapped over the piano lid. Andy said, 'A minute. A minute. You'll tear the blinkin' hap.'

'My arse in parsley. It'll not tear!' said Wullie with a masculine confidence in technical matters that Andy thought misplaced. He murmured, 'If you could sook as hard as you can blow' – and stood back, looking at the job, his lips pursed in a silent whistle. Then he said, 'We'll walk it.'

'*Walk* it?'

'Aye.'

'It's a piano, not a bloody horse. Have you noticed it's got no legs?'

'Ach, use the few brains the guid Lord gave you. Lift your end and I'll lift mine. Right?'

'Right!'

'Now tilt it on your corner and I'll swing it round. Right?'

'Right!'

'Now tilt it onto my corner and *you* swing it round.'

In this way they moved the piano until it swung over the back of the lorry and tilted onto the skids. They slid it gently to the ground, pushed it upright on its castors, then with an effort got it onto the pavement.

'What do we do now?' Wullie asked. Said Andy, 'Run upstairs with it and slip it through the letterbox.'

He went into the cabin and came back with furniture slings. They rolled the piano on its castors into the close and at the bottom of the stairs slipped the slings under the piano, tied them behind their necks, then lifted. Andy was first to climb the stairs, an awkward job because he had to walk backwards, though Wullie was taking most of the weight on his big shoulders.

'Two up did you say?' panted Wullie.

'Aye, two up.'

On the last flight of steps a young woman appeared above pushing a pram down toward them.

'Ye cannae get past,' said Andy more abruptly than his normal courtesy to women with prams allowed, for the weight on the sling round his neck made speech difficult.

'What's happening?' said Wullie behind the piano, easing some weight off his shoulders.

'Keep going,' croaked Andy and continued backing upward a step at a time as the young woman pulled the pram up the next flight of stairs. Both men grunted and sighed with relief when they got the piano onto the landing and took the slings from their shoulders. The woman said, irritably, 'Tt, tt. I'm in a hurry for my messages and I can't hold this here all day.'

'We'll not be two shakes of a lamb's tail – and I'll give you a hand doon.' Andy said, knocking on one of the landing doors. Wullie folded his arms on the piano top, leaning heavily with his chin resting on his wrists. The young woman was still clicking her tongue.

*   *   *

The door had been skilfully stained, varnished and artificially grained, and its old-fashioned, well-polished brass plate bore the name 'Alec C. Anderson.' When Sadie Anderson opened it she was plainly embarrassed and started apologising to the younger woman saying, 'I'm haudin' ye back, Mrs Matheson,' then opened the door wide saying, 'In ye come!' and backing into the lobby. The men pushed the piano in far enough to let the young woman past. Andy lifted the pram's front wheels and helped her take it downstairs. Again Wullie leaned on the piano while Sadie, blushing, tugged at the other end as if it was something she wanted to hide away, embarrassment giving the lines of her face a strange undefined look.

'You'll rupt ... I mean, the piano's too heavy for you Mrs Anderson,' said Wullie, 'We'll wait on Andy.'

'But it's half blocking up the landing.'

'Andy'll not be a tick.'

Sadie murmured about 'the bother' she was causing. Andy returned and the men tilted up the piano enough to swing it round in the tiny lobby and push it into the kitchen while Sadie fussed around, giving it little tugs she hoped were helpful or anxiously twisting the bottom of her apron in her hands. When the piano was finally standing against the back wall of the kitchen Sadie wanted to make the men a cup of tea, saying, 'I've given you a lot of bother. I didn't know a piano was that heavy.'

'Well, you see, they're full of big bits of cast iron,' Andy said.

'Oh I'm sorry.'

'It's all right. We've moved pianos before.'

Sadie took two pounds from her purse and held them out saying, 'Here – take this.'

'But we agreed on thirty bob.'

'No, but take this. It'll pay for your extra bother. The two of you are baith sweating.'

'Don't give *him* money,' said Wullie, 'he's got enough already. Gie it to me.'

He held out his big paw but when she offered him the notes he grinned and said, 'Away you go.'

Sadie laughed shyly, gave Andy the notes and when he tried to offer ten shillings change she took him by the shoulders and turned him to the door saying, 'Naw, naw. Keep it and buy yourselves a drink.'

The men left, grinning and shrugging.

For a while Sadie stood in the middle of the kitchen, looking at the piano, until there came a knock at the door. She opened it to Andy who said, 'Here, we forgot the piano stool.'

She took the stool inside, set it before the piano and sat on it silently, again simply looking. Then she opened the lid and timidly struck middle C with her thumb. After another moment or two she started to pick out a melody with her forefinger in the key of C. She did not notice a pathos in the infirmity of the tone and in the rhythmic hesitation of her single playing finger. But the melody was recognisable: Brahms' lovely little waltz in A flat.

Sadie was worried because she had told neither her husband nor sons that she had bought a piano, and in that small kitchen it looked huge. She had not appreciated its great bulk before the coalmen half jammed it into the lobby. She saw that the display cabinet filling the space between the piano and a corner looked ridiculous and would have to be shifted. All this had happened through a moment of exuberance the previous Friday morning.

It had been a beautiful sunny day. After Alec and the two boys had gone to work she was tidying away the breakfast things when she heard Schubert's overture *Rosamunde* on the wireless. When it ended she switched the set off but the tunes kept running in her head when, as usual on Friday mornings, she went shopping. While standing in the Co-op pay queue, her baskets full to the brim with groceries, she remembered the many years when she had had to budget carefully. Nowadays she was able to shop without thinking too much of the cost, and bought many things that once seemed extravagances – soft toilet paper and kitchen tissues, for instance. She now enjoyed shopping. After buying staples like sugar, butter, flour, salt, tea, vegetables, it gave her a wonderful sense of opulence to wander round the store picking out something unusual in the way of biscuits, table figs, a tin of crab. When Alec asked her, 'What's for tea?' her standing joke was to say, 'Something nice, and no' common.' She enjoyed picking out uncommon things without thinking of the price. Alec and the boys didn't mind her branching out a bit sometimes, as long as they were frequently fed with mince and doughballs, Scotch broth and rhubarb tart.

She was passing the newsagents with the straps of the shopping bags biting her fingers when she saw a card in the window offering a piano for sale. She had taken the bags home, left them unpacked on the kitchen table, returned to the newsagents and asked for the address of those selling the piano. She had then walked through several streets toward it, thinking nothing of the absurdity of buying a piano, of the fact that the kitchen would be too small for it, and it would have to be explained to Alec and the boys. She meant to play it, and they would certainly demand an explanation for that. They would think this urge whimsical and erratic in a timid, working class housewife, and their kindest reaction would probably be amused tolerance because she was nearing the menopause. But she walked along a busy Glasgow pavement on that sunny Friday morning, crossed the road at Parkhead Cross, went down Springfield Road to one of the streets behind Celtic Football Stadium, and enjoyed a clear, lucid specific happiness at the thought of owning a musical instrument. It could not be explained by her outward circumstances, or character. She walked onward, not thinking about it but remembering Anna who she had neither seen nor heard of for over thirty years.

Archie Hind

You could see the Irish in Sadie. She was small, freckled, with good bones, frizzy auburn hair, a small straight well-formed nose, a large mouth with big strong teeth which nearly parted her lips so that in the act of closing them her mouth took on a clear shape which gave her face some beauty, and gave her expression both compassion and irony. Her intelligence was questionable, for that is often, at least in maturity, a matter of how one acts. As a child she had been a gamine, unquestionably bright, and her smiles had been brilliant. Without this gamine quality she would probably never have got to know Anna Bermant.

Sadie had always been at the top of the class until one day, when she was nine, Anna was introduced to the class as a new girl by the headmaster. Sadie's first impression was that he had brought a splash of colour into that roomful of working-class Scots children with their frayed woollen cardigans, snot-encrusted sleeves, scuffed and worn boots. Anna positively blazed. Sadie could still remember the tangerine coloured moiré silk dress, the off-white sash which bound Anna's waist, fastened not in the convenient bow but in a tie-knot which left two trails of silk, also the black patent-leather pumps. All this against Anna's cap of straight, thick, glossy black hair, the straight level eyebrows, the dark long eyelashes set against eyes such a light blue as to seem at one moment blank and pale against her dark skin and the next to glint and pierce like sparks from the trolley of a tramcar. When Anna sat down near her Sadie studied her with shy, underhand glances which discovered a curious little fault in Anna's beauty. From the middle of her brow, across her left temple and down her cheek was a pinkish stain under the skin, a fault in the pigmentation, slightly mottled yet definite in outline.

Sadie thought this fault, this delicate stain unbearably enviable and beautiful and she thought of it always as Anna's 'tan' in contract to her own plebeian fault – the big orange freckles saddling the bridge of her nose.

At playtime that morning one of the rougher boys, witlessly attracted by Anna, had pulled at her sash and she had immediately and soundly thumped him.

'You're a *big* boy? You're brave? You fight with girls?'

All the little girls in the class had their repertoire of sarcastic remarks, a defensive equipment kept hands to use on the boys and sometimes each other. It was usually delivered in an intonation of annoyance or displeasure, but Anna shouted in a mocking rhythm, her voice pitched high on certain words so that the rhetoric in her questions was controlled and sure and comical, so the other girls burst into laughter. She disclosed another exoticism to add to her 'tan' and silk dress, for her accent was unusual, not posh, not English, but nothing like the broad nasal speech of other children in the playground. It sounded foreign. She was fascinating. Sadie had been awed, then envious, and had then fallen in love with her.

We fall in love with personality, not with moral characteristics. Attraction is mysterious, but the mystery creates strong curiosity, a desire to know more, and this curiosity can be life's most exciting and important thing. So Anna went around in a glorious amoral blaze while Sadie, behind her dull orange-coloured freckles, felt that excited curiosity. She experienced it stoically, perhaps because it expressed something in Sadie's own brilliance, sometimes shown in the heart-warming smile that drew Anna toward her with a kinder love.

So the two children entered a friendship that was quite normal for all its intensity. Children's emotions are too keen and anarchic to be classified and can only be labelled sexual by transferring them into adulthood where they would accommodate to a social pattern, or else into another milieu where they would be labelled crushes. But these were children in a co-educational, working class Glasgow school where the word 'crush' was unknown. They were free to follow their inclinations in questions, handclasps, secrets, giggles and tiffs. Otherwise Sadie, thirty years later, would never have allowed herself to remember her friend.

Anna had immediately taken Sadie's position at top of the class and Sadie was content to follow as second top, but kept trying to better Anna, less from competitiveness than from feeling that if she did better she would share some of Anna's brilliance and really know her. It was a long time before she beat Anna in any way, and when she did, and realised she too had some mastery, it was a moment of glory. This sense of mastery made her remember Anna years later as she walked the dusty Glasgow streets that sunny morning in search of a second hand piano. But she had discovered it only after visiting Anna's home.

Sadie had lived in the room-and-kitchen tenement flat where her mother had died when she was a baby. Her father drove a Glasgow Corporation tramcar. She had an eldest sister who looked after the home, two older sisters who went out to work, two older brothers who occasionally worked. This family, in its own estimation, was not poor because the father's job was steady and the district where they lived, like many out-lying parts of the town, contained wealthier and poorer homes. It was a mixture of sandstone room-and-kitchen tenements, others with four or five room flats with interior bathrooms and gardens in front, council houses and, near Sadie's home, a street with a row of large grey stone houses, each with a big wall-enclosed garden. In one of these houses Anna had come to live with her parents. She was the only child who went to the local school from that area of big houses. Sadie and Anna went to and from school together, meeting and parting in the street, but for several months saw nothing of each other after school hours, so for the first weeks of the summer holidays Sadie did not see Anna at all.

Because her father was on shift work and her eldest sister did not control her much Sadie, during these weeks, became mostly a creature of the streets. Perhaps in recollecting that period Sadie's memory united it with earlier summer holidays, giving that time a density which her later adult years did not have. Perhaps the life of the streets in childhood *was* as rich

and teeming as she remembered, with its peever beds and
ball games, the chalked love messages on tenement walls,
the rounders, kick-the-can, leave-oh, the back-court concerts.
Above all she remembered the songs, the street ballads.

> Down in yonder meadow where the green grass grows,
> Sits Sadie Maxwell a-telling all her woes.
> She sang, she sang, she sang so sweet
> That she sang Alec Anderson from across the street.
> Sadie made a wedding cake, she made it awful nice,
> She cut it up in slices and gave us all a slice.
> Saying, 'Taste it, taste it, don't say no,
> For tomorrow is my wedding day and I must go.

The voices of her companions would become mocking and
shrill as they shouted out her name and the name of some boy,
but that mattered less than the song's mysterious suggestion
of sweet and heart-catching expectation. The most glamorous
song was the one that started,

> There came a Prince a-riding, a-riding, a-riding,
> There came a Prince a-riding, long a-go.

When they sang these songs she felt a strange sad warmth in her
throat, a nostalgic happiness attached to no previous memory
and experience, which explained the sadness in them. Perhaps
only those who never sang them recognise how sad they are,
with a kind of sadness only felt by those who learned them as
their first songs. They took their power from the density of
childhood in streets through which no glittering and specific
prince ever rode. The street ballad is a powerful, naive art
whose power came from children whose simple life-energy
depended on naivety – that energy which goes on hoping and
believing in life through pain and disappointment. For most
of her life, Sadie would be one of those whose desires and

ambitions would attach to nothing specific because nothing very specific existed for her. Her life-attitude would always be hopeful rather than expectant. This attitude, more than anything else in life, diminishes intelligence by preventing its use, for intelligence has to grapple with the concrete by creating new individual expectations and situations – too great a risk for ballad singers who sing:

> Sadie Maxwell says she'll die,
> For the want of the Golden City.

Art which suggests real possibilities has to be self-conscious.

So the children played and sang in the hot dusty streets during long weeks of summer and Sadie sang with them. The boys scuffled after their footballs, kicking and dribbling their way through the rings made by the girls. Together the boys and girls twisted and dodged one another on the pavement, slipped through gaps in the railings in the backyards. Their voices clanged up and down the closes and stairways. The sun shone and the dust rose and when the buskers came to play the children sat on the pavement edges as if in orchestra stalls. All day long like motes in a sunbeam until dusk – sometimes afterwards under the streetlamps – through the warm summer holidays the children teemed and swarmed.

Early one morning after the holidays began Sadie wandered through intervening streets toward Anna's home. She had no conscious intentions until she found herself in Anna's street and decided to call on her. For a while she stood uneasily outside the heavy iron gate, then timidly opened it and walked up a curved path through the garden, mounted a broad step and pressed a doorbell. Anna's mother opened to her and Sadie spoke the ritual words, 'Is Anna coming out to play?'

For a few moments Anna's mother stood regarding the grubby little girl now standing nervously in her faded cotton print frock and frayed, lilac-coloured cardigan. The cardigan was unbuttoned and Sadie was twisting the hem in her fingers.

'Come in, come in!' said Mrs Berman, 'Anna is practising just now. You can wait until she finishes.'

She brought Sadie into the hall. From one room came the very faint sound of piano playing, from another the rumble of a man's voice. Mrs Berman opened a door and said, 'Anna has a visitor.'

Again there was a man's deep rumble and Mrs Berman closed the door, smiling, then said, 'Would you like something while you wait? A biscuit and some milk perhaps?'

For a moment Sadie could not forgive her for this question. Babies were offered food and drink, but offering them in those days to a working class girl might imply that her family could not feed her properly. Sadie had never before encountered such formal hospitality and said, 'Naw, I'm no hungry.'

Mrs Berman's eyebrows went up so comically that Sadie nearly laughed in spite of the offence and her nervousness.

'*Hungry*? You need to be *hungry* to drink a glass of milk and eat a biscuit?'

She led a forgiving Sadie into a kitchen and gave her a glass of milk and (not a biscuit but) a strange kind of spicy bun.

The kitchen was tidy but busy. The end of the table where Sadie sat was dusted with flour and covered in bowls, bags of flour and broken eggshells. From a big pan in the cooker came the heavy smell of deep frying.

'And which one of Anna's friends are you?' Mrs Berman asked, tidying the table very efficiently, putting floury utensils on the sink's draining board, putting away eggs and transferring paper bags to a cupboard.

'Sadie Maxwell.'

'Oh, you're the one who *sings*?' – Mrs Berman sounded pleased – 'You are the one who *sings*?'

'Me?' – Sadie was genuinely surprised – 'I cannae sing Mrs Berman.'

'But Anna tells me that you are the best singer in the class.'

But Sadie was a poor singer because in schools like hers teachers seldom persuaded children to project their voices confidently enough for anyone, including themselves, to know if they could sing or not. Even now the middle-aged Sadie remembering all this tended to speak through a tight throat when outside her usual milieu. She could, however, sight-read music with uncanny facility, just as outside the classroom she could easily follow any melody at any required interval – could 'harmonise'.

Having tidied the kitchen Mrs Berman asked if Sadie would like to hear Anna playing and Sadie nodded her head shyly. They went back into the hall and Mrs Berman opened another door just as Anna played some ringing octaves, the notes sounding out with such boldness, such brio and flair that Sadie found herself gasping. The piano was on the far side of the room and Anna played with her back to them with such delicious entrancing motions of arms and head that Sadie felt a rush of love for this friend who was responsible for such glorious sounds. It was that lovely, satisfying and unequivocally good response we call admiration.

'It's lovely,' she said. While Mrs Bermant smiled, the notes rang out, Anna's childish wrists rose and fell and Sadie, in her grubbiness, cotton-print dress and twisting her fingers in the hem of the frayed cardigan, found an emotion isolated within her which henceforth she would always recognise with a shock. She would never give it the name – aesthetic – but it became, nevertheless, there, fully formed. Anna was playing one of the Clementi Sonatinas with no more than some childish physical panache. She went on to play a few little classical pieces which are all the more touching for having been written by grand distant masters for the fledgling hands and ears of little girls with frayed lilac cardigan hems twisted in their fingers.

Perhaps it was an outrageous and unwarranted interference in Sadie's life that two years later Mrs Bermant taught Sadie to sing some German lieder. Better to have left her to her ballads because the Bermant music room had a thick Indian carpet, polished wooden floor, Buhl cabinet, bow windows hung in velour, a Bergère suite, an inlaid escritoire, silver display and music drawers. The big dark polished upright Bechstein was surrounded by the privileges on which appreciation of Mozart, Schumann, Schubert, or Wolff depended – the formal musical art of Europe. Yet it stopped feeling foreign to Sadie. A year later she and Anna learned a song they performed together at the class concert held before the summer holidays. It was Mozart's 'The Violet'. Then Sadie wanted to learn something more difficult, but Anna could not manage the very difficult accompaniment to Schubert lieder. So though Sadie eventually, in her weak but true voice, sang 'Heidroslein' and 'Auf Dem Wasser zu Singen' Anna's mother was to accompany her. Mrs Bermant was puzzled that Sadie could read the staff notation so easily, for she knew that the school had not taught her this method. She never found out that Sadie simply learned the key signatures, then transposed the intervals into sol-fah.

So, when a year had gone Sadie knew Mrs Bermant considered her Anna's musical superior. Sadie was musically better than the beautiful blazing Anna who had sat before her in the arrogant pianistic pose, lifting her hands high, the lax wrists making those delicious, entrancing curves over the keyboard, her head jerking proudly as she thumped the chords. Mrs Bermant said so one day with Sadie sitting on the very edge of one of the Bergère chairs. Anna had just left the room when her mother struck middle C on the Bechstein and asked, 'What is this note Sadie?'

'Doh.'

'Is it? What is this one then?'

She struck the G above.

'Soh.'

'What are these notes then?'

She struck the G major chord. Sadie paused before answering, then said slowly, a little puzzled, 'Soh, lay, ray?' and frowned anxiously at Mrs Bermant as if asking 'Am I right?'

Mrs Bermant frowned too, then struck the chord again and held it while singing 'Doh, mi, soh –' Then she turned to Sadie who, having suddenly realised something, smiled at her and said, 'It's not the *real* doh, mi, soh. But you can call it that if you like.'

'If we called it that, what would this be?' said Mrs Bermant, striking again this little trick. Without hesitation she said, 'Now you could call it fah.'

After that Mrs Bermant worked through the key cycle until she got to F sharp major.

'Where's *your* Doh now?

Sadie put her hand to her face and giggled at Mrs Bermant through splayed fingers, then hummed and haw-ed a bit and shook her head. Mrs Bermant struck a couple of arbitrary chords before hitting C.

'That's it!' Sadie shouted triumphantly, at which Mrs Bermant announced 'The gal who found the lost chord!' and also had a fit of giggles. But when she finished laughing she asked why Sadie called that particular note Doh. Sadie came to the piano and showed it was the only piano note she knew by saying, 'You have to start here to play the scale,' and played the C major scale with one finger.

'I see.'

Again and again Mrs Bermant tried to catch her out but Sadie always knew where *her* Doh was. Mrs Bermant then explained that neither herself nor Anna (not Anna!) could do that simple thing, remember their Doh.

'Very few people can do it. It's as if, you see, you had a perfectly tuned piano inside your head, so can always hear exactly where it is being struck. It's called, having perfect pitch.'

Sadie nodded gravely as children do in face of adult seriousness. She was neither particularly impressed nor interested.

'It means –.' Mrs Bermant shrugged. 'Wouldn't you like to learn to play the piano, Sadie?'

'Naw, Mrs Bermant,' said Sadie, smiling and shaking her head.

*　　*　　*

It would not be impertinent to remember here that teeming street, the room-and-kitchen tenement from which Sadie came, her frayed lilac cardigan, nor the street ballads she and other girls sang in the street that summer.

This tonic note – this Doh – ran almost unconsciously through Sadie's life, a life that needed no talent or perfect pitch. In Anna's house she had glimpsed a lucid world of new possibilities from the moment she had heard Clementi's octaves ringing and repeating beneath Anna's fingers on the keyboard, but she only experienced that lucidness as a line of feeling, attractive to her because she recognised the complex artifice producing it. This, which required training, mastery of technique, active conscious control, was all a belief in human freedom and choice. And that belief Sadie didn't have.

A child of teeming street, she was saturated with brave but passive ballad wisdom, teaching her to thole and not expect. She had no model of dominance, no close example allowing her to believe that athleticism – style in action – the physical imposition of fingers in a keyboard performance could be hers. She perhaps half-believed what Mrs Bermant told her about her magnificent ear, her gift, but had no sense of grace and beauty this could give her. Pianism belonged to Anna's exotic world – to *her* blaze, her beauty, her tan, whose stain was on her brow and not, like Sadie's vulgar freckles on the bridge of her nose. So she said, 'Naw, I wouldn't like to learn the piano, Mrs Bermant, I couldn't.'

The other banal, pathetic reasons – poverty, no money for lessons and the *price* of a piano, no space for it in a cramped room-and-kitchen where seven people lived – were only practical difficulties. Sadie's urchin fatalism made it really impossible, that terrible and common denial, not essentially from Sadie herself, but from her circumstances and history, her life, if you like. Thirty years later, the sudden weakening of this denial made her walk through the dusty summer Glasgow streets clutching her purse.

'We want rid of it,' the woman selling it said, 'It hasnae been tuned for donkeys' years. Anywey, naebody can play the damn thing. It's just a burden – I'm sick of dusting and polishing it. All we can dae wi it is keep photies on top. *He* says we've tae get rid o't.'

'It's a lovely looking piano.'

'Oh aye, my goodness, aye, a bonnie instrument and nothing wrang wi't. My faither used to play it before he was took. Then *I* had to look after it.'

It certainly was a nice looking instrument, and it badly needed tuning. When Sadie tried some of the keys the strings buzzed and sang with a sour, astringent discordance which dried the roof of her mouth.

However, only half an hour after Andy and Willie had delivered it to her the piano tuner arrived. He worked on the piano for nearly the whole afternoon and it cost her as much to pay him as it did to buy it. Several keys had to be fixed and both the pedals. As he worked through the tuning cycle Sadie herself could hear the piano coming together and she felt a new excitement. When he finished tuning and before he put back the front panel the tuner played a few arpeggios. Sadie was thrilled by the sound.

'By God,' he said, 'it really needed that.'

Sadie laughed, 'Aye, the people I got it from hadn't had it tuned for years.'

'Aye? Still it's not too bad,' (he played again) 'even though it's been neglected. It's amazing how mucky the inside gets.' (He had extracted dust with the small nozzle of Sadie's vacuum cleaner.) 'How much did it cost you, if I'm not being too cheeky?'

'The owners wanted rid of it so they only asked a couple of pounds.'

'Och, well, you weren't done. Mind you nothing much goes wrong with pianos if they stay out of draughts and don't get too much beer spilled on them. A bit like ourselves, I suppose.'

'The owner seemed to think it was mair of a burden than anything else. It does seem a big brute of a thing, noo that I see it in the house.' Sadie regarded the piano anxiously for a moment.

'I suppose so. In these wee kitchens. Is it for one of the kids?'

'Oh no. *My* kids are out working and one is married –' Sadie paused then smiled. 'No, you see – I'm going to learn to play myself.'

'You?'

'Aye. Why no?'

'Nae reason,' the tuner shrugged, 'It's just unusual.' He paused and looked at her for a moment. 'Are you serious?'

'Aye. I'm going to learn to play.'

'Have you got a teacher?'

'As a matter of fact I was going to ask you about that – if you know anyone. A good teacher, like.'

'Well, I do. I know a really good teacher – but I don't know –' He hesitated. 'I'll give you his address. And you can go and see him. The only thing is – you see, he's always pretty busy and he might not take you –'

'Because I'm oe'r auld?'

'It's a bit unusual, you must admit. But never mind, go and see him anyway. I'll write his address on my card and you can tell him I sent you. OK? If he doesn't take you there is no harm done.'

'I'll try him. Thank you very much.' Sadie took the card after he scribbled the address.

'Part of the service. Oh, and I might say, if you're using it, I'll have to have another look at this piano in a few months. If you learn to play on it you'll want it kept in tune.'

When the tuner left it was nearly time for tea and Sadie hurried to set the table. She pulled out the leaf of the dinner table, spread the cloth and noticed how cramped the room looked then fried fish in batter, heated plates, masked the tea, listening all the while for the sound of a key in the lock. She wanted the tea ready before Alec and the boys came home. When Alec's key rasped in the outside door lock the fish and chips were keeping warm in two big tissue-lined dishes in the oven. The tea was ready for pouring, the draining board clear for cooking dishes. The table was set with sliced bread, fruit loaf, scones, tomato sauce, and a sponge cake with cream filling. When Alec entered the kitchen Sadie smiled nervously and said, 'You in then?' Alec grunted, 'Aye, I'm in.'

She turned her back to him and wiped the draining board with a cloth, then rinsed the cloth in the sink, turning on the tap too hard and spraying water over her arms and apron front. She waited tensely for Alec to notice the piano.

He was a small man, not much bigger than Sadie, dressed in a serge suit, with a head of very thick auburn hair which was kept cut short and always beautifully groomed. He was full of masculine bonhomie, dapper, with a small man's spryness, but very fit, small boned but well-muscular. As he stood in the kitchen doorway Sadie couldn't help half-noticing, as she always did, the lovely set of his head on his thick youthful-looking neck.

Yes, even in middle-age Alec was handsome, his fine grained skin still clear and fresh. He noticed the piano right away and the skin wrinkled around his eyes. But her back was toward him when he said, 'F'r Pete's sake! Hey Sadie?'

Sadie turned towards him with her temper ready to let loose at him defensively. 'What is it?'

'I don't know Sadie. There's a big thing standing there against the wa' wi' a great row of shining teeth. Grinning at me. What is it?'

'It's a piano. A big, shiny, brown piano wi' brass candlesticks stuck to it.'

'You're right! – it is a big – shiny – brown – piano – wi' brass candlesticks stuck to it.'

'Then that's what it must be.'

'Yes, I suppose that's what it must be.'

Sadie turned back to the cooker, her back stiff. She brought the teapot to the table and put the cosy over it saying, 'Boys'll be in soon. The sink's clear, you can wash your hands.'

Alec hung his jacket in the lobby and came back to the kitchen, unbuttoning his waistcoat. He still wore galluses striped blue and red longitudinally, and his shirtsleeves held back from his wrists by old-fashioned sleeve bands. While he washed his hands at the sink Sadie took the warm plates from the bottom of the oven and set them at their places on the table. Alec stood watching her while drying his hands on a towel at the back of the cupboard door, then he quickly looped the towel back on to its hook and turned to her, his arms out and palms uppermost, then he shook his hands up and down in a gesture of florid appeal.

'Och, *Sadie. C'mon*? You're not saying anything. I mean, where did you get it? Whit did you? – no!' The lines crinkled round his eyes again and he clenched his fist and stuck his brow. 'No, don't tell me. Wait a minute. Ye won it in a raffle?'

'No, I didn't win it in a raffle.' She spoke in a huffed tone. 'As a matter of fact I bought it.'

'Bought it? Gave good money for it?'

'Aye. I did.'

'F'r that?'

'Aye. For that.' Again she turned away from him and stooped before the oven door. She lifted the bottom of her apron, twisted it, wiped some sweat from her upper lip then spoke in a flat matter-of-fact voice. 'It didn't cost much. It was advertised in a card in the paper shop window so I went to the woman selling it and she wanted to get rid of it to make room for a new sideboard getting . . .'

'So you decided to gie it hoose room?'

'So I got it for a couple of pounds and paid the coalman a couple of pounds to bring it on his lorry while he was doin' the rounds. They brought it up the stairs wi' these strap things round their shoulders.'

'Ah see.'

'I just got this notion –'

'It'll be a gey heavy notion when we humph it back down the stairs.'

'But I want to keep it!'

'Keep it? Sadie! You should have put that money towards something – like, you know, to help you in the kitchen, or a new coat.'

'We're short of money then?'

'It's not that. I mean look at the room it takes up. And it'll need a fair bit of polishing.'

'It's me that'll polish it.'

'And dusting.'

It's me that'll be dusting it. You'll have nothing to complain about on that score.' She looked round at the small, cramped, immaculately kept kitchen. Then satisfied, she repeated, 'Nothing to complain about on that score.'

'It'll get in the road when we're trying to sit doon at the table. It makes the kitchen look awful wee. There isnae room to swing a cat.'

'You can squeeze past. And forbye, there's no need to be swinging cats.'

'Just kiddin' like.'

'Well, Alec, I wish you wouldn't.'

'All right then. But it does make the room look awful wee. It is a big brute of a thing.'

That had been worrying her ever since she saw it looming at her on the landings so she became exasperated. 'I *ken* it makes the room look awful wee. But you can get used to it. I'm getting used to it and it's no' a couple of hours in the place. This time next week you'll not even notice it.'

'I suppose so. If maybe you just kept the lid shut?'

'No, I'm not having the lid shut. I like to see the keys. It looks like a big coffin when the lid's shut.'

A few moments later the door bell rang and Alec answered it. Their sons Colin and Hugh came in.

Colin was unlike either of his parents, being tall and slim. He had his father's thick well-groomed hair, but so dark it seemed nearly black. His mouth was wide and thin with the lips unusually defined for a man, which gave his features a dry, sarcastic expression. He wore a modish, quite expensive brown suit. Like his father he was an engineer but unlike Alec he had also studied at night school. His firm had transferred him to its computer section and was training him for it. Hugh, a few years younger, resembled his parents, having something of Alec's powerful physique and Sadie's big Irish teeth, but he was bigger than Alec and slower moving. It was hard to know if he was intelligent, for he was diffident, good-natured and deferred a lot to Alec and Colin. He drove a delivery van. Hugh, as usual when he came from work, was thinking of his tea and only eyed the table. Colin had noticed the piano immediately. His green eyes gleamed but he said nothing. Instead he sat in a chair facing his father, grasped his forehead between thumb and forefinger so that the palm of his hand was over his eyes, and started to shake with laughter.

Hugh was saying, 'Is the tea ready –' when he stopped speaking and his eyes popped. He said to Colin in a careful suspicious voice. 'Hey Colin. Look!'

'I'm looking,' Colin said, his voice sobbing with laughter.

'It's a piano.'

'So I see.'

'It's no' half a piano either! Where did you get it Ma?'

'She's been rakin' the middens,' said Colin still laughing. Said Sadie, 'Och, you're awful pass remarkable. It's just a piano I bought second-hand, and that's that.'

'Well, you've got a few quids' worth of timber anyway.' Colin went over to the piano and wrapped his knuckles on the top. 'Lovely tone.'

'But it makes the room awful wee,' Hugh said.

'I *ken* that,' Sadie's exasperation had brought her near to tears. 'I know it makes the room awful wee.'

'Mind ye, Sadie.' Alec tried to placate her. 'It wouldn't be so bad if we shifted it over there again the wall. We could move the wee bookcase ben the room, then when you opened up the leaf of the dinner table there would be mair room.'

'No. You can't put it there. It would be between the door and the fire. There would be too much draught.'

'A draught? Alec asked amazed.

'You're afraid it'll catch cold?' said Colin, 'Or pneumonia?'

'Aye, it's probably delicate' said Hugh. What dae ye feed them on?'

'Cream crackers,' said Colin, 'Dirty great cream crackers a yard long. Imagine it crunching into them wi' that set of wallies.'

'Aye,' Alec chuckled. 'Think of the crumbs it'll leave all over the carpet. I hear they're very messy feeders.'

'You're a' awfu' sarky,' said Sadie, 'It's just a piano.'

'It'll need exercise tae. Somebody'll have to take it oot at night.'

Colin and Hugh had both moved over to the piano for a closer look. Hugh put his hand out timidly towards the keys and Colin suddenly shut the lid and gave a little feminine scream. Even Sadie laughed at the way Hugh jumped like someone backing away from a wild dog. 'Oh, the brute! It'll have to be muzzled.'

Sadie was by now half laughing and half in tears and she said, 'I don't know what all the fuss is about. It's just a plain, old, ordinary upright piano that I've always wanted to have for years and years and years –'

'We're never noticed the want of one before,' Alec said, half indignantly, 'We've sometimes wanted a fitted carpet, or the room papered, or the sink boxed in –'

'Well, you see, these things –' Sadie interrupted Alec, her

voice pitched in irritation. She stopped and frowned then spoke slowly. 'These are sensible things – but some wants are harder to put a name to – until something happens.'

'And you happened to see an advertisement for this bloody great monstrosity –'

'Ach, Da. Wheesht!' Hugh had begun to realise how much the teasing was upsetting his mother. 'Everybody wheesht.' It's all right kidding. But look!' He sat on the piano stool and examined the instrument slowly. 'C'mere, Ma. Look, Colin, Da. Come here and have a good look. Look at those candle-brackets and the work that's been put into them. And that inlay with all those bits of mother-of-pearl. See how the beading round these panels is mitred. Ye cannae see the joints.'

'It's well done,' Colin admitted.

'Well done? It's better than that. They don't put computers into cabinets like this I'll bet you. This is craftsmanship. Nobody bothers to do that nowadays. Look at that fretwork round the music stand. You know, Ma, I could wire up these candlestick bulbs and put them in them.'

'Och, ye're making a fool of me again.'

'Naw, I'm serious. You can buy special bulbs that look like candles, wi' a wee bit black wick on top and the sides looking like melting wax. It would be nae bother to pass a wire up through the brackets and fix in sockets where the candles should go.'

I suppose that would be nice,' Sadie conceded though privately she didn't want her piano mucked about with.

Hugh had suddenly become enthusiastic about the piano. 'Look' See these medals fixed inside of the lid. See what they say. Hey Colin, listen to this. Gold Medal – Lou – is – i – ana purchase Exposition. Something – Internationale –'

'Arise, ye starvelings –'

'Shut up. Something – Republican Français. Universal Exposition. St Louis. The United States of America. And then there's a date. M-C-M-I-V. I think. Whit date would that be?'

'The year of the ark – tae look at it.'

'Never mind him Ma. It's a lovely bit of furniture. Come and sit doon on the stool. There. Now just look at it. It *was* a bargain. I'm sure.'

'Aye, but I still think it's a gey big bit of furniture just for to haud up some photies,' said Alec.

Sadie sat on the piano stool, running her hand along the lid. 'It *is* a lovely thing. But I didn't get it to put photies on. The tuner came in today as well and fixed it up. You see, I got it for playing.'

'Who's going to play it?' Alec asked. 'Naebody in this hoose can play a piano.'

Sadie struck middle C, smiled, played a scale with one finger then said, 'I'll play it.'

'But Ma, you cannae! You never learned a note of music in your life.'

Sadie struck middle C again. Her Doh. She pounded the key several times then shouted at Colin. 'How do you know? You're only a boy. You haven't known me all my life. Anyway –' and she played her Doh again, 'I'm going to learn.'

Hugh came over to her, looked in her face and said, 'It's all right, Ma.' But Alec burst out angrily, 'For goodness sake wumman. At your age? Wantin' tae play the piano. I mean you're pushing fifty.'

'That's right. I'm pushing fifty. Though it would have been just as easy to say that I was leaving forty.'

'Ach.'

'Ach. Who are ye ach-ing at? Whit harm would it be daeing? Your dinner'll still be on the table when ye come in. Well, ye can all go and ach away to yerselfs.' Sadie burst into tears and went into the lobby slamming the door behind her, leaving the men embarrassed and silent. Then Alec shrugged.

'Well, well. Your ma's in a right tid tonight.'

'Aye,' said Colin. 'That's us told, I suppose.'

'Nae wonder,' Hugh was feeling remorseful though his part of the teasing had been more out of genuine merriment than the others. 'We deserve it. A bit of kiddin's all right but we went over the score.'

'I don't see how,' said Alec to justify himself. 'I mean you come home to face a bloody great monstrosity of a contraption like that that makes the hoose look like a telephone kiosk. It's a good job we have got a sense of humour.' He paused then went on speaking with his voice adapting to tolerance, concession. 'Still and all. Maybe you're right. I suppose she can't help it. It's just that women get to a certain stage. Well, it's got to do with their age. You know what I mean. It's her *age*.'

Colin suddenly realised that his father was trying to refer to the menopause and burst out laughing. 'Oh, aye, aye. Yes. Of course. It'll be her *age*.' He phrased the words 'her age' in parody of Alec's mysterious tone but Alec was too embarrassed to react.

Hugh, worried about his mother going ben the room in a huff said, 'I think she just wants to learn to play the piano.'

'Christ, you're a help.' Alec was becoming irritable again, for the argument was threatening to stop them eating appealingly. 'Have some common sense. She just wants to learn the piano? At fifty?'

'She's not fifty yet,' Hugh cried. '*For* – get it! *For* – get it!' said Hugh, then added in a parody of his own Glasgow accent. 'Let us not forget that us yins have not had wur tea.'

'It'll be bloody cauld. And we'll have to put it out ourselves,' grumbled Alec.

'Well, we're not paralysed,' said Hugh, 'We can stir our ain teacups, I suppose.'

This remark contained enough bitterness to start another argument, but at that moment Sadie came back. She marched into the kitchen, her cheeks red where she had dried her eyes with the apron, and still sniffing said, 'Ye'll be wanting your tea?'

She took the dishes from the oven, banged them on to the table, and started serving the fish and chips. Her anger was evident in her every movement. The plates rang and clattered under her serving spoon. She poured out tea and passed the cups in such a careless movement that the liquid slopped into their saucers. She served herself a few chips and a tiny piece of fish, then sat picking at the batter with her fork and projecting her upset appetite round the table. Colin smiled and ate unperturbed. Hugh first picked at his fish, peered anxiously round the table, then started eating as if out of duty. Alec, though sometimes glaring at Sadie, ate his fish and chips with gusto then helped himself to a big slice of cream sponge.

When Sadie went to bed that night she lay awake longer than usual. Alec, as usual, lay at the back of the bed, his face to the wall, sound asleep. Sadie always lay on the outer side of the bed, being the last to go to bed at night and first to rise in the morning. She often lay awake, not thinking she had insomnia, but if the boys were out late, assuming that she was listening for them to come home. When the key clicked in the lock she would sigh, turn on her side and sleep. In these waking periods she took stock of the day, anticipating the next, planning meals and chores to be done. She would worry a little and sometimes reminisce.

It would be hard to say that Sadie was happy, for she often worried at lot and was anxious at times. It would also be hard to say she was unhappy, for she had no words for such estimations, not because she did not understand them, but because they did not seem to fit her situation. She spoke with a Glasgow accent but was never guilty of solecisms, except when her speech was vigorously idiomatic. She knew the meaning of 'happiness' or 'insomnia' and even 'aesthetic'. But as she herself said – 'Some things are hard to put a name to'. Not *find* a name, but *put* a name to. For that would be a breach of these carefully worked out limitations, those precariously established boundaries set by Sadie's cultural background, where wants are expressed without being named. Such naming establishes possibility, it changes vague hope to precise expectations, and to have these beyond the limits set by life is only to suffer.

Sadie's marriage avoided naming precise wants so she and

Alec thought it a good marriage. It had brought them years of unease, hardship, and small day to day disappointment, but they judged its success by their satisfaction and relief at avoiding worse.

She had known Alec most of her life for he came from the same teeming street of her childhood. She first saw and disapproved of him when she was small and he one of the bigger, rougher boys, just ready to leave school, wearing long trousers, climbing up rone pipes at the side of buildings and fighting with other boys. Their first close contact was when she too was nearly ready to leave school, her breasts beginning to grow and after her first periods. One Sunday afternoon some older boys were hanging around the street on their bicycles. They gathered in a group, half sitting on the saddles, one foot on a raised pedal, one leg stretched out to brace the tilted bicycle. Sometimes one of them, or a pair, or a whole group would break out of the knot, cycle slowly up the street, then turn and come back. Sometimes they cycled round so slowly that the front wheel wobbled from side to side and the plane of the spokes alternately darkened and lightened in the sunlight. Some with fixed wheel clogs occasionally rode their bikes with only one foot on a pedal and raced up and down the street with their whole bodies going up and down with the turn of that pedal in an awkward see-sawing motion. The younger children gathered round the knot of boys and begged to be taken rides on the bar of someone's bike. This was a great excuse for the cyclists to invite older girls to sit on the bars and some girls were notoriously reckless at this game, they sat sideways on the bar between a boy's arms, stuck out their legs, leaned back and incited the boy to go at more and more reckless speeds. It was quite a spectacle to see a boy tearing down the street with a squealing, giggling girl perched unsafely on the bar, her legs flapping wildly. Then the brakes were jammed, they skidded to a stop, the girl nearly head over heels but held safely in the boy's arms. The game expressed their young physical vigour, and the horseplay was an excuse for physical contact. When bikes fell the boys would try to grab a girl's breast or tip her over to expose as much of her legs as possible, even her crotch. Alec was one of the worst or best at this game, but Sadie didn't like horseplay with bigger boys, and was too shy to expose her knickers like some of the girls.

Alec, however, kept riding up to her, stopping beside her, inclining his head sideways and saying, 'C'mon Sadie Maxwell and I'll gie ye a shot on my bike,' and when she shook her head he would taunt, 'Are ye feart?'

'You would tumble me,' Sadie had said.

'Away ye go, I'll not tumble ye. I haven't ever scaled anybody yet.'

'Would you go slow?'

'If you want I'll go slow.'

So Sadie was coaxed on to the bar of Alec's bike. She sat carefully sideways on to the bar and balanced herself while Alec held the bike steady; then he put his arms round her to grab the handlebars, thrust down on the pedal and she felt herself carried away in a delicious surge of motion. After that she hardly noticed the movement of the bike, so unprepared was she for what she would feel. Sadie had played, along with the other children, at games of truth and dare, and at night in the back close she had occasionally kissed and giggled and held off a fumbling, groping boy. Alec however, in carrying her on his bar, directed all his physicality towards controlling the bicycle, and being less aware of her his movements were powerful and frank. His knees pumped up and down with the pedals and each time she felt his left knee under her thigh. She felt the hard violent movements of the muscles in his arms as he controlled the front wheel and the broad, hard curve of his chest on her back, rising and falling. His breath blew on her cheek, his chin was nearly in the crook of her neck and shoulder, and she could smell the mint from the chicklets he was chewing. She felt the rough, rhythmic exhalation in his throat each time he pushed down on a pedal and had a sense of being lifted and carried in the rhythm of his uninhibited vigour.

For a few seconds, just as Alec pushed off, this shockingly intimate juxtaposition with Alec's body made her shiver, a sharp slightly unpleasant sensation, then as the goosepimples came up she found a strange conditional pleasure in the feeling. She held her body balanced between the nearly unpleasant sensation and a desire to lean back limp against Alec's big hard chest, a balance easier to hold if she breathed like him with each thrust of the pedal. When he finally let her off she heard him laugh awkwardly as he said to one of his friends, 'That Sadie Maxwell, she's a nice wee thing, getting –' and for a minute or two could hardly pay attention to anything else going on around her.

Sadie had been a few months from her fourteenth birthday then. Less than five years later she was pregnant by Alec so they married. Ann, their only daughter, was born, then Colin, then Hugh. They had been brought together by sharp, clamorous specifically genital sexuality that had eventually died, leaving them with pleasantness, decency and habit keeping them together. Both came from a generation and a class which considered any break in marriage vows utterly disgraceful. This was not out of principle or religious belief, but from sound, ingrained knowledge that good behaviour was all that was economically possible. Perhaps there was also a strange and deep collusion between that original sexual clamour and the later transformation of its binding energies into a mature and stable economic arrangement. Until the boys got older Alec was sometimes not a very good husband, becoming neglectful, indifferent, irritable, sometimes angry and occasionally vicious, but nobody doubted that the marriage should be tholed. Sometimes Alec would say, conventionally, standing in some bar, 'Ah well, if I was single again,' and Sadie, perhaps more dangerously would reminisce, but that was all. Eventually Ann had married, Colin gained his apprenticeship, Hugh and Alec were both earning good wages. There were good carpets in the house, Sadie could splash a little at the Co-op, a routine had been established – some sort of contentment reigned.

Yet at night as she lay sleepless Sadie still reminisced. That period of youth had gone when clamorous energies obliterate our histories for a while, and now she found herself consciously returning to these vague hopes and lucid glimpses of childhood and measuring against them her adult life. Now as she lay listening for Colin's key to rasp in the lock she associated these lucid glimpses with the big piano looming on the other side of the dark kitchen.

The following Wednesday morning at eleven o'clock Sadie went to see Mr McKay, the music teacher whose address the piano tuner had given her. She arrived ten minutes early. McKay lived on the outskirts of the city in a quiet street of bungalows with their backs to a golf course. When she rang the bell McKay opened the door, ushered her brusquely into a front room off the hall, muttered something about still having a pupil and left her. From a room at the back came the sound of a piano being played – brilliantly, it seemed to Sadie.

She sat in an armchair, awed and a little discouraged by the brilliant runs and crashing chords. The soft easy chair took her comfortably and disconcertingly back into its depths so she got up again and sat on a dining chair beside the music-strewn table by the window. She felt easier sitting upright on the hard chair and looked around. The neatness of the house from the outside impressed her, but this room was anything but neat. Though not exactly dirty it seemed dusty and drab. The sideboard was obviously not used as a sideboard. Along the top lay piles of music, books, scores. Both doors lay slightly open, and Sadie got the impression that the inside was crammed with old newspapers. Table and chairs were the only other furniture apart from bookcases. One complete wall was taken up to the ceiling by bookshelves made of untreated wooden planks. What Sadie thought should have been used for display cabinets were recessed into the wall on each side of the fireplace and were also crammed with books. Only a wall containing bay windows and one behind the sideboard were clear of books and they were cluttered with pictures, framed photographs and drawings. Above the fireplace, which held a small tile-framed gas fire, hung huge plates and dishes of coarse looking make, all with the same reddish ornate pattern. Beside the hide covered easy chair on which she had first tried to sit there was an ugly adjustable lamp fixed to a bracket on the wall, and lying beside it in the ash strewn fireplace was a small nude blatantly sensual statue of a woman carved from greenish stone. She was covered in cigarette ash and where her hands met, delicately clasped across her stomach, lay a cigarette butt.

This disappointed Sadie as had the sight of the big man who had brusquely let her in. He struck her as coarse. She could still hear the piano stopping and starting, playing a certain passage over again, and that made her feel more confident because somebody was obviously learning from him.

The piano finally stopped playing. She heard Mr McKay in the hall letting out his pupil, so she opened her bag and took out the piano tuner's card and held herself armed with it in her hand.

McKay was certainly big and Sadie's first impression of coarseness was perhaps justified. He seemed in his late fifties; his block of a body seeming mostly bone for it was not over fleshed. He had thick grizzled crew-cut hair, large ugly ears with heavy lobes, his bottom lip stuck out beyond the top one as if he were continually considering a problem. What most gave the impression of coarseness a brick red complexion, like that of a farm labourer or bricklayer who worked outside in all weathers.

He entered the room, squinted against the smoke that rose into his eyes from a cigarette between his lips. He blew away the ash without taking the cigarette from his mouth and immediately started dusting it off his front. Sadie stood up and handed him the card. He studied it while rubbing the bristle on his head with one hand. Again he squinted at the smoke and took the tiny stub from between his lips and, after looking unsuccessfully for an ash-tray, threw it into the fireplace beside the little nude statue. Handing Sadie the card back he shrugged and smiled brightly as if to say, 'What's it all about?' But he didn't speak. Sadie decided that she didn't like him at all.

'Mr Martin recommended you to me. That's why I phoned.'

'Aye.' Sadie again felt disappointed, she didn't expect this broad 'Aye' from a music teacher.

'Well, I mean, I've come to see you.'

'He recommended me to you?'

'Yes. Uhuh.'

'Aye. Well –' he didn't continue but stood staring at the floor, rubbing his stubble. It was like a scrubbing brush, Sadie thought, and she felt anger like a spark rising in her breast at this ugly ill-mannered man who stood there not speaking. Keeping me hanging, she thought, just keeping me hanging. She snapped her bag shut.

'You want to take piano lessons?' he asked after quite a long silence.

'Yes.'

'C'mere.'

McKay walked out of the room and Sadie followed. They crossed the hall into the back room from where the piano had sounded. It was a big room, practically bare except for a Steinway grand piano, a few chairs, a small occasional chair against a wall and a metal music stand in one corner. The wooded floor was well polished and covered by a light carpet. Sadie thought she would have had a different impression if she had first entered this light and airy room instead of that grubby little den. By the time she came timidly through the door McKay was standing in the middle of the room with his back to her. Then he walked to the piano stood and slumped there with his back to the keyboard, legs stuck straight out, heels on the floor, toes pointed upward, hands clasped between legs. His movements seemed too dramatic, too boyish for a man of his age. The thought of that grubby little room made Sadie realise that McKay was unmarried or a widower, and she wondered if his underclothes were clean. The thought brought a rush of sympathy for him with some embarrassment on his behalf, and the realisation that he too was embarrassed.

'D'ye think I'm a silly auld woman?'

'No, no, no. I don't think you're a silly auld wumman.'

McKay said this rather insincerely, then looking up at the ceiling said almost to himself, 'At my age I'm not keen on calling anyone old and I've learned better than to call anyone a fool. At least no' without evidence.'

He grinned and addressed her for the first time in a fairly civil tone. 'I expected you to arrange lessons for one of your kids. It's unusual to find someone of your age wanting to learn the piano.'

'Thank you,' Sadie's sarcasm was all the more telling, coming out of her diffidence.

McKay wasn't exactly a bully, but like a few good teachers he had something of the bully in him. Though mostly patient and kindly he used his status to sound off private ideas and often hectored pupils in a semi-ironic, humorous way. He knew and enjoyed a rough demotic style, using colloquialisms and dialect. To certain older pupils he would swear like a trooper and to some others he pretended it was an accident. He was successful because most pupils enjoyed his flamboyant tempers, his parodies of irritation; they were attracted by his colour and the expressive and vigorous language. His memorable imagery drove the music he taught into their minds. His fault was in talking too often over their heads. But his style was almost automatically provoked by any sign of rebellion and Sadie's sarcastic thanks immediately brought it out. Though he was less heavy than he would have been on a pupil he knew.

'No, I've no prejudices on the subject, Mrs –' he snapped his fingers at her.

'Mrs Anderson.'

'If you want to pay for expensive (and I'm expensive, no two ways about that) piano lessons it's up to yourself and I've no objections to taking your money – I'm a professional teacher Mrs Anderson. But I won't lie to you.' He arose and walked up and down the bare room. 'Frankly, I think you're daft. You don't realise what's involved. Hours of practice and concentration, hours of sheer drudgery and boredom. Do you know – have you any idea of the things you'll have to do? First you'll have to learn musical notation.' McKay illustrated this point by shoving a sheet of music in Sadie's face and thumping the sheet with the back of his hand. 'You'll have to practise finger exercises.' He went to the piano and played some very unsteady five finger exercises as if he was a learner, his brow furrowed. 'Then scales passages –' this time he fingered chromatically up the keyboard in a swift peremptory run. 'And the kind of music which I teach –' (he rattled off the first few bars of *Rondo á la Turque*) '– is what is called classical piano.' He rose from the piano again. 'I'm not going to charge you expensive fees to teach you to vamp with your left hand while you pick out a tune. You'll get studies by Czerny, pieces by Beethoven and Clementi – all that kind of old rubbish.'

'But I want that!' Sadie cried out, thrilled by the mention of Clementi. 'Oh, I know what you mean – you think I want to learn to play the piano like someone in a pub but I don't.' Sadie was now appealing to him, for when he had ripped off that chromatic run she had lost some of her dislike. 'I want to learn to play properly.'

'What's properly?' he asked her. His question seemed rude and blunt again but she answered simply, though her voice rose in pitch as she tried to break through what she thought his lack of sympathy. He seemed to her taking up the same attitude as her family.

'I want to play music that isn't all fuzzy. I'd like to play – you'll laugh at this –'

'I might, but say it just that same.'

'I'd like to play something like Brahms' waltz in A flat.'

'Well, well. It's a nice wee tune.' He considered for a moment. 'It's not impossible – but.'

'For a woman my age.'

McKay laughed at her directness. 'Aye, for a woman of your age.'

'And that makes me an old fool.'

'Och, now, Mrs Anderson. It's not that –'

He sat on the piano stool looking at her and rubbing his stubble again. She could see his puzzlement, his not wanting to turn her down and hurt her.

'But you think it's just some kind of notion I've got into my head?'

'Well, yes! It must be!' For a while he sat, still and silent, his decision, his bottom lip protruding further and further in puzzled exasperation, then he seemed to come to a decision, stretched his arm out with forefinger pointed, and said in a brisk, hard, worldly wise way, 'I tell you Mrs Anderson, I'm a professional musician. I learned my skill through hours, days, weeks, months and years of continuous hard work and concentration. I had to train like an athlete and study like a monk; I had to develop the manual dexterity of a juggler and I had to learn to count like a bookie; I had to combine the cold intelligence of a mathematician with the hot emotional temperament of the artist; the idealism of a saint with the cynicism of a criminal; the patience of Job with the restiveness of a child. Above all I had to work, work, work and work. At twelve years of age I was playing euphonium with the Salvation Army. Oh aye, Mrs Anderson – round the back courts every Sunday morning farting and blasting guid folk oot of their Sunday rest, excuse the language. And all this not in the Praise of the Lord but to harden my lip. I was an apprentice fitter in the shipyards but I was a fully time served tradesman before I was able to buy one of these damned jangle boxes. Twenty three years of age. Twenty three! Though by that time I knew music. Crammed that fu' wi' it that I was sneezing semi-quavers, with a G clef on my brow instead of a kiss curl. When I *laughed* it was in figures like an Alberti bass. But it was still hard – and in the end I have never been within a kick in the arse of – whit? What? Certain standards –'

'In a sense I was a fool. I'm not all that out of sympathy with you. If I had known what was ahead of me I wouldn't have been able even to try. I had to be fool enough not to know and fool enough to ignore my elders and betters when they tried to tell me. Music making – it's the most demanding and abstract and concrete of all human skills. To start doing it is to be a fool, to continue is to be a bigger one. But I believe it's a serious pursuit, Mrs Anderson. That's why I'm a good musician and a good teacher.'

'All these things you said –' Sadie looked wan, then suddenly she smiled, brilliantly, showing her big Irish teeth. 'I might have said the same for marriage, Mr McKay, and that's why I'm a good housewife.'

McKay put his head back and laughed, guffawed. 'That's me told. I see what you're telling me. Don't brag.'

'And what you're saying is that I don't understand. Oh, I've been laughed at, don't worry. It seems you've got to be a fool to try anything in this world – except what's ordinary. But if what you're saying is right then it's just as well if I don't understand, because I'm fool enough to try.'

'I suppose so. But why now? Why – a woman of your age – why do you want to start now? Why wait all that time?'

'Because I've never had a piano before, and now I've got one. I was good at music when I was a wee girl at school. The teacher used to say I had a marvellous sense of pitch. I could sight read and render any tune into sol-fa, right away, singing it, even the teacher couldn't do it as good as me – and I can still do it.'

McKay wasn't very impressed but was listening attentively.

'Then I used to sing these songs for fun (I couldn't really sing) by Mozart and Schubert and that. But I always listened to the piano accompaniment. Do you know Mozart's song *The Violet*?'

McKay nodded.

'I can only vaguely remember the words, haven't remembered them for years, but I still carry the notes of the piano in my head. A girl in my class at school who used to take piano lessons was my friend. Do you know this district very well Mr McKay?'

'No, I wasn't brought up here. I'm from Govan originally.'

'Well, I was brought up in the very street I'm living in now. When I was a wee girl there was a field down the street where the factory is now, with cows in that field. It's all built over now. Anyway, if you went down the side of the field you came to a sort of cul-de-sac with big houses where this girl lived. Her folks were nice, nae side, and sent her to the same school as the rest of us. She used to play Clementi. I'll never forget that, for her mother used to shout, 'Anna, have you finished your Clementi?' Sometimes I waited in the kitchen, sometimes I sat in the room and listened. There was one piece, I remember, where the notes kept repeating themselves in octaves –'

McKay grinned at her. 'Did it go anything like this?' He played a quotation from near the beginning of Clementi's 1st Sonatina where the G repeats itself eight times in octaves followed in the next bar by a little ornate figure.

'That's it!' Sadie reacted by lifting her face, a little sensuous smile on her lips. 'It was like getting ice on your spine.'

McKay laughed. 'Sounds like a cure for a nose bleed.'

'Och!' Sadie dismissed the remark impatiently. I even felt that way when she played exercises and scales and made the piano ring out like that. I'd have given anything for to do that. You talk about drudgery Mr McKay. But learning's not drudgery. I've been a housewife for coming on nearly thirty years and brought up three weans in a room-and-kitchen and there's application and work, work, work and work in that too. And warnings that you're fool enough to ignore – then scrubbing and cooking and nursing and tending. Wiping snotty noses and washing nappies and teaching and caring. They say a housewife's work is never done –' Sadie laughed at this, a short laugh, grim and rather bitter. '– It's true. You can't keep anything you put your heart and soul into. People change and grow away from you. And all the time the dust and the oos* come floating back down. It's messy. But you only have to play the piano with your fingers! After *your* drudgery you are left able to play, and even the scales and exercises you need to play are clear – and, I don't know –'

'You think I only play the piano with my fingers? You think sound is less amorphous than living?' McKay shrugged.

He had been impressed by Sadie's long speech. He spoke slowly and musingly as if to himself. 'Well, Maybe. I suppose I shouldn't brag.' Then he shook himself, all brisk movement again. 'No! It's ridiculous! Look, a long time ago you took a fancy to the piano. You like music. You can't balance that against your age. I mean, what else have you got?' McKay's question was purely rhetorical but Sadie answered.

'Perfect pitch. If that's any help.' She was sarcastic again. 'Against my age.'

'Perfect pitch?'

'Aye.'

McKay stood up, put his hands in his pockets and started to walk up and down the room again. 'You've got a bloody cheek. You really have.' He faced her and flung his arms around in flamboyant exasperated gestures. 'Not only, one,' he struck an index finger in the air, 'have you got a broader, harder, wiser, wider and more intense experience of life than I have. But, two,' he stuck up two fingers, 'you tell me you've got mair natural ability as a musician. Well –' He anticipated her protest, 'that's what perfect pitch means. Perfect bloody pitch!' He sat down at the piano. 'My arse in parsley. Do you know the names of the chords?'

'You don't have to swear!'

'That's not what I asked. Do you know the names of the chords?'

* Oos (rhymes with goose): Glaswegian for fluffy dirt

'No. But I know the names of the notes, now that I've a piano.'

'Right. What are these notes?' He struck a chord.

'D, F sharp and A.'

'Jesus Christ!'

Sadie stood up this time. 'I still don't think that there's any need to swear.'

'Don't you believe it. Don't believe it for a minute. I mean, f'r Chrissakes, you were right. And anyway the process of learning is not so pure and abstract as you seem to think. If you're going to be my pupil you'll find there'll be a lot of cursing and blinding done before we're finished.'

Sadie nodded.

'So don't criticise my methods. Ach, tae hell. You've got me admitting the possibility.' He came over to her and took the handbag she had been clutching in both hands. 'Take your coat off.' He took the coat and handbag and laid them over the small table. 'Right. C'mere to the piano.' Sadie came to the piano and they both sat down on the bench-like stool.

'So now you're just another wee lassie wanting to learn the piano. OK? Let's see what you've got. You like music?'

'I like – what you called – classical piano.'

'You've got a good memory – you can carry a tune in your head?'

'Yes.'

'So you've got these, a love of music, a good memory, and (if you'll excuse me, Jesus Christ) you've got perfect pitch. All you need now is to pay attention, for everything I tell you when you're sitting on this stool, even when I'm cursing and blinding, is important. All you need beside the other things is a pair of hands – *you* said it, you play that piano with your fingers. We'll leave the dust and oos out of it. No rubato*. Now the hands – let's have a look.'

'I'm afraid they're not pianists' fingers.'

---

* Rubato: musical term for blurred, distorted rhythm

'The only people with pianists' fingers are pianists. See these paws?' McKay held up his big, strong, masculine hands, raw and knuckled and hairy. 'Oh, the nails are cut short and they're nice and clean – but otherwise they're a navvy's hands – like my father's – or a tattie picker's – like my mother's – or a fitter's – like my son.'

'I always thought that long tapering fingers were best.'

'Oho? And elegant? There's nothing elegant about piano playing – you watch any concert pianist writhing about the stool with sweat dripping off his nose. No. Or see any book of pianoforte technique. Wait a minute.' He rose from the stool, disappeared, and returned a minute later with a book he propped on the music stand. 'These are pictures of great pianists' hands. They took plaster casts of them you know. There's a rogues' gallery for you! Some wi' paws like lumps of mud, some wi' hands like emaciated chicken claws. One or two of them are reasonable, Chopin's, Mendelssohn's, but look at these big mitts of Liszt's. Rather like my own, if I say it myself, without the lumps.'

'Rubenstein had hands like an overfed baby's. Richter – plain, ordinary looking hands you wouldn't give tuppence for. It's only when they play that they become beautiful. Oh, no! Your lovely tapering fingers are frail and need strength, and the wee stubby fingers that fly up and down scales and runs have to learn to stretch and the big broad hand that can compass octaves has to learn speed. You have to work for your advantages just like in real life. Now sit here on this stool – don't crouch! – it's a keyboard, not a bloody scrubbing board – make yourself comfortable so you reach the keys without bending forward or back. Take some balance on your feet – it's like playing snooker, hmm, you wouldn't know – we might as well start you off right. *Now*, let's see what *your* disadvantages are. Play there – from middle C – with the left hand – like this.' McKay played the first simple five-finger exercise, slowly. 'Now you try, with both hands.'

Sadie played, halting and stumbling. 'I thought so. A good

middle-aged housewife's hands – strong, competent, but with no independence in the fingers. No independence. Right? So, that's what the exercises are for. We'll have to get a book of exercises that'll soon put that right. Your drudgery book full of scales and exercises that'll soon have you limbered up.'

Sadie was sitting at the piano and the beauty of the instrument, the rows of soft-coloured keys, the polished case, the elegance and definition of its lines, most of all McKay's words – all seemed to heighten and add savour to the thrilling drudgery McKay was offering.

'Ach, tae hell. If you don't put your line in the watter ye never catch any fish,' McKay said. 'For Chrissakes, we can be two auld fools thegither.'

The big old piano loomed and bulked across the kitchen, its polished wood and brass reflecting the dim and flickering lights from the fire like the lucid gleams in her mind. Much of her time was taken up by her appetite for drudgery at the keyboard, but there were still other things in her life that could not be ignored.

The dust and oos which she had mentioned to McKay was a reality in her life and a powerful image in her mind. Like any housewife she had an intimate acquaintance with them, and she felt the disorder they represented as an injury, though her own childhood had not been unusually harsh. Mary, her eldest sister, had seen to that, for Mary had the gift of husbandry, the purse-clutching bitter art of those times. She kept the home clean, clothes washed, let out seams, patched trousers, mended second-hand shoes, walked miles to the cheapest butchers for ham-bones and mince, brought coarse oats and lentils and peas in bulk and the misshapen batch ends of loaves from the bakery. She was prim, light-lipped, tart tongued, a mistress of mean economies and paring, a scrubber, polisher, darner and patcher. These had been necessary skills in those callous and mean-minded times between two World Wars. Her dour fight for what she called 'decency' had distorted her life. She often said, 'Smiles are cheap.' In her stiff work-chapped hands gutting and frying herring for the family dinner there was as much love as in the flowing lines of a free polymorphously per- verse body – however pathetically expressed in huge quantities of ham-bone soup, pease brose, thick porridge, clean patches, and neatly let out seams.

Sadie learned none of Mary's skills. From leaving school until marriage she had worked in a grocery store, leaving home in the morning at half-past-six and returning at night well after tea-time. During that period in her teens both her brothers had left home despairing of ever finding work. The older one went to Canada where he simply disappeared, the younger one to Birmingham where he found work as a mechanic. Sadie's lack of domestic experience had created difficulties in the first years of her marriage. Alec, fortunately, had never been out of work for long, but with a young family and her inability to cope properly at first with ordinary household tasks (cooking, cleaning, keeping their cramped little room-and-kitchen tidy) their life and been hard. They got into small, niggling debts. They quarrelled a lot – lived from hand to mouth without proper routines. Eventually she learned better and things became easier, but she remembered these years as stolen from her in some way, and attached a great deal of value to the order established in her domestic life. So she rose every morning at half-past-six, visiting her father and mother and her sister Mary every Thursday and her daughter Anne on Sunday afternoons. The carpets were hoovered each morning before nine, her washing fluttered on the line in the back court every Tuesday afternoon, bed linen was changed on Monday, shopping done on Friday morning, windows washed once a week, mince and dough balls served on Saturday at dinner-time.

Yet she did not pay much attention to these things; though she would never have dreamed of stopping giving her hours and energies to them. The routine was so well established that she found it easy to live her inner life as she went through tasks and chores.

On Thursday morning the day after first seeing McKay she visited her father who now lived on the ground floor of a tenement further up the street from where he had supported his motherless family. Mary still lived with him and had insisted on shifting to a ground-floor flat where he need not climb stairs. Before the visit Sadie bought cold meat, tomatoes for the tea that night, an ounce of thick black tobacco and a packet of chocolate biscuits, then collected from the newsagents a stack of illustrated weeklies ordered regularly for her father.

The front door of his house had been flushed with hardboard and painted with a rich maroon gloss finish. A new chrome letter box had been put in and a combination name plate and bell-push was lit by a little bulb fixed in the door frame. Instead of pushing the bell Sadie rapped the door with her knuckles. She hated the sickly noise made by the chimes, and knew Mary and her father would know it was her by the knocking.

Mary was making a pot of tea with deft movements between sink and cupboard while Sadie took off her coat. One leaf of the kitchen table had been opened and Mr Maxwell, Sadie's father, sat there writing with a ball point pen. Mr Maxwell not only worked out form for dogs, horses and football teams but entered every competition he saw in newspapers or magazines – crossword puzzles, spot-the-ball, questionnaires. He even wrote letters to the papers, especially to cheap Sunday papers that print and pay money for declamatory opinions. He had started doing this after retiring and both Sadie and Mary had encouraged him thinking that it was good for him to be occupied with something, but they found that Mr Maxwell actually made a profit by these activities, carrying them out with amazing competence. The letters he wrote to the papers were totally cynical and he used to laugh when reading them aloud and saying, 'Pro Bono Publico has earned himself another quid.'

Mary would tell him proudly, 'You're a cunning old bugger.'

The electric kettle Mary was boiling up for the tea came

from one of his ploys. He often talked of his ambition to win the big one, the treble chance, the magic number.

Sadie took from her bag the biscuits, papers, plug of tobacco and put them on the glass topped coffee table. Beneath the glass was a large coloured photograph of a Highland stream fringed by autumnal birches, Mary's idea of contemporary décor. In the fireplace stood a small metal figure of a man in armour carrying a pike, which could be ingeniously dismantled into a hearth-tidy. The chimney piece was hung with paper printed to look like a rubble or dry-stane wall. The other walls were papered bright cream with a pattern of leaves and fragile branches filigreed over it. Against this hung little wooden frames holding narrow shelves on which glittered Mary's collection of glass animals and figurines – cute dogs, coy fauns and plump innocent birds. All woodwork in the room was gloss-painted off-white, and the draining board topped with a hard, bright washable plastic. It was all too shiny for Sadie's taste, but she also felt it was cheery and bright and (as the houseproud Mary made sure) clean.

Sadie enjoyed these morning visits to her father and sister. Mary had a tart, worldly hard-headedness expressed in words for which Sadie would have been apologetic. She'd dismiss the chimes on the door, the gloss paint, the glittering animals with a cynical laugh saying, 'It's not Buckingham Palace but it's bright enough.'

In the times when she had brought up a motherless family she had ensured, after each weekly struggle, that there was always twopence for the cinema matinee and sweets on a Saturday afternoon, saying, 'The weans must enjoy themselves' as if this was a matter of fact, of necessity, which it wasn't in many homes. When Sadie's daughter Anne brought her two little daughters to see Mary she would take down her precious glass animals and let the girls play with them. 'Children are only weans, they don't mean to break things,' she'd say in her sharp worldly tone, as if too adult to care that children might break a couple of small glass animals. She spoiled neither the children not adults around her with her bitter, cheery, cynical tolerance and kindness.

While Sadie tried to undo the knot in the string round the bundle of newspapers and magazines Mary put plates with biscuits and tea things on the glass surface over her Highland burn. Then she sat across from Sadie, poured tea, added sugar and milk, stirred the cups and handed one to her father with a tea-plate holding a wrapped chocolate biscuit.

'Well, did you go and see your man?' Mary punctuated this question while sipping tea to show her question was neutral and casual. She knew Alec and Colin had been putting Sadie through a barrage of destructive persiflage about her music teacher.

'You mean the piano teacher?'

'Aye.'

'I saw him all right.'

'Well – how did you get on?'

'Fine – except that he's a funny sort of man.'

'How come?'

'He seemed different from what I expected – I mean, he was awful abrupt – and then' Sadie started to giggle, 'he cursed and swore.'

'Cursed and swore?' said their father looking up from his writing, 'A funny sounding music teacher.'

'Yes, he has an awful coarse Glesca tongue on him, but at other times he speaks quite proper – he's got letters after his name.'

'Is he any good though?'

'He's marvellous!' This judgement broke out of Sadie with unwitting enthusiasm. 'Of course, as I said, he's a bit coarse – but he knows a lot about music.' She paused, then laughed. 'Actually he's quite funny wi' it. He told stories about how he learned music himself and had a comical way of putting things. I thought at first he wasn't going to take me, because of, you know –'

'Because how?' said Mr Maxwell, slicing the plug of tobacco

with the sliver of blade left in by the filthy old pocket-knife. 'Is your money no' good enough?'

'It's nothing like that, faither. It's just that it does look a bit funny, I suppose Alec's quite right. I mean, at my age –'

'Aye, the man's not going to be wasting his time, and quite right.' Mary said this as if assuming that in taking Sadie he wouldn't be wasting his time.

'I got the impression that he's quite a keen sort of teacher. I don't think he's impatient or anything. Oh, and Mary, you should see the piano he has, a huge Steinway grand. Anyway, the thing is, I'm going twice a week, Monday and Thursday mornings. I start next Monday.'

'Thursday morning?' Mr Maxwell asked.

'Aye. That's the thing. I'll have to get another to be coming here, if that's all right?'

'Well, Sadie. We're aye gaddin' about that much that I don't know if we can fit you in.' Mary took another biscuit and grinned a sarcastic wee smile. Sadie laughed, thinking that Mary was always sensible and easy.

She got home at lunch-time made herself a couple of tomato sandwiches and a cup of tea, then sat down and reflected on the problem of fitting things in. McKay had told her that, if at all serious she would have to practise a little every day. How could she manage things so that she had some time every day for the piano? She had arranged to visit McKay in the morning at ten o'clock. Monday was all right for she had nothing definite to do that day after seeing McKay in the morning. But on Tuesday she went to the steamie, the public wash-house, because Tuesday was her turn to use the drying space in the back-court. Of course, nowadays, with big spinners and drying cupboards she didn't need so much time for drying, but she was used to doing her washing on Tuesdays. While she sat chewing at a tomato sandwich she'd wondered if she could start sending her sheets, towels, curtains to the bag wash. They would come back a bit damp, but she could quickly iron them dry. Unless she took the bag-wash stuff to the steamie with her for it was a big advantage to be able to use the calendar. She would have to think about that. There was still the underwear to be ironed on Tuesday night, but Alec and the boys were usually out then and she could manage easily. There wasn't much to it, especially since Alec had at long last given up expecting starched collars. Wednesday mornings she could visit Mary and her father, getting his thick-black on the way, and she didn't really need to collect his papers on Thursdays. She only did that because she was passing the shop. The rest of that day there was nothing much except for an occasional baby-sit for Anne and her man. Thursday morning she'd see McKay again and there was nothing much else that day. Friday was crammed, for that day she shopped, changed some laundry, gave the house a thorough going over, washed the inside windows and, once in three weeks, the stairs, stairhead windows and the lavatory on the stairhead landing. And Friday was the night when Alec always went out for a drink. The weekends didn't have as much routine, so there was always the odd hour for practising. She knew that in spite of routines everything couldn't be anticipated – there was the occasional night when she'd go to the pictures with Mary, weekend visits to Anne and her grandchildren, or to one of her other sisters, there was always an odd bit of mending to do. She'd have to cope with these things as they came.

When she had finished her lunch Sadie washed and tidied away the plates, not even leaving the cup and saucer to dry on the draining board. She had rinsed them in such hot water that the dish towel slid smoothly over the warm surfaces. Several years before Hugh had seen an electric geyser in the wash-room of the ware-house where he worked, and had bought one and wired it up for her. This was now one of her great pleasures – cleaning dishes in such hot water that they almost dried off themselves. She loved the feel of a dry dish towel skiting off a warm plate. It was additional pleasure that plenty of hot water made it possible for her to now think of her piano.

Sadie had expected McKay to give her a piano tutor from

which to work but instead he had given her a cyclostyled pamphlet in which the rudiments of musical notation were set out and had ordered her flatly to learn the value of the notes, the meaning of the time signatures and a few common musical signs. 'I mean, you've had enough gumption to bone up on a few rudiments without my help. I'm going to teach you to read music, Mrs Anderson, but that doesn't mean wasting my time telling you what a semi-breve is, or a crotchet – it's all in there, so you get it learned up, by Monday if possible, right? Oh, and you can have a go at these five-finger exercises, seeing as how you're gasping to get your fingers on the keyboard. That should keep you amused till Monday.'

Sadie had spent the previous night reading through the pamphlet, feeling some of that appetite whose edge had been honed by McKay. Now she had the afternoon free and, feeling the same hunger, she took the book of exercises, put it on the fretted music stand and sat down on the piano stool. McKay had told her how to practise.

'Remember you are looking for speed, security of rhythm and intonation. That's what you're after, right from the beginning. And you've got to get over the feeling of strain in your muscles. Now, on Monday, when you come back here, these'll be the only things you will be able to play – but you'll play them like they were wee tunes.' He demonstrated on the big Steinway, to Sadie's delight. 'Playing exercises is a bore, you know, your drudgery –'

She had interrupted him at this point, just by looking at him as if to say, 'I can face that.'

'Oh, I ken,' he waved his palm in front of her face disclaiming interest in anything she was going to say. 'I know, you're a hardened housewife. But nobody learns anything bored. Boredom is your attention straying. Now, what you've got to do is this! Drudge, drudge, drudge away. *But*! Anticipate and relish what it is going to bring you. Nae oos and dust coming back down. But freedom and liberation in these auld fingers and muscles. You must take pleasure in the movement of your fingers and with the drudgery that pleasure will increase. It's the only way to learn. Enjoy yourself, enjoy your fingers. That's a lesson for a marriage-hardened house-wife, eh? Harder than you think. Anyway, when you come here on Monday –' as Sadie sat at the piano she had to smile at this recollection of McKay, 'I don't want any of this.' He had sat at the piano, intense concentration on his face, tongue out to the side of his mouth, playing a blocked, stumbling series of notes. 'Even if it's well played it is not enough. I want this.' He smiled arrogantly, swaying his head easily on his neck burlesquing a gallant expression of nonchalant physical anticipation then, first flourishing his hand languidly above the keyboard, he played, the keys rippling under his hand while a brilliant cascade of notes sang out from the magnificent big Steinway. 'Like a wee virtuoso, right?' Even as the flashy spray of notes chilled her somewhere, like eau de cologne on the skin, she had to laugh at his comical mimicry.

Yet though this recollection made her smile, she sat at the piano feeling reluctant to begin. Sadie had a tremendous amount of physical vigour which made her able to tackle domestic drudgery without hesitation, but the music before her made her uncomfortably aware that she would have to read the bass clef, something she had never done before. But more than the difficulty of tackling something new was the ground of her inertia. It was a weird social embarrassment like the diffidence some people know before picking up a fork in an expensive restaurant. The cluster of black notes on the paper, hard and black and defined against the paper's whiteness, suggested nothing of sound to her and the keys beneath her hand, ordered and strict, seeming somehow untouchable and hygienic. Yet she screwed herself up, and forgetting McKay's example, his casual and familiar bashing of the keys, out of her own act of will she reached out a struck middle C with her right thumb. Not over the keys, as McKay had shown, but with the stool too distant from the piano she reached out and touched the note. It sounded, like a sparrow cheep, meek and ragged, then lost itself in apology. She had sounded her Doh and broken that silence of many years standing. Sadie came out of a dwam of concentration about an hour and a half later, unaware that she had pulled her stool in to a comfortable distance in that time. She looked at the clock on the mantelpiece, closed the exercise book and sat still on the stool feeling slightly dizzy and numb, as if wakened from oversleeping. Yet she could remember that sleep, remember every note within the range of her exercises in the bass clef which had so frightened her, remember with her fingers every figuration of the five notes she had been playing and with her thumb the precise moment of crossing to play the C major scale. She felt neither tired nor impatient but simply a warm sense of accomplishment that some grist had been broken under the mill of her effort. And on Monday when she saw McKay there would be more, which was what she desired – more and more and more.

McKay never locked his front door when at home, so most of his pupils waked in and yelled their arrival, but Sadie always rang the bell, and when he opened she remained standing on the threshold like a hare about to run. She wore a tweed coat, a head scarf, and carried a big leather shopping bag with zipped pouches in the sides. On her face was a characteristic look of alert wariness. He had to invite her in and she never followed him straight into the music room, but stood in the doorway, watching him. He had to tell her to remove her coat, and where to put the bag. She moved with a constraint that McKay privately called 'the close-mouth shuffle'. He had seen hundreds of these women shuffling up and down Glasgow tenement stairs, crouching over their breasts which they held clutched in their forearms like valuable parcels. Women who confined themselves, or were confined, to their purdah, their families, their neighbours, their domesticity, their streets, their shops. Outside these they all wore the same self-conscious closed face as like Sadie's when she stood in his hall waiting for him to tell her where to put down her bag, hang up her coat. She had stood in the hall furtively taking everything in without moving her eyes but giving herself away to McKay by the slow panning movement of her face as she looked around. Another purdah characteristic, he thought. She was too polite to stare knowing that sight was a critical faculty, yet too wary, too apprehensive outside her habitual surroundings not to desperately, surreptitiously, familiarise herself. For a moment he had been alarmed, almost angered at this small, persistent, dowdy woman – and he wished he had not taken her on as a pupil. But he remembered their previous interview and how much he believed in formal musical education and the formal tradition of European musical art, while maintaining that its source was a vulgar musicality which could be found anywhere and he refused to be surprised at its origins. 'Have you ever tried to play a *Jew's harp*, for Gawd's sake?' he'd say and speak of boys he'd heard sitting on a close step playing jigs on mouth organs, the bowler-hatted work's foreman who played a sweet and fluent cornet, the Scots fiddler busking in the street. He was prepared to appreciate and admire musicality however expressed, and was never surprised at its unexpected appearance, even in this dowdy little purdah woman. Even (if asked) in a little girl with a frayed lilac cardigan.

Yet when Sadie came creeping into the music room he had to make a conscious effort to accept her presence there. She was like an awkward guest at a dinner party, he thought. Everything about her denied the possibility of performance. Her movements were the neat, exact, movements of a seamstress, now that she had become a little more at ease, but with none of the expansiveness needed to play a bloody piano. She had cast off some of her dowdiness with the tweed coat and headscarf and McKay was slightly disturbed by her physical attraction. Irish, he thought, with those teeth and that thick auburn hair. Her skin was of a type which goes so well, yet so seldom, with auburn hair; freckled, not dark but with a surface opaqueness in contrast to the usual pale, dry, transparent skin of red-haired people. It had no youthful bloom but a reliable adult evenness of colour and texture. The taut skin over her strong-boned face verged on gauntness but the rest of her body was strong, almost plump and her breasts, high inside the short sleeved shirtwaist blouse, were big in contrast to the small rib-cage beneath. If she stuck them out, thought McKay, she'd be a right little pouter pigeon. He had a drill-sergeant impulse to shout at her – 'straighten up, arse in, chest out.' Which was what he would really have to do. For this quiet little woman really wanted to play the piano.

So she was astonished when near the start of the lesson, after playing all her arduously learned exercises, McKay screwed his eyes in disgust, covered his ears and yelled at her, 'Oh my Gawd, my Gawd!'

She stopped and turned to him, dismayed. He lifted his arms high, dropped them to slap his thighs, grinned at her, turned up his eyeballs to the ceiling, shook his head and laughed. 'What a nice little domestic sound *that* was! Like a spoon tinkling in a tea-cup.' He walked over to the piano and with an expansive salesmanlike gesture he patted and caressed the woodwork with his huge hand, leaning over and speaking to her while rubbing a corned of the woodwork sensuously, as if easing an itch with the middle of the palm of his hand. 'This, Mrs Anderson, is a piano. It is not a musical cigarette box, nor a Swiss chalet, but a big strong noisy instrument built to take abuse. It will not come to pieces beneath your hands.'

I was playing too quiet?' Sadie sat with her hands clasped in her lap, looking straight at McKay, her lips pursed, her eyes suddenly dewed with anger. In the whole set of her body was a different question: Why not say what you want and cut the cackle?

McKay smiled, said, 'Don't look at me in that tone of voice. Do you think I'm being o'er sarky?'

Sadie tossed her head like a young girl and said, 'I get enough of that at home.'

'You have my apologies. Just play the bloody thing louder.'

Sadie positively thumped the piano and the notes sounded out, uneven, ragged, infirm, harsh.

McKay smiled again and leaned forward grinning provocatively and said in his broadest Glasgow accent. 'And that sounded like you was scrubbin' claes on a washin' board.' Then he looked at her, his head flirtatiously to one side, his shoulders set in a frozen shrug, full of blatant charm.

Sadie's response to his outrageously false manner this time was to turn her head away, as if to say, 'He's hopeless.' But a little smile strayed round her mouth.

He said, 'I'm embarrassed. I don't know what to say to you. I might give you the sack.'

'You're giving up already?'

'No, not really.' He waved his big hand, reassuring her, then he walked up and down the room pouting, standing for a while thinking, tapping his bottom lip with his forefinger so that it made tiny fleshy smacking sounds. He spoke as if to himself.

'I'm wondering what would be the best approach.'

Suddenly he turned on her in the middle of a stride and shot out a question.

'Are you intelligent?'

'Intelligent? I don't know – I was clever enough at school.'

'Ach, that's not what I meant. If you had real intelligence you would understand that question.'

'Thank you.'

'What I meant was *gumption*. You know. Gumption. You know what that is?'

'I know. I might even have some –'

'Then you should know why I shouted at you. That sound you made was not a tune. Tea-cups and scrubbing boards. That was your autobiography. In which I'm not interested. Forget the dust and oos. No rubato. You play with your fingers, not with your life.'

Sadie nodded and muttered, 'Aye', darkly, and McKay stood and looked at her for another long moment. Then he came over and sat down beside her on the stool. 'Shove o'er a bit.'

'Forget about exercises just now,' he said, 'I'm going to tell you something.'

Since she had faced up to his shouting without wilting she might be all right – and it would serve another purpose. She was too old, he thought, for slow learning. She simply didn't have the time. If she could take in the rudiments quickly then he would be able to make music interesting to her. He suspected that her physical relationship with the piano was her weakness, the athletic act of playing. But the mere question of sight-reading music, counting, relating the stave to the keyboard had to be dismissed, brutally and quickly. McKay explained all this to her.

'I can't do this with a young pupil because they'd find it too painful. Your age is an advantage for if my teaching hurts then you're old enough to understand why. What I'm going to show you involves study so intense that you'll have to learn it in a few weeks. Are you prepared to face that effort?'

'Uhuh.'

'It'll be worth it, you know.' McKay spoke almost pleadingly for it was something he had often wanted to try out on the right pupil. Perhaps one that didn't matter too much.

'All right,' said Sadie.

'But first of all, so that you get the point, I'm now going to teach you all about music in one lesson. For it's as simple as that. You can learn it all in one lesson.' He nudged her and put on his flirtatious act. 'Of course that's only in a manner of speaking. We start by playing this note, holding down this single key. Give it pedal, if you like. And there it is, the whole thing. If you listen you can hear it all in the one note – everything!'

He went on to show her how, from the sound of a single string, the greatest European major-minor harmonic system was built up. He showed her the key cycle, letting her work through it herself when she caught on. He explained the triad and its place in simple harmony; he demonstrated the nature of the intervals, their change of mood in augmentation and diminution, the relatedness of the major and minor keys. Though he did all this quickly, discursively, treating the whole thing in a general way, he realised he had caught her. A warmth swelled up in him towards her as he noticed her excitement. It was as if she had already heard all this and had been waiting for it to be articulated. Waiting for a notation to be put upon it; and with that neat and exact quality which was in her she was catching and ordering that notation to what she could hear with her (and this struck him more and more forcibly) magnificent ear. And he too had excitement to communicate, an excitement at stretching his pupil's powers, which is the true mark of a teacher. He enthusiastically demonstrated that great feat of analysis by which European music created the world's greatest art tradition, teasing out and separating the complex sound of a single string to re-assemble them in the Bach fugue, Mozartian counterpoint, the Beethoven sonata, the Wagnerian opera; he spoke even of the great modern puzzle, the Twentieth-century fear of the tonic.

And he showed how it had all evolved from the middle C which he thumped over and over again. Sadie's Doh.

McKay's assessment of Sadie was not quite right, though to teach her he conceded that she might have something individual (apart from her magnificent ear) which should be taken seriously. His doubts were strong for he recognised in her that refusal that had taken place all these years ago, on the morning when Mrs Bermant tested her ear. Of course he had not seen it as a specific occasion, but as generalised denial of a type well known to him. He too came from those teeming streets – in his case a slum in Govan, and he too had overcome an inheritance of inertia. His expectation of her failure mingled with hope for her success but expectation was strongest.

His judgement was proved not quite right by Sadie standing up for a month to his brutal assault on her capacities. He had forced her to count her ta-ta-ti-fi through numerous scores, counting bar by bar, drumming and tapping, accenting and skipping, beating and tripping, in that strange activity which was at once an intellectual exercise and physical co-ordination, arrest and movement, analysis and synthesis, arithmetic and rhythm. For hours she sat at night with a difficult piano score borrowed from McKay on her lap, poring over it, finger under each bar, foot tapping, lips moving silently; one, two, one, two-and – in Alla Breve and Waltz, compound and simple, common and triple – wrapped in a concentration outside which lay the arithmetic dust and oos. It was, McKay had said, like breaking stones with one hand and setting jewels with the other, or (more coarsely) 'like rubbing your belly and pattin' your heid.' But these rhythms in their opposition and merging were more familiar to Sadie than he knew. Her body remembered the streets of her childhood, the clapping of hands, the smack of a ball, the swish and slap of a skipping rope ca'ed in duo; the counting, the common time –

'Eenty, teenty, halligollum,

Pipe clay, up the lum.

Urky, turkey, torry rope,

Ram, stam, toosie jock.'

The triplets, one po-ta-to, two po-ta-to; tempo ad libitum – plainie, clappie, rollie, backie, high Scottische, low Scottische, touch the ground, birlie round; tempo giusto – German boys are, awful fun-ny, this is how they, earn their mon-ney; and so on – one, two, three, aleerie – five, ten, fifteen, twenty, you are out and the game's a bogy – every measure and rhythm from the strict to the syncopated scliff-*thump*, scliff-*thump* as the rope and the scuffed shoes raised dust from the pavement while all the little girls skipped. And playing for keeps, there was that adagio swing, that fundamental rock, back and forward, of plain misery, loss and grief. Besides all this – Sadie could dance. Whatever disuse so many of her faculties had fallen into there was this wry fact – that she had suffered no atrophy of the rhythmic sense, and all this measure she had learned *a piacere*.

In the question of measure, therefore, Sadie found assistance in past experience. The formal absorption of musical convention she found more difficult, and in the difficulty even more satisfaction. Her concentration, her involvement in learning threw up round her barriers outside which were life's limitations – her age, kitchen, family, domestic duties – all that restricted her intelligence, if intelligence is an active, confident spirit which would not stand waiting in a doorway. Inside these barriers, inside the learning, she was capable of sharp and sustained intellectual effort, and after all, it was only a question of remembering a few conventions.

McKay was agreeably surprised at her success, at the attentiveness, eagerness, the refusal to be exhausted she displayed. Yet when she stood in the hall before the start of each lesson, and more slowly than she learned music, relaxed into familiarity, the signature of her talent emerged, a childish capacity to absorb appeared in her very gaucheness – her awkwardness. But, as McKay told her during these laborious weeks, signatures can mislead, you don't know what key it is in until you play it – it might be minor. And Sadie had always known how to diminish.

McKay had began his pounding by simply taking a piano score, pointing to a note and asking her to play it on the keyboard. Sadie had difficulty with the bass clef and the ledger lines. It was a boring, routine technique but presented Sadie with a labour she was in the mood to undertake if McKay sat with her on the piano stool for half an hour, forcing her to these exertions – that one, and that one and that one, over and over again, that one and that one – Sadie herself was able to sit at night until the stave, with its 11 lines, unrolled itself before her with each space and line separate and clear and the black and white piano keys a reflex of these notes. He made her work over the key cycle until the keys and their relationship became a fixed pattern in her head; he gave her bundles of old scores in which she marked the chords and intervals in pencil until a sound had its reflex in a position and shape, and the sharp, black visual notes had their reflex in sound. At the end of that month Sadie had reached the stage in learning to read music where comprehension had set in, when it ceases to be a crude effort of memorising and was becoming a question of honing and refining the act into habit and speed. She was making more than tentative efforts to read a score.

All this pleased, puzzled and surprised McKay who had been prompted to try out this method of teaching Sadie because he thought he had seen some quality of intelligence in her sparking at times through her bland shyness; seen it in occasional flashes of sarcasm and dryness, in knowingness expressed in a grim worldly smile. 'Do you think I'm too auld?' or in an equally grim laugh, no more than a snort, an exhalation through the nostrils, 'A housewife's work is never done.' She had surprised him by a greater speed, a greater formal intelligence than these few signs had appeared to warrant. So he attributed her success and her endurance to her gifts. This seemed to him a sufficient explanation, but if ever there was a questionable matter it is this one of gift and it appears a less simple matter when we look at it in the form in which it is bestowed and the conditions it may demand. Sadie too had her richnesses, her complexities and her gift with its overtones. She remembered something of these and suspected how they would manifest themselves in what McKay was about to teach her – or give her, for he called it her reward.

During that month he didn't curse so much but still blinded a bit. Over the sound of Sadie's practice his humorous, bullying voice now sounded coaxing, and wheedling.

'Good. Not bad. Up with the wrists a bit. Don't pull the keys, you're not dusting the mantelpiece-up-up. That's better.'

Weeks went by and his voice became more coaxing, more exhortative – displaying an urgency on her behalf – so the fingers became more and more secure.

'Aye, you've got that thumb moving right – keep your elbow in though, it's waving like a flag. It's your thumb you move – just slide it under – uhuh – not bad.'

And so on and so on until the reward was earned.

This was Beethoven's little sonatina in G.

Aside from the loosening of her fingers Sadie was also finding it less and less necessary to maintain her shy stiffness with McKay. Against his subtle blustering she gradually relaxed until she too could let herself in and announce 'I'm here, Mr McKay', hang up her coat, dump her big leather shopping bag and take out her music. And eased into familiarity she also started pattering McKay back. In her fifth week, after McKay had listened in silence as she played slowly but firmly a set of scales, he said, 'That's fine. You're doin' well. You must have been practising.'

'I have been.'

'I always give my pupils a reward if they practise well.'

'Am I doing well, Mr McKay?' and Sadie had laughed and attempted, nearly successfully, to ripple a cluster of notes under her hand. 'Like a wee virtuoso?'

He laughed. 'Oho. And getting big-heided with it and all. Never mind. Good enough for your reward.'

McKay put a book on the music stand, opened it, and Sadie was taken aback. 'Sonatina – by – Beethoven. Beethoven? Have I to learn to play that?'

'No, Mrs Anderson. You haven't to learn to play it. That's what scales and exercises and studying notation are for – the drudgery – to *learn* to play it.'

'It looks awful hard.'

McKay treated this brusquely and impatiently. 'Aye, and it looks hard to me when I look at the whole page at once. Take it a bit at a time. You read music, you've exercised your fingers, have a bash.'

Have a bash was what she couldn't do. She panicked. She felt the return of that old feeling that the notes were hygienic and untouchable. The wood of the piano took on the same aloof, polished air as the counter in a bank. As her fingers hovered over the keys and she read the first bar she felt about to take unwarranted liberties with some massive dignitary. She tentatively pressed the keys, playing the first chord, stumbled over the following grace note and played the wrong harmony with her left hand, C instead of D-seven, then rattled off the four quavers much too fast. She only tried the first bar then she snatched her hands away from the keys looking at McKay, terror stricken.

'Aye, aye,' McKay said, 'what's the matter?'

But Sadie only shrugged and looked helpless.

'What a wumman,' McKay said. He walked up and down with his thoughtful bottom lip out, then stood looking at her for while grinning with great good humour. 'Well, I suppose if I'm going to teach you music I'll have to teach you –' He hesitated, then completed his thought, '– well, music.' With a gesture of his arm, expressing mock disgust he waved her away from the piano stool. 'Away and sit on the chair and I'll play you a tune.'

McKay sat down and played *Für Elise* while Sadie sat stiff and upright on a hard chair, her hand clasped in her lap. As he played her face lost some of the hard blank look which had come over it. In the middle section, at the *ritardando*, the marked slackening of speed where the introductory figure is repeated and this time divided between the hands, McKay emphasised the pause and turned to grin reassuringly at Sadie. He did so again in the middle of the chromatic run down into the last section, and she smiled back, sharing their pleasure in the music.

When McKay played those dozens of consecutive staccato As in the bass her stiffness changed to athletic tension in sympathy with his drumming fingers and the sudden dramatic heightening of the music; during the last chromatic run she had felt the notes like loving fingers playing delicately on each knob of her backbone. Moved by a strange feeling of power, she returned to the stool and sat with McKay as if possessing a capacity for richness, for complexity of feeling.

Insights had become available through the clarity; an emotional idea made perfect sense. She knew what it meant and appreciated Beethoven's sly double use of the piece, which was for Elsie in the concession to young unlearned fingers and that it was for Elsie in that it seemed to express, sensuously, her young bloom, all that was virginal and fresh and downy-cheeked; all that innocent impatient energy, the laughter, the sudden changes of mood, the skittish pauses, the chromatic complexities of feeling, the dreaminess, the indefiniteness, the petulance and questioning of youth – and in approval to put itself with a tender, smiling good-humour in sympathy with all of it. It was a reminder of that tenderness felt by experience towards innocence and freshness; a tenderness which was more than a mere instinct, more than a mere biological determined maternity but the tenderness felt by all existence for its preludes; a tenderness felt by all that is complete for that which is only half-formed, that which is becoming, that which is hovering shyly on the verge of experience; a tenderness which was more than a mere nostalgia for youth; it was, from a sense that the incompletion, the striving, the curiosity characterises more than just youth, a tenderness for the very stuff of life itself.

Sadie watched fascinated while McKay played – this big uncouth-looking man, sitting there at the piano, his bottom lip pendulous in consideration, peering and grimacing through the smoke which rose from the butt-end of the cigarette in his mouth. The ironic smile which twisted his bottom lip was not, she knew, simply an expression of technical assurance, but his recognition and assent to Beethoven's idea and also a sly hint to her, Sadie, that for all the dignity and pride of *Erotica*, the agonising complexity of the late sonatas, the icy intellectual heights of the last quartets, this coaxing little piece was written by Beethoven not just to persuade and wheedle the unformed hand into mastery but to assert common human feelings in which all true grandeur was based. It was an assertion of that essential approachability on which genius rests.

She felt touched to be the recipient of this tenderness, and of McKay's generosity. All the more so for her own capacity to feel the same nostalgia and affection for growth. Even if she had not, inevitably, been reminded of that time more than 30 years before when she had sat on the cushion in the big Bergère arm-chair and listened to Anna playing, even without that particular, and to her moving reference she would have still felt, isolated and clear, that nostalgia and affection.

When McKay finished playing he had turned to her. 'You know that wee tune, I suppose?'

'Oh yes,' she said, 'Fur Sadie,' and it wasn't until McKay put his head back and laughed that she clapped her hand to her mouth.

'Fur Sadie,' he said, laughing, missing out the umlaut and so turning the word into Glaswegian, 'Fur Sadie.'

When the alarm went off Sadie stretched her arm out past the curtain and touched the button to shut off the strident noise. Alec as usual grumbled and turned in his sleep. The alarm always disturbed him though he never woke to it if Sadie was quick to cut it off. When she was not he always grunted and nudged her with his elbow.

Sadie got up at once for it was Saturday morning and she had plenty to do. After half dressing in her slip she went to wash at the sink. The kitchen window faced due east and a pale yellow light filtered through the sash curtains which were still drawn. She washed thoroughly, splashing much cold water on her face as she did every morning, even in winter. When a little girl her sister Mary had told her it was good for her complexion. This was one of several ascetic habits Sadie had learned from her sister, though oddly enough Mary hardly ever practised them.

Before going to bed Sadie always brushed out her long auburn hair and before washing in the morning always hastily pinned it up into a bun. As she turned to dry herself she exposed, intimately, the tender nape of her neck to the diminished sunlight; the little unruly fronds of hair were darkened with damp to chestnut and the slight frizz round the mass of her head caught the light to make the golden aureole.

As she stood in that quiet morning kitchen she might have been a young girl, her naked shoulders lit by the sun, the small shoulder blades sliding fluently beneath the unflawed skin as she dried herself – or some neat, clean, glossy animal unselfconsciously grooming.

After drying herself she put the kettle on to boil, finished dressing and by seven o'clock had wakened Alec and the breakfast was nearly ready; the tea was masked, the eggs on to boil, the toast being buttered. If he had awakened earlier she would not have stood so easily, her big breasts pouted as she raised her arms to pin her hair, nor as she stood vigorously drying her face and neck, nor would her spine have curved so grandly, swerving down like a clef into the small of her back and flaring out into the mass of her buttocks. Instead she would have crouched and hurried, her face averted, hands covering the deep cleft between her breasts.

Just as Alec, when he rose, turned away to drop his pyjama bottoms. He put on his trousers with his back to her, bending over so only his buttocks were visible through his underpants, and the big hairy thigh, strong and braced as he lifted a foot to put inside his trouser leg. Meanwhile Sadie deferentially buttered toast.

She did not consciously turn her eyes from him. Over the years they both established this routine in deference to one another's modesty, just as they had a routine for going to bed at night. They had never seen one another naked and both wore their underclothes at night – Sadie her pants and bra under her nightdress and Alec his vest and pants under his pyjamas. Neither had a reason for shame. Both, given some naturalness, could have shown each other a splendid nakedness. Yet even during the most passionate connexions of their early married life Sadie had only pulled her nightdress up over her thighs. Always, after the assuagement of sexual heat, modesty returned. Over the years, with the dying of this connexion, modesty had increased.

It was a terrible modesty that excluded everything from the

sexual act but stark genital facts, the ache for detumescence, the need to release tension. It was a terrible modesty that excluded sexuality from the commonplace acts of the day and, denying ordinary acts of touching and looking, denied a way of expressing tenderness. It was a terrible modesty that, in denying exposure, authorised ignorance and secretiveness. The modesty was increased by the memory of the act it sought not to recognise, the act made more brutal by the modesty surrounding it. So Sadie and Alec protected themselves from consciousness of all this by the coy morning clothing routine, moving about the kitchen doing essential chores so that their faces seldom turned to one another. Alec quickly grabbed the key from its hook in the lobby because, until he visited the closet in the stairhead and emptied his bladder, he always had a slight erection. This would not have been an occasion for wifely amusement on Sadie's part if she had noticed it, but a shameful reminder of their shameful relationship.

This particular morning she was reminded of this relationship by the absence of the piano from the kitchen. Moving the piano to their sons' bedroom had been prelude to an evening that had ended in Alec's drunken rummaging inside her while she gasped and pushed towards that consummation she had almost forgotten existed.

Sadie was boiling the eggs when Alec returned from the closet. He was suffering a slight hangover and they did not speak until sitting down to breakfast and after she had poured the first cups of tea. Only on Saturday mornings, when Colin and Hugh slept late because they did not work at weekends, did Sadie and Alec breakfast alone.

'Do you want an aspirin?' she asked.

'No. No. Tea'll be fine.' Alec spooned out the last of his egg, spread his toast thick with marmalade, laid another slice of toast on top and ate vigorously. Sadie said, 'It hasn't affected your appetite.'

'You know me. Can always recover.'

If Alec had time for a smoke after breakfast he always left, drawing fiercely on his fag, blowing smoke at the chimney and tapping ash carefully into the grate, for he hated the sight of ash. Only when leaving for work did he mention the previous night, standing near the door with bonnet on, tapping his pockets to make sure he hadn't forgotten anything.

'That Joe Pringle,' he said, 'he can fairly play the piano.'

'Aye,' said Sadie.

'It was a good night,' Alec said, 'well, I'm away.'

He left and as she heard his footsteps, light and pattering, go down the stairs, Sadie recalled that it had not been a good night for her. Not a good night at all.

Maybe things had begun to go wrong when McKay, a fortnight before, had given her the Beethoven sonatina to play. In his usual way he stressed the lesson he had tried to impart by playing *Für Elise*.

'Right. He's a great composer, but don't let that frighten you. He understood growth you see – and he wrote this piece especially for people like us. Now look, what does it say? Moderato – not too fast. The key signature?'

'In G,' Sadie said.

'One sharp, Mrs Anderson. You don't know if it is in G until you play it. Common time – you know what that is. So you take it just a bar at a time. And the changes of harmony – read the chord and not just the separate notes. Like I showed you – you don't read, you recognise. Now off you go –'

And Sadie, reassured, had tried again to play the sonatina, but this time without fear. She had gone home and practised the piece and then had tried to play it to Alec and the two boys. Until then she hadn't fully realised how much Alec and Colin disliked her piano lessons, because they didn't fit their idea of her. Their objection was no less strong for having no specific grounds. When Sadie had played to them, 'just to show how I'm getting on,' they couldn't restrain their jocular remarks.

'Listen to Myra Hess,' Alec said.

Colin, who felt he had some right to musical taste because he enjoyed a collection of records by Thelonius Monk, Coltrane,

Mulligan, Brubeck et al, was too sophisticated for the little sonatina and did not try to hide a response that mingled indifference with amusement. When she stopped he had taken her seat at the piano and played some staccato chords, among them the inevitable flattened fifth. Then he had laughed and played that chord again, exaggerating the affected jerk of the right shoulder and stylishly splayed fingers of many jazz pianists, saying, 'Aye, how about playing some *music* Ma?'

Sadie suspected how McKay would have snorted contemptuously, dismissing Colin's display as infirmity, but Colin brought authority to his blues chord because of its supposed unpretentiousness, because it was not Beethoven. 'You want to get with it Ma,' he said and moved from the piano stool with a kind of sarcastic elegance.

Sadie was hurt and disappointed. For all of Hugh's 'That's great, Ma, you're doin' really great,' she knew he appreciated her playing less than he wanted to soothe her, which was no defence against the aggressive indifference of the other two.

Then Alec said, 'Clash the pans Sadie, we're a' hungry.' For a day or two after she had to force herself to the keyboard and in spite of her stubbornness the playing had faltered.

And now the absence of the piano in the kitchen reminded her of a further check.

They had been sitting at their tea when the doorbell rang. Hugh got up to answer, returned and had jerked his thumb towards the lobby saying, 'There's a wumman to see you, Ma. I think she's from the next close.'

Sadie went to the door and recognised Mrs Anthony, whose kitchen was through the wall from hers. It seemed likely that she wanted to borrow something for she stood with folded arms, smiling ingratiatingly until Sadie smiled back. Then Mrs Anthony opened her mouth and after a huge intake of breath said, 'Mrs Anderson I'm awfully sorry to bother you Mrs Anderson but –'

Then came another great intake of breath held for a moment with open mouth before the words came in a rush: 'Is-there-somebody-in-your-house-plays-the-piano?'

'Well, yes,' Sadie answered, 'I – somebody was practising.'

'Aye.' Mrs Anthony's voice then rose to the pitch of complaint. 'It's just that I can hear it in the kitchen.'

'I'm very sorry Mrs Anthony. I didn't think it would be disturbing anybody.'

'Oh, its no' disturbing *me*.'

'And it hasn't been played at any unreasonable times.'

'It's no' that but – you see my man's on constant night shift.'

Sadie suddenly felt shocked and hurt. She had always tried to give no cause for complaint and was appalled by this new mundane objection to her piano. Her eagerness for music was being dragged onto the stairhead, made a reason for unpleasantness. She tried to answer but instead opened her mouth and silently moved her lips, her hands twisting the corner of her apron. The woman said, 'I'm sorry but you understand he's got to get his sleep.'

The woman's cringing manner irritated Sadie. Her hurt changed to anger only shown by the prim line of her mouth. She said, 'I'll see that it doesn't happen again.'

'I'm sorry but – I don't want you to think I'm complaining. But it was an awful noise and I mean Sam had a sore head going to his work and I thought to myself there wasn't any necessity for it –'

Sadie's temper broke. The complaint was unfair because Mrs Anthony's man (as she called him) could have slept in the front room if the piano disturbed him so much. Sadie didn't point that out. Almost in tears she protested, 'But you are complaining!'

Mrs Anthony's mouth opened but her intake of breath was cut off short. She shut her mouth, swivelled her face slowly round to look at Sadie, averted her eyes and smiled again. 'I'm not trying to cause trouble Mrs Anderson.'

'I'm quite sure you're not,' Sadie said, 'I'm quite sure you're not. It'll no' happen again. Don't worry.'

Sadie shut the door in the woman's face and went back into the kitchen and burst into tears. 'The sleekit auld –' she couldn't continue for she was gasping with indignation. 'She was complaining about the piano.'

'Aye, we heard her,' Alec said. 'But you can't blame her if her man's on the night shift.'

Sadie just said 'Oh!' and stamped round the table and sat down violently on her chair. She was crying and lifting the hem of her apron to wipe her face. It was, unusually, Colin who saved the situation. He spread his hands apart and shrugged.

'If he was a' that bothered why'd he no' sleep ben the room?'

'Aye, right enough,' Alec said.

'*You* might have thought of that,' said Sadie through her tears.

'It's no that but –' Colin said and he grinned at his mother, 'we want our tea in peace.'

'It's no' that but – you don't want to greet about it Ma,' Hugh said.

Alec grinned too. 'It's no that but – pass the salt.'

'It's no that but – so it is.'

Sadie sniffed and smiled a little and Hugh said, 'It's no that but – blow your nose Ma.'

She blew her nose.

'It's no that but – do you usually blow your nose on your apron Ma?'

Sadie started laughing with tears still on her face. She tried to say, 'It's no that but,' and burst into a fit of giggles.

'Wipe your face Ma and don't worry about it.'

As they were finishing their tea Sadie said, 'We'll have to move the piano ben the room.'

Alec and the boys nodded. Alec had gone to sit in the chair by the fireplace, taking his cup of tea. He had lit a cigarette and was reading the evening paper. When Sadie made it clear she wanted the piano shifted at once he folded the paper and slapped it on his lap.

'The night? F'r Gawd's sake, Sadie. It's *Friday* night.'

'Ah know it's Friday night,' Sadie said, 'but I practise on a Friday night when you're a' oot. And I'll feel uneasy if I think I'll be disturbing anyone.'

'But auld Anthony'll no be sleeping the night. He'll be away oot for a drink.'

'I suppose so. But if we put if off it'll no get done o'er the weekend. And you'll keep putting it off.'

'I'm supposed to be goin' oot the night.'

'We're a' supposed to be goin' oot,' said Colin.

'You've plenty of time. It's only the back of six.'

Alec sighed. 'All right,' he said, 'in a minute. I'll just finish my fag.' He rattled his paper open again.

While he read and smoked and Sadie cleared the tea things Colin had tried the piano for weight. Standing at one end he gripped it, tugged vigorously and nothing happened. He then tried lifting the end with no more success.

'Either I'm a seven-stone weakling or this damn thing's glued tae the wall.'

'Nonsense,' Hugh said. 'Oot the road and I'll have a bash.' He shuffled up to the end of the piano and keeping his back straight, bent his knees and gripped it low down. When he straightened his knees one end was raised several inches. He swivelled the end out and let it down gently. 'I reckon you must *be* a seven-stone weakling.'

Colin felt admiringly the bicep Hugh boastfully offered him. 'Aye,' he said, 'it's well seen your Ma feeds you.'

'She disnae feed me,' Hugh said, 'she puts it out on a plate and I feed myself.'

'I know. She leaves it on the bottom of your cage.'

The two boys began wrestling and Alec put his newspaper down, his reluctance to help shift the piano gone now it had become a matter of physical demonstration. 'Ach,' he said, 'I've got mair years than the baith of ye.' Without any more ado he got up, took the other end of the piano and lifted it so that the instrument now stood parallel to the wall. 'There,' he said, flexing his shoulders like an athlete limbering up. 'It's just a knack.'

Sadie had gone ben the room to clear a space for the piano. The recess here held a big double bed hidden by curtains. Though Colin's and Hugh's bedroom it was also furnished as a sitting room with a TV set, big uncut moquette sofa in the middle of the floor. Beside the fireplace was a wardrobe tall as a man with deep blanket drawers underneath. One wall was clear, except for a long narrow table with an empty flower vase on a strip of embroidered cloth. This table, of highly polished dark wood, Sadie moved into the bow of the window, then pulled the heavy velour curtains across and noted that they hid the table almost completely. She went back to the kitchen.

'You can bring it though now.'

The castors on the piano were stiff and could not run freely on the thick pile carpet. Alec and Hugh, with small lifts and turns, advanced it steadily ignoring Colin who accompanied them crying, 'Heave ho me hearties! Port her helm, three points to starboard!' Suddenly Alec yelled, 'Put it down,' and dropped his end.

'Whassamatter?' asked Hugh.

'I've just remembered,' Alec said, 'the TV's ben the room.'

'Oh, f'r Gawd's sake!' Hugh clutched at his temples. 'I thought you'd broken your back.'

'Aye, but the TV's ben the room.'

'It'll no' matter. I'll no' *play* the piano when you watch TV,' said Sadie. Alec looked at her sceptically until she said, 'I've never even practised when you're in the house, never mind when you watch TV.'

'Right enough,' Alec conceded, then spat on his hands and stooped.

'Gangway,' Colin shouted, 'they're at it again.'

Alec said, 'Standing about chirping doesnae help.'

'It's called division of labour,' said Colin, 'you shove while I grunt.'

'Division of labour?' said Alec. 'Stick the handle of the brush up my arse and I'll sweep the lobby floor on the way through.'

'Alec!' said Sadie, 'There's nae need for that language.'

They got the piano into the lobby where its castors ran freely on the linoleum until it stuck against the big wooden coal-bunker. Alec and Hugh lifted one end and swivelled the instrument round to get it past, but as Alec was gripping the strap across the piano back the castors suddenly moved and his hand was jammed again the wall. He yelled, pulling the hand out and stuck it under his oxter.

'Jesus O'Connor Daly Mulligan O'Christ,' he said, 'I've skint my knuckles.'

Colin and Hugh started laughing then saw he was annoyed, having taken one of those knocks on a sensitive part where pain is out of all proportion to damage. He stood shaking the hand loosely, gasping, his eyes bright with pain and indignation. 'Bloody laugh!' he said, 'I've only had a square yard of skin off the back of my haun.' He looked at the knuckles. Skin was knocked from the top of each and a dark bruise was spreading on the surrounding skin. He went to the kitchen and turned on the tap over the hand. Sadie filled the basin with hot water and Alec plunged the hand alternately in the basin water and under the cold tap. After a while he said, 'That'll dae,' and dabbed the injured hand carefully with a clean towel while Sadie hovered anxiously watching. When his hand was dry she fixed strips of sticking plaster across the knuckles.

Colin and Hugh swaggered back into the kitchen brushing their hands jauntily together. 'Nae bother,' Hugh said.

Alec, putting his waistcoat on, told Colin, 'I'm glad to see you finally got working.'

'Oh, you can aye depend on me when the chips are down.'

Alec, scowling and huffy, flexed the fingers of the hurt hand, saying, 'These'll stiffen.' He slowly started fastening the buttons of his waistcoat, ostentatiously favouring the fingers with the skinned knuckles. Colin said, 'Well, we've earned our pint the night.'

They all put on their jackets and left.

Sadie washed and put away the dishes, then carried the piano stool from the kitchen into the room. Opening the lid she took out her music and put it on the stand. Instead of practising the sonatina she played a few scales then sat, hands in lap, back slumped, shoulders lax, her head thrown back, staring at the blank wall above the piano. She had been upset by Mrs Anthony's complaint, then by Alec's injury, and the scales showed the piano responded to her mood and sounded flat, toneless, as if the action was clogged. She felt in herself a kind of grittiness, almost physical, like the unpleasant feeling when emptying the grate and coal-ash blew into her hair. As if life was a frictional process always throwing off this abrasive, coarse dust which clogged her own action.

Editor's Postscript

At this point, sometime in the early 1970s, Archie Hind stopped writing *Fur Sadie* and gradually or suddenly lost interest in completing it, lost it so thoroughly that he retained no copy. The preceding fragment has been edited from a photocopy of pages he gave in the early 1990s to John Linklater, then Literary Editor of *The Herald*, who occasionally commissioned Archie to write book reviews. Even that had some pages missing from the centre, but these were found printed in a 1973 edition of the *Scottish International* magazine, so though lacking a conclusion, the start is continuous.

In January 2008, when John Linklater asked Archie why he had not finished the book. He answered in the words of another writer, 'It developed a slow puncture.' I had discussed the book with Archie thirty years earlier, having read enough to have fallen in love with the heroine. Archie had then been definite that the novel was going to end (unlike *The Dear Green Place*) on a triumphant note. How this would be achieved he now refuses to speculate, which makes it inevitable for the readers to do so. Sadie's piano playing has brought her domestic life to a crisis. She can no longer keep it out of her family's earshot and even a neighbour has started complaining. How can her talent – her *life* develop without splitting up what, by any decent standards, is a good marriage? For it is obvious that the important men in her life, husband, sons, and that great teacher McKay, cannot be reconciled.

Yes, the theme of this book is also in Dickens' *Great Expectations*, Hardy's *Jude the Obscure* and most novels by D. H. Lawrence – the conflict between warm but constrictive working communities and an imaginative freedom that operates like a curse, for how can it achieve emancipation without the freed spirit joining the damned *upper* classes. Sadie, however hard working and talented, is too old to have become a concert pianist, and it seems unlikely that she would ever join a band of popular musicians. Could she become a singer's accompanist? Might she have found support in her sympathetic older sister Mary? Her friend Anna vanished completely when Sadie's schooldays ended – might she have reappeared, and to what effect? None of these questions can be answered. To present a problem our society has still not solved, and present it believably and sympathetically in mid-twentieth century Glasgow, is as much as could be expected of a writer having to earn a living in many other ways.

This book ends with an article from the *Scottish International* of August 1973. The owners of the Upper Clyde Shipyards had announced the end of Glasgow shipbuilding, as they were preparing to invest in yards outside Scotland. The Glasgow shop stewards led their workers to occupy the yards in a well organised work-in. This was the first and biggest attempt to save a major Scottish heavy industry, and for several weeks that event brought Glasgow and its working-class spokesmen into the centre of British political news. The eventual failure of the effort heralded the steady closure of every other major Scottish industry (coal mining, car manufacture, steel production) through the rest of the century. This article shows Archie giving historic perspective to his eye-witness report.

Alasdair Gray
January 2008

'Men of the Clyde'

(from *Scottish International*, August 1973)

THE UPPER CLYDE – it was just a little strip of river, barely half-a-dozen miles of it and only yards in width with hardly enough draught to take a barge. On its banks a few small burghs, a few small villages and the small city of Glasgow, dependent on commerce, textiles, a little manufacturing and tobacco trading. Further inland there were coal seams and iron ore lying beneath the farmlands and ducal estates belonging to the effete, mad or absent aristocracy. Otherwise nothing but a wet climate, a shallow river and, even then, long, long miles to an indifferent and alien government. Nothing, unless we consider the men and their inheritance. Men whose fathers had failed disastrously in the ambitious imperial venture at Darien, their hopes blocked and thwarted by English intrigue; men, evicted from their homes in the Highlands by absent landlords to make way for sheep; men driven from their Irish steadings by famine; and men – weavers, artisans, mechanics – unemployed and impoverished, their living standards brutally assaulted by new technical advances in the weaving and textile industries. The hard men, the men of this cold, northern, wintry land who had learned to take a special view of reality, a sour view, a harsh view; men whose characters were as obdurate as the reality which had formed them; men whose history had been violence, shock and dispossession. Dour, repressed, unimaginative, they had iron in their religion, in their memories, in their souls. It was not for them to express themselves in soft marble, or build in wood, or create in flimsy. Just as their spirit attained malleability only in the white heat and high pressure of passion so they chose their material which would shape only in the white heat of the foundry, the furnace, the forge and bend only under the repressed and contained force of the steam hammer. Their imagination was limited to reality and that reality was a world waiting for expansion. They were the first of the modern emergent nations. So they dredged the Clyde to take great draughts, they built the berths obliquely onto the cramped river, they dug into the earth for the coal and the iron and then subjected the world to an incomparable holocaust of design, invention and industry. It was more than a revolution – it was a renaissance. Watt introduced to the steam engine and the world the governor, the condenser, reciprocating motion. More than mechanical inventions these were models of containment, direction and timing taken from the psychic economy of the Calvinist soul. Cook gave the steam ship, the blacksmith Napiers, the iron hulls and the first great iron building yards; Neilson, the hot blast; Murdock, gas lighting; McIntosh, industrial chemistry; Rigby, the steam hammer; Elder, the compound engine; Kincaid, screw propulsion; MacAdam, the modern road surface.

These men built first in everything – in steam, in iron, in steel, in screw propulsion, in turbines, in hovercraft. And they built beauty and extravagance – the *Cutty Sark* and the *Spindrift* which seamen called the giblet pie 'all wings and legs', the great steamers which took the Atlantic Blue Riband, and the custom-built jobs like the Russian Royal Yacht *Livadia* which out-imagined Captain Nemo himself. They built the clippers for the China Tea runs and the Australian wheat races; they forged and carried the rails which would unify nations in the Old World and great Atlantic steamers which would populate the new. Clyde dredgers howked out the ports and berths and docks of five continents; Clyde stern paddles forced the Congo, the Mississippi, the Irrawady, the Yellow River. Clyde pleasure boats abandoned their beautiful estuary to break the American blockade; Clyde-built ships carried Clyde-built locomotives onto the American prairies, the Russian steppes and the Indian plains; out of the tenements of Parkhead poured the shifts to forge and turn and bore and rifle the great guns which would give rough collateral to British Imperial expansion; from the closes of Fairfield, Govan and Clydebank came an energy and a pressure which woke nations from their dreams; from here, on the Clyde, came the vehicles which carried the meliorative force of Western technology and science to the world and in a last refined ecstasy of creation Scottish engineers brought those harbingers of the McLuhan age to the global village – the electric speed of the telephone and television. Amidst all this in an ironically reductive and bathetic act of which only the west-coast Scot is capable they even had time to invent the bicycle.

Yet history is only a swift dramatic flourish over the long arduousness of men's lives. The men of the Clyde lived out that arduousness in the room and kitchen tenements of Clydebank, Govan, Tradeston and Parkhead. The shipyards, forges and engineering shops were their bread and dripping, socks and semmits for the weans and schoolbooks in case the oldest boy turned out to be a man o' pairts. And that expansive historical heat came from a fire which could easily rake into cinders. Between 1920 and 1933 the tonnage launched on the Clyde dropped to a twelfth – 672,000 tons to 56,000. The caulkers, the riveters, the fitters, the carpenters, the riggers, the engineers, the experienced and skilled tradesmen of the Clyde were out on the streets, their bread and butter taken from their mouths. The shipyards and forges and lathes and ingots were still there but capitalism had reached that stage where its movement and action were no longer initiated by the direct confidence of energetic men in their machines and materials. The shipyard owners no longer stood among the fumes and steam and clatter of their yards but behind that shifting chimerical mist which is finance. Their confidence and understanding had gone in the face of 'the theological subtleties and meta-physical niceties' of commodity production. Action transmitted through the mysterious system of cash relationships, gold standards and fiscal policies were as effective as a rubber prop shaft. If the shipowners did not understand, the men did, for they had learned through years of hardship in the Glasgow tenements an addition to the harsh reality which they had inherited. That addition which was at once a dream and a tool – the idea of Socialism. From Camlachie, Bridgeton, Partick, Clydebank and Govan they discovered men like Maxton, McLean, Kirkwood, Campbell Stephen, McShane, Shinwell, Wheatley, who took black-balling, imprisonment and poverty in their stride to go and argue the dream and idea of the Red Clydeside tradesmen. They indicted the owners, the government, the capitalist system itself and fought for the living standards and jobs of the men they represented without the mean and narrow-spirited advocacy of special case. They had the fire which came from a moral belief in a political idea as expansive, generous and as hot as the head of steam in a boiler.

We have a kind of safety valve in this country which lowers pressure of this kind. Perhaps it is just that the style of life in which a living has to be wrung from the world makes for men to whom work is always a preferred alternative to extremity. These men in the yards may have been possessed by a dream of Socialism, but they had their daily lives with wives and children and rents and groceries. They had a stake in life which was more domestic than dramatic. In the mid-1930s work recommenced on the Cunarder. There was preparation for war, there was the war itself when their homes were pulverised by German bombs. Afterwards there was the rebuilding and a gradual but steady increase in living standards. Socialism was deferred in favour of more immediate and urgent victories. Not only in the yards but elsewhere, the trade union movement won battle after battle with capitalism without ever engaging in a war. Its political and moral passion became, at least in form, the possession of the political wing of the Labour Movement – the Labour Party. Without the heat of domestic crisis they too were content to win only battles. In the separation of the two wings of the Labour Movement the political implications of industrial and economic action were lost and ironically the two wings came time and time again to bitter confrontation over the special cases and claims of particular groups of workers.

In the 30 years following the period of the Red Clyde, shipbuilding on the Clyde began to die slowly of a kind of malnutrition. It suffered from absentee ownership, bad management, lack of capital investment. And shipping itself was changing – in the decade after the war the passenger lines began to feel the pinch of competition from the airlines. In time the passenger services were taken over completely. Freight-carrying ships were becoming bigger, and as docking became more and more mechanised, the bigger ships became more economical. They were also more profitable to build, cheaper to run and more in demand. The custom-built job which was the Clyde's speciality requiring imagination and flair and engineering skill and experience were no longer in demand. The Spanish and Japanese were turning out the huge production jobs needed for modern freightage and turning them out in coastal yards where there was room to launch the massive tonnage. They were building in covered yards where the weather did not interfere with their schedules. They did not have an expensively skilled and well organised labour force with a trades structure that would lead to dispute and demarcation. Nor did they need them. The pools of cheap and captive labour were sufficient for the kind of job they were doing. They were building to schedule, they were costing realistically, they were getting the big profitable tonnages, they were making money and they were putting it back into the industry. Under the severity of world competition the Clyde shipyards simply declined – Simon-Lobnitz, Harlands and Wolff, Stephens, Babcock and Wilcox, Denny's, Barclay Curle, they either went or reduced themselves drastically. In the early 1960s the Geddes Commission found a management which could not face the realities of modern shipbuilding. Its recommendations led to the foundation of a consortium which is the present day Upper Clyde Shipyards.

UCS inherited a legacy of bad worker–management relations, inadequate yards and machinery and berths, the same narrow river which could and should have been widened, and a commitment to jobs whose schedules and costings were the fruits of panic and desperation. In its history over the last half-century of mismanagement, meagre investment, technical ineptitude, a venal leech of profit, and brutal indifference to its work force the ship-building industry was comparable only to the old privately owned railways and mines, but under new management the men of the Clyde showed what they could do. Contrary to their image in the tabloids, the unions and men behaved with a complete lack of that bloody-minded intransigence with which they are so often accused. Demarcation disputes were settled, a fair wage structure was agreed and agreement honoured, management–labour relations became rational and resilient, the work force was cut and tonnage figures soared. The UCS began to pay off a half-century load of other men's debt. Compared to the bleeding and leakage of the previous half-century its losses were trivial. It had begun to turn towards viability.

Until the day Mr Heath's government announced through their Minister for Trade and Industry Mr John Davies that UCS was to go into liquidation. Why the government chose to act like it did in refusing the £6m cash asked for by the UCS is an interesting speculation. Interesting because it shows that a rampant and bloody-minded Tory ideology is consistent with the shifts and dodges of high finance and the directions of cash towards the whizz-kid industries and the fast buck. If capital floats around waiting to settle only on the lucrative high return investment then many of the resources of the country are bound to fall into neglect, a neglect which this government is apparently prepared to sanction with acts of flagrant and callous omission.

When the men's leaders reacted to the news of the impending

liquidation by announcing that they intended to continue working the yards in spite of the liquidator's presence and in spite of any act of the government several even more interesting things happened. On the face of it the co-ordinating committee of shop stewards are only decent men trying to defend their right to earn a living. Men like Reid, Airlie, Dickie, the workers' spokesmen, are indeed decent, humane men defending their own and their mates' livelihood. They have gentle eyes and workmen's faces and Glesca voices and there is no room in their style for any relish of upheaval or apocalypse. Yet this announcement awoke a few memories of that history of the Clydeside adumbrated here; it restored a few energies and aroused enough visionary fantasy to go around the whole comminuted* variety of left-wing groupings.

Certainly it was an original kind of industrial action but it was forced on to the men by the nature and circumstance of their plight. It could be seen simply as an imaginative attempt to call the attention of the Press of the country to this plight, to confront the government and in this way force concessions, save jobs, get a deal. Yet in fact the implications of this act of direct and immediate control of physical capital, the carrying on of work and activity and production without the initiation of cash is to strike at the very root of capitalism. It clears our eyes from the abstract mists and obfuscations of finance and capital production and proclaims a new reality of machines, tools, materials and men to work them. It is an act of revolution. Whether these implications are realised or conscious is another matter and depending on this consciousness will be the issue of whether this act is or comes to be either a mere confrontation with this government on this issue or a confrontation with the capitalist system itself. If the spectres of Daniel de Leon and Syndicalism stalk the Clydeside then their nebulous substance has not yet shown in the acetylene fumes.

It is a hellish and lonely burden which rests on the shoulders

---

* Comminute, verb meaning, to pulverise – reduce to small particles.

of these men in the yards. Hellish and lonely because the movement they represent – and it matters nothing here whether we mean the Labour Party, the trade unions, or the militantly middle of the road Communist Party – this movement has no ideological commitment to, and still less experience of, this kind of action. It is an act committed not only in the physical isolation of their plight but in their historical isolation in the Labour movement; a possibility lost in that wide gap between the industrial and political wings. The stewards are out on their own. If the government continues in its obstinacy then their task may be a little easier for they can go on fighting to either win or lose. If the government concedes they have won a victory. If they are offered a deal, concessions, a bargain, then they have the difficult choice to make between the immediate humanity of saving some of the jobs and the more distant humanity of an act of critical revolt. It is not for us to tell them how to choose.

Meanwhile the feeling at John Brown's gate is one of waiting. A few of the fantasy makers and dreamers are about. The fancy London media boy with his rag-bag of left-wing commitments, with his lifestyle and indulgence and expense account and dolly-bird and total lack of a sense of authenticity envying the boiler maker for the authority of his crisis. There are the hard men from the tabloids, the realists, whose only sense of actuality is what is – and can be written in one paragraph. There are the middle of the road media men who must film shop stewards against a crane jib. Aside from the media men there are the VIPs who storm through the yards exuding sympathy and solidarity and keeping their cards close to their chests. And then there are the skelfs and splinters of the left wing – the Trots, the Mao-ists, the IS, the IMG, the SLL: their eyes avid for the upheaval and cataclysm which will herald their arid millennium.

The public arguments are bald and unsubtle. On the Monday morning when the men from Govan return from their Glasgow Fair holidays there are mass meetings held at every yard. In John Brown's at eleven o'clock after the mass meetings there is a Press conference and statements are given to the Press.

The TV arc lamps are glaring and someone is making cracks about make-up. The committee of stewards sit in a row watching the Pressmen come and make gallus remarks in a language only understood by the locals. Anyway they might not understand the humour which in its gutsy, muscular origin and workaday imagery owes nothing to Monty Python or any kind of sophisticated English whimsy. The questions asked by the Press are just as bald as the statements but afterwards in Connelly's bar the arguments reach a Mediaeval degree of subtlety. Behind the scenes one imagines the stewards must be arguing with their own brand of finesse. But there is a gap between the two Mediaeval groups which goes all the way from sophisticated anguish to plain bloody worry. Wandering round the yards talking to the tradesmen you seem to meet nothing but quiet, peaceful, patient men with families who have worked all their life on ships. They are staunchly behind the stewards. It seems heartbreaking not to leave them in peace to work and live out their ordinary lives. Elsewhere you meet people hot for action and you think of these men and their families. The stakes are higher than in a lunchtime game of brag and it is these men who will have to pay.

Yet the hopes and the fantasies clustered round the Clydeside could become real. The argument about the viability of the shipyards can only be dismissed brusquely. No one really believes that the Clyde can't earn a living, probably least of all the government. What has come to be the issue is whether or not the Socialist movement is capable of growing in stature over the events on the Clydeside. There is the extreme left of the movement impotently defying the system at a level of personal morality and lifestyle, fighting the police over social and racial issues, thumbing noses at university courts, desperately whipping up a sense of revolutionary crisis over issues like women's lib, or abortion, or gay power, or the right to print porn or smoke pot. While the GEC grows larger, the Tories return to confident power, the guitars belt out their revolutionary message, the left politicos dream of workers' control – and lose their grip on reality. On the other hand the unions clamber over one another for a bigger slice of the capitalist cake while the Labour Party ties itself to the realism of a mixed economy and lets the Socialist dream go. With Jimmy Reid's announcement of the workers' intention something happened – round that announcement there crystallised a lot of hopes. Many people saw in it the possibility of a kind of action which could unite the radical left and make Socialism not just the sour and unrealistic hope of a few lonely men but a radiant possibility for many. The ghost of the old Clyde arose in the imagination of many men.

As I write this there have been no pay-offs, no redundancies, no attempt to remove materials or machines or stop the people working. When that happens we'll know where the stewards are going. Whatever way they chose we can only assent, for as well as the choice of revolution they have the plight of thousands of their comrades and their families to think of. The shame and agony of this choice has been the Medieval schisms of the left which has left them alone in their decision. If they do chose to dig in it will be a greater shame to this country's left (greater than the previous self-defeats of the general strike and the coalition government) if they are not supported wholeheartedly by every member of the left-wing spectrum from the long-haired hippy and life-style dandy all the way to the front bench of the Parliamentary Labour Party and the TUC executive.

I am not, it seems, exempt from fantasy myself. If I were to have one to articulate it would be this (in contravention of the Unfair Industrial Practices Clause, incitement to, in the Industrial Relations Bill) – that one day a ship would be permanently berthed on the Clyde, as in the *Cutty Sark* at Greenwich and the *Queen Mary* in the States. In front of the gangway would be a notice, or plaque, which would say: 'This is the first of a long line of ships built by UCS workers at John Brown's shipyard in defiance of a reactionary government, permanently berthed here to commemorate and honour those same workers who brought life back to British Socialism.'

'The Dear Green Place'

In 1971, Archie Hind's review *Through with a Flourish* was presented at the Edinburgh International Festival and contained the following song written in collaboration with Peter Kelly.

Tenements of black and grey
Fill the city where I stay
Still you'll always hear me say
'Glasgow, the dear green place'.

In the streets the children play
Games of lands so far away
For they know they'll leave one day
Glasgow, the dear green place.

The people came down from the north
From Ireland's shores they came across
And settled by the riverside.
And in their tongue they chose a name
The city changed but just the same
Gleschu is the name that stays
Glesca, that's the dear green place.

People passing by this way
Look around then go away
Never knowing why I say
Glasgow, the dear green place.